Sweet Justice

Sweet Justice

MARK INKLEY

Copyright © 2022 by Mark Inkley.

ISBN:	Softcover	978-1-5035-4162-7
	eBook	978-1-5035-4161-0

All rights reserved. No part of this book may be reproduced or transmitted in any form or by any means, electronic or mechanical, including photocopying, recording, or by any information storage and retrieval system, without permission in writing from the copyright owner.

This is a work of fiction. Names, characters, places and incidents either are the product of the author's imagination or are used fictitiously, and any resemblance to any actual persons, living or dead, events, or locales is entirely coincidental.

Any people depicted in stock imagery provided by Thinkstock are models, and such images are being used for illustrative purposes only.
Certain stock imagery © Thinkstock.

Print information available on the last page.

To order additional copies of this book, contact:
Gotham Books
1- 307-464-7800
www.gothambooksinc.com

Contents

Introduction..9

Chapter One
Yuma Hell Hole 11

Chapter Two
The Beginning 26

Chapter Three
Independence Day 45

Chapter Four
The Long Hot Summer........................63

Chapter Five
Bad News from Lincoln 83

Chapter Six
Memories 97

Chapter Seven
Frontier News 119

Chapter Eight
A Blast from the Past........................142

Chapter Nine
Hell's Angels.......................................162

Chapter Ten
The Loss of a Friend........................186

Chapter Eleven
Voices on Paper 210

Chapter Twelve
Changing of the Guard 230
Chapter Thirteen
Justice Comes to Town 243
Chapter Fourteen
Bittersweet Goodbyes 257
Chapter Fifteen
Visit from an Angel 270
Chapter Sixteen
The Call of Love and Duty..................................286
Chapter Seventeen
The Demon Dog..306
Chapter Eighteen
Indian Troubles 327
Chapter Nineteen
Running Out of Time 345
Chapter Twenty
Showdown at Daybreak......................................358
Chapter Twenty-One
From Hunter to Hunted 369
Chapter Twenty-Two
The Last Stand 390
Chapter Twenty-Three
Going Home..409
Epilogue..417

Disconnected

No dial tone, heart beat or hip-bone connected to
the thigh-bone, no Siamese, no love to talk about.

No television, no vision at all, friendships are gone,
family blood all dried up, no talking just a
muted catatonic body in the corner.

No gravity, floating into nothingness, can't eat,
food won't stay down, can't sleep, laser beam eyes
watching, glowing in the dark.

A no man havin' demagnetized, chastised by life
broke down, busted and disgusted, half-dead chick
who woke up pissed off.

The spigot is rusty, tongue is tied lips sealed,
cross-eyed high on negative thoughts. Can't strike
a match, fire-breathin' bitch with an attitude that

keeps everyone in her wake sucked in the abyss
of her black heart. She's disconnected, no cord,
no pulse, no tears, no spit.
She's all dried up like the Mohave desert, prickly like a
Cactus. A pissy lot who can't hold a tune in bucket, the
notes run from her.

No fingerprints, no hair follicles, no blinking,
no snaps from her fingers, her joints are out of whack.

The tin man has more swag.

Hot to Death and Still Kickin'

Staccato cries shake her body like
an earthquake. Tears show steam from her
hot flashes. A teeter-totter
going from zero to sixty.
Her Jekyll and Hyde personality
catapults her into a
psychotic state. Everyday
she is someone different.
Insomnia makes her become
a restless zombie swinging in
between life and death.
On a suicide mission to
kill the lady that came before her
so, she can become the Grand dame
to rock it out in a post-apocalyptic state
surviving the aftermath
of transition that makes
men-all-pause.

The Glutton

Gorged on crime, sex, porn, and can't get enough.

A belly full of hate moving up her esophagus

spewing chunks of despise, indignation, and

wickedness leaving a bitter vile taste on her

coated pinkish-gray tongue. She's willing to

inhale all the devastation and tragedy until she

fills up on more trash than a landfill.

Constipated from all of society's woes like the

poor, the homeless, the down-trodden, along with

the scathing scum of the earth. She wants to

gobble them up until her seams start to burst and

when she finally blows, chaos will take hold like a

leech draining all the life out of this dreadful world

giving gluttony a severe case of diarrhea, a drainage

of mess that will spill down through the ages until

she turns back into the dust she was created from.

Inside Job

I feel my heart ticking like a clock

gone cuckoo. Sometimes it feels like a

bomb that has detonated and left behind

a grave yard. The inner workings of atoms and

cells with hardhats are scrambling to

reconstruct my organs that were

decimated from the blast.

On the outside, I'm Miss Hollywood, the

name my uncle gave me, a girl without a care

walking around like an android that just

looked straight, shoulders back, a ruby red

lipstick smile moving with automated grace.

My friend anxiety, drops by to cause chaos

And frenzy, I call her Tornado Jane because she

Leaves destruction behind in her wake.

My hardhat friends drop by to clean up and

call for a state of emergency.

I'm a mess in there, but I'm also a work in progress.

I'm under construction, getting prefabbed, rebuilt,

redone. I feel my friends at work knocking around

vital organs trying not to hit main arteries.

My meds are lifted down on scaffolds to soothe

the ills of my soul. My inside job is something I

cannot retire from, it is an ongoing project.

Or, at some point, will I become brand new?

Stay tuned for the next chapter of my progression.

CPSIA information can be obtained
at www.ICGtesting.com
Printed in the USA
BVHW031353130921
616657BV00010B/270

Artwork by Mark Inkley

INTRODUCTION

BILL SAUNDERS HAS FOUND HIMSELF in Yuma prison for a crime he swears he didn't commit, watched over by guard hell bent on seeing him hang. What in all Bill's years of running from himself since the end of the Civil War could he have done to make a man he's never met or seen before hate him this much? Can the mayor's beautiful daughter help him prove his innocence before the noose wins the race? Can he help the men who share his cell before their fate is the same? And if he does find his freedom, can he find the courage to return home after what happened at Gettysburg? To keep his mind off his perilous situation Bill shares his stories, taking us to the territories of the Wild West, before fences penned people and animals out and the bars of the Yuma hell hole penned him in.

CHAPTER ONE

Yuma Hell Hole

"WHAT YOU IN FOR?" THE question seemed to echo from a distant realm, that place that you pass through on the journey between sleep and consciousness. "What you in for?" I heard him say again, followed immediately with a kick to my foot. Not one that hurt, mind ya, but enough to annoy anyone, especially when bein' yanked out of a dream. Dreams were the only escape from the hell hole I was in, and I sure didn't like the return trip. I looked up to see who was talkin' to me and realized it was the kid they'd brought in on the prison wagon late last night.

"Who wants to know?" I said, in a not so friendly voice. You learn quickly in this place to assert yourself as someone who doesn't take guff from anyone, and I wasn't obliged to take it from a kid.

"Easy," I heard 'im say. "I was just tryin' to make conversation."

"By wakin' me up?", I said in a softer tone. "Good way to start your time here with a black eye, I reckon."

My words took him by surprise and sent him into defensive mode.

"Pretty big words, considering you don't know who you're talking to," he challenged.

I laughed out loud, to a point that begged him to start somethin'. He started to lunge at me as if testin' the waters. I stood up and met his gaze, fists clenched in anticipation. He stood about an inch or two taller than me and grinned when he realized it. I smiled back and asked him if he wanted to eat lunch before I knocked his teeth out or after. Not that it would matter. Most days you could drink the slop they served around here. The only time you really needed to chew was when the mayor's daughter, Miss Emily Watson, brought pie to the prisoners. She brought other things too, like bread and cobblers, but it was the pie we looked forward to. Yes sir, she sure could make a good pie, and we all waited in anticipation for those days.

I could never figure out how a dung hole like Yuma could ever have someone as sweet and beautiful as Emily Watson livin' in it, but on the days she was allowed to come, I sure was obliged to see her. I wrestled in my mind which one I liked most, the pie or seeing her face. It was a toss-up 'cause both had their own way of fillin' a void.

The first time I ever saw her was at the courthouse the day they brought me in. I was accompanied by a cast of hard-lookin' riff raff. They were guilty of everythin' from cattle rustlin' to bank robbery and murder. I watched her look at all of us very carefully and came to the conclusion that she was lookin' for someone specific. When her eyes met mine, I smiled. It seemed to take her by surprise, and she hurriedly looked away and went quickly back to studyin' the rest of the group. I continued to watch her, wondering who she might be and who she might be lookin' for. My mind wondered, reflecting on what kind of act would be so bad as to bring someone like her to a gathering such as this.

As I came to my conscious mind and surroundings again, I noticed her lookin' at me. I bowed my head, as was the customary Southern gentlemen thing to do. She stared at me for a moment as if tryin' to figure me out, smiled, curtsied, and turned to the sheriff.

"He isn't here," she said, then quickly gave me another look and walked away. After that all of us were ushered into the courthouse, except two hard-lookin' Mexicans who were immediately taken to the gallows, as near as I could tell. Even though I knew what they were guilty of, I couldn't believe they weren't goin' to get a trial. Not that they didn't deserve hangin', mind ya, but I remember thinkin' to myself, *William, what have you gotten yourself into?*

"You're pretty confident for an old man," the kid said smugly, snapping me back to reality.

"And you're pretty cocky for a smart-mouthed boy," I shot back, emphasizing the word *boy*, followed with, "I was beatin' the hell out of tougher men than you when your pa was still whoopin' your ass for stealin' the corset pages from the catalog in the outhouse."

Some of the men in the room snickered. Most kept their silence, though, sensin' the tension. I don't know if I just got his goat because he wasn't used to people talkin' to him that way or if I'd actually come closer to the truth than he cared to admit, but his face turned red, and he threw himself at me like an ornery bull. I stepped out of the way, leavin' my foot there to trip him as he passed. He went down hard. Everyone started laughin' at that point, and it just made him madder. He came at me again, more aware of my actions, but he lacked the experience to protect himself. I met him with a stiff uppercut to the chin, and before he even knew what hit him, he was on the floor again.

"I don't want to hurt you, kid," I said. "Just stay down there and cool off."

He could hear the others laughin' at him, and he said, "If I had my guns—"

I shut him down before he could finish. "If you did, you'd be dead," I said. "It pays to know who you're dealin' with before you open your mouth. If you learn that lesson now, you might live to get outta this place."

His anger made him want to get up again, but his hand rubbin' his chin told me he wouldn't, so I sat back down in the straw, pulled my hat back over my eyes, and tried to go back to sleep.

******

It was the beginning of July or thereabouts. I could tell because if I stood on my tiptoes, I could see the decorations on the courthouse. July meant that it was gonna be hotter than usual, and that was saying a lot, considerin' it was always hot in Yuma. And one thing's for certain: if it was hot outside, our cell was even hotter, like an oven. Most of the prison was made up of two-man cells that opened to an outside corridor, but because of overcrowding, some of the minimum risk prisoners were lumped into a room that was probably built for storage, and the only ventilation was a little hole in the wall that faced the courthouse. The best way to pass these days was to sleep. It didn't make it any cooler, but if I was lucky, maybe I'd dream of bein' in the high mountains back in New Mexico.

I'd just started to doze when I heard the kid's mouth runnin' again. He was tellin' the guys around him how fast he was with a gun. Ted told him to shut his mouth before he had to prove it.

"That's Bill Saunders you tangled with. You might be fast, kid, but I know he is. I heard he drew on one of the Clanton boys in Tombstone, and if he didn't have a cool head, that feller'd be dead. There was a man who used to be in here, God rest his soul, that was in the saloon the day when Clanton decided he didn't like the way Bill was lookin' at him and tried to start a fight. Bill told him to calm down and that he didn't recall lookin' at him but if he had he was sorry.

"The Clanton bunch think they own and run Tombstone anyway, and their reputation makes them cocky. Bill's apology was seen as cowardice, and Clanton took courage from it and kept on taunting him. When Bill wouldn't feed his fire, he got mad and spun him by the shoulder and at the same time took a cheap shot at his nose. Bill shook it off and returned with a punch to his face so hard it put him on the floor. Then he told him to let it rest. That Clanton fellar got up and went for his gun. He told me the speed of Bill's answer to his challenge was truly something to see. He calmly said, 'One of us can die here today, or we can pretend this never happened. You make the call, sir, but choose wisely.' Clanton could see he was in no position to push his luck and quickly backed out of the saloon. So you might be fast," Ted said again, "but word has it he definitely is. If 'n I was you, I don't reckon I'd push my luck."

A hushed silence fell over the room. I glanced from under the brim of my hat towards where the kid was sitting. He seemed a little pale, maybe from the information he'd just received or possibly from the blood he was losin' every time he spit. Whatever it was, the quiet it created allowed me to try and sleep once again. It was short-lived, though, because no sooner had I dozed off the prison guard came to the door and yelled, "Lunch time, scumbags. Form a line."

"Virgil," I muttered.

Virgil, the prison guard, and I had friction between us. He was the one who drove the wagon I was brought in on from the train station. It wasn't normally his job, and you could tell by his attitude that he wasn't very happy about bein' pulled into the hot sun to perform it. He was extremely rough, both physically and verbally, and I reckon he didn't win any friends that day. Certainly not with me anyway. I guess my reputation preceded me because he was out to cut me down to size from the moment we met. When we were leaving the station, the shackles on my ankles had a smaller than normal chain between them, so I had to double step about every three steps to keep up with the other prisoners. He decided that I wasn't movin' fast enough and cracked me with the butt of his rifle. I turned to him and whispered that if he did it again, I would beat the hell out of him. I should've kept my mouth shut. He just grinned and said, "We got us a tough guy here." And just to show that he was in command, he hit me again, only this time in the

SWEET JUSTICE 17

ribs, crackin' them so hard that it was two weeks before I could draw a breath without wincing in pain.

Everyone stood up to form a line for lunch. Even the hardest among us formed an orderly line because we knew that Virgil was always itchin' to use the club he carried around. The kid didn't know that yet, however, and wasn't quite as orderly as Virgil thought he should be. "Boy, I said form a line. Are you too stupid to know what that means?" Then Virgil opened the door and took the opportunity to let his stick teach him a lesson. I felt bad when he hit him, loudmouth or not, because I knew I had already given him enough pain for the day. The kid took it like a man though, and I could tell he had grit.

As Virgil was plopping food on his tin tray, he noticed that the kid's mouth was bleeding. Never being one to pass up a chance to administer his own brand of justice, he asked, "Who done that to ya?"

The kid spit on the floor and said, "Done what?"

"Don't get smart with me," Virgil said, "or I'll crack ya again."

The kid replied coldly, "Well, your honor, I have a disease that causes my mouth to bleed uncontrollably, but don't worry, the doc says there's only a fifty percent chance that it's contagious." Virgil pulled back when he heard that with the funniest damn face you ever saw as the whole cell broke into laughter.

Virgil yelled, "Go ahead and laugh, scumbags, but I'm the one who serves your food, remember that." And then he spit in the pot.

Slim muttered, "Horse's ass." And we all broke into laughter all over again.

I realized then that the kid was alright; he was just cocky and had some learnin' comin' his way.

I had just sat down to eat when Virgil came back; only this time he was opening the entire door. Everyone stiffened because they only did that when someone was bein' taken to the courthouse or, worse yet, the hangin' gallows.

"You," he said pointing at me. "Get up."

"I just started eatin'," I said.

"Get up and quit whinin'," he replied.

I hesitated a little bit, unsure of why, when he said, "Dammit, Saunders, hurry up, or I'll shoot you where you sit."

I walked over to the cell door, and true to form he shoved me against the wall. "No funny stuff, Billy," he said in a mocking tone. "The world would be better off without you in it." He put me in wrist shackles attached to a belt. "I'd probably get a medal for ridden it of you."

"Wouldn't care if you did," I said. "It'd beat the hell out of another day lookin' at your ugly mug, and maybe I'd get a chance to keep my promise I made ya by takin' you with me."

He looked at me, and I could see fear in his eyes. He masked it by saying, "Just give me an excuse, Billy. Just give me an excuse."

I stared at him coolly and could see him try not to shrink.

"Get goin', tough guy," he said as he quickly moved behind me with his rifle.

I was unsure where he was takin' me and could feel the palms of my hands sweating. Every day was already filled with a dread that it might be my last, and his hatred for me seemed more extreme than usual that morning. I breathed a sigh of relief, however, when we turned down the hall that led to the courtyard. I squinted as he opened the door. As I stepped out, I could see a figure against the far wall, but because my eyes hadn't adjusted to the light yet fillin' the cell, I could only see what appeared to be a shadow. I instinctively went to throw my hand up to shade my eyes but then realized that the chains on my shackles wouldn't allow me to.

"Take them off," I heard a pleasant female voice say.

"But Miss Watson, he could be dangerous," Virgil replied.

"Come on, Virgil, he's not going to attack me in the courtyard," she said in an exasperated tone. "Especially with you holding that gun. Take them off," she said again, "and leave us."

"I'm not supposed to leave the prisoners unattended. I could lose my job."

"Then stand in the doorway out of the sun if it will make you feel better," she shot back with what seemed like a little irritation in her voice.

Virgil walked back across the courtyard; he seemed almost dejected as he assumed the post at the door.

"What's your name?" she asked me.

"Bill Saunders. What's this all about?" I asked.

She continued as if she didn't hear my question. "Is Bill your real name?"

"No," I said. "It's William."

"That's a much better name for a man from the South."

"How did you know I was from the South?" I asked.

"I figured you were Southern by the way you tipped your head to me the day we first saw each other."

"Then am I to believe you were once a Southern bell by the way you curtsied back?" I asked.

"Yes, Mr. Saunders, you are."

"Ma'am, I don't want to sound ungrateful for gettin' me out of that cell and into the breeze and sun, but I find it hard to believe you had me brought out here to make small talk. What's the real reason for your visit?"

"Mr. Saunders," she said seriously. "I look at every prisoner brought into this place, and I can see the hate and guilt in their eyes."

"Yeah, I noticed that. What or who are you looking for?"

"That is a topic that can wait for another visit. Mr. Saunders, today I want to talk about you. As I was saying," she continued, "I can see guilt, hatred, pain, and remorse when I look into a man's soul."

"That must be quite a gift," I said.

"Don't be flippant, Mr. Saunders. I'm here to help if I can," she said coolly.

"I'm sorry, ma'am. I didn't mean any disrespect. Please go on," I coaxed.

"I didn't see it in yours," she responded. "A little sadness perhaps but not guilt."

"Well, I said I know you've probably heard it a thousand times, but I ain't guilty, and if they'd talked to the witnesses I sent 'em to, they'd know that. Instead I'm rottin' away in this hell hole, waitin' for tuberculosis or some other disease to win the race against the noose. Either way I'm as good as dead if I can't afford a lawyer, and I can't, so forgive me when I say, whether you can see guilt or not, my fate is still the same, and there ain't a damn thing I can do about it."

"Well, maybe I can, William," she said.

"Why would you want to help me?" I asked. "What if I'm lyin' to ya? And I actually deserve to be in here? Why would you stick your neck out for me?"

"Because I don't think you are guilty, and I believe that, given a chance, you would do good things with your life. I would like to help you, William. Can we meet again?"

"On one condition," I said. "What's that?" she asked.

"That you bring pie when you come," I said, half joking. "That, Mr. Saunders, is a promise I shall keep."

She called to Virgil, almost coldly, and said, "We are done for today, sir. You may show me out."

"For today?" he asked in a puzzled tone. "That's what I said," she snapped.

"But Miss Watson, this man is a hired gun. He's not worth your time," he said.

"Are you not in your own right just a hired gun, Virgil?" she said coldly.

The comment shut him down. "I expect you to treat this man with respect until I return. Now show me out," she demanded.

Virgil looked at me, and I flashed him a broad smile. He scowled at me with more hatred than ever before as he let her out the courtyard door. And even though I knew that this would make him more abusive towards me, I had to chuckle inside myself.

As we walked back to the cell, I could tell that Virgil seemed preoccupied—first by the fact that he didn't put shackles back on my wrists, followed by the realization that he didn't have any smartass comments spewin' out of his mouth. This was something I'd never experienced.

Virgil was like a small dog; he thought that barking a lot would somehow mask the fact that he was a coward and make people think he was tough. I'd seen his kind a lot in my life and knew that you always wanted to keep a keen eye on this type of man because one of the symptoms was an itchy trigger finger, and rarely did you ever see them without a gun. I thought to myself that if I was ever goin' to try and escape from this place, this was certainly a good time to try: his gun was down, and I didn't recall ever hearin' him cock it.

The thought quickly left my mind, however. What I'd told Miss Watson about bein' innocent was true. Not that I hadn't run with a tough bunch, but I didn't commit the act I was imprisoned for, and if she was really going to help me, tryin' to escape would put an end to anything she might accomplish. *Besides,* I thought, *it's not like I don't have skeletons in my closet. Maybe my kind deserves to be here anyway.*

By the time we reached the cell, Virgil was back to bein' his old rotten self, and he showed me by shoving me extra hard into the hell hole once again.

I took a step or two when he called me back. He pulled me in close where he could whisper in my ear and said, "I don't know what Miss Watson said to you, but you keep your distance when she comes 'round, ya hear? Don't even look at her," he said sharply, "or so help me I'll kill you, understand? I'll kill you deader than dead!"

He shoved me again and shut the door extra hard. As I listened to his boots echo down the corridor, it all came to me. Virgil was shinin' on Miss Emily Watson. All his actions made sense. No wonder he looked so dejected when she told him to return to the doorway. I smiled at the discomfort I'd created in him and hoped she'd return soon so I could do it again.

It was a win-win for me. Not only was Miss Watson easy on the eyes, she was also a vehicle to get under Virgil's skin, and I'd tangle with a room full of bobcats to do that. Yes sir, maybe two rooms.

All eyes were on me as I found my way to my straw pile. It was sweltering inside now, and after bein' out in the open air, the smell of seven men who needed a bath seemed twice as bad. At least under the window I could hope for a little air movement.

"What was all that about?" Stumpy asked.

I pulled my hat over my eyes and pretended not to hear him. Stumpy was half Mexican and was the kind that had to know everything—probably a result of the rowdy bunch he rode with. They fed themselves by holding up the wagons that would haul silver from a mine that was actually in Mexico but was being worked by Americans. Stumpy never saw it as stealing, though, because it was on property supposedly owned by his family ever since Spain controlled things. It was right on the border, so ownership was always in dispute. In the end, however, American guns won out, and Stumpy and his brother had to flee for their lives.

His brother made his way to Wickenburg. I heard tell he'd found some gold there, but Stumpy, he just got mad and decided to be a bur in the saddle of those he claimed were stealing what was rightfully his. "Come on, Bill," he said again. "It's not like the saloon dancers are gonna come in and entertain us or nothin'. You're the only one I seen hauled outta here that wasn't goin' to no swingin' party since I been in here. Did they figure it was you who popped the kid?" he prodded.

"You don't look beat up or nothin'."

After a long pause he asked the same question again. I looked at him from under my hat with a look that said give it a rest, and the motion of him settling back into a lyin' position told me he got it.

I shifted my eyes and said, "Hey, kid, your silence today showed me you have courage and spit. Thanks for not telling Virgil I was the one who hit you. And if it's worth anything, I'm sorry I did."

"It's alright, Mr. Saunders," he replied.

Mr. Saunders, I thought, as I closed my eyes again. *Kid learns fast. He might just get outta here yet.* My thoughts turned to Miss Emily Watson as I drifted to sleep, and before I knew it, I was in the cool alpine country on my favorite horse.

The next sound I heard from the real world was the night guard announcing supper. I must've fallen asleep with my mouth open because my first coherent thought was how thirsty I was. Going to the water barrel first meant that I'd be last in line for the vittles—if you could call 'em that—and that was never good. The last man always got what could be scraped off the sides of the pot or chiseled from the bottom, but my thirst won the battle. I drank from the tin dipper and watched the line grow smaller. The night guard looked beyond the last few men in line and saw me.

"Hey, Bill," he called. "I understand you got a visit from Miss Watson today. Sure did put a powerful stick in ol' Virg's craw," he continued laughing. "He was still grumbling about it when he left."

SWEET JUSTICE   25

I stuck my tin out to get filled, expecting the burnt offerings, but when I pulled it back through the slot, I found a beautiful piece of strawberry pie.

"Compliments of Miss Watson," he said. "Virg was goin' to eat it, thought it was for him. Imagine the color of his face when Miss Watson told him to keep his hands off it. Picture a redhead that fell asleep in the sun, and you'd be 'bout halfway there," he said with a laugh that continued all the way back to the end of the corridor.

"Who's Miss Watson?" the kid asked, as I turned to find a place to sit down. "Is she that pretty gal that seemed to look right through me last night? Hey, where'd you get the pie from?" His last question trumped the two previous as he looked back to what was on his tray.

"How come you got pie?" some of the others questioned. "Because I asked for it," I said.

Jed, known to be a little dimwitted, yelled down towards the guards. "Can I have pie too?"

"Shut up," was the reply back. He turned with a perplexed look on his face, and the lot of us broke into laughter.

Chapter Two

The Beginning

Everyone watched me as I ate my pie, so I made sure I made each bite as enticing as possible, just to drive 'em crazy. The kid spoke up, tongue in cheek. "Mr. Saunders, if I was to ask you why you got that pie, and if it had something to do with your disappearance today, would you hit me again?"

"Call me Bill, kid," I said, "and I told you I was sorry."

"Yeah, I know," he replied. "I was just tryin' to ruffle your feathers." "Then try it when I'm sleeping," I joked. "Fact is, kid, this here pie

has everything to do with my trip to the courtyard today."

Slim, sometimes called Four Fingers, spoke suddenly. "You were in the courtyard, outside and everything?"

Slim had acquired his nickname by playing pharo with a man wielding a bowie knife. Turned out the man was faster at catching a cheater than Slim was at cheating. Those in the saloon said that he drew that knife faster than any gun slinger drew his gun and that before Slim had a chance to yell in pain he had the knife back in its sheath.

"Yes sir, I was," I said, gloating just a bit.

Slim had been here longer than any of us and was in the beginning stages of tuberculosis. Add that to the fact that he shot the man who took his finger, and it meant he probably wouldn't get outside again until it was his turn to swing.

"I'd give anything to feel the breeze and sun again," he said.

Jed, trying to get a laugh, yelled, "You'll feel the breeze when they hang ya, Slim."

Everyone told him to shut his mouth. I half expected to see Slim go after him, but this place and the knowledge of his fate had broken him. He slowly settled back to a half lying position. I tried to rub some of the luster off my statement by sayin' there wasn't any breeze and the sun was hot and then something' 'bout how my eyes still stung from the light, hopin' to make Slim feel better.

There was an awkward silence before the kid spoke again. "Why did she come to see you?"

"She said she wanted to help me prove my innocence," I said. "But I'm not sure if that was her real motive or if she even can at this point." "You have to be innocent to be found that way, don't ya?" he said with a laugh.

Everyone started to poke fun at me with comments after that. "I'm innocent too. I don't know how that gun got in my hand," one said, followed by another saying, "Sheriff, someone must have put that silver in my saddlebag. I'm bein' set up."

The best, though, was "I'm sorry, your honor. I target practice by shootin' cans. You know, peach cans, bean cans, Mexicans—I had no idea it was against the law."

They all got a good laugh at my expense, and I waited for them to quit laughin' before I continued. "Boys," I said. "I'm not going to claim that I haven't done things to be ashamed of, but I truly am innocent of the crime they said I was involved in."

"You mean to tell me that you've been here for three years for a crime you didn't commit?" Stumpy asked. "That's tough," he continued. "All of us earned our way here. Makes the time tolerable to think you're payin' a debt, but to sit in here when you should be free must be unbearable."

"I've learned to deal with it," I said. "I got no place to go if I got out—well, no place you'd call home anyway."

"Where's your family?" the kid asked.

"Still in Texas, I reckon. Least, that's where they were the last time I saw any of them, that is."

"Why did you leave in the first place?" asked Jed.

"There were a lot of reasons, I guess. My pa brought us out to Sherman to start a wheat farm when I was thirteen. But I was never content to be a farmer; my dreams were farther into Texas. When I was a teenager, I wanted my pa to try his hand at raising cattle, but his love was farming."

"Why didn't you just leave then?" Jed asked. "That's what I'd a done. I always wanted to run from what my pa was forcin' me to become, but my pa was a drunk and mean as a badger. He used to beat the hell outta me, and I was always afraid of him."

"I did eventually," I said. "But not to raise cattle. It was the war that took me away."

"You ain't been home since the war?" Slim asked.

SWEET JUSTICE

29

"Can't say I have. Well, that's not exactly true. I did go home right after the war, but battle had messed with my head. I was carryin' around demons that haunted me and memories I couldn't shake. "War is hell, boys," I emphasized. "There's things that you see no man should have to and things you do in the heat of the moment that you regret, things that you wish you could change, but you can't. Dead is dead, and there's no going back on dead. After the war I headed that way, even got about a hundred yards from home but couldn't talk myself into finishing the journey."

The room was silent at that point, and I continued. "I just couldn't answer the questions or face possible rejection, so I sat on the hill and watched them load our stuff on wagons. My ma kept goin' to the road, watching. For me, I guessed. I saw Pa and one of my sisters come out to get her. They escorted her to the wagon, and I watched them pull away. Part of me wanted to get up and go after them, but my feet wouldn't move. It was like a dream, but I just sat there and watched 'em go."

"Do you know where they went?" the kid asked.
"Yeah, my ma left a note for me on the door."

> *William, if you find this letter in time, we've gone to a new settlement in the northwest corner of Texas. We waited for you as long as we could, but your pa sold the farm to the neighbor just north of us. The courts said we had to be off the property by sundown. Please come as soon as you can. Love, Ma.*

"About ten years ago, I saw them again from a distance on our way to San Antonio, but I didn't talk to any of them. Looked like they were doin' good. My pa always had a nose for where the next opportunity would be, and his instincts were right. Time I finally got there, a town had sprung up. Amarillo they call it, and it sure was pretty."

"Why in the hell would you go home and not talk to your family?" the kid asked.

"It's complicated, kid," was my answer. I wasn't sure I wanted to open those wounds again, and I found myself wishin' I'd just kept my mouth shut.

There was a long pause until Slim broke the silence. "If you ever get out of here," he said, "go home, Bill. Forget the reasons why you can't or why you won't. Just do it." He seemed to look past the wall as he said it. A tear formed in the corner of his eye and lingered there 'til he noticed it and briskly brushed it away. "I left home when I was eighteen and never looked back. Unlike Stumpy, I didn't have a reason to run; I just did. I thought about home sometimes, but it seemed that every path I chose took me farther and farther away from it."

"My point, Bill, is this," Slim continued. "I'm pushin' fifty, in the beginning stages of tuberculosis, facin' a hangin' for killin' a man that if I'd gone home would still be alive." He paused a moment. "It's too late for me now, and it's one of my biggest regrets. My ma and pa are dead, died without knowin' where I was or why I left. That ain't right, and they never done nothin' to deserve it. Even if I could get outta here, I wouldn't have a clue how to find my sister and brother if they're still alive, and it sure as hell looks like I never will now." He looked at me intently. "Find a way to prove your innocence and go home." His last sentence seemed to fade into the darkness forming with the sunset. "Just find a way and go home," he said again.

Everyone sat in silence, each reflecting on the paths they'd chosen. The silence was almost deafening. Then out of the blue, Stumpy said, "That's the most words I heard outta Slim since I got here." Everyone chuckled, but the mood stifled any jubilant laughter.

After that most of the men drifted into sleep, probably thinking of home. I lay there awhile, listening to the crickets and the distant flow of the Colorado and wondered what my family might be doing at that moment. How could I ever go home after the things I'd done? I thought if they found out what happened at Gettysburg they'd never forgive me. The thought of it made me uncomfortable. Maybe I don't want Miss Watson to get me out of here after all, was the last thing I remember thinking before sleep found me too.

*****

Morning came, and it was already hot. I sat for a moment, shakin' the sleep out of my head.

"Must be the fourth of July," the kid said, standing at the hole in the wall. "They's people everywhere, and they're hangin' flags as far down the street as I can see. Dang I wish I was out there now," he continued. "Looks like a heck of a hoedown comin'."

"Well," I said, "unless it's Virgil workin' today, we might get to go to the courtyard. 'Least, we did last year, anyway."

"Don't count on it," Slim chimed in. "I've been here six years, and it's only happened twice that I heard of—once right 'fore I came and last year 'cause Virgil was sick."

"Well, we can always hope he gets sick this year," I said. "Let's hope deathly sick," Stumpy said.

We all started to laugh when we heard Virgil at the door with breakfast and a look on his face tellin' us that he'd heard our wish. "Might be I'm so sick I spill these beans all over the floor," he said. "I was thinkin' 'bout letting you into the courtyard today, but that comment cost you that, sure as shootin'."

Jed and Ben started to gang up on Stumpy for sayin' it. "Let it lie," I told them. "He was never goin' to anyway."

"You sure 'bout that, Billy?" Virgil said. "You sure seem to know a lot about me. You must be some kind of mind reader."

"It doesn't take a mind reader to know an asshole, Virg," I said sarcastically.

"One of these days," he shot back, "your mouth is gonna get you killed, William," he said, tryin' to egg me on.

"Well, I take comfort that it won't be you, because without your gun and those bars to protect you, you'd be hidin' with the school girls," I said.

"That just cost you breakfast, Bill, and maybe lunch as well," he said smugly.

"Make it dinner too, Virgil, because I stand behind my words."

Everyone got their breakfast and sat down. Virgil stood starin' at me through the slot, savoring his punishment against me.

SWEET JUSTICE   33

"I'm not like you," I said with a smile, "so if you're waitin' for me to start cryin', you're wastin' your time. 'Sides that, my hunger pains will hurt me a lot less than the pain you'll feel today every time the truthfulness of my words echo in the back of your mind."

Virgil slid the slot door closed with a snap and walked away. Stumpy said, "He's going to make things rough on you, Bill."

"I'm beyond caring. I never wanted to kill anyone out of sheer hate, but he comes close."

Stumpy turned to Slim and asked, "How's it you been in here for four years, puttin' up with ol' Virg? They forget about you or somethin'?"

"You mean why ain't they hung me yet?"

Stumpy tripped on his words, "I didn't mean to bring up a touchy subject. Just tryin' to make conversation is all."

"It's alright," Slim replied. "Truth is, they can't find a jury that'll convict me. I was caught dead to rights, killin' the son of a bitch that took my finger, but folks don't see it as murder since he pulled his knife first. And come on, who doesn't cheat at pharo? So he didn't really have motive. Self defense, they call it."

"Then why ain't they lettin' you out?" I asked.

"Well," Slim replied. "Turns out the man I shot was a friend of an important judge. I can get lawyers to defend me 'til the cows come home. But when it comes to fightin' for my release, they all lack the brass to go up against the judge. So it gets wrote down as a mistrial, and they send me back here. Only time I get another crack at it is when some new rookie lawyer thinks he's gonna make a name for himself. But somehow by the end, their own butt becomes more important than justice, I guess. Can't say I blame 'em," he added. "It's not like they're gonna make any money off me. Spent it all on women and whisky, and the rest I just wasted." His comment earned a round of laughs from us all.

"Have you tried an appeal to a higher court?" I asked. "A what?" Slim asked.

"An appeal. If the courts can't reach a verdict or prove guilt, you can ask to be tried in a different court."

"No one ever told me that," Slim replied. "Don't matter much at this point, I reckon. The first nail's already in my coffin, what with the TB and all."

"That's bull," I shot back. "You can live a long time if you could breathe real air. This here hell hole is just killin' ya faster. It's killin' us all."

"I think that's what the judge wants, my friend," Slim said with a forced smile.

"Well, you just hang in there, partner. If and when I get outta here, I'm a gonna find a way to get you out. You deserve to die a free man." "If you keep rubbin' Virgil the wrong way, you'll never get outta here either," Slim said. "There ain't no justice in Yuma. No sir, none at all."

*****

I looked over at the kid who was again standin' at the window, pining to be on the other side of the wall. "What you see, kid?"

"It's hard to see, but they must be settin' up for some kinda feast. They's people carrying food down the street, but they disappear 'fore I can see where they're goin'.

SWEET JUSTICE   35

"Real food," he went on, "not the beans we eat in here. There's a pig for the spit and all kinds of fruit. Boy, what I wouldn't give to have a piece of that bread with real butter, yes sir. They're eatin' good tonight, that's for sure."

The kid's description of what he saw reminded me that I hadn't got any breakfast, and my stomach growled somethin' fierce.

"Hey, there's your girl, and she's got a mess of them pies," he continued, oblivious to my hunger.

"She ain't my girl, kid. But I sure wouldn't complain if she was." "Sure wish I was out there," he said again.

"Why ain't you?" I asked.

"'Cause I'm in here," he said matter of factly. "Funny, kid. That's real funny."

He smiled, proud of his wit. "I'm not out there 'cause someone needed a lesson," he stated defiantly. "And I was just the one to teach it to 'em."

"Well, considering you're in here and they're out there," Ben teased, "maybe it's you doin' the learnin' and them doin' the teachin'."

His comment surprised me. Ben was a quiet type, content to let others do the talkin' for the most part. I chuckled at his comment. I had asked him once why he never talked. His reply back to me was words of wisdom we'd all do well to remember: "It's better to keep your mouth shut and be thought a fool than to open it and remove all doubt."

I could tell his comment irked the kid a little, so I drew his attention away by askin' what the lesson was. He said, "All I wanted was a job. I went to the company that hauls the ore from the mines to the crushers and told them I wanted to ride shotgun. They laughed at me and told me I was too young. I told them I could shoot better than anyone they had workin' for them. And to show them, I pulled my gun and proved it. Scared a couple of mules and caused them to drop their loads. Boy, did that get some fellers excited. The boss told me there was more to ridin' shotgun than being able to shoot and then told me I'd probably be doin' myself a favor if I was to leave."

"You ever shoot your gun when someone was shooting back at ya?" I asked.

"Can't say I have."

"Well, it's a whole different game, kid. Most men that ride shotgun have been on the wrong side of a gun, and they have learned not to panic when lead's flyin'. Could be that man saved your life. Ever think about that?"

"No," he said. "But I got sand, Bill, and I needed a job."

"Don't be in a hurry to get yourself killed, kid," I said. "I watched boys younger than you in the war bleed out and die, wishin' they'd a stayed home instead. Life becomes real precious when it's ending too soon, real precious indeed."

I could tell my comment caused him to think, so I gave him a moment to absorb it before I added, "Well, they didn't send you here for scarin' mules, so what's the rest of the story?"

He hum-hawed a bit, as if the stupidity of his deed was coming clear for the first time. "Well, when they wouldn't hire me to ride shotgun, I decided I'd switch sides and make the man ridin' it earn his pay."

"Did you kill him?" I asked.

"No, but I could've. But as I was ridin' up on the wagon, the two guys that was helpin' me came over the hill too fast. The one in front took a shotgun blast to the face. The driver took the other with his revolver. I was just comin' up the back side of the hill when the first shot was fired, and my horse took a piece of buck shot to the eye, went down harder than a bottle of frontier whiskey. I went over the front of him in a tumble and rolled to a stop with a shotgun pointed at my head. They had me dead to rights. The rest of the story kinda tells itself."

"Well, consider yourself lucky, kid," I said. "Two or three years of prison beats the hell outta bein' dead."

"That's tough luck," Stumpy commented.

"No, that's good luck," I replied. "If he'd gotten away with it, he'd be on the run, wanted for murder and robbery. If he got caught after that, they'd hang him, and if they didn't catch 'im, he'd spend the rest of his life lookin' over his shoulder. A few years of that and you'd wish they'd a caught ya. That's no way to live, always scared and edgy."

As I was finishing my sentence, the kid broke in. "Sounds like you're speakin' from experience."

"Not quite," I answered. "I rode herd with some fellers on the Chisholm Trail that were always lookin' behind 'em. Never could relax, those two. My foreman, Marty, told them one night that they ought to just take the night watch for the entire night 'cause they didn't sleep anyway. Made one of 'em real mad, and he pulled his gun on him. Fortunately for Marty, I saw it comin' and had my gun in his face 'fore he broke leather. I told him to sit down and shut up. That's what lack of sleep gets ya, kid. Messes with your judgment, makes you do things you usually wouldn't.

"Anyway," I continued, "Marty came to thank me later and said, 'We'll have to keep an eye on those two, Bill. Somethin' ain't right.' I said to him, 'You hired 'em. Where did they say they come from?' 'I didn't ask' was his reply. So I said, 'You mean to tell me that you hired two men for a cattle drive without getting any background on 'em?' I couldn't believe it, so I says to him, 'That's mighty dangerous, Marty.' 'I know,' he snapped back at me, and then proceeded to justify his actions. 'Boss hoped he could count on you and your two men to show up come drive time, but when you arrived with just one, we was short a hand. Then his damn nephew decided to chase after some gal going to Santa Fe. Promised he'd be back, but he didn't come. Who knows where the hell he is now, but it sure ain't here.' Then he said to me again, 'We gotta watch 'em close, Bill. Somethin' ain't right when a little razzen causes 'em to pull a gun.' I told Marty I'd keep my eye on 'em, and then I tried to calm him down by sayin' maybe he's just havin' a bad night. But truth was I was a little skittish from their reaction myself."

"So did they give you any more trouble after that?" Stumpy asked.

"Well, they didn't really get the chance to. Turns out they were on the run, and the next afternoon the posse caught up with them. See, lookin' over your shoulder doesn't guarantee you ain't gonna get caught, kid."

"Did they arrest them?" the kid asked.

"No," I replied. "They decided they were too far from any town, so they hung 'em right then and there. Marty started gripin' about bein' shorthanded, which made me laugh, considering he wanted rid of them the night before."

"So how did you get the cattle to market?" Stumpy asked.

"Well, as luck would have it, two members of the posse asked if they could finish the drive with us. Smart fellers. Full pay for half the drive." "How many times did you get to ride the Chisholm Trail, Bill?"

Ben asked.

"How many times did I have to, you mean? Ever been on a cattle drive, Ben?"

"No."

"Well, it ain't all that you think it is, believe me. Herdin' cattle is hard work. They are one of the orneriest, dumbest animals on God's green earth."

"I've herded cattle before," he shot back with a little irritation in his voice.

"I didn't mean any disrespect, Ben, but herdin' cattle is a whole different kettle of fish than drivin' 'em. Bringing cattle in from one range to another is tough, sure enough, and if you've really done it before, then you know how they like to bolt and run and how they'll circle back to where you started from. If it's an unfamiliar herd, you can spend a lot of time doin' it 'til you figure out which ones are the herd bulls. And until you do that, you'll chase the same damn cows over and over. But at the end of the day, you get to eat somethin' real, somethin' hot. You get to lay your head down in a bunkhouse with a roof to protect you from the comin' rain, and when Saturday comes, you can head into town for some fun and relaxation. The Chisholm is three months of hell. It's sun up to sun down, chasin' stupid cows out of bushes, finding the ones smart enough to realize that if they can hide from you they won't have to walk anymore."

"I get your point," Ben said.

"No, I don't think you do. There's blazin' sun and downpours that you can't explain to someone who's never been in one and rattlesnakes as big around as a man's fist. Have you ever tried to stop a herd from runnin' when they smell water?"

"Why would you have to?" the kid questioned. Ted and Slim let out a snicker.

"Don't laugh at me," he threatened.

"Keep your hat on, kid," I said. "The trick to any cattle drive is to get the beef to the rail head with as much fat on their bones as possible. Plus when you run 'em, it gets the adrenalin coursin' through them."

"So what does that do?"

"It affects the taste of the meat," I replied.

"Big deal," he said. "Who's gonna know that before you sell 'em?" "Doesn't matter," Slim interjected. "They'll know eventually, and so will the ranch you're herdin' for. The buyers might not want your beef next season, and the boss won't be as apt to hire you even if they did." "And once you get 'em to water, you gotta get 'em across," I continued. "You have to search for quicksand. There's calves that ain't never crossed a river before. They panic and get themselves buoyant, river carries them off. Crossin' a river with cattle is a dangerous game, my friend, and you'll earn your pay on them days, I assure you. But the worst part is at night you'll climb off your horse, sore as hell, eat your food, half asleep, and when you're finally gettin' the rest your body's been beggin' for, last man on watch is kickin' you to get up and take your

Sweet Justice

41

turn. Probably one of the reasons why I was so cranky the day you kicked me, kid. But the worst and most dangerous thing that can happen is a spooked herd. You get them cattle riled up, they're going to bolt. Cows ain't like a horse; they don't care what's in front of them.

A horse won't step on a man. A cow, on the other hand, will turn you to sausage."

"Stampede, they call it," Slim chimed in. "What causes that?" the kid asked.

"Lots of things," I said. "Thunder, wolves, cougars, a stick snapping in the dark if the herd's uneasy, or maybe your worst fear, rustlers milling around in the shadows."

"That does rub off some of the luster," Ben said.

"And that's just the first day," I said jokingly. "You got eighty-nine just like it, come sunup."

"There are advantages though. There's a freedom ridin' the range. Some of the most beautiful country you ever laid eyes on is another. If 'n you want to see land that's so pretty it hurts your eyes, go up to Montana and ride the trail to where the Belle Fourche, Red Water, and Hay Creek create a fork. Them black hills have ponderosa pines as far as the eye can see. It's not hard to see why them Cheyenne defend it with their lives. A man could live out his days there, happy as a flea on an old dog's back, sure enough, and there are some of the best new spreads I've ever seen being homesteaded as we speak. But the best part I'd have to say is when the ride's over and the cattle are sold, the boss comes up and hands you fifty gold dollars that you earned with blood and sweat and tells you thanks. There's certainly a pride factor that makes a man feel good about himself."

"Fifty dollars for that?" the kid said. "Sounds like more work than it's worth."

"Maybe, but it ain't stolen," I replied, looking him in the eye with a stare that made him uncomfortable. "And there is no shortage of places to spend it in a town with a railhead, I can assure you of that. It ain't what a man makes in dollars that makes him who he is, kid" I went on. "It's knowin' that he's been a part of somethin' bigger than himself in the end that matters."

"Did you ever have to fight any of the Injuns, Bill?" Ben asked. "More than once. Truth is, most don't want to fight you; they just want to be left alone for the most part. It's when we break promises we made to 'em that they get excited."

"Yeah, but they're savages, and they kill women and children. My pa says that the only good Indian is a dead one."

"Well, Ben, I sure don't condone them killin' women and children, but before you condemn a whole race of people to death, you have to stop and look at it from their point of view. They're just tryin' to hold on to what they think is theirs. And you and I would do the same, I reckon, if the tables were turned. Hate is a wedge that in the end destroys both sides.

Stumpy asked excitedly, "You really been all the way up to Montana, Bill?"

"Yep," I said, "and a whole lotta places in between. I might just go back there if I get the chance. There's a man up there named Seth Bullock who swears there will be a railhead there some day and is so sure about it that he's buyin' up property left and right. A man with money, grit, and sense would do well up there, I reckon."

SWEET JUSTICE   43

"Ever been to Laramie?" he prodded.

"Yes sir, I've gotta few stories to tell about that place. That's one wild town indeed."

"Well, go on and tell 'em," Jed shouted.

I was more than happy to because talkin' and thinkin' about the other side of the wall was a nice escape and a distraction from the oven-like heat that was upon us.

I started to reflect, lookin' for a place to start when Virgil slid the cell door slot open and yelled, "Lunch! Form a line, you bums. That is, everyone but you, Billy. You can just stay sittin'. I ain't got nothin' for you."

"Still eatin' at ya, huh, Virg?" I asked defiantly.

"Not like them hunger pains you're courtin'," he replied. "I'd imagine they's powerful bad, what with the smell of free-people food wafting in through the window."

"My hunger will die with the changing of the guard, Virgil. Your hunger for a back bone will pain you the rest of your miserable life."

He opened the door and came at me, stick in hand, and I stood up to meet him. The realization that he was surrounded by prisoners that had no love for him and the fact that he could see I wasn't scared made him think twice, and he doubled-stepped back to the safety of the door.

"More hunger pains, Virgil?" I asked as he slammed the door. "Shut up," he said as he hurried away.

"You can have some of my grub, Bill," the kid said. "I'm not sure I can stomach it after looking at all that real food outside."

"Thanks, but no thanks," I said. "I wouldn't wanna give Virgil the satisfaction."

"You got a powerful hate for 'im, don't ya?" the kid asked.

"Me and you share somethin', kid," I responded. "We both became acquainted with his stick the day we met him, and neither one of us deserved it. A man like that needs to be knocked down to size. His kind deserves to be on this side of the wall."

"He wouldn't last three days," Slim commented.

Everyone got a chuckle out of that, and as they ate, you could see their minds imagining what form of justice they would dish out if given the chance.

CHAPTER THREE

Independence Day

It must've been about three o'clock when I heard heated words coming from the front office.

"They ain't goin' out, and that's final," I heard Virgil say.

The other voice was hard to make out, but I could tell it was a woman speaking. Virgil was easy to hear, however, because he talked loud anyway, especially when he was angry.

"I'm in charge, Miss Watson, and I said no."

Miss Watson must have realized that a ladylike approach wasn't going to change his mind because when she replied you could hear her plain as day.

"My father says they are, Virgil, and last time I checked, you were a long way down the chain of command than he is. Don't make me go and find the sheriff on his day off," she threatened in a voice that if I hadn't heard it with my own two ears I'd a never believed it was possible.

Virgil's voice became quieter after that, and he said, "Emily, men don't learn lessons here if you go soft on 'em."

"And they don't learn if you treat them like animals either, Virgil," Miss Watson replied. "It's Independence Day," she said in a softer tone. "Let them have a little too." Virgil started to protest again, and Miss Watson talked over him, "I will go get the sheriff and my father if you force me to, and I would imagine neither one of them is going to be happy when they get here. So do us both a favor and let them out."

I heard the door from the office open and footsteps coming down the corridor. "Fine, Emily, they can go to the courtyard. But not Saunders; he's being punished."

All the men were up at this point. They could hardly contain themselves. "We're gettin' out!" Slim said, as giddy as new colt. "We're gettin' out," he said again.

"What's Mr. Saunders being punished for?" I heard her ask. "Causin' a riot," Virgil said as he started to unlock the door. "Okay,

boys. Guns at the ready," he said to the other guards. "They're comin' out."

Virgil swung the door open and said, "Listen, you're going to the courtyard. I don't want any funny stuff, or I'll put you right back in here, understand?"

Everyone formed the straightest line you ever saw. There was no way they were missin' out on a chance to feel the sun and breathe fresh air. They exited, and Virgil was about to shut the door again when Miss Watson said, "I would never question your authority to punish a man who has broken the rules, so I won't ask for Mr. Saunders to be released also."

Virgil smiled and again started to close the door. He looked at me with a face of victory. Miss Watson continued, "However, I do have business with William, and you certainly wouldn't want me to go in there, now would you?"

Virgil lowered his voice to almost a whisper at this point. "Miss Watson, there is nothin' you can do for him. I don't know why you would want to anyway. The man is a hired gun and a killer."

"Do you know that for sure? Or are you now a judge as well as a prison guard?"

"He had his day in court, and the jury found him guilty."

"A jury that was handpicked and armed with partial evidence," she exclaimed. "He was appointed a lawyer that lacked the courage and moral ethics to go up against a judge that had already decided he was guilty before the case even went to trial, simply because of his reputation. Have a heart, Virgil. All the witnesses William claimed could prove his innocence were omitted from the proceedings by somebody for reasons I intend to uncover. We do believe in justice in this country, don't we?"

Virgil reluctantly nodded.

"I think his case deserves another look. If the man is guilty, then you're right. He should be in this dreadful place, but if he's not, he deserves to be free. This can't happen if I can't get his side of the story." "He can't right now," Virgil said. "He ain't comin' out of that there cell today, and that's final."

"Okay," she replied. "You have relented enough by lettin' the others out, so I guess I'll have to go in there and speak to him."

"Now Miss Watson, you can't go in there. I won't have it."

"Well, then, whatever shall we do?" she said in the sweetest voice she could muster. "I do have things to discuss with him, and a fine gentleman with strength and authority like you, Virgil, has already shown that he has the decency to not allow a lady to enter that cell." Her Southern belle charm was working its magic, and it reminded me of bein' home.

Virgil was trapped like a fly in a web. "Get up, Saunders," he said. "The lady has requested a visit."

I was careful not to make eye contact with him as I passed and started toward the courtyard. Virgil was in a trance that could easily be broken with the slightest hint of smugness or victory from me. After all, Emily had worked so hard to spin it. But the labor it took to not chuckle was almost more than I could bear.

After we arrived in the courtyard, Miss Watson told the other guards to bring in the feast. Virgil started to protest but quickly changed his mind when Emily said, "Now make sure that Virgil gets the blueberry pie. I made that one especially for him."

To make sure that he felt like he was gettin' the best prize, she emphasized that it was the only one she made because blueberries were hard to come by this time of year. Virgil's countenance changed, and he said, "Why, thank you, Emily."

I rolled my eyes and smiled at her ability to play him and at what a gullible idiot he was.

Miss Watson excused herself to go make sure that the tables and food made it to their proper place. I scanned the courtyard until my eyes found my companions. The guards had them herded up at the far end. I watched them turnin' their faces to the sun and breathin' in fresh

SWEET JUSTICE 49

air in big inhales and then slowly lettin' it out again as if it was going to be the last breath they ever took. It was good to see Slim enjoyin' himself like a kid on Christmas morning, and I reflected on the lousy hand of cards he'd been dealt and at the same time admired him for not lettin' it turn him bitter. I took in a few deep breaths myself and enjoyed the slight breeze that had come up, closed my eyes, and turned my face to the sun, drinkin' in the energy it seemed to fill me with.

"Come and get it," Miss Watson hollered.

Every one turned to see what they were comin' to get. When their eyes saw the tables, they looked like kids at a general store starin' at the candy. They all started running when Virgil realized that the order he liked so much was coming unraveled. "Stop!" he yelled. "You will form a line and act like civilized men, even if you have to pretend. Guards, you will stand at the ready until the prisoners have their food and are seated. Do I make myself clear?"

"Yes sir," the guards said almost simultaneously.

The prisoners must've understood too because they were startin' to impress me with how perfect a line they could form. Everyone put as much on their plate as it could possibly carry without snapping in two and found a place to sit in the shade.

"Boys, we're eatin' good today," I said, and they all grunted in agreement.

Jed stopped stuffing his face long enough to exclaim that it was probably the best he'd eatin' in his life. Even Virgil was half human and seemed to forget I was supposed to be going hungry. Miss Watson stood on the sideline, watching the joy and momentary freedom she had brought to all that were in attendance. It seemed to please her, and with the combination of the smile on her face, the blue and white dress and the light from the sun in her hair, she looked like an angel. I looked back at the feast and the men that received it and thought how at this moment everyone was happy. There was no contention between the guards and us; we were all on the same side of the bars. Even Virgil seemed half human. And combined with blue skies and a breeze, I decided Miss Watson didn't look like an angel; she was an angel. An angle in the middle of a hell called Yuma, Arizona.

Emily caught me lookin' at her and flashed me a smile. I got up to walk over to her. As soon as Virgil saw my intentions, he told me to sit down and leave her alone. I sat back down again, feeling a little embarrassed.

"Leave it to Virgil to suck the joy out of somethin' good," Stumpy muttered.

"He thinks I'm makin' moves on his girl," I said.

"Well, are you?" the kid asked.

"What would a fine woman like Miss Watson ever see in me?" I replied. But in the back of my mind, I wished it. There was somethin' different about her, compared to other gals that'd come and gone. She had a way of makin' me want to be better than what I was, and she was damn hard to get out of my mind.

I realized at that moment how much I wanted to be where she was and share the same air she breathed. It made my heart hurt, and the feeling irritated me because I had never felt that way before.

I glanced back at her and saw her movin' towards me. Virgil quickly stood up and rushed to her.

"I'm much obliged for the hospitality, Emily," I heard him say.

She told him there was really no need to thank her and that it was her pleasure. She started my way again, and Virgil asked her if she'd like to come out of the sun and sit a spell. She politely declined and reminded him that her business at hand was with me and started to make her way to me a second time.

Virgil said, "Miss Watson, I cannot let you go over there. They are hardened criminals. I don't need to remind you that this is not a social event."

You could hear the underlying desperation in his tone when he said, "We have protocol here."

"They are boys, Virgil, and a few men who may or may not be guilty. I would hardly call them hardened criminals."

"Well, just the same," Virgil said. "I can't let you go over there." "Billy!" he yelled. "Miss Watson would like to talk to you. Get your sorry butt up and show her some respect. Guard, I want that man in shackles while he's talkin' to the lady."

I felt kinda bad for him because he didn't have the sense to realize what an ass he was makin' himself look like.

"Virgil, if you wanna have any chance of catchin' her eye," I muttered, "you'd need a ladder to get outta the hole you're diggin', and instead you have a shovel."

Miss Watson protested as they put the shackles on me. Virgil told her that he needed all the guards to escort the rest of the prisoners back to the cell and that he wasn't goin' to take any chances.

"If you want to talk to him so bad," he said, "it'll be on my terms."

I told her it was all right, that I liked the look of the shackles. "They match my boots," I said. Miss Watson seemed amused, and it irked Virgil, which in turn amused me. It made the shackles tolerable.

"Fine, Virgil," Miss Watson said. "Then I guess there's no reason for you to hover over us."

That sentence might as well've been a knife in his heart, and it wasn't hard to see that his petty punishment turned the tables around and had him wishin' he'd've thought it through before acting so hastily. His worst nightmare was coming true—not only was I goin' to talk to her against his will, but his actions had eliminated him from the picture, and any protest by him at this point would have no foundation.

He stared at me with a look that could kill as he excused himself. "Very well, Emi—I mean Miss Watson. You have one half hour."

We watched him walk away. Miss Watson waited for him to get out of earshot and then turned to me and said, "He's an exasperating man."

"He seems to have a shine on you."

"I know. He has since the day my father and I moved here. We were classmates all through our school years."

"How long ago was that?" I asked. There was a pause, so I quickly said, "I'm sorry, that's none of my business."

"No, you're fine, William. I was just thinking about the day we came here. It was such a drastic change from my childhood home."

"Where was that? If you don't mind my askin'—I mean *asking*." "Georgia. It was so beautiful there that I remember getting off the stage coach and thinking that there couldn't be an uglier place on earth than Colorado City."

SWEET JUSTICE 53

"Ma'am, I don't mean to sound stupid, but aren't we in Yuma?" I asked.

She let out a laugh that was music to my ears and explained that the town's name wasn't changed to Yuma until 1873. "When I came here, it was claimed by the state of California. In fact, that's how my father sold me on coming here. The simplicity of youth had me thinking of oceans, beaches, and gold. I never pictured California as having deserts, so you can understand my first impression."

"Yeah, it isn't the prettiest place on earth. In fact, it's the ugliest place I've been."

"Oh, it grows on you with time, William. The sunsets are beautiful, the cactus in bloom is magnificent, and the Colorado River has a rugged, powerful beauty. You should see the steamboats running up and down her. It reminds me of home."

"I never got the chance to see that part of it. I came into this town hurtin' somethin' fierce, thanks to Virgil and his gun, so I wasn't really in the frame of mind to drink in its hidden beauty. I saw the courthouse and then my home for the last three years—that fancy hotel room I share with five other guys."

Miss Watson laughed and told me I had a great sense of humor, considering the circumstances. "Well, I hope you get the chance to see it from the other side someday. It's a busy town, the only place to cross the river for miles. The military uses it frequently, and the canyons leading to San Diego are filled with a rugged majesty. You should see the Pacific Ocean as you make that last bend coming out of them. It's so blue and vast. Have you ever seen the Pacific, William?"

"Can't say I have, ma'am." "Please, William, call me Emily."

"Alright, Emily. The closest I ever came was Carson City, Nevada." "You do get around Mr. Saunders," Emily replied in surprise.

"That's a long way from here."

"Call me, William," I asked. "I like the way it sounds when you say it. Most people call me Bill, and I haven't been called William since I left home in '62. And yes, I do get around. Been to just about every territory in the West, I guess. That's what happens when you're runnin' from yourself. Hard to put down any roots when you're movin'—I mean *moving*."

Emily chuckled and said, "You don't have to try and be proper, William, but thank you. The slang and drawl of the Western man has grown on me. I've been here longer than I lived in Georgia, after all."

"Well, that's good. I was startin' to sound like I stuttered or somethin'."

We both broke into a laugh, and I felt some of the fear and anger leave me for the first time in years.

"You never did answer my question," I said, and she looked at me quizzically, tryin' to put her finger on it. "How long ago it was when you came here remember?"

"Oh, yes," she said with an embarrassed laugh. "I do have a way with running on when I enjoy the company. Please forgive me."

"Not at all. I could listen to you all day. Heck in just a few minutes, you've sold me on Yuma, and I ain't even seen it yet."

Emily seemed to be blushing a bit. "We came at the end of 1862," she said. "I was thirteen years old. My father left his store in Georgia to my mother and came out to open one here. He has a mind for business and could see that a place such as this would always flourish because of its importance and location. Turns out he was right; we have done extremely well here, I must say."

"Would I be too forward if I asked why you're ma didn't come with you?" I inquired timidly.

"My mother was never what you would call a domestic type. She was only happy when she could be center stage and was always looking for the next social gathering to feed her needs. She loved to have the gentlemen fawn over her and was content to allow our nanny to raise me so she could maintain her social status."

"How did your pa feel about that?"

"My father is a saint. We were always close, even though he was extremely busy, and I think he felt he had to make up for the neglect of my mum. He fell under her beautiful spell and charm, and I think he really thought he loved her. She, however, knew that his family owned the mercantile and property, and I believe that's where her heart was all along, although I would never say that to him. My mum played the part to obtain what she really desired, but even as a young girl, I could tell that my father saw through it and that his heart was broken."

"So he gave her what she wanted and moved on?"

"Sort of." She hesitated at this point and then said, "I'm not sure if I want to tell you why we left in the end. It could be hard on my father in his political circles if anyone knew the reasons."

"Well, I don't want to pry. I'm just happy you're here."

"Me too, William," she said as she reached over and touched my hand. "Me too. But enough about me. I do have a way with going on about myself when the real reason I'm here is for you." She reached into her bag and pulled out a scrap of paper and something to write with. "I need to know the names of the witnesses that can prove that you were not involved in the act that landed you here, and I need to know who the sheriff was that arrested you, as well as the year and details of what really took place."

"That's where there's a problem; the witnesses are either dead, or chances are they've moved on."

"Well, give them to me anyway. At least it's a place to start." "Well, Miss Watson, I haven't been known to run with high class people. So please don't think less of me."

"Sometimes, William, high class people aren't any better. They just hide their deeds and actions behind money and prestige, but the truth has a way of finding the surface like a festering sliver."

"Well, you could start with the saloon girls at the Bucket o' Blood. I s'pose there might be some of them still there. After I left the boys I rode into town with, I went downstairs for a drink. I don't know if they'd remember me by name, but I'm sure they'd sure remember the night; after all, it was one of their friends that was the victim."

"The victim of what?"

I flashed back to that night and tried my best to remember the details. As the flood of buried memories came back to me, my mouth just started runnin'. "Them bastards started passin' her around and gropin' at her. At first she was okay with it, but the drunker they got, the rougher they got. She asked them nicely to stop, but they didn't."

"And you weren't apart of it?"

"Hell no!" I said sharply. "I told them to settle down a few times, hopin' to quell the situation, but when the poor girl screamed and told them to leave her alone, I stood up and told them to knock it off. Keith told me to shut up. I said, 'Make me, Keith. You think you got it in ya?' Then I felt a sharp pain on my shoulder blade from the butt of Simon's gun. I grimaced in pain as he flipped his gun barrel and stuck it in my face. We had been in town about three days, and my partners hadn't stopped drinkin' since we got there, so Keith was extremely drunk by this point and told me to mind my own business or he'd let Simon shoot me. Then he said, 'Simon never liked you much, Bill, and has been itchin' to see if he's faster than you. Maybe when were done here, we'll find out.' 'Anytime you think you're man enough, you let me know. And if you hurt that girl anymore, I might shoot you anyway,' I told them. "Simon cocked his gun and looked to Keith for instruction; Keith started in with a taunting laugh and told me to get out of the room. I didn't have any choice, Emily. I'm sure they would've shot me, so I backed out of the room. The girl begged me not to leave her there with them, so when I reached the safety of the door, I assured her I was goin' after help. I made my way downstairs and asked the bartender where he thought the sheriff might be. He let out a belly laugh and said, 'Sheriff? What sheriff? You're in Tombstone, son. There's no law here.' So I asked him if the girl upstairs worked for him. He said she did, so I told him what was going on up there. He told me she was alright and not to worry about it. Then he motioned some of the other girls over, to keep me from makin' a scene, I guess. I told them I thought their friend was in trouble, and they replied that she was tough and could handle herself. About twenty minutes later, I saw them come out of the room and saunter down the stairs. I knew somethin' just wasn't right when they left the saloon without comin' to get a drink, so I made my way upstairs and peeked into the room. What I saw I'll never be able to get out of my mind as long as I live. I seen a lot of dead people—some I killed myself—but to see an innocent girl lyin' dead, knowin' I had the power to stop it is somethin' I'll never forgive myself for."

Emily put her hand on my shoulder and told me that there was nothing I could have done. "Some people are just born bad, William," she said, trying to comfort me.

"I know," I said. "But when I looked in that room, her head was turned toward the door, and her eyes were wide open, starin' at me. I could hear her voice in my head sayin' please don't leave me. I immediately ran down the stairs and out the door to see if their horses were still there, and they were, so I tried to figure out which way they had gone. The commotion of me leaving so abruptly must've caught someone's attention because I heard one of the girls yell, 'She's dead!' This brought people out into the street; I continued slowly walkin' down the boardwalk, lookin' in the shadows for them. I wanted to kill 'em, Emily. I wanted to kill them bad. All of a sudden, Keith and Simon came out of the alley on a dead run towards their horses. In the chaos someone said, 'There they are!' I don't know why they ran for their horses. It was definitely a drunken move because a sober man would know they didn't stand a chance. Once the shooting started, it was mayhem. They filled them so full of lead I don't know how they picked them up."

"That's good news. The bartender would know you were not involved," Emily said excitedly.

"Maybe," I said, "but if he testifies of that, he'll have to also admit that I told him about it and that could make him seem guilty of neglect because she was working for him."

"I didn't think about that."

"When you surround yourself with people from the under belly," I explained, "you learn fast that you can't count on many because they all have secrets to keep. Besides, there's no proof that she wasn't dead before I came downstairs the first time."

"Well, I'll have someone question him anyway and check to see if any of the saloon girls remember anything. So how did you avoid getting shot?" she inquired.

"I was down the street in the shadows. I guess they couldn't see me. At that point I didn't think anyone thought I was guilty. I came up as the crowd was dispersing to see the bodies as they were pickin' them up. A man named Waylon—no that's not right," I said flustered. "Wes."

Emily cut me off. "Wyatt," she said.

"Yeah, that's it. Wyatt. How did you know that?"

"His brother is the sheriff of Tombstone now. He and his brothers have managed to bring some law to the lawless."

"He didn't have a badge on when I met him," I told her. "How long ago did this happen?"

"About three years ago, give or take."

"He wasn't sheriff then," she said. "That would have been about the time they came to Tombstone. Apparently, they came to run a saloon and gambling tables, but I heard he was sheriff in Dodge City for a time, and it looks like it must be in their blood because he is again."

"Anyway," I said, "Wyatt came up to me and said, 'Rough lot you rode in with.' I turned and told him that I didn't have any idea how rough until tonight. I didn't like the way he was eyin' me, so I told him I didn't have anything to do with her death. Someone on the boardwalk shouted, 'Bullshit! You were up there in that room. I saw you come out.' I defended myself and said, 'I came out at the end of one of these fellers' guns. I was trying to stop it.' 'Doesn't look like you tried very hard,' he yelled back. 'The girl's dead.' I didn't do it,' I told him. 'Then why did you run out of the saloon so fast?' he taunted. By then people were starting to gather. 'I was tryin' to find the ones who done it.' 'To run away with them, I'll bet,' he said accusingly. 'No! To kill them for what they done!' I shouted. Wyatt said there was a lot of holes in my story and suggested we go to the jail and sort it out before the crowd got ugly. I didn't know what to do, so I turned to run."

"That was probably a mistake," Emily said.

"Yeah, I know that now," I agreed. "I didn't get far, however. Wyatt let me have it on the back of the head with the butt of his rifle. That's the last thing I remember before wakin' up in the town jail."

"It doesn't look good, William."

"I know. It didn't matter how much I pleaded with the deputy to go and check out my story either. I kept tellin' him I was innocent, and he kept tellin' me that the territory marshal would know what to do when he came to town. When he finally did, though, he brought back some Mexican bandits that'd been stealin' beef and runnin' it across the border—not that that was worth his time. The two men I was with and I, we'd've just stolen them back, if they could have stayed away from the tequila, that is."

Emily broke in. "You were stealing cattle?" she said in a surprised tone.

"Not really stealin' them," I explained. "More like stealin' them back. That's why I was down here in the first place. A rancher was tired of the Mexicans thinnin' his heard, so he hired cowboys that could shoot to come and stop it. He was payin' good money too, but my partners turned out to be drunks, and we never got to finish the job."

"I'm glad you cleared that up," Emily said relieved.

"Well, I'm not a thief," I assured her. "Anyway, he was expecting the train from Yuma to transport them because instead of just stealin' cows, they attacked a stagecoach and killed everyone on it."

"I heard about that," Emily said. "That's why Virgil had to bring the wagon down to the station that day."

"I guess those two really gave the marshal hell when he was trackin' them 'cause he came back lookin' like a wornout mule. I told him my story briefly, and he said he'd look into it, but when it was time to meet the train, they loaded us all in and sent us here. The marshal never did look into it, and the deputy sent the statements from the witnesses that put me with Keith and Simon and at the scene of the crime but not any that said I tried to stop it. My story never came up in court. It took the jury less than twenty minutes to find me guilty, and the rest is history." Emily wrote it all down and put the paper back into her bag. We spent the better part of the next hour talkin' about our childhood days and a number of other things. I remember thinkin' I could talk to her all day.

About that time Virgil came and yelled, "Time!"

"Probably not much you can do for me," I said to Emily, "but I'm much obliged that I got to finally tell my story."

"Don't give up hope, William. There's always a chance," Emily said. "I'm not quitting, so you can't either."

"Hope is all that's kept me goin'. That and the fact that I know I'm not guilty."

"I know you're not, too, so that's two of us."

"Come on, Billy," Virgil interrupted. "That's enough of your sob story."

"I'll see you again, William," Emily said as she turned toward the exit.

"Emily," I said quickly, "that was a good thing you did for us all today, and I'm much obliged to ya."

"You're welcome, William. And happy Fourth of July."

Chapter Four

The Long Hot Summer

Virgil shoved me in the cell and said, "Don't think you got one over on me, Billy. The only reason you ain't still hungry is because Miss Watson is a friend of mine."

"That or you were scared of facin' the sheriff and the mayor," I said, tryin' to get under his skin.

"You think you're so smart, Saunders," he shot back, "but if you think that Miss Watson is going to be able to help you, you're dumber than dirt. She's always been the type to bring home stray dogs and injured birds, and you're just another dumb dog to her, so don't get your hopes up. She may think you're innocent now, but the jury found you guilty because you are, and when she finds out the truth, that will be the last you see of her, sure as shootin'."

His tone turned meaner than usual, and he said, "You're scum, Billy, worthless trash, and I'll do everythin' in my power to make sure Emily Watson never comes back to see you and that you hang for your crime. So keep your lip flappin', tough guy. Oh and Bill, tomorrow when you're sweatin' your life away in here, I'll be out on the street talkin' to her." His last sentence he repeated all the way down the corridor, "and the day after that, and the day after that, and the day after that."

I kept my mouth shut—partly because I was done listening to him go on and on and partly because if *I* didn't stand a chance with a girl like that, I knew his chances were even smaller. But mostly because my stomach was full of the best food I'd had in years, and I was ready for a nap. I piled some straw to lie down on and pulled my hat over my eyes.

Slim said, "Man, what a day. That's the closest I've come to freedom in a long time, and I'd almost forgotten what real food tasted like. Yep, that was some day."

His comment got them all talking' 'bout their favorite part of the meal and how good the sun felt. Stumpy said, "I didn't realize how bad you all stunk until I got some fresh air." This brought on a rousing wave of laughter as they accused each other of bein' the smelliest one in the lot.

The kid asked me how my visit with Miss Saunders went. "It was okay," I said and left it at that.

"Are you going to tell us what she said?" he prodded. "Not tonight, kid."

"Well, that sure was a nice thing she did for us today, seein' she coulda spent the day with friends instead."

"Yep," I said. "She's an angel."

That was a mistake 'cause everyone started cracking off remarks about how I was shinin' on her. The teasing comments started flying across the room from every direction; it reminded me of grammar school all over again.

"An angel, he says."

"Bill's got him a girlfriend." "Is that wedding bells I hear?"

"The infamous Bill Saunders is settling down." "Shut up and go to sleep" I said jokingly.

Someone said, "Ooh, I think we hit a little close to home there, fellas."

They all started laughing, and it was a good thing my hat covered my face because I could feel my cheeks blush a bit, and I couldn't keep the smile off my face. I laid there listening to the revelry and celebration from the other side of the wall and thought, *What if she really could find a way to get me out of here? Would she be interested in a man like me?* I convinced myself that maybe she would and started imagining what it might be like as I drifted off to sleep.

*****

The next morning I woke up to Jed and Ben arguing about why the Civil War happened.

"Don't be stupid, Jed," Ben said. "We only went to war 'cause you wanted to abolish slavery, and it was none of your damn business what we did in our states. We didn't try and make you have slaves in the north."

Jed shot back that that was a simpleton way of lookin' at it. "The war was because you Southerners thought that the federal government favored the north."

"They did!" Ben shouted. "That's why slavery was on the chopping block, because Washington was caving to pressure from the north."

"Bullshit. And if the government felt they had to please the north, it's because our economy produces way more money than the South's, and we were footin' more of the bill than you, even with your slaves workin' for free. Maybe you should've gotten off your lazy asses and done some of the work you were forcing black people to do. They're not animals; they's people."

Ben shot back, "Maybe if you northerners tried to remember that we are separate states, you'd have realized it was none of your damn business what other states were doing."

Jed got in his face and said, "If your people would've pulled their heads out and seen with their own eyes that enslavin' human beings is wrong, the north wouldn't have had to force you to end it."

"Well, if *your* people had minded their own business—"

I jumped up just as they were about to go fist to cuff and stepped between them. "Knock it off," I said. "You're about to start the damn war all over again."

"Have you ever been whipped?" Jed shouted, looking around me to Ben. "And I don't mean with the back of your pa's hand. I mean really beat good because someone thought you was slacken?"

"No."

"Well, maybe you shoulda been. Maybe then you'd know what it's like to live in fear everyday and to have no freedom to choose for yourself."

"My pa never whipped or beat any niggers, if that's what you're aimin' to say."

"Well, most that owned 'em did, and bein' on the wrong end of lots of whippin's by my pa," Jed said passionately, "I can tell you it ain't no way to live. Bein' kept from schoolin' when ya want to go so bad it gnaws

SWEET JUSTICE 67

at ya, and watchin' all your friends get to, was a small taste of what your people made them Negros go through everyday."

"Well, I still say it was none of your business. No one was forcin' ya to have slaves," Ben replied.

I could see this was goin' to continue all day, so I grabbed them both behind the neck and told them to knock it off. "War's over, boys," I said, "and the fact of the matter is you both have some good points, but that's no reason to turn on one another."

"Well, it's clear to see that they didn't learn their lesson by gettin' their butts whooped," Jed answered. "Maybe they need a little more learnin'." His words made me want to backhand him, and I shouted, "Shut up! You don't know what you're sayin'."

He shot back that he knew full well what he was sayin' and that he meant every word.

"You ever watch a friend die or get his leg blown off?" I yelled in his face. "Have you ever seen a man with kids at home get a bayonet shoved through him, knowin' his youngins would never see him again?" I paused a moment. Jed was lookin' at me wide-eyed. I touched his shoulder to put him at ease and calmly said, "Well, I have—and worse. The nightmares that remain for those that lived I wouldn't wish on my worst enemy. Killin' someone that had it comin' is one thing; killin' someone 'cause you don't agree with their politics or way of life is another." I wanted them both to understand how precious life was. "I watched men die violently because some leader stirred them up to anger with half truths and flat-out lies."

I paused a moment, collecting my thoughts before I continued, "They ain't ever goin' home again, boys, or feel the warmth of the sun in spring, and they ain't ever goin' to get the chance to chase their dreams ever again. The cost of communication breakdown and compromise has robbed them of life forever. Jed, you're right; men don't have the right to make other men slaves. And Ben, you're also right; in America no state should have the right to dictate what happens in another state. And it doesn't matter which states are payin' the most taxes because each state has pledged to stand united for the protection of our constitutional freedoms and the union that makes us strong. If the union had been allowed to fall apart, odds are both sides would've collapsed. Countries like England, Spain, and France might be tempted to attack us if our ability to defeat them were cut in half. We need each other to survive. That's what the war was really over— brotherhood, despite our differences. The absolution of slavery was a product of a much bigger problem that'd been growin' for a long time. It was festering long before the first shots were fired. The constitution guarantees freedom to all—not just white men—and I believe that if we don't offer it to all, eventually, we'll all lose it. But the way to fix it is in our courts and through our political system, not by killin' men that should be our brothers. And for hell's sake, not by fightin' with someone you have to live with everyday. Too many good men and boys were slaughtered in that conflict. It's time to bury the hatchet and find common ground." I stopped to take a couple of breaths and to calm down a smidge, and I then said, "This heat and confinement will make us turn on each other like rabid badgers if we let it. So we're not going to, ya hear?"

"I'm sorry," Ben finally said. "I don't know why I got so riled up. My family never owned slaves anyway. Hell, we was so poor we was almost slaves ourselves."

Jed took a few minutes more to simmer down but eventually offered his hand to Ben and said, "I was wrong to come at ya. It's just that my pa used to beat me so bad when he'd get drunk that I feel for anyone who's in a position to get the same."

"I never knew that's what the war was over," the kid jumped in. "I always thought it was about slavery too. And I had no idea you was so smart, Bill. I thought you was just another dumb cowboy that was good with a gun."

"Well, I ain't goin' to claim to be real smart," I said, "but when I was a boy, my pa made sure Jim and I got an education, even if he had to work twice as hard on the farm to ensure it. I think that's why my desire to raise cattle put us at odds sometimes. He worked hard to make sure we could be more than farmers like him."

"Jim?" Slim spoke up. "I thought you said you only had sisters." "I did, but I had a cousin named Jim—Jimmy we called him. His pa died when he was young, and he came to live with us when he was eight. We were like brothers, him and I. We did everythin' together—workin', schoolin', huntin', and, my favorite, gettin' into trouble."

"Is he still with your family?" the kid asked. "No, he died in that damn war."

"I'm sorry," Jed said. "I had no idea. Otherwise I'd never—"

I cut him off before he could finish his sentence. "I know, Jed, it's okay."

Slim said, "I'll bet that was hard, Bill, findin' out you lost a brother like that. How'd ya come to know about it?"

Tears formed in my eyes, and I turned my head. "I was there. He died in my arms."

"Man, that's tough, Bill," the kid said.

"You have no idea," I replied, choking back tears. "No idea at all." I attempted to change the subject to something brighter by teasin' Ben about his sudden choice to talk. "You been in here a little over a year, Ben, and I think I've heard more come out of your mouth in the past three days than all the rest of the days I've known ya."

Some of the boys that'd been here awhile laughed and agreed with me.

Ben spoke up, "I'm usually a quiet person, have been all my life. I can still hear my pa tellin' my ma that there must be somethin' wrong with me. 'It ain't right,' he told her. 'Youngins his age ought to talk more.' It ruffled his feathers somethin' fierce, which is funny 'cause his bein' stern and loud is probably part of the reason I'm so quiet."

"Well, you sure weren't a few minutes ago," the kid said. "Damn near woke up half the town yellin' at Jed there." Everyone chuckled, including Ben.

"Yeah, I know. Been that way my whole life. I bottle it up for so long that when it finally comes out, it's like a powder keg."

"No need to tell us," Slim said. "We all witnessed that fact with our own ears, or what's left of them anyway." Everyone laughed at his comment.

"My pa used to frustrate me," Ben continued. "My ma told me it was because we were so much alike. That bothered me some because I didn't want to be like him."

"How do you mean?" I asked.

"My pa was gruff, and his comments had a way of diggin' at ya like a sliver in your trousers. They didn't really hurt so much as they rubbed and poked at ya. You know how you don't notice it's there most of the time, and then when you think it must be gone, you suddenly feel it again? His comments were like that—they'd bother ya when they was bein' said, and then I'd bury them away for a time, but in quiet moments they'd come back and echo in my ears."

"My pa was the same," Jed said. "I learned how to make his words bounce off me. I sure wish I coulda figured out how to make his belt do the same."

"I'm real sorry that's how your childhood was," Ben said to Jed. "Kinda makes mine seem like it weren't so bad. My pa wasn't the kind that would spend time with ya. He expected you to learn by watchin' him, and then he'd watch as I'd do it. 'Don't you know how to pay attention, boy?' he'd say, or, 'Somethin' must be wrong with you.' The ones that hurt the most though was when he'd push me out of the way and say, 'If you can't do it right, I guess I'll have to do it myself.' Somehow by fillin' my head with little sayin's, he decided he was doin' his job as a father and that somehow I was learnin' somethin'. But the truth is, when he died I didn't know how to do much."

"What did your pa do for work?" Stumpy asked.

"He was a carpenter, or at least that's what he claimed to be. But truth is he was a tinkerer, kinda good at some things but not real good at anything. Anyway, I grew real tired of bein' run down all the time, so I guess I stayed quiet so that I don't open myself up to bein' made fun of or bein' railed on. That's part of the reason why I'm in this hell hole. After my pa died, my ma didn't stay around much longer. I don't know what she saw in him, but after he was gone, she just seemed to draw into herself and became real sad. One morning I came to see if she wanted somethin' to eat and found her dead in her bed. The doc came and said he couldn't tell how she died, but he figured she died from stress and a broken heart."

"How old were you?" I asked.

"Seventeen. Anyway, we had chickens and a milk cow, so I thought I'd be alright with the money my ma had hidden in the jar above the fireplace. My grandpa had given it to her when he died, and she didn't tell my pa about it. She'd give me some sometimes when my pa wasn't lookin'. But when I went to see how much was there, I found it empty. Turns out my ma had been tappin' into it for a while to make up for my pa's lack of consistent work, and it wasn't long before I started to find out how much we were in debt. I had to sell the chickens and the cow and eventually the property. I didn't know how to do much, and the work I could pick up paid pittance wages, so eventually I started stealin' what I needed to survive. When I saw that I was finally good at somethin', I decided I could rob a bank and then I'd be set. That was dumb though. I lost two friends that day and wound up here. And the worst part of it is I still don't know how to do nothin'."

"Ben, when you get out of here, I'll give you the name of someone I know that owns a ranch," I said. "You go find him, and he'll teach you to be a cowhand. It don't pay much, but it's an honest living."

"You'd really do that for me?" Ben asked. "I'd be much obliged, Bill."

"Now hold on," I said. "If I do this, you have to promise you won't steal from him. He's a friend of mine, and dealin' with cows ain't no walk in the park. You're gonna work for every penny you earn."

"I can, Bill. And I won't, I promise. I swear I won't, Bill, I swear." "Alright, Ben, keep your hat on. I'll write him a letter as soon as I can."

Ben sat down with a smile on his face like he'd just found a twenty-dollar gold piece. Jed gave him a little friendly nudge that knocked him off balance, and I could tell they'd come to understand each other a little better and that things were gonna be all right between them.

"Stopped the war before it got out of hand," I said to myself. "Where were you in '61, Bill?" The thought made me smile.

"So Jed, everyone's spillin' the beans about why they're here. What's your story?" Stumpy asked.

"Stealin' horses," Jed answered without hesitation.

"Stealin' horses," I said with just a little disappointment in my voice. "And I was just startin' to like ya."

"Well, I had a good reason."

"Jed, stealin' a horse is like stealin' a man's woman. You're lucky you're here and not swingin' from a tree someplace."

"I know, but the folks that caught me knew my pa." "Friends of his?" Stumpy asked.

"Not at all. If 'n they was they'd a hung me for sure but not 'cause they was honest. My pa's friends was bad people, and my pa weren't much better."

"They were folks from the town we lived by, and they were all aware of my pa and what he did to me. They knew the bad things he did too but could never prove it. But more than once I caught the glint of the sheriff glassin' our place, tryin' to catch him as he'd slip away and slip back in. One thing about my pa, he was damn good at what he did."

"And what was that exactly?" I asked.

"Don't rightly know, but I can tell ya it weren't good. I used to slip away and go to the schoolteacher's house. She done her best to try and teach me in spurts whenever I felt I could disappear. Wasn't often, but I know some of my letters and a little math. Never did learn how to make letters say anythin', but it felt good to learn somethin'. She taught me about the war and why it happened and about how we got our freedom from them red coats, but mostly she just made me feel like I had a chance and that I didn't need to be like my pa. Most my lickin's came after I was sneakin' back from her place, but I didn't care about them ones."

"So why were you stealin' horses?" Slim asked.

"My pa made me do it. Some men showed up at our place in the middle of the night. Their horses looked like they'd been run pert near to death. My pa woke me up and said we didn't have enough horses to give 'em fresh ones and told me to go and get some. I asked him from where and he told me the Hendersons' place. I told him that the Hendersons were my friends. Then he got spittin' mad and told me to man up and get goin', gave me a swift kick, and said, 'Hurry up and get.'"

"Why didn't you just go to the sheriff?" asked the kid.

"My pa woulda killed me had I done that. And I mean kill me for real. You don't cross my pa, no sir. I went and got them horses lickity split and brought them back just like he told me. But it turns out they was watchin' our

SWEET JUSTICE 75

place, and when I came in with the horses, the sheriff and some of the folks from town had them all corralled with their hands in the air. That was the last time I saw my pa, and I sure ain't missed him, that's for sure. The sheriff put me under arrest for stealin' horses. When Mr. Henderson said, 'He was just followin' his pa's orders. I think we can let it slide,' the sheriff said he was aware of that, but since I was seventeen, I had to be held accountable for my actions. And he ventured a guess that a little time behind bars might make me fly straight when I got out. So here I am."

"Well, after hearing your story," I said, "I ain't goin' to hold it against ya."

"Bill," he said, "I got no place to go when I get outta here." He paused for a moment.

I noticed Jed tryin' to say something. "What is it, kid? Spit it out."

"Well, sir, do you think I might be able to try that cowboy stuff too? If not, it's okay, I'd understand," he said.

"Can't see how puttin' two names on that there letter could make much difference," I replied, "but same goes for you as it does for Ben there, understand?"

"Yes sir. Yes sir indeed," he answered excitedly.

About that time Spencer, one of the guards, slid the cell door slot open and yelled, "Breakfast!" It was music to my ears to hear that it wasn't Virgil. And it must've been to everyone else's too because the line seemed a little sloppy.

"Good news, fellas," the guard said. "There was pie left over from yesterday, and Virg isn't here to say no. So I'm gonna let you have some come lunch."

Everyone let out a cheer but me. The word pie made me think of Emily and how much I'd like to see her again. Spencer just made it worse when he said, "Bill, I don't know why, but Virgil wanted me to tell you that he'd be talkin' to Miss Watson today. Does that mean anything to you?"

"Yep," I replied. "It means Virgil's gonna make himself look like an ass again." We all started to laugh, including Spencer, and I continued, "That poor bastard doesn't have a prayer." I tried hard to convince myself that it was true, but my innards were all tied in knots.

I attempted to eat my breakfast, but my mind kept stewin' about what Spencer had said, and it made me lose my appetite. I stirred at it awhile, and then I heard Ted ask if I was gonna eat it or draw pictures in it. I told him I wasn't hungry and said he could have it if he wanted it. "Hell, yeah," he said. "I'd never pass up food. Seems like I spend most of my time bein' hungry 'round here."

Ted wasn't one that could be accused of being skinny. He wasn't so much fat, but he sure wasn't skinny either, probably because he lived with mostly Mexican people before he wound up here, and Mexican food has a way of sticking with a person, especially when they're not a Mexican. He was from New Mexico and lived near the border all his life, so he spoke English and Spanish. Funny thing, though, he didn't speak either of them very well. But boy, could he use a rope. If you were goin' to spend the day branding cattle, Ted would be the one you'd want to partner up with. One day he talked the guards into bringing him a lariat. Took some coaxing and bragging to get 'em to do it, but he claimed he could dance with it and rope anything they wanted him to. No one believed

Sweet Justice

him. They thought he was tryin' to get the rope for somethin' else, and they didn't want to be responsible in case they were right, but he kept on boastin' 'bout how good he was with one. I think they finally gave it to him so he'd shut up. Either way they promised that next time Virgil wasn't working they'd bring one to him. It was a couple days later at lunchtime when the guards opened the door and threw one to him. "Let's see if you can do what you claim," they said in a heckling tone of voice. Ol' Ted, he'd really built himself up, and I think they just wanted a good laugh when he fell on his face. Ted held that rope like it was a newborn baby, and his eyes seemed to sparkle, and when he got that rope a twirling, dang, what a show. Turns out he was better than he claimed. I never saw anyone do with a rope what he could, jumpin' in and out of it as it spun and then makin' it go up and down while he stood in the center of it. It was truly something to see.

"What else can you do?" the guards asked.

"Well, if you give me double lunch rations, I'll show you," he said. The guards thought about it for a second and said, "Okay, Ted, it's a deal, but if you fail to impress us, you don't get lunch tomorrow, deal?" "Deal," Ted said. Well, he got that rope twirling down by his feet and then brought it up to his side. The loop got bigger and bigger until it was almost as big around as he was tall. Then he told the guards he was goin' to jump back and forth through it. They laughed and said they didn't think he could do it, so Ted reminded them of the deal then jumped through the spinning rope. Not just once either; he jumped through the other way too and then kept doin' it back and forth. It was truly somethin' to see.

One of the prisoners started running in a circle and yelled, "Let's see if you can catch me with it."

Ted said, "That's too easy. I'll catch your foot."

The guards laughed and said, "We'll give you double rations tomorrow if you can pull that off." Ted got a big grin on his face, threw the rope, snagged his leg slicker than slick, gave a little tug, and down that feller went. The whole cell busted up laughing, except the guy lyin' on the ground, that is; he didn't think it was so funny. And seein' him sit there staring at us while we laughed just made us all laugh harder.

Ted was a decent kind of guy. He knew how to work hard, obviously, because he had kept the same job for about thirteen years.

Most cowhands drifted and hired themselves out to the one payin' the highest wages, so rarely did anyone stay around that long. He seemed honest enough too. Not the kind of guy you'd figure to be in here. He kept to himself for the most part but was eager to help anyone if they needed it. He'd've been a great mediator because he had a way of gettin' people in a confrontation to see the other's point of view. That is, until it turned heated and violent. In those cases he was more than happy to hang back and let it play out on its own. If someone had a problem with him, he was just as content to give them their way rather than argue with them.

So when I found out what he was in for, it took me by surprise. Turns out that he worked on a ranch owned by an Irish immigrant that was close to the border. When Ted came lookin' for work, his potential boss told him that he only hired Mexicans because he thought they were better with cows than Americans. He said it loud enough for all his hands to hear, gave Ted a wink, and whispered, "I don't have to pay them as much to do the same amount of work." Ted bet him that he could rope, ride, and handle the cattle better than his other hands and promised he'd be loyal as a 'coon hound. Then he swore he'd stay on as long as there was work. "I don't know," he was told. "I got some real good hands workin' here," shooting off another wink. So Ted challenged him. "How about a wager?" he asked. "If I can out do them, you give me a job with a fair wage." And if you can't," the owner replied, "what do I get?" Ted thought for a moment and told him, "You can have my horse, deal?" The two shook on it and headed for the corral.

Well, needless to say he won the wager, and the owner of the ranch was damn glad to have him, made him boss that very day. It didn't sit well with the hands that were already there though, so Ted was never accepted as part of the group. They did work hard for him, however, because they all knew he could outdo them and proved he would work alongside and as hard as them. Besides, their boss liked having him around. He told me that he liked the job a lot, except for the fact that they all poked at him with negative remarks all the time. It didn't take long before they all knew that he didn't like confrontation, so they were always stirring the pot and questioning his authority. Ted took it for thirteen years and performed his job well in spite of it. Until one day he just snapped.

There was an argument about who was goin' to bring the cattle down from the foothills to the lower pasture. Ted had assigned four men to go, but when it came time, they put up a fuss. It was raining, so no one wanted to go out in it. They started griping that the only fair way to decide was drawing straws or something. Ted told them that the call was already made and that they needed to just get it done.

They ganged up on him and started yelling about how he should be the one that went. "You're the big shot boss," they said. They claimed he only got the job because he was an American and started calling him a boot licker. Ted fell apart and started to lose control, and the more he broke down, the more they came at him. I don't know if he had a nervous breakdown or if it was momentary insanity, but when one said his ma was a puta, he pulled his gun out and started shooting.

There were Mexicans running everywhere. They were diving behind anything that would provide cover. By the time his boss heard the shooting and could get out to stop him, three of them lay dead and four more were hurt bad. Ted was yelling things no one could understand and shooting his guns off without bullets. They took him to the closest doctor because no one knew how to help him. He was still talking nonsense and seemed oblivious to what he had done. They sent him here without a trial. I don't think it was for shooting the Mexicans though. I guess they just didn't know what to do with him and felt that he wasn't going to hurt anyone if he was locked up. But without a trial, there was no clear date set for his release, and no one could tell him if he ever taste freedom again.

I couldn't keep my mind off what the guard had said, no matter how much I tried. I looked over at Ted who was polishing off my breakfast and then around the room at the others. Slim was sleepin', or at least appeared to be; Stumpy was talkin' to Ben about mining and what kind of rocks to look for if one was to be looking for silver and gold; Jed was drinking water from the barrel; and the kid was back at the window again, longin' to be on the other side of the wall.

Artwork by Mark Inkley

Chapter Five

Bad News from Lincoln

"Hey, kid," I said, "time goes by faster if you can keep your mind off the things you can't be doing. It'll eat you up."

"Can't help it."

"Why don't you take this time to decide what it is you're gonna do when you get outta here and what you're gonna do so you don't come back again."

"What do you mean?" he asked.

"Life's tough, kid. A man needs somethin' to do that gives him purpose. Somethin' he enjoys doin', even if it doesn't make him rich. When a man can take care of himself without needin' to rely on anyone else, he can look in a mirror and like what he sees and can live out his days knowin' he matters. You need to decide now how you're gonna spend the rest of your life. And what it is you're gonna do with it. Somethin' that doesn't include robbin' or wagons."

"Don't know what I want to do," he said.

"Well, I can tell you this. If you're plannin' on makin' your way with a gun, get it outta your head. There's always gonna be someone faster or luckier than you, and," I emphasized, "it becomes real blurry when you're tryin' to decide if you're workin' for the good guys or the bad, and that's real important." I looked at him and established eye contact then continued, "You can find yourself on the wrong side of the law and the wrong end of a gun quicker than hens lay eggs. Now, I'm not sayin' that you can't make a livin' hirin' yourself out as some form of security—you could be a body guard or somethin' like that."

"How did you do it, Bill?" he asked.

"Well, I always made sure I knew who I was workin' for and what the objective was. And then I followed my gut. If you're gonna end someone's life, you need to make damn sure they have it comin'."

"I could do that."

"Let me just warn you—enemies multiply fast, and there's always gonna be someone who wants to know if they're faster than you. The problem with that is the only way to find out is one of you has to die, and the one that doesn't has to live with himself."

He turned back to the window and without lookin' at me said, "I don't know how to do anything else. My pa is a blacksmith, and I never wanted to do that."

"That's a noble job, kid, and you'd always be busy, that's for sure." "But it's just not in me."

"Well, there are other things. Have you ever thought about workin' for the railroad? They're sure layin' a lot of track nowadays."

"That looks like too much work."

"Kid, don't ever be afraid of work. Anythin' worth doin' is worth doin' well. Besides, if you think bein' a hired gun ain't work, you haven't thought it through very well." There was a minute or two of silence while he drank in my comments. So I asked him, "Do you want a family?"

"Hadn't thought about that. Hell, I'm just a kid myself," he said. "Which reminds me, how come you call me *kid*?"

"I guess you never told me your name," I reminded him. "And you remind me a lot of a sassy kid I met about three months before I wound up here, up New Mexico way. We was all shootin' to kill some time, and I was enjoyin' the attention I was gettin' for bein' the best when he pulled his gun out and gave me a run for my money. 'Nice shootin', I said. 'What's your name?' 'They call me Billy,' he said with just a hint of arrogance. 'Well, Billy, that's the best shootin' I ever saw from a kid your age. Billy the kid who can shoot is what they ought to call you,' I told him. He said that sounded good to him since it was true. His cockiness made me chuckle. Anyway, he started his adult life with no direction and a list of mistakes just like you but got lucky enough to find a man I worked for once in a while named John Tunstall. He's a British fellow that made it his duty in life to take young men and try to steer them right, give them another crack at it, you might say. Has himself a right nice ranch and a dry goods store outside of a town called Lincoln. "Tunstall," the kid said out loud, more to himself than to me. "That name is familiar." All of a sudden his eyes lit up as it came to him. "Was Billy's real name Bonny?"

"Yeah! How did you know that? William Bonny, but he asked me not to call him that. Threatened, really.

Kinda easy to remember, considering it's my real name too."

The kid spun around when I said it and excitedly exclaimed, "That's why that name's familiar. Bill, I don't know how to tell you this, but Tunstall is dead."

"Dead? How?"

"Well, apparently he was gunned down by some men that worked for a guy named Murphy, I think."

"Yeah, that would be right. Rotten son of a bitch too," I said. "He also owns a ranch and store in town and wasn't very happy when Tunstall came along to give him some competition."

"Why's he rotten?" the kid asked.

"Where do I start? First thing I guess would be that he was able to worm his way into a government contract to supply beef and vegetables to Fort Stanton and the Apache Reservation because he was a soldier in the war, but the bastard never even saw combat. Then he got caught selling property to farmers on credit, and it wasn't even his land to sell. When the poor bastards couldn't make the payments, he'd foreclose on them and took their property, crops, and cattle to fulfill the contracts to the military. And he got away with it too," I said angrily, "because he had contracts with the Santa Fe ring."

"What's the Santa Fe ring?" the kid asked.

"Not what, *who*. Just more corrupt politicians who think they're above the laws we all have to live by."

"Well, now you can add his involvement in a big war to your reasons to hate him. It's goin' on up there right now," the kid said. "That Bonny fella's goin' by the name of Billy the Kid. Must've stuck when you called him that. He's part of an outfit callin' themselves the regulators. I heard they shot the sheriff up there 'cause they claim he had somethin' to do with Tunstall's death."

"Probably did," I said. "Murphy owns everyone in Lincoln. I never did like him much. Did some work off and on for a Mr. Chisholm, and he told me if I was ever lookin' for work to go and hire out to Murphy, but I never did. I just couldn't stomach the guy."

"Maybe that was a good thing."

I let the information roll around in my brain for a moment before I spoke again. "Damn, I knew there was tension between Tunstall and Murphy, but I had no idea it would come to killin'. Old man Chisholm, is he tangled up in it too?"

"Hell yeah, he is. The papers make it sound like everyone up there is," the kid said. "He wasn't at first, but he kinda got drug into it when Billy started killin' everyone. He's siding with Murphy now, I think."

"That can't be good. Bonny is damn good with a gun and cocky to boot. That could turn into a blood bath real quick. Tunstall had some boys workin' for him that ain't gonna take his death lyin' down."

"If'n what I heard is true," the kid went on, "they weren't. Someone deputized them to go and arrest the men that done it, but they was just killin' 'em as fast as they could find 'em."

"What about a man named Garret?" I asked "Him and I are distant friends."

"Garret was runnin' with the regulators, but he ain't no more. They made him a sheriff after the shootout in Lincoln. Even the military came in for that one. They shot it out for three days and finally burned 'em out. They only got one of them though and killed Tunstall's partner. Last I heard Garret was huntin' them all down to bring them to justice. I can't believe you ain't heard this. It's been in all the papers from San Francisco clear to New York City."

"Yeah, well, you'll find you don't get much news in here. Bonny knows New Mexico like the back of his hand, and he speaks Spanish. They could hunt for him a long time; that is, if he's not already in old Mexico."

"They was already, and then they came back. It looks like it ain't goin' to be over 'til everyone's dead."

"Damn, that's too bad," I said. "See, kid, that's where the gun can take you, and it'll take you there fast."

"You sure know a lot of people, don't you?"

"Yep, s'pose I do. That's what happens when you're a rollin' stone, kid."

"Bet it's taken you a lot of places, ain't it?" "I've been a place or two, that's for sure."

"Did ya ever see the salt sea in the desert?"

"Yep, I followed the Bear River almost to its bank." "What took you up there?"

"Drove some cattle to Fort Bridger from Laramie and decided if I was that close I might as well go and have a look see. Heard tell them Mormons had a right nice city in the middle of the wilderness. Turns out they had a bunch of them."

"I heard they have horns. Is that true?"

"No, kid, it ain't," I said with a laugh. "Actually, they have some real pretty girls runnin' around. And they've turned that desert floor into some mighty nice farms. There are people from all over the world livin' there, and they've gotta be some of the most industrious people I ever came across."

"Where did you go from there?"

"A man in Salt Lake City told me that a fella named Porter Rockwell was tryin' to find someone to drive a few cattle to a rancher outside of Virginia City. And since I seem to be drawn to wild towns, I took the job. Now kid, if you want to meet a man that'll put us both to shame with a gun, he'd be the one to seek out for sure. Man's got nerves of iron and has probably been more places than me. Has a hide of just about every animal you can think of, includin' a big ol' grizzly. I'd venture a guess that man ain't scared of nothin'." Then just to make it sound more adventurous, I added, "He lives on the route of the old Pony Express. In fact, that's the trail I followed to get to Virginia City."

"I think I could find myself wanderin' to see what's out there," the kid said.

"Oh, you do, do ya?" I replied with a chuckle. "Gets mighty lonesome at times, and you have to have a way of feedin' yourself while you're doin' it."

"How do you do that?"

"Well, I moved a lot because of the cattle business, but there was money at the end of each adventure. I was never content to stay workin' in one place for very long or for one man as far as that goes, so over time I got to know a lot of people that knew they could trust me to get the job done, and when I'd finish a job, I didn't have to look very hard to find another."

"I can shoe a horse and shoot a gun," he replied, "but I don't know much about cows."

"I'd sure be happy to teach you when you get out, that is, if Miss Watson can find a way to get me outta here first."

"Sorry to bring up a sore subject, Bill," the kid said, "but why are you in here?

"They convicted me of accessory to murder," I told him. "Don't they hang you for that?"

"Only if the jury votes to, kid, and they didn't get a unanimous decision in my trial. So unless some lawyer decides to take it to trial again, I'll just rot in here for who knows how long."

"Didn't they tell you in court?"

"Yeah, they gave me ten years, but I don't think a man can stay healthy enough in this place to make it that long. And if Virgil has his way, they'll put me back on trial. Then I'll hang for sure."

"Are you really innocent, Bill?" he asked with a little hesitation. "Yeah, kid, I am."

"Well, I hope you get out then." "Me too, kid, me too."

"Well," the kid said, "I know I won't get outta here for three long years. They was pretty frank when they passed judgment on me."

"Three years ain't so bad, kid, if you use the time to learn from what you did. Two men are dead because of your bad decision, remember that." I grabbed his ear and tugged his head so he had to look in my eyes and said, "Take this time to make it right, ya hear. Make it right in your heart, and make damn sure you make yourself understand it, or you'll wind up like Bonny. That ain't no way to live. And when your time is done, you come find me. I'll teach ya about them cows, and you can shoe my horse or somethin'."

He laughed when I said that and then got a real serious look on his face. "I don't know if I can make it three years, Bill."

"You'll make it, kid. It don't seem that long. Take it from someone who's done it, ya hear?" There was a pause as he stared at the floor. "Ya hear?" I asked again as I nudged him a little.

"Okay," he replied. "But, kid."

"Yeah?"

"You gotta quit lookin' out that dang window." "I'll try, Bill, I'll try."

Wasn't long after that the guard on duty yelled for lunch. After passing on breakfast, I was hungry, so I stood up like all the rest and got in line. When they started serving, however, the pie that was promised us wasn't on the tin.

Jed said, "Hey, where's the pie we was promised?"

The guard said, "Sorry, boys. Virgil came by a while ago and saw it and said there was no reason for it to go bad sittin' here, so he took it. The new guy told him that we were gonna give it to the prisoners."

"What did Virgil say to that?" I asked.

The guard hesitated like he wasn't sure he wanted to say and then blurted it out. "He said those worthless scum bags don't deserve it. Good thing I came by before you wasted it like that."

"That man is a son of a bitch," Jed said.

"Don't say that too loud, boy," I told him. "He feeds off the punishment he dishes out. Could be he's outside that window right now just to drink it in." After I said it, I could've sworn I heard someone hurry away from that very spot.

"Dang it," he said quietly. "I was lookin' forward to that all morning." "Me too," I said, "but life's like that. Let it slide. If you don't set your sights too high, then the disappointment is easier to swallow, and the rewards are sweeter."

"I'm not sure what you mean," Jed replied.

"Well, it's like this. You're gonna find in life that sometimes what's promised doesn't always come, that tasks that are laid at your feet aren't always gonna happen on sunny days. You might have to work in the rain sometimes. Ain't that right, Ted?" I asked.

It took him a half a second to get what I was sayin', and then he replied, "Yeah, that's for sure."

"The point is, Jed, life's gonna come at ya from all directions—sometimes soft, sometimes hard. And if you learn to take it, no matter how it's dished out. The peaks aren't as high, for sure, but the valleys don't seem so low either, and then the journey becomes easier, you know what I mean?"

"Think so," he said.

"Kickin' against the pricks," I continued, "just makes your feet soar, and the pricks like Virgil just laugh at ya, so don't give 'em the satisfaction."

"I'd take the sore feet to have a round of kickin' if it was Virgil at the other end of my boot, I'll tell you that for sure," Stumpy said.

Everyone sounded off in agreement as they ate their lunch. It was quiet after that. I think everyone was a little disappointed, but after what I'd told Jed, they were content to suffer in silence.

Finally, the kid broke the quiet and asked, "Bill, you ever get in a scrape you thought you might not get out of?"

"More than one," I answered. "I was in the war, remember? When the second day of Gettysburg came around, I was sure it'd be my last."

"How so?"

I hesitated, not sure if I was ready to think about it. I'd found a place deep inside me to lock those memories away and was content to let them rot there.

"What was the war like?" Ben asked.

"It was hell, Ben, pure hell." Once I had cracked the door, the words escaped and formed on my lips. "There was so much chaos and noise," I said. "And it seemed better to keep movin', even if it was in the wrong direction because those that hesitated seemed to die before my eyes. It was like you spent every minute waitin' for your turn to have parts of you blown off or to be the next bloody corpse lying in some twisted unnatural heap on a fence or rock wall. And to make matters worse, minutes seemed like hours." I paused a moment, not sure I wanted to talk about it anymore. My gut said stop, but my mouth kept running. "Men screamin', smoke everywhere, and those cannons, those damn cannons, keepin' time with the horse hoofs pounding the hell out of the blood-saturated ground. And every time you think you'd found a place where you could stop a moment and collect your thoughts and reset your bearings, they'd come out of the trees. Trees filled with smoke that was huggin' the ground like some eerie scene straight from hell, with their sharpened bayonets that look like the teeth of some monster that has to kill the one comin' at it. And you find yourself partly hopin' you fall to it so you can leave the terror that surrounds you behind because you can't remember green pastures anymore and all happiness has been ripped from you. Then you're sucked into an abyss where all you can see is the fear and terror in the eyes of man in front of you as you take away from him all he's had and all he's ever gonna have ever again."

I put my head in my hands at that point, trying to wrap my head around what for so long had only seemed like a nightmare I'd had once, screaming in my head for it to leave me alone. After a few minutes, I looked up and came back to my surroundings. They were all silently looking at me in disbelief.

"Holy shit," Ben said, "now I can see why I had a smack comin' yesterday. I guess I never thought about the reality of it all. I'm really sorry, Bill."

"It's okay, Ben. It felt good to let it out. I carry those memories around inside me, and they eat at me like a cancer. I guess they always will. It's been eighteen years since that day, and it still haunts me like some kind of a demon I can never escape from. There were other battles after that, but none came as close to hell on earth like that one. If there were ever a day God turned his back on the earth, that was it."

Talkin' about it for the first time forced my mind to focus on the worst moment of my life, and before I could stop it, the thought had made its way to my mouth. "That moment," I blurted out, "changed my life forever." I hesitated and then broke down in tears, sobbing uncontrollably, my darkest secret so close to my lips and the horror of my hidden deed desperately clawing to get out and destroy me. I felt someone's hand touch my shoulder, and I tilted my head towards it and broke down again, ashamed that I'd lost my composure.

It took a few more minutes before I could talk again. When I finally could, I said, "That day was hell, boys, but what I'm about to tell ya I've never told anyone before. The moment that made it impossible to go home, the moment that's kept me runnin' from myself all these years." I hesitated and caught my breath that begged to be released. "The moment," I paused, "when I killed my brother." The tears formed in my eyes again, and I brushed them away because for the first time since Gettysburg I felt free, like an overbearing weight had been taken off my back.

"When you killed your brother?" Slim said in disbelief. "Why, Bill?"

"I didn't know it was my brother," I replied regretfully. "In the heat of the moment, it was just another soldier. In those moments it's kill or be killed. About the time I felt my bayonet hit bottom, I looked closer at the man I'd killed. We recognized each other in the same instant. 'William?' he said in a voice that said so many things in one word. 'Oh, shit! I'm sorry, Jimmy!' I cried out. 'I didn't know it was you!' I screamed above the hellish noise. 'It's good to see you,' he gasped. 'We all wondered what happened to you.' I looked down and could see blood pourin' out of him. 'Hold on,' I told him. 'I'll get a medic.' He grabbed my arm to stop me from leaving. 'I love you, Bill,' he said. I sat in a pool of his blood, starin' in disbelief as I watched his life slip from him. 'I love you, Bill,' he said again, and then he was gone forever."

I started to cry again, but this time it was tears of loss and closure. And even though I could hear the others talking, it seemed to be distant and vague. I sensed them movin' away to give me room, but in my state it felt more like I was the one moving, like I was bein' pulled into some kind of tunnel, and everything around me seemed to disappear until I was all alone.

I spent the rest of the afternoon in quiet reflection, thinkin' of the times we shared, smilin' one minute and sheddin' tears the next. But finally, I'd found comfort and peace as I came to grips with a secret that was now on the table. I felt free, and for the first time, I couldn't feel the demon that had chased me for so long, clawing at me with its cold fingers. I'd run from it long enough, and I found myself longing to see my family again before they were gone too. My sadness and melancholy turned to desperation and a feeling of bein' trapped. Damn, how I wanted out of this hell hole.

Chapter Six

Memories

The next two weeks went by in a blur. I didn't feel much like talkin', and I think the others could sense it, so they pretty much left me alone. I spent a lot of time thinkin' about all the adventures Jimmy and I had, and a flood of memories that'd been buried underneath the stress and responsibility of the last eighteen years came to the surface. I drank them up like fine wine, treasuring each moment. I closed my eyes, and we were thirteen again, swimmin' at the hole and playfully teasin' the girls. I could see Elizabeth's face like it was yesterday. She was a pretty girl, and Jim knew I was shinin' on her. He was waitin' for her to get to the rocks, which was a good place to jump in because the water was deeper there, but to get to 'em you had to walk on a narrow strip that was bordered on one side by the water and on the other a hedge with the rock wall at the end of it. When Elizabeth made her way towards it, Jimmy told me to follow her. When she got to the jumpin' off point, she hesitated to get the proper footing before jumpin' in. Jimmy had followed me down the trail, but because of my fixation on Elizabeth, I didn't know he was there. All of a sudden, I felt myself bein' propelled forward, and with no place to go I was pushed up against her and the rocks. We both looked at each other in shock. When she realized Jimmy's trick, she smiled at me and then jumped in. Jimmy laughed and stood there with his thumbs tucked under his armpits like he'd just accomplished the greatest feat in history.

To this day I can clearly see his toothy grin, his freckled face, and his zest for life. Boy, how I loved that kid, and truth be told, I was glad he pushed me that day. She turned out to be my first love, and we spent every free minute together after that. Unfortunately, it was only a couple of months later that my pa announced we were moving to Sherman. I could still feel the regret of leavin' Elizabeth behind.

My mind went to the time we snuck into Farmer Wilcox's pasture full of Texas longhorn cattle. We took a plank with a rope tied to it and formed a loop at the other end. The thought was if we could get the rope around the cow's horns and get it to run, we could catch a ride on the plank sleigh we had built. Problem was, once we got the rope around the cow, which was no easy feat, mind ya, the stupid cow just stood there. Jimmy got the idea to go and get a long willow stick to use as a whip. It worked like a charm, and that big fat cow took off like a bullet. Reckon I laughed harder and longer that day than any other day in my life. When it was Jimmy's turn, however, he somehow whipped the cow's ear, and that cow jumped and took off on a run that might be the record for the fastest bovine ever. Jimmy was hoopin' and hollerin' and laughin' so hard he could hardly catch his breath. When the cow came to the fence at the one end of the pasture, I thought it'd just stop, but boy was I wrong! Instead a jumpin', it made a sharp 90-degree turn without losin' speed and, due to the length of the rope, whipped Jimmy around like he'd been shot out of a sling shot. He was havin' the time of his life until he hit a gopher mound. It launched him so high I thought I was gonna pee my trousers laughin'. Jimmy must've rolled twenty times or more before he came to a stop.

I ran to see if he was alright 'cause he'd stopped laughin'. But when I got to him, I could see clearly why the demise of his laugh had come: Jimmy had come to a stop, head first, in a big pile of cow shit. The look on his face was priceless, and I fell down on the ground and laughed so hard I thought my stomach would never stop hurtin'. About that time Wilcox saw what was going on and started after us. We both jumped up and started runnin' as fast as we could to avoid the whippin' he'd threatened to give us. I thought my heart would pop out of my chest before we made it out of the field, but we finally cleared the fence and arrived in the safety of the trees, both of us bent over gaspin' for breath. When we felt like we weren't goin' to die from a lack of oxygen anymore, we looked up at each other. Seein' half of Jimmy's head still covered in crap, I started laughin' all over again. At first he scowled at me but then quickly joined in the revelry.

*****

For two weeks I didn't feel much like rilin' Virgil, and it never dawned on me that he figured it was because of his threats, until he came to the door one morning and announced breakfast. When it was my turn to have my tin defiled, he said, "Looks like I finally taught you your place, Billy."

"How's that?" I asked.

"By showin' ya that I'm the boss and that I control everythin' from the outside." Then he asked in a mocking tone, "Has Miss Watson been around to see you lately?" Without waiting for an answer, he continued, "I seen her every day, and we're gettin' real close, her and I."

"Is that so, Virgil?"

"Sure is, boy," he laughed. "I think I got her convinced that tryin' to help a loser like you is a waste of her time."

"You sure you're not just havin' wishful fantasies, Virg?" I asked. "It's you that's wishin'," he replied. "We've been takin' some real nice walks together, and we went to dinner last night. Could be I got her talked into puttin' you on trial again, and maybe on the day you swing, we'll get married so we can celebrate two milestones on the same day every year."

"Just give me my damn food, Virgil." "That just gets at ya, don't it, Billy?"

"No, Virgil, it don't. I think you're a damn liar, and a worn-out mule would have more of a chance with her than you. But you keep on havin' them there fantasies, if that's how you've come to deal with your self loathin'. Even a worthless piece of shit like you deserves to have some hope."

He got defensive at that point, and his voice went up an octave. "Well, ya just can't know that for sure, can ya, William? Maybe if you could get out of that cell—Oh wait, I seem to have the keys in my pocket." He started to laugh in a mocking tone then continued, "In fact, I have lots of your future in my pocket, Billy, and there ain't a damn thing you can do about it. Now, if you'll kindly excuse me, I have a date with Emily."

I turned around, and everyone was lookin' at me. "That man is lower than the ass on a worm," I said.

"Don't let him get to ya," Jed said.

"He didn't, Jed. To tell ya the truth, right now, I don't care."

"Don't go givin' up on us, Bill," Ben said. "We all look to you for our strength. You're the one that gets us through most days 'round here." "Well, you might want to start lookin' for a higher caliber of hero,"

I said. I sat down to eat, and I felt like all the wind had been taken out of my sail. I ate in silence, but my mind and heart were fightin' each other. My heart kept tellin' me there was hope, but my mind kept tellin' me that Yuma was the end of the line. And then for a moment, my heart convinced me that Emily would find a way to prove my innocence. But in the end my mind won and convinced me that Virgil would get the last laugh. In defeat I pushed my tray away from me and said, "Hey, Ted, you want my breakfast?"

Slim came and sat next to me. He was older than the rest and had the wisdom to partially understand what I was feelin' and the experience to offer some kind of exit from it. "You've had a hard couple weeks, Bill. I don't think the kid meant to bring all this on you with his question, and I think he kinda blames himself."

"I know he didn't. I'll talk to him," I said. "Actually, gettin' it off my chest has been good for me, so he did me a favor, if you want to know the truth."

"That's a lot to carry around."

"Tell me about it," I replied. "What's really gettin' me now is bein' trapped in here."

"We're all trapped," Slim reminded me.

"I know," I said apologetically. "I didn't mean it like that. It's just that before I told anyone what I'd done, I could deal with bein' in here. It kept me from runnin' from myself, and it was hard, but I'd learned to deal with it. And I kept tellin' myself that even though it wasn't for the crime they accused me of, somehow I was payin' for what I'd done to Jim. But now I feel like I could possibly find the courage to go home and begin to let the wounds heal, but I can't because I'm trapped here, and it's become a livin' hell. You know what I mean?"

"Think so," Slim replied, "but you can't give up hope, Bill. Maybe Miss Watson can help you and you'll be able to do just that."

"I don't even know if she's still tryin', Slim. I haven't seen her in almost three weeks."

"These things take time, Bill. Tombstone's three hundred miles from here."

"You're right. It's just that for the first time in three years, I feel trapped, and it's killin' me."

"That I can understand. I'm the old guy here, remember?"

"Oh dammit, Slim, I'm sorry. I was so caught up in myself I forgot who I was talkin' to." I reflected for a moment on Slim's fate and his willingness to try and help me anyway and then put my hand on his shoulder and said, "We've got to get the hell outta here, Slim."

"I don't think that's in the cards for me, Bill. But if it is for you, don't you forget what I told ya to do, ya hear? You go home and bring your ma some peace."

"I think I can now, Slim. I finally think I can."

"Promise me, Bill. Promise me that you won't let the paths, trails, or excuses keep you away." He sounded so sincere when he said it, so I made sure that I looked him in the eye.

"I promise, Slim."

Slim had made me feel better, and I decided then and there not to let time, heat, or Virgil suck the hope out of me. I told Slim thank you, and he turned and smiled in acknowledgment. I tapped his leg a couple times and said, "I'm gonna go have a talk with the kid."

"He could use it. He's been pretty hard on himself lately. I think he admires you, Bill."

"We're gonna have to get him better role models then," I said. Slim chuckled and replied, "I think he's doin' okay."

The kid didn't see me comin', so he jumped a little when I snuck up behind him and asked, "How's the window problem comin', kid?"

He spun around and said, "Oh hey, Bill. It's pulled me in a couple of times, but each time your words of advice ring in my ears, so I sit back down."

"That's good, kid," I told him, "That's real good."

"Bill," he stammered, "I didn't mean to bring up those bad memories.

I'm sorry."

Don't you worry one minute about it, kid. In fact, I owe ya one." "Owe me one, why?" he asked.

"Because I never had any reason or any desire to tell anyone about that day, and it was becoming a burden to carry."

"Well, you're welcome," he said tongue in cheek. "To tell you the truth, Bill, I was afraid you were goin' to haul off and hit me again.

And just between me and you, I've never been hit that hard in my life and wasn't lookin' forward to it again."

"Who says I'm not?" I asked. The look on his face made me chuckle, and it took him a moment to see I was just pullin' his leg. He tried to smile, but it wound up lookin' more like he had just inhaled something rotten.

"I wouldn't hit ya, kid. Fact is, you remind me a lot of my cousin Jim. He was witty and cocky too, but I knew I could always count on him in a scrape. I'd like to think that even though our first encounter wasn't pleasant we've become friends and would have each other's back if the opportunity presented itself."

"Hell yeah, Bill. I'd stand with you anywhere," the kid said absolutely.

"I'm glad to hear that, kid. I haven't had much of a chance to make many friends. Seems I'm better at makin' enemies."

"Hey, Bill," the kid said quietly. "You plannin' somethin' I should know about?"

"Yea, I'm plannin' on gettin' out of here." "Do you really think you can?"

"Yep. Just as soon as Miss Watson figures out how to spring me." "Oh," he said with a sigh of relief. "I thought you was gonna try and break out of here or somethin'. I was thinkin' that's why you asked me to have your back."

"There's no way outta here, kid. I just needed to know I had a friend that's all."

"Oh good," he said relieved. "You got a friend in me, Bill, and I'm damn proud to say it."

SWEET JUSTICE 105

"You need better friends, kid," I said as I gave him a friendly shove. He smiled at me and tried to shove me back, but I dodged him. "I hope you're faster than that with a gun, or you're not gonna be much good to me."

He shook his head with a smile. "Next time, Bill. Next time."

*****

The rest of the day went by pretty much as usual. The heat was unbearable, so we all looked like hounds sweatin' and pantin' through the dog days of summer. The best thing to do in this situation was to find a comfortable place to lie down and try to keep your mind off of it.

"Tell us about Montana," Stumpy yelled across the room.

"It's cooler," I said.

"Come on, Bill," Ben said. "Tell us more than that. What made you go there in the first place?"

I sat there fanning myself and said, "Wyoming and Montana are cooler. They get hot too, but nothing like this, and generally you get the afternoon breezes because of the mountains. And on the days you don't, it ain't too far a ride to change your elevation considerably. One thing about the Rocky Mountains," I told them, "sometimes it seems you can climb twice as many feet in one step than the distance of the step itself. At that rate you can be a thousand feet higher in no time at all.

"This heat and talkin' about mountains," I continued, "reminds me of a fire I experienced in Helena, Montana. I was there in '69 when the whole town damn near burned to the ground. I hadn't been there long and was thinkin' that I liked it there and was contemplating stayin' when all of a sudden someone yelled *Fire!* Within an hour there wasn't much left to like anymore. It was kind of disheartening too 'cause all I'd gone through to get there."

"Now you're talkin'," the kid said. "Go on and tell us."

"After the war, and when I'd convinced myself I could never go home, my paths took me first into the heart of Texas where I learned the art of the cattle industry. The need to run from my past kept me from stayin' in any one place for very long. So when word got out that findin' jobs in Montana's booming cattle empires was far from difficult, I hooked up with some other casualties of war and headed north. What initially started out to be exciting and adventurous turned sour in a hurry. There were four of us the day we left—Barney, Danny, Russell and myself—but by the time we hit the Montana Territory, we were down to one and a half."

"One and a half?" Ted interrupted. "How in the hell could there only be a half?"

"Just let me tell the story, Ted. The year was 1867. After we put Texas behind us, our first major destination was Fort Sumner in New Mexico. We figured we could stock up on supplies there, and since we'd left in the spring, we hoped that we could hire out to brand cattle as we journeyed. Gettin' the work didn't prove to be as easy as we thought it'd be, but we managed to do alright.

"When we finally hit Fort Sumner, we must've been a sight. Four straggly kids, real worn out from hard work and the trail. All of us decided to put our money together, and we trusted Russell to manage it so we were

SWEET JUSTICE   107

sure everyone paid an equal share for the supplies we'd
need to get to make it all the way to the gold fields in
Helena. Everyone was given enough to get a bath and
a drink or two at one of the saloons, and then we were
to meet up at one of the hotels where we were gonna
splurge for a room since none of us had slept on anythin'
but hard ground for over two months. The plan was
perfect, or so we all thought. Problem was, we didn't take
into account thieves that preyed on new people in town
known to have their money on them. All was going well
until Russell decided to shortcut through an alley to save
himself fifty steps. He was confronted by some Mexican
bandits who knew just how to play the game—roll 'em,
rob 'em, stab 'em, and then disperse separate ways and
meet up later to split the take. The rest of us went to the
hotel and talked the owner into lettin' us go up to the
room with the promise that our partner would be along
soon to pay him. After 'bout two hours, the owner came
up to see what was goin' on and then told us we'd have
to leave unless someone could pay him. We told him we
would go and see what saloon he was lost in and that we'd
be back, but by the time we hit the boardwalk, we could
see a crowd of people gathered down the road. I knew in
my gut that somehow it was Russell, and sure enough I
was right.

"So there we were in Fort Sumner, three men out of
money and summer right around the corner. We couldn't
go back, and we couldn't continue on. All that was left
to do was pull on our boots and go find a job. We asked
around to see if anyone might know someone who was
hirin' cowhands. The blacksmith told us that the best
place to start would be the Chisholm Ranch and then

pointed towards its general direction. Little did we know how far it was. I guess we thought it was at the end of the finger that pointed it out. Needless to say, without money we were mighty famished by the time we arrived there, and it was a good thing he needed us 'cause I don't think the three of us could've gone much farther.

"Mr. John Chisholm was better than a good man to work for. He worked us hard but paid us well, and grub time was nothin' to shake a stick at. In fact, I put on a little weight. I didn't notice so much, but my trousers and horse seemed to. We worked for him through the summer, keepin' watch on the herd for intruders and breakin' the new horses we had rounded up from a herd of wild mustangs. When fall came 'round, we looked forward to our first cattle drive. Had I known how much work it really was, I probably wouldn't've been so excited. The drive to Abilene went pretty smooth as far as drives go, or so they told me, and it was a good thing too because I was about as ready as I could be for it to be over.

"Mr. Chisholm knew we didn't have anywhere to go for the winter because through the course of our time there, he'd come to know our story. In fact, he paid to have a headstone made for Russell's grave and attempted to find his family so they would know where he was and what had happened to him. But none of us could tell him where he was from. That was the only time he seemed irritated with me all summer until I explained that Texas was full of men from the South, as well as the north, and that we found it easier to just not ask. My comment seemed to satisfy him because he didn't ask again after that. He told us that he usually only kept a few men around in the winter to protect the herd from

SWEET JUSTICE 109

the Indians. They get hungry, he told us, and if he didn't protect the cows, by December there wouldn't be any left to make calves come spring. Then he asked if we were any good with a gun. We all chuckled and reminded him we were all in the war. 'Well, then, I think I can find a place for you,' he assured us, and then he said, 'Boys, let's go home.'

"The winter was cold but not terribly. I'd felt colder during the war because of the humidity, and I took to the drier climate like a fish to water. We spent most of our time ridin' fence and scoutin' for Indians. Mr. Chisholm told us to protect the herd but said we weren't to kill any Indians unless they started to take too many of his cows. 'They need to eat too,' he said, 'and if I let them have a few to get through the winter, I won't have to worry about raidin' parties comin' to take the whole lot all at once.' I admired him for what seemed wise to try and coexist, rather than wastin' time fightin' Indians that could be used for more important things. Fightin' Indians all the time would be like swattin' at mosquitoes all day, I thought. You might kill some, but most of them would just slip away from you and return in bigger swarms.

"For the most part, the bulk of the winter was uneventful, but there were some things that made it memorable. The damned skunks under the bunkhouse would get skittish if someone dropped somethin' on the floor or slammed the door too hard, and they'd get to sprayin'.

Sometimes tryin' to sleep after they'd filled our quarters with their powerful stink finally got to be more than we could stand, so we decided we was goin' in after them. It was quite a battle for a week or two, but we finally won the war. There were some casualties, however; two of us got sprayed full on, and everyone had no problem gettin' up and out in the morning just to get some fresh air. Christmas was nice, too. Mr. Chisholm put out a banquet that was right tasty and gave us all new hats as gifts.

"But then there was the wolves. We had a pack come in and take a couple cows in the night, so until we could kill them all or chase them away, we had to do night shifts to protect the cattle. The days, for the most part, were mild, but nighttime was cold. We spent a lot of our days tryin' to hunt them so the night watch would come to an end sooner. Eleven wolves we took before the problem stopped. After that, the bunkhouse seemed cozier just knowin' we didn't have to go out in the cold and dark anymore.

"As spring came around, I reminded my partners of our endeavor to get to Montana, and after stayin' in one place as long as we did, all three of us were ready for a change of scenery. None of us, however, wanted to go and tell the boss of our intentions because we knew calving season was right around the corner, and, after all, he'd made room for us through the winter. So for a few days, we went through the daily routine, tryin' to work up the courage to drop the news in his lap. About that same time, Mr. Chisholm came and found us in the bunkhouse one night and asked us if we were plannin' on stayin' or continuin' north. I was the first to speak after a moment of awkward silence. 'Well, Mr. Chisholm, we are mighty grateful for what you done for us and reckon we sure wouldn't want to leave on bad terms, but we got a hankerin' to see that Montana Territory. If not for ourselves, maybe for Russell and to know we finished what we set out to do.' 'Well, first of all,' he said, 'you fellers call me John, you earned that much; second, boys, I remember what it was like to be your age and know full well that if you don't go, you'll regret it; third is probably the most important and will fit right nicely into your plans: I just happen to need some cowboys to take ten beef stock bulls up to a feller outside of Denver and was hopin' you'd take the job on your way.'

"We all breathed out a sigh of relief and told him we'd be proud to do that for him and even offered to do it in return for his puttin' us up for the winter. 'No, boys, you done me proud and earned every penny I paid ya. Besides, it's a long way to Denver, and I don't want you thinkin' I cheated ya after you find out just how far.' 'Well sir,' I said, 'you can count on us to get it done.' 'I know,' he said. 'If I didn't think that, I'd a never have asked ya. When d'ya think you'll be leavin'?' 'Three days ago,' I said laughing. 'Well then, you boys best go and pick you some nice horses to take. I think the ones you rode in on are plumb tuckered out.' 'Really?' I asked surprised. 'You goin' to give us horses?' 'Not so much give,' he replied. 'I'd hoped it would be a down payment to entice you to come back and work for me if you ever get back this way. They say Montana is double pretty, boys,' he continued. 'Pretty to look at and pretty damn cold. You might like it up there in the summer, but when those northern winds blow come fall, that's an invitation to come make another run to Abilene and spend a milder winter here.' 'We're much obliged for the offer,' I said. "You get some rest tonight after you get your things together,' he said. 'I'll have some of the others get that herd rounded up, and you can leave tomorrow. Now get goin'. You got a long ride come sun up.'

"By the time the sun rose the next morning, we were already packed and ready to move out, anxious to be on our way again and happy to have a purpose. All the supplies we were going to buy with the money that was stolen, Mr. Chisholm gave us before we left, so we had new horses, new hats, and a pocket full of money. We were proud as turkeys and cocky to boot. Our next projected stop where we could resupply would be a trading post at a place called Pueblo. The mountain men frequented the place and had built a fort of sorts there. Later, the Colorado gold rush made it a good place to set up for business. But between us and Pueblo was a range that took us higher in elevation than any of us had been before, and when we camped those few nights, it felt like we were back to winter again.

"I saw my first bull elk on top of that pass and swore when my hands weren't so full I was going to come back and hunt one. Coming from Texas I had no idea that there was anything that big, and it sure looked like a nice trophy to bag. But we had promised to get the job done, so I regretfully watched him lope over the hill. We finally got to Pueblo, which was about halfway, and got ourselves a decent meal and a few supplies, then continued our journey to Denver. We had seen some Indians on a hill, but they seemed content to let us pass on through. It kinda made the hair on my neck stand on end, so needless to say, we kept a sharp eye out after that. We sure didn't need to tangle with no Indians.

"On our last night of the journey, we sat around the fire, tryin' to decide how many days it'd taken us. As near as we all could agree, we decided that five weeks was close enough for future storytellin'. As we sat there reflecting on moments and highlights, Barney commented that we should count ourselves lucky that we hadn't had any major mishaps or accidents. Danny chimed in especially with them Injuns. Barney and I agreed with a sigh of relief, and then I got up to go get more wood for the fire. About the time my eyes had adjusted to the dark, I thought I saw movement in the trees. I hunkered down and scanned the trees along the river for farther movement for a few minutes and came to the conclusion that talkin' about those Indians had me skittish, so I brushed it off, collected the wood, and made my way back to the fire.

"I was the last on watch before morning and, truth be known, was dog tired. I awoke with a start just as the thin line of light on the horizon was announcing the birth of a new day. I rubbed my face vigorously, angry with myself for falling asleep, and as my eyes came into focus, I saw what looked like a human form moving through the trees. The trunks and branches had grown close together in their attempt to rob the precious river water from each other, so you could only see flashes of movement. Whatever it was it sure wasn't walkin' on four legs. I kept on watchin' but couldn't see it again, so I started countin' heads. At first I could only see nine, and I started to cuss myself when the tenth stood up out of some tall grass. 'Present and accounted for,' I said in self consolation. 'No harm done.'

"I started to gather them up when Barney and Dan joined me. 'Let's finish this job and head for Montana, boys,' Dan said. We all let out our get goin' whoops and whistles with smiles on our faces and started off. We had gone about a mile or so when the beauty of the morning was shattered; from out of nowhere an arrow found its target deep in Danny's side. We instinctively followed his body to the ground, and the soldiers in us took over. 'There, just over the bank!' Barney yelled. 'I see them!' I shot back. One stood up to release his arrow, and I took him with my rifle. He fell with a yelp. I told Barney that he needed to keep their attention and that I'd try to slip away in the tall grass and come up behind them, so he started takin' wild shots to force them to keep their heads down and stop them from seein' me slip away.

"I hadn't got more than a hundred yards away when they decided to charge Barney's position. Thinkin' we were both still there and knowin' the meadow behind us offered no real protection, I guess they figured they had us dead to rights. As they started their run over the bank, they found out real fast what three years of war will teach ya. Barney took the one in the lead; the other three kept comin', committed to finish what they'd started. I cracked off a shot from my position and hit one of them in the hip. This surprised them and threw them off because they thought I was still with Barney. It was two against two now, so I jumped up and started runnin' at 'em. The one in front kept headin' for Barney, and the other focused his attention on me. He pulled his knife because I was gainin' on him too fast for him to use his bow, and I met him on a dead run, crackin' him across the head with the butt of my rifle. He tripped me as I went by, and I tumbled to the ground, rollin' over just as he was ready to pounce on me. My speed and skill with a revolver saved my life that day. I shot him just below the neckline, and he was dead before he landed on top of me.

SWEET JUSTICE   115

"I quickly threw him to one side and ran to see if Barney needed my help and found him ready to take the scalp of his victim. In what must've been a moment of insanity and terror, that Injun had run headlong into a hail of bullets from Barney's gun. I told him he shouldn't do that, and he replied that it was worth money and went back to work. I sat down next to him. 'Haven't we seen enough slaughter without makin' it worse?' I asked him. He looked up at me and said, 'I guess you're right, Bill. Come on, let's round up them cattle.'

"We got 'em gathered and buried our friend, then finished the job. After relaying our story to the rancher, we delivered the cattle too. He invited us to stay on and work for him. We told him we were much obliged but that we were hell bent on seein' Montana before winter came, so he insisted we stay for some of his wife's cookin' and suggested we set out in the morning. 'Ya'll can make Denver in a day from here, and then you won't have to find camp tonight,' he said. Barney and I looked at each other and were in no hurry to run into the friends of the Indians we'd killed in the night, so we said, 'You talked us into it.' "We decided to spend a day or two in the newly formed Denver 'fore makin' our way to Cheyenne. From there we would continue north to the North Platte River then turn northwest and wind our way to the southwest corner of the Montana Territory, following the Bozeman trail.

There were gold and silver camps and towns that dotted that part of the country. That way, we had it figured, if there were people, there'd be a need for cowboys and guns, and if we had down time we could try our hand at panning for some of that easy money they was pickin' up in the river bottoms. To set the record straight, none of those three jobs turned out to be easy, but I did make some money doin' all three. Panning for gold had its rewards, if you can get past the sore back and cold feet. Bein' heavy with a gun paid well but sure was dangerous, and sometimes when the smoke cleared, you was left wonderin' if you were fightin' for the right side or if both sides just needed killin'. Bein' a cowboy didn't pay as well as the other two, but it was consistent and a whole lot safer.

"Barney and I made it to Cheyenne and had ourselves a couple wild nights there and met some men that told us the best route to our destination and who to contact once we got there. Barney managed to find us a fight the night before we were slated to move on, so we left town hung over, beat up, and a little poorer than when we came. So needless to say, we was happy to put Cheyenne behind us. We made it to Fort Casper and picked up the gold trail to Montana from there. We were told that it passed through Indian Territory and that it'd be a whole lot safer to travel in bigger numbers than just two. Barney and I were in no hurry to go up against Indians again anytime too soon, so we started askin' around to see when there might be a larger group going that way. "We found an army captain that would be takin' a garrison that way in a couple of days. After he found out we were Civil War veterans and handy with a gun, he invited us to come along. Neither one of us was too upset about that because, to tell the truth, we were both plumb tuckered out and could use a couple days to rest. Two days later we was on our way again. And as luck would have it, we didn't see any Indians until we were almost to Montana, and even

SWEET JUSTICE 117

then they didn't want to fight; they just wanted to stir the pot and remind the military they was there by takin' some wild shots at us from a distance. No one was hit, but Barney's horse spooked and stood up on its hind legs, causin' him to fall off backwards. Barney landed with his leg twisted, forcin' the tip of his spur into his leg about three inches below his butt. It bled somethin' fierce, but he swore he was all right, and other than changing the dressing a couple times, no one thought much of it.

"When we finally arrived in Helena, Barney had developed the chills, and no matter what we did, we couldn't get him warm. He was havin' a hard time walkin' on his injured leg, and his skin seemed to be a yellow shade, so the Captain told me I best take him to a sawbones. Little did I know how right he was; the doctor took off his bandage and sniffed the wound, said it smelled like cheese and told him he'd have to cut his leg off or he was gonna die. Barney asked him to give him a night to think about it. The doctor told him he wasn't sure he had a night but assured him it was his decision. Barney and I spent that night talkin' about our journey and the friends we'd lost along the way. Then he got real serious and said, "Bill, I ain't gonna be any good to no one without a leg.' 'You can still do stuff,' I told him. 'And I'll help you. We're partners, remember?' Ol' Barn refused to let the doc amputate his leg the next day, and another night soon found us.

"It was about three in the morning when he grabbed my hand and said in a raspy voice, 'Bill, it was good to know ya.' Then he closed his eyes and died. I cried as I held his hand. I hadn't cried over my other two friends, but realizing I had lost three out of the four that'd left

Texas two years earlier and reflecting on the fact that the better part of their lives had been taken from them too damn early was more than I could take. So I held his hand and quietly cried until the sun found its way through the window.

"I quickly found a job with a local cattle rancher. He was gruff and hit the bottle a lot but was good to pay and let me go prospectin' as long as he got a quarter of anything I found. But by the time August was half over, I knew where I wanted to be, and it wasn't there. So I drew my final pay and headed into Helena for a drink. 'One for the trail,' I told myself. I went back and forth, wonderin' if I was makin' the right decision and had half decided I liked it here, and after all, I told myself, one place was as good as another. All of a sudden, the shout of fire quickly made its way through town. I barely had time to get to my horse and get the hell outta there before it seemed the whole town was alight. It didn't take long, seein' as half the town was canvas tents, and what wasn't, was built out of dry pine—easy to light and hard to put out. I sat on the outskirts, watchin' it burn and ponderin' on the irony that a town whose main street was a river was burnin' to the ground. There were people desperately runnin' to and fro, tryin' to save it, and I thought to myself, 'Well, there's your answer, Bill,' as I spun my horse towards the Bozeman trail once again."

CHAPTER SEVEN

Frontier News

WHEN I WAS DONE TELLIN' my story, I spent the next hour answering questions.

"You been back since then?" Slim asked.

"Yeah, a few times," I told him.

Ben wanted to know more about the Indians and a better description of the elk I'd seen. I told him I'd hunted many since that day and promised that if we got the chance, I'd take him to hunt one of his own. For the most part, everyone wanted me to describe landscapes, rivers, mountains, and formations I'd seen, and I tried to paint a picture with my words as best I could. But ultimately in exasperation, I told them that I couldn't do it justice and that they'd just have to go see it for themselves. The questions kept comin' though, along with a plea for me to elaborate, and I was happy to do so, just to take my mind off the heat. Lunch and dinner had come somewhere in the middle of it all, and their inquiries were still comin' when the sun went to bed.

The next morning Spencer came and announced breakfast. When I asked him if he could post a letter for me, he said, "I didn't know you could read and write, Bill." I assured him I could and asked if he'd help me put pen to paper. "I'm not supposed to give you any sharp objects," he told me.

"Who made that rule?" I asked.

At the same time, we both said, "Virgil."

"I don't want to get you in trouble," I told him. "Maybe you could just write it for me, and I'll tell you what to say."

He sheepishly looked at me, and I could tell he was embarrassed. "I'll do my best to get you some when I think it's safe."

"Don't you know how to read, Spencer?" I asked him quietly. "Not so good," he confessed. "I never got much of a chance to learn.

My pa thought it was a waste of time. He didn't think a farmer would ever need to know it and filled my head with knowledge about how to grow stuff instead."

"Well, that's good to know. After all, you can't eat books." He laughed and asked me not to tell anyone. I promised I wouldn't and then told him I'd be happy to teach him.

"Virgil wouldn't let you." "Virgil doesn't have to know."

"That'd be somethin', Bill. I'd be too embarrassed to ask anyone in town," he said. He looked down to put my food on my tray and asked, "Do you think we could start today?"

"You bring me the stuff to write a letter, and I'll teach you anytime you want."

He started to leave and then turned around and said, "Hey, Bill, Miss Watson has been here a couple times to

SWEET JUSTICE 121

see you, but Virgil told her you were in solitary and that you couldn't be seen. I'd lose my job if he knew I told you that, but I thought you should know anyway."

"I won't make trouble for you," I said, "but thanks for telling me.

It's good to know."

"If it's any consolation, the last time she was here, she told him that she wouldn't take no for an answer next time, even if she had to bring her father. That got Virgil agitated, and he seemed mighty uncomfortable the rest of the day." He paused for a moment, searchin' his mind for somethin' he might've forgotten before he continued, "Anyway, I'll bring some paper after lunch. If we ain't seen Virgil by then, odds are we won't."

I ate breakfast and thought about the information Spencer had shared with me. Why was Virgil so hell bent on not allowing Emily to help me? There was more to all of this than just him seeing me as competition for Emily's affection. He seemed to be out to get me from the moment we met, and I never did anything to him, least not that I knew of. How was it possibly going to hurt him one way or another if I was to get out of here? If anything, I'd more than likely just leave town, remove myself from the picture altogether and leave him to pursue Emily the rest of his days. Not that he stood a chance, but at least he wouldn't have to worry about me. The questions kept coming, and I tried to put it all straight in my head. It was like a pile of puzzle pieces shy of the picture they were supposed to create. *If I get the chance to see Emily again*, I thought, *maybe she could help me at least connect the edges so I could fill in the rest.*

It was hot by the time I finished breakfast, so I laid down to try and sleep. *Maybe,* I thought, *I could escape to a higher climate in my dreams, and if I was lucky possibly figure out the answers to some of the questions I had rollin' around in my head.* Ben came over and wanted to know more about fightin' Indians. I looked out from under my hat and said, "Not today, Ben. You plumb wore me out yesterday," and then I smiled at him and promised I'd tell 'im later. I must've been tired for real because I never remember him leavin' before my dreams had me back in the saddle.

The call for lunch woke me up, and everyone stood to get their grub. I was groggy, and it was so hot I didn't really have much of a hankerin' for food, but when I saw what was on everyone's tin, I was glad I stood in line. The beans were the same, but there was a slice of buttered fresh bread to go along with it. "Has Miss Watson been here?" I asked.

"Yes sir," Spencer said. "She wanted to see you, but only Virgil has the authority to allow visitors. She did leave a message for you though."

"Good news or bad?" I asked.

"Good, I guess." Spencer paused to take a bite of his bread. "Well, aren't you goin' to tell me, Spence?" I asked impatiently.

"Oh yeah," he said. "Sorry about that. Miss Watson sure makes good bread, don't she?"

"The message, Spencer. What was the message?"

"She said that Wyatt Earp claimed to remember the incident in Tombstone and that he didn't think you were guilty, but unfortunately, he didn't have any way to prove it though."

SWEET JUSTICE 123

"That's good news? How d'ya figure?"

"Well, Miss Watson seemed excited about it, and she wanted me to be sure I told you."

"Is that all?" I coaxed.

"No, there was somethin' else. She said that there was testimony that claimed you had no part in the murder, but it left Tombstone the same time you did."

"Dammit. I wonder why it wasn't brought up in my trial." "Don't know, Bill, but she was gonna try and find out." "That is good news, Spence, thanks for the message."

"I got more," Spencer exclaimed. "I also brought your paper and pen, but if Virgil shows up, you'll hide it, right?"

"Absolutely," I assured him. "Are we still on for readin' lessons?" "Hell yeah. I'll be back a little later. I just wanna make sure Virgil's not comin'."

Spencer came back about an hour later. I was done writing the letter for Ben and Jed and hoped it'd help them find a better life when they got out of here. Spencer stuffed it in his shirt pocket and assured me that it would be on the next stage.

"Thank you, Spencer. I 'preciate ya stickin' your neck out for me. That letter could change the lives of two of my young friends that deserve a second chance to get it right."

"Glad to help, Bill. Don't you fret about it one minute." "Speaking of boys that need a second chance. The kid you brought in a few weeks ago tells me there was some kind of war up in New Mexico and that one of my friends was killed. Do you know anything about it?"

"Sure do. Which one was your friend? They's been more than a few kilt."

"Tunstall," I told him.

"Yeah, I'm sorry to say he was right," he said sympathetically. "He was the first. After him, all hell broke loose."

"Any word on a young kid named William Bonny?"

"He's dead too. Happened just a few days ago. Some feller named Garret claims he finally got him in Fort Sumner, but there's already talk that he got away."

"Wouldn't surprise me. I know that for a time there was a bond of sorts between 'em."

"Well, Bonny was going by an alias. Called himself Billy the Kid, and I guess he took a few with him 'fore he went."

"What about that son of a bitch Murphy?"

"Last I heard he was in Santa Fe, fightin' a cancer," he replied. "Serves him right," I said boldly. "Anyone that starts somethin' like that out of sheer greed doesn't deserve to breathe air, as far as I'm concerned. Thanks for the info, Spence. It's a shame that's what happens when mouths quit talkin' and guns take over, I reckon." I tried to change the mood after that, so I smiled and said, "Let's do somethin' productive and teach you how to read."

"I don't know how we're gonna do it. I can't come in there without informing another guard, and I can't let you out without permission."

"We can do it right here at the door," I assured him.

"Yeah, but then they'll know I can't read," he said, lookin' over my shoulder.

"Well, I wouldn't worry too much about that, Spencer. Odds are most in here can't read either." I hoped

SWEET JUSTICE 125

that realizing he wasn't the only person in the world that couldn't read and write would put his mind at ease and take away some of the apprehension he was feeling.

"Okay. Where do we start?"

"Do you know any of your letters?" I asked.

"Some of them, I think. That is, if I can see them. I ain't got 'em memorized or nothin'."

"Well, let's start there then. I'm gonna write 'em in order, and then we'll memorize them. How's that sound?"

"Sounds good, Bill," he said excitedly. "Sounds real good."

I handed him the piece of paper I had written the letters on. "That's a big word, Bill. I don't think I can read that one," he stated timidly.

I held back my urge to chuckle and explained that when they were all written that way together it didn't make a word. "That's a list of all the letters we use to read and write. It's called the alphabet."

"That's all of 'em? Hell, I thought there were at least a hundred.

That don't look so tough, I guess."

"We're gonna say them out loud and in order. After we've been through them enough times, it'll be like a poem of sorts in your head. Are you ready?"

"Reckon so," he said, sounding a little unsure.

Spencer struggled with a few at first, but as we continued to repeat it, it came easier to him. After the second or third time through, Jed came over and asked if he could do it with us. "Sure," I told him. "Let me write you a list too." I quickly jotted them down for him, and we continued to say them out loud. One by one, everyone in the cell made their way over and wanted to learn as well. I was only able to make one more list, however, before I ran out of paper, so I told 'em they'd have to share. What a sight! Two groups of men lined up to see the paper in front of them. I laughed inside myself when the thought that they looked like men singing in church crossed my mind. *Hell's Yuma Choir*, I thought in my mind as the alphabet rolled off our lips.

We worked on reciting the alphabet for about an hour or so before movin' on to vowels. I made Spencer write them himself this time, under the alphabet list I'd written earlier. This seemed to please him, and he seemed right proud of himself when he showed me his writing. To tell you the truth, they looked pretty good.

"What makes 'em different than the rest of 'em?" Ben asked. "Those are the letters that give the word its sound," I said because I couldn't think of a better explanation. "What?" a couple of them said in unison.

"Let's not get ahead of ourselves," I told them. "I want everyone to keep practicin' your letters. Spencer, I want you to write all your letters at least ten times tonight and your vowels at least five, ya hear?"

"Why? I have them written already."

"It will get your hand and mind in the habit of workin' together," I said, with a newfound respect for the teachers I had given hell to when I was in school.

About that time we heard the night guard come through the door, lookin' for Spencer. As his boots echoed down the corridor, we all could tell it was Virgil's step by the sound and rhythm bouncing off the walls. "Everyone hide those papers," I said in an urgent whisper. Spencer stuffed his down his pants and in an afterthought quickly put my letter there too. Everyone tried to look natural as they scattered across the cell. "What the hell are you doin' back here, Spencer?" Virgil yelled.

Spencer choked, tryin' to think of a reason, so I quickly said, "He came back to tell us to shut up. I guess we was makin' more noise than the other prisoners wanted to listen to."

"Is this true?" Virgil asked, as he pulled open Spencer's shirt pocket to have a peek.

"Yeah," Spencer answered, "they was yellin' somethin' fierce about somethin' or another."

Virgil eye-balled us all, and everyone had a guilty look about them. "I don't believe a damn word you're sayin'. I better not hear a peep outta any of you tonight, or you'll face my stick, ya hear." He turned on Spencer. "It's your quittin' time," Virgil snapped. "Get the hell outta here."

Spencer double-timed it back to the gate that led out of the corridor. Everyone could tell Virgil was in a worse mood than usual, and I think Spencer wanted to get away before Virgil found a reason to search him further for the answers.

Virgil looked at me and said, "I'm not sure what's goin' on back here, but I'm watching you, Billy." After a couple seconds, I heard the door shut, ensuring that Spencer had made a clean getaway, so I said, "Watch all you want, if that's how your windmill spins, Virgil."

"Why, you son of a bitch," he said defensively. "I can't wait to see you swing, Saunders. It's closer than you think, tough guy." He stared at me with eyes full of hate, so I gave him a stare right back. He shrank as usual, pulled out his stick, and smacked it on the cell door. "Not one peep, ya hear," he threatened as he walked up the corridor.

"That was a close one," the kid said, "I wonder why he's workin' tonight."

"Don't know," I replied, "but he sure ain't happy about it, is he?" We all quietly chuckled.

"You think he'll work the truth out of Spencer?" asked Slim.

"I doubt it. Spencer really wants to learn how to read, and I don't think he wants Virgil to know he can't."

"He's out to get ya," Stumpy said. "Maybe you ought to lay low on teachin' Spencer."

"I'll take my chances," I said defiantly.

"But Bill, he really wants you dead. Don't you think laying low might help get him off your back?"

"He wants me dead; there ain't a thing that's gonna change that. And I ain't gonna give him the satisfaction of thinkin' he's broke me. That I can guarantee you."

"It's your neck," Stumpy replied.

"There's more to Virgil's hate than Miss Watson wanting to help me," I continued. "It's been that way since the day he unloaded me off the train. At first I thought he was just a coward with somethin' to prove, but now I'm not so sure. Not that he's isn't a coward, but his hatred seems to focus on me."

"What do you think it is?" Slim asked.

"I'm not sure, but for some reason he wants me quiet or out of the way. He seemed content to watch me rot away in here until Miss Watson took an interest in securing my release. Now I don't think he'll rest till I swing or until he can think of an excuse for shooting me."

"Could it be he was tied up with a common enemy from your past?" the kid said.

"I doubt it," I replied. "Miss Watson told me she met him when they were nine years old, and she didn't say nothin' about him leaving Yuma."

"What ya goin' to do?" Stumpy inquired.

"Somehow I've got to see Miss Watson again," I said. "Maybe she holds the missing pieces or can shed some light on Virgil's past."

"What makes you think she knows anything?" Slim asked.

"I don't know. Somethin' in my gut, I guess. Virgil's been workin' overtime to keep her away. That and after she came around, Virgil started actin' skittish like he was tryin' to keep somethin' hidden. It might be the heat, but I've seen that look before, usually when pointin' a gun at someone who's been caught doin' somethin' they shouldn't have." "No offense, Bill, but how can you be sure he's keeping her away?"

Slim asked reluctantly. "Could be she just isn't comin', and Virg has nothin' to do with it."

"Spencer told me she's tried to come a couple times, and Virgil told her I was in solitary," I replied.

"Why in the hell do you suppose he'd do that?" Stumpy asked. "Ain't he smart enough to know the truth would come out eventually?" "That's what's got me troubled. When someone's cover starts to be exposed, they get agitated and start to make mistakes. Could be he hoped I'd be dead before it did."

"You sound like you could've been a sheriff, Bill," the kid said, laughing. It seemed to tickle everyone, and they started to chuckle with him. They didn't laugh long, though, when I told them I'd been a deputy in Wyoming for six months.

"Dang, Bill," Slim said. "Just when I think I've heard it all, you come out with somethin' like that."

"Well, it sure wasn't a job I went lookin' for; I just happened to be in the wrong place at the wrong time."

"How long ago was that?" the kid asked. "About seven years ago, I reckon, give or take."

"Ain't got nothin' but time," Ben hollered from the corner. "Spill the beans."

"It was in Laramie," I started. "I was ridin' for an outfit that wasn't real big, but the boss had big dreams. Problem was he shared water with big ranch called the M&T that didn't like him movin' in, even though he had the right to be there, and the sheriff sided with the big boys because they paid the bills, if 'n you get my meanin'. So when the big boys started pushin' the little ones, and it became apparent that the sheriff wasn't gonna do anything about it, he hired some of us that were as good with a gun as we were with beef."

"That led to a standoff, and for a while it worked because neither side wanted to fire the first shot, but the friction seemed to get worse everyday."

"Did it come to shootin?" Jed asked.

"Not at first, but there sure was some brawls and fist fights down at the saloon, that's for sure."

"How in the hell did you go from that to bein' a deputy?" Stumpy asked.

"I'm gettin' to it, Stumpy, I'm gettin' to it. After everyone had been lickin' their wounds for a while, the fights became less frequent, and everyone involved hoped that maybe the two sides were about worn down and ready to come to some kind of understanding. That is, until horses started disappearing."

Sweet Justice

131

"Is that when the shootin' started?" Jed asked excitedly.

"You sure got a hankerin' for shootin' tonight, Jed. Keep your shirt on. I'm gettin' there." Everyone chuckled, and Jed seemed a little embarrassed. "They met us one morning down at the creek and accused my boss of bein' a horse thief. 'I ain't stole no horses,' he said. 'You're a liar,' they shouted back, 'And we aim to come find 'em.' All of us cocked our guns at that point, and for about ten minutes, we aimed at each other, jus- waitin' for the shootin' to start."

Jed shifted his position and just about opened his mouth but thought better of it and settled back down. I smiled at him and shook my head in a teasing manner. When he saw me, he motioned with his hand like he was buttoning his lip.

"It's comin', Jed, just hang on," I said. "Finally, my boss told 'em to come on ahead and see for themselves if it'd make them feel better, and then he told us to lower our weapons. None of us did though. When you use a gun to settle your differences, you don't open yourself up to be shot at. So we kept pointin' 'em 'til the boss on the other side told his men to put theirs down too. 'You better not let us catch you with our horses,' they yelled, 'and if any more disappear, we'll be back.' Then they turned and rode away. The boss told me and another fella to stay and watch for a while in case they doubled back."

"Did they?" Stumpy asked.

"Not that day, they didn't. About two or three days later, some of our horses disappeared, and my boss figured they'd done it in retaliation. I can still hear him sayin', 'Dammit! I can't afford to lose no livestock.' Then he told us he wanted two riders out, around the clock. That didn't sit well with some of the boys, and they suggested we just go get them back and be finished with it already. He said, 'There will be no shootin' unless you catch 'em on my property. If we keep an eye out, we'll catch 'em eventually. Then you can do what you want.'

"It was about a week later that the sheriff rode out and told us that more horses had disappeared from our rivals and that he was gonna arrest our boss for horse thievery. We all knew he hadn't stolen any and that if he was taken into town they'd hang 'im for sure. He told us that he didn't have a choice and that he'd get the cavalry down here if he had to. We talked amongst ourselves and decided that it didn't matter how good we all were with a gun; we didn't stand a chance against the army. So I told him he could take 'im without a fight, if I could come to town too and help protect him until there had been a complete investigation. The sheriff got angry and said, 'I'd have to deputize you for that.' I shot back, 'Well, you ain't takin' him unless you can guarantee his protection, that's for sure, so you best get to it.' He smugly told me that he'd deputize me but said he wasn't gonna pay me. 'If I'm goin' to do your job, you better damn well pay me,' I shot back, 'or I'll stay here, and you can fight me when I come to bust him out. Sheriff, we've had horses disappear too, and no one is gonna hang 'til we figure out who's takin' 'em. So you make the call right now. I need to know what I'm doin.'

"I told two of the boys to stay there and keep an eye on things. I had the other three come hang out in town and told them to keep a low profile in case anyone came

SWEET JUSTICE

133

to start somethin'. We saddled up, the sheriff deputized me right then and there, and we left for town.

"The ride into Laramie was uneventful, other than my boss thankin' me about ten times for ridin' along. After the sheriff locked him up, I left to go get supplies so I wouldn't have to leave the jail anytime soon. On the second day, some of the riders from the M&T came into town and headed for the saloon. I told the sheriff that they'd gone into one of the saloons and warned him that they were probably gonna get a shot or two of courage and to expect trouble. He said, 'I know those boys. They ain't goin' to start nothin'. Your hankerin' to fight is gonna get you killed, cowboy.' 'You're wrong,' I told him. 'Bein' ready for a fight at the drop of a hat is the reason I'm still alive. Your confidence in your so-called friends could be the death of you though, sheriff.' He claimed he could take care of himself and that I didn't need to fret none about it. I warned him that the men ridin' for the M&T don't have friends; they make their living from the friendly side of a gun. 'You'd do yourself a favor to realize that when the fightin' starts, their loyalty is to the man payin' the wages. And the man that ain't will be on the unfriendly side without any hesitation.' Sweat formed on his brow as the truthfulness of my words sunk in. He sounded nervous when he said, 'If you fellers hadn't stole them horses, we wouldn't be in this mess.' I got defensive and told 'im, 'We didn't steal no horses, sheriff, and my boss gave 'em permission on the first day to search his ranch to prove it. They're not the only ones who lost horses; a couple nights later we did too and figured they was just getting back at us. Someone is stealin' horses, and maybe if you'd a done the job, these people pay you to do, we wouldn't be in this mess. Did you ever think about that?'

"My accusation didn't sit well with him. 'I do the job they pay me for,' he shouted. 'If they want more, then they need to pay me more.' 'You seem to do pretty good, judgin' from your belongings,' I pointed out. 'Most sheriffs I've come across don't seem to do as well.' He got real defensive and said in a louder voice, 'I do this well because I supplement my earnings. It ain't from my sheriff's pay, I can assure you.' 'How can you possibly find time to do anything else?' I asked him. 'You're the only law here. That's kind of a full-time job, I'd imagine.'

"He told me he had a deputy up until recently but he'd been killed when they was ridin' over the pass to Cheyenne. 'Who killed him?' I asked. 'Don't know,' he answered. 'The shot came outta nowhere. When he was knocked out of his saddle, I took off on a dead run back to town.' I asked him how come he came back to town if he was ridin' for Cheyenne. His reply back was that it wasn't important enough to get killed over.

"Somethin' in his story didn't sit well; it wasn't like Cheyenne was just around the corner, and a trip there would certainly require some level of importance. So I asked him how somethin' important enough to pull the only two lawmen out of town for had become not so important all of a sudden. He got extremely agitated and defensive at my question and told me he wasn't payin' me to question the way he did his job and that he didn't appreciate bein' put on trial in his own jailhouse. I told him to calm down and assured him I was only makin' conversation.

SWEET JUSTICE

135

"I waited a few minutes before I asked him if his deputy was the kind to make enemies that might want to see him dead. The sheriff told me that people in town seemed to like him and that he got along with him too until he didn't want to play by his rules. He shook his head before he continued, 'I told him that he could be sheriff some day soon and then he could run things the way he wanted to, but he was so damn bent on goin' by the book.' The gnawing in my gut told me there was more to his story than he was sharin', so I asked him, 'What rules you talkin' 'bout, sheriff?' His reply back was short and final, 'You ask too many damn questions, cowboy.'

"I let it lie at that point. He seemed to be gettin' nervous, so I put my feet up on the desk where I could watch the entrance and tried to make some sense out of what the sheriff had told me. He lived pretty high for a man on a sheriff's wages. He claimed to do other work to make the added income, and his deputy was shot for reasons that had no basis by a mysterious stranger that seemed to fade away as quickly as he'd come. On top of that, the deputy seemed to play it a little closer to the book than his boss wanted to. And apparently, he was plannin' on leaving his job soon.

"I rolled it around in my head for a while until it hit me. I stood up and told him I was goin' to go stretch my legs and peek in on our friends down at the saloon. The sheriff seemed all too happy to let me. I don't know if it was because he was content to stay in the safety of the jailhouse or because my questions made him nervous, but he didn't put up a fuss either way. I made my way down to the livery stable where I figured my partners might be, and sure enough they were there doing just what I'd asked them to do. I told 'em I had a job for one of them. They objected a little because they saw the men from the M&T ride into town, and none of 'em wanted to miss out on the fight they figured was comin'. I told them that my two days with the sheriff had shed a little light on things and that I needed one of 'em to ride out like they was headed for Cheyenne without the sheriff seein' 'em and to be real stealth and quick because I was sure the rest of M&T's boys would be comin' to town for a showdown. One of them asked me what he'd be lookin' for. I told him if my suspicions were correct, he should find a new trail, headin' for a canyon or trees or possibly smoke from a fire comin' from a strange place. I told 'em my gut was tellin' me that the sheriff was involved in the disappearing horse mystery. 'If I'm right, you'll find the stolen horses. Try not to make any noise or draw attention to yourself, and head back here. If you find them, put a piece of red cloth in the loft window at the livery so I know.'

"It was a couple of long days later when the anticipation got me antsy, so I decided to stretch my legs. I made my way up the street and quietly stepped up to the saloon's swingin' doors. I could hear some of the M&T boys talkin' big about how they was gonna come pull my boss outta jail and hang 'im right there in the street and that if the sheriff got in the way, they'd make him disappear too. It didn't surprise me much because I figured they would; the question was when. I decided to go and get a real meal and a bath before returnin' to the jail, in case it was gonna be a few days more before they worked up the courage.

SWEET JUSTICE   137

"The gal that served me my food was a curious type and noticed the star on my shirt. She asked if I was the new deputy and told me she was real sorry to hear about the old one. She said everyone liked him and that he did his job real good. She also told me that the folks in town didn't have much respect for the sheriff because he seemed to make his deputy do everything and that he didn't seem to be in town much. When I was finished, she said, 'I hope you can figure out who killed our last deputy; the sheriff sure hasn't tried.' I assured her that I was already working on it and hoped I could too. I made my way down to the bath house, and the man that ran the place pretty much told me the same thing that she did, only he used more colorful words to describe the sheriff and what he thought of 'im.

"The information I gathered just reaffirmed my suspicions and made me hope my companion would be able to find the proof. On my way back to the jail, the M&T boys left the saloon and rode out of town. When they saw me on the boardwalk, they made sure to let me know that it wasn't over and they'd be back. I covered the star on my shirt because I didn't want 'em to know I would be in town. Better to let them think I was leavin' too, I thought. I found my way to the jailhouse and settled in to wait for the fight I knew was comin'.

"It was two more days before we saw three of them come into town again and head for the saloon. I figured the rest would be along shortly, so I let them get a couple drinks in them before headin' for the spot where I had overheard them the last time. They were gettin' pretty drunk by then, which made 'em loud, so I hung out for a while to hear if I could figure what their plan was.

"One of them said, 'Let's go kill that damn horse thief and be done with it.' The rest told him to shut up and have a drink and reminded him that nothing was gonna happen 'til the rest arrived. His intoxication gave him courage, and he said, 'It's only one sheriff; we can take him.' 'One sheriff with lots of guns and adobe walls to protect him, stupid,' another answered. 'Don't worry, when we're all here, he'll be dead soon enough, and so will his prisoner.' I took comfort in the knowledge that they didn't know I was there and more in the fact that they didn't have any idea that I had two more in the livery. All of a sudden, I could hear horses comin' into town, so I backed into an alley to see who it was. I was glad I did because it was three more riders from the M&T. I waited for them to enter the saloon and join their friends before I hurried to the jail. I cussed myself for sendin' one of our boys off on what could easily turn out to be a wild goose chase and was a little worried about 'im because he'd been longer than I thought he would be. I hoped he'd be back soon, no matter what he found because if they started the fight now, it'd be four against six, and I didn't like them odds."

"Did they?" Jed said in anticipation. We all turned and looked at him and busted out laughin'. He stared at us for a second then joined in.

"Sorry, Bill, keep goin'," he said.

"Yeah, Jed, they did. About the same time I got back to the jail, I could see 'em comin' down the street. I ran in and told the sheriff they was comin' and what I'd heard 'em say. He grabbed his gun and said, 'They don't pay me enough for this shit.'

"They stopped in front of the jailhouse, and one of 'em yelled into the sheriff that if he didn't want to get

SWEET JUSTICE 139

killed he best step aside and let the hangin' commence. I could hear the townfolk scatter for cover and heard doors slammin' up and down the street. The sheriff looked at me and said, 'Maybe we should just let 'em have 'im. It ain't worth us dying, is it?' I called him a chicken shit weasel and yelled out, 'If you want 'im, come and get 'im!' My voice threw them off, and obviously they weren't expecting it because they quickly hit the boardwalk and took positions that provided cover. One of 'em stepped up and kicked the door open. I figured it was the one that was liquored up because you'd have to be drunk to do somethin' that stupid. It was the last thing he ever did. I blew him back into the middle of the street with a blast from my shotgun and pushed the door shut with my foot. The rest of 'em ran across the street and took cover behind whatever was available. They didn't know my two boys were comin' up the street, however, so when they started shootin' at them from the other direction, they had to scatter again before they could return fire. I told the sheriff to go back to the cell and protect my boss and assured him that if he was killed, I'd hunt 'im down and do the same to him. He quickly took the gun and headed that way.

"The shootin' continued out in the street, but one of 'em had made his way to the rooftop and had a vantage point down on my partners. The only way I could get a shot off was to step out on the boardwalk where I'd be a sittin' duck. I wasn't about to let him take one of my friends though, so I rolled out on my side into a sitting position and took him out with the Winchester then dove back into the jail. That quickly brought the odds down to four against four, if we counted the sheriff, and I liked them odds a whole lot better.

"We continued shootin' at one another after that, but we was just wastin' bullets at that point. I poked my head around the corner to see if I could see the livery and saw our man wavin' a red bandana frantically in the air. I yelled for my men to stop firin', which brought the return fire to a stop too. I called for the sheriff to man up and help bring it to a close before anyone else got killed. He was happy to do so just to save his own ass, or so he thought anyway. I yelled that we were comin' out, and if they'd let me have two minutes to speak my peace, I'd let them into the jail to do what they saw fit and then walked out where they could see me. I threw my guns down and told the sheriff and my men to do the same and invited them to meet us in the center of the street. They came out from where they was hidin' and walked down the street towards us until we was all face to face. The town folk allowed curiosity to outweigh their fear, and they slowly started to gather as well.

"'I have some news you might find interesting,' I told them. 'I think I know where your horses are and who shot the deputy.' The sheriff turned to slink away, but I caught 'im by his vest and said, 'You might wanna stick around and hear this too, sheriff.' I called in my friend that had confirmed my suspicions and asked him to enlighten us all. He quickly told 'em what he'd found and how to get there but urged them not to go rushin' in 'cause as near as he could tell, there were at least two men with guns keepin' a pretty close watch on things. 'There's at least ten different brands in the mix,' he added. I turned to the sheriff and asked if he wanted to finish the story. He looked around and saw that the people from town were gathering and told me to go to hell.

SWEET JUSTICE   141

"The boss from the M&T asked what the hell was going on. I said to him, 'Well, as near as I can tell, your sheriff here has been moonlightin' as a horse thief, which would explain the extra money he seems to have and why he spends so much time out of town.' The sheriff yelled and said, 'You can't prove that.' I told him that I didn't have to and reminded him that now it was he who'd have to prove he didn't. Then I went on tellin' the people in town what my suspicions were. 'Your deputy wasn't killed by a stranger; he was killed by the sheriff here when he didn't want any part in his night job operation. I suspect that he got wise to it and arrested the sheriff when he found out about it. That's why he was takin' him to Cheyenne to see the marshal, and I believe the sheriff 's men ambushed him and shut his mouth then and there. And I'll bet if you start askin' other ranches if they're missin' horses, you'll find they all are.'

"Then I turned to the sheriff and asked how close to the truth I was. He started ranting that the people in town didn't pay him enough and that he had to do somethin' and then said that if the deputy would've just kept his mouth shut he'd still be alive."

"What happened then?" Slim asked.

"They hung him then and there," I told him. "Didn't even have to make a noose; they just used the one meant for my boss. And since they no longer had a sheriff, I got the job until they could replace him. And the boys from the M&T were all too happy to go and get their horses back. I never had to put those men in my new jail, so I think it's safe to say that frontier justice stopped 'em from ever stealin' horses again." "You're full of surprises, Bill, that's for sure," Stumpy said. "Plumb full, I reckon."

Chapter Eight

A Blast from the Past

As near as I could tell from countin' days, it was now August. It was always nice to see July come to an end in Yuma. It meant that the hottest month was over. Not that August wasn't hot too, but its companions were generally wind and rain, which had a way of cooling things down a little. The monsoon season did come with irritations, however; high wind, if it came from the right direction, had a way of findin' its way through the window the kid liked so much, and since our floor was straw, there were hours sometimes when it was better to just keep your eyes shut rather than take a chance of fillin' your skull to the hilt with blowin' debris.

Rain could also bring its own irritant and danger when it came. Usually, it'd come in very few drops. Most of it would evaporate before hitting the ground because of the heat and sun; the rest of it would just make things dirty. But occasionally, it would win the battle against its rivals, and when it did, the rain would come down real hard. This brought the potential for flash flooding. The water didn't bother us so much in here, but when it got wet like that, it'd bring the scorpions up out of the sand, and they would scurry to find refuge somewhere, and somewhere meant the straw we used for our beds or into our boots while we slept.

The men in the regular cells weren't as affected by them as those of us in the overflow because they had beds that were elevated up off the ground, but those of us sleepin' at floor level were exposed to anything that shared the ground with us. But on the bright side, we had room to move around and some protection from the elements. Besides, the friendships I'd developed were worth the effort to watch out for any critters that might come to visit once in a while. The first year I was in here one of the guys got stung by a scorpion and suffered so bad from the pain and swelling that the rest of us learned real quick to check and double check before lyin' down. I'd heard tell of one man dyin' from the sting he received. I don't know if it was true or not—stories that go from one man to another have a way of gettin' bigger with each telling. Nevertheless, the story ensured that no one else was goin' to allow themselves to fall victim to the same fate, and we all had killed more than our share.

August had a feeling of doom about it too. For some reason there seemed to be more hangin's this time of year. I don't know why; maybe it had somethin' to do with the fact that the intense heat had a way of gettin' people's nerves riled up, and they were ready to take their frustration out on something or somebody. I don't know for sure, but the gallows sure seemed busy when the summer season grew old.

This knowledge had my stomach in knots because I knew Virgil would sleep better if the gallow's eerie thump was accompanied by the sound of my snapping neck, and I knew he would do everything he could to ensure that my case came up for trial again.

I ate my breakfast, stewin' about it and hopin' Emily was puttin' forth as much effort to prove my innocence as Virgil was, tryin' to convince those around him that I wasn't.

My train of thought and worry was broken by the sound of the prison wagon pulling up in front of the courthouse. You could always tell when the hell on wheels was comin' from the train station because it had its own distinct sound about it. If you couldn't pick it out from that, you could almost always count on the vile words bein' shouted as it made its way up the street. I looked towards the window and could see the kid tryin' his best not to run to it, but the desire to see what was goin' on finally got the best of him, and like a moth to a flame, reason won out and curiosity took its place.

"What you see, kid?" I asked.

He turned sheepishly towards me and replied that he couldn't help himself. I laughed when he said it and told him that I didn't mean he couldn't ever look out it. He smiled when I told him that, like some form of freedom had just been handed back to him. He commenced to describe the play-by-play of all that was goin' on.

"They's five men comin' in," he said, "accompanied by the marshal and four guards with guns, keepin' a pretty close watch on things. One of the prisoners has a bandage on his leg. Looks like he been shot by the way he's limpin' and the amount of blood saturating the bandage. Two of the others look like they's been beat up pretty bad. They have them lined up on the steps for some reason," he

SWEET JUSTICE 145

continued, "like they're waitin' for somethin'. Hey, there's Miss Watson!" he shouted suddenly.

In a flash, I was up and takin' my place next to him. This opened me up for a little teasin' from everyone, but I didn't care; I was missin' her somethin' awful and was glad to be another moth if it meant I could see her flame again.

I watched her as she looked intently at their faces and then saw her confirm to the guard that she didn't find what she was seekin'. I wondered again who it was she was lookin' for and surmised that something tragic must've happened in her past. As far as I knew, she never missed its arrival, day or night. She started to leave when she paused and looked towards the place where I was standin'. There was no possible way that she could see me with the sun in her eyes, but I took comfort from her glance and hoped that perhaps I was on her mind.

The prisoners were quickly ushered into the courthouse, and after lookin' at the added guards that accompanied them, I had to wonder how many were lookin' at their last day and if any would be the newest tenants of the Yuma hell hole. My time at the window abruptly ended with Virgil's call to lunch. Little did I know, however, that I wouldn't be joining my friends for today's tin of slop; Virgil had other plans for me, and I was escorted in full shackles to a place in the prison I'd never been before.

Upon arrival Virgil cracked me with his stick he loved so much, and my vision was blurred from the pain in my head.

"Go ahead and cry for help," he said. "Ain't nobody gonna hear ya; they're all at the courthouse."

"What the hell's this all about, Virgil?" I asked.

"This?" he said. "Why, William, this is a social call, a chance for you and me to come to an understanding, you might say."

"Well, take these damn shackles off, and you and I will get acquainted then."

With that he smacked me with his stick again, bein' real careful to hit me where it wouldn't show. I drew a breath after wincing from the pain.

"You're a coward, Virgil," I said. "What the hell's your problem with me anyway?"

"My problem is your conversing with Miss Watson." He threw his stick and made full contact with my lower ribs. "I want you to stay away from her."

"And if I don't?" I asked, grimacing in pain.

"If you don't, Billy," he threatened, "I'm gonna kill you, but not before we've had a few more of these here parties."

"You've been tryin' to kill me since the day I got here, Virgil. Tell me somethin' I don't know," I said angrily.

"And I'm gettin' close too," he said. "Just about got a lawyer and a judge convinced that you're a threat and that overcrowding might be a good excuse to get rid of you."

"The only problem you've got with that plan is Miss Watson, Virgil," I surmised. "Seems to me that the only chance I got to stay alive is to keep talkin' to her."

He poked me in the sternum with his stick. "You'll never see her without my permission, tough guy."

"I've got a deal for you, Virgil. How 'bout you take these shackles off, and I just rid the world of a yellow coward. I'll keep it fair—you can have your gun and

SWEET JUSTICE 147

stick, and I'll take my chances with my fists. If you kill me, your problems are solved, and if I kill you, I'll go to the rope with a smile on my face."

I watched his face turn red with anger and then watched the color drain away as he realized he lacked the courage to meet my challenge. His voice became shaky as he spoke again. "Listen, Bill," he said in desperation, "you promise to stop talkin' to Emily, and I'll promise to do all I can to get you out of here. But only if you promise to ride outta town and never come back. Hell, I'll even give you a horse," he added, trying to sweeten the deal.

"That sounds good. The only problem you got is I don't believe you, so if it's all the same to you, I'll take my chances with Miss Watson."

His face turned bright red again, and he angrily stated that I was makin' a grave mistake, and then he smacked me with his stick again once in the ribs and twice across my head. The last one split my head wide open as I fell unconscious to the floor. I don't know how long I laid there, but my next semi-coherent realization was staggering back to the cell with the aid of Virgil and then bein' shoved back into it. I remember takin' a couple of steps, and then I must've fainted from the pain and loss of blood again because I don't remember hittin' the floor. In my subconscious state, I found myself back at Gettysburg, fightin' for my life. Everything was in slow motion as I watched my friends die around me, and the faster I tried to run to save 'em, the slower I seemed to move. I watched in horror as men were blown to pieces and bayoneted on both sides of me. It was like I was immune to any harm and that my part of this scene from hell was to witness the destruction of all that I loved and cared about. I realized I could see guns firin' and cannons goin' off with bursts of smoke and fire, like demons bein' released in waves hell bent on destroyin' everything in their path, but I couldn't hear the sound of any of them.

I watched men screamin' in horror and boys curled up in fetal positions, yellin' for their mamas as tears of desperation streamed down their faces, but all I could hear was a muffled wind rushing in my ears. I tried to run away, but no matter which way I turned, there was some form of absolute destruction and violence blocking my path, so I stood and watched all hell break loose right in front of my eyes.

I looked at my hands covered with blood, and no matter how many times I wiped it on my torn uniform, the blood just kept comin' back. The nightmare silence was deafening, so I screamed until my stomach ached, but no sound could overpower the eerie wind in my ears. All at once they came out of the smoke on a dead run with their shining bayonet's dripping with blood. I went for my weapon to defend myself and realized I didn't have one, so I turned to run out of their path, but my feet were stuck in what felt like quicksand, and the harder I tried to move, the more stuck I became.

When they were almost on top of me, I saw men runnin' from the other direction. As they met each other in battle, their fingers turned to claws, and they were rippin' each other to shreds. It didn't matter how many fell; there were two more to take their place. Pretty soon it wasn't North and South fightin' each other anymore; it was just an awful scene of kill or be killed, with no rhyme or reason, playin' out before my eyes. I tried to close

SWEET JUSTICE 149

them, but some unseen force wouldn't let me, and the harder I tried, the more focused they seem to become.

In the middle of the mayhem, I could see the fightin' crowd give way to somethin' that was movin' through, like a ship breaking water as it takes its place of dominance. Like the water, they quickly moved back as soon as it passed. I looked at the men directly in front of me and saw they had turned to demons. As the coming entity that was moving through them was almost upon me, they turned to look, as they gave it the right of way, with sinister grins full of blood-stained, sharpened teeth.

As the approaching doom came through the last of 'em, I could see that it was my cousin Jimmy, still bleedin' from the fatal wound I'd inflicted on him. He looked down on me as I was slowly bein' pulled into the black pond of quicksand that surrounded me. I put my hand out to him, hopin' he could pull me out, but he just stood there, starin' at me with hollow eyes and a blank stare. I cried out for his help, but he didn't move. Suddenly, my pa was there and behind him my ma and sisters, but they just watched me as I slowly sank farther. There was no sadness in their eyes, not a trace of emotion on their faces. *Help me*, I cried out, *please*. But there was still no sound—just that damn rushing wind.

Then outta nowhere, Virgil was standin' over me with an evil grin. He put his foot on my shoulder and began to apply weight to it. I searched frantically into the faces of my family to see if they would stop 'im, but they just stared blankly. As I looked back at Virgil, Emily was standing next to him. I saw her take his hand. Then at last the silence was broken: *I told you, Bill. I make the rules. I'm the boss, and your fate has been in my hands all along.* The last thing I heard as my head oozed into the black abyss was Virgil yelling, *You all stay the hell away from him; he brought this on himself.*

As I sank deeper and deeper, I couldn't breathe anymore. Seein' that my family didn't care, I decided to stop fightin' it and let the cold hands of death take me. The next thing I felt was someone slappin' my face. "Damn it! Fight it, Bill. Come on, partner, stay with me." I could feel a cold cloth on my face, and I opened my eyes a little. "Come on,

Bill, stay with us," I could here Slim say.

"Get the hell away from him, Slim," Virgil yelled through the cell door. "He did this to himself."

"Go to hell, Virgil," Slim shot back. "You'll pay for this, you bastard."

"Pay for what, Slim? It's not my fault he tripped in his shackles and hit his head," Virgil shot back.

"You're a damn liar, Virgil, and you know it," the kid said.

"Well, you'd have to prove that, wouldn't you," Virgil said smugly, "and it'd be my word against yours. Who do you think people are gonna believe—me or some kid that tried to rob an ore wagon?" He let out a laugh that echoed down the corridor.

I don't know how long I was out after that, but I could tell from the location of the sun that it was the next day. When I heard a familiar voice from my past ask how I was, in my state I had a hard time placin' it but was sure I somehow knew who it belonged to.

"He's hurt pretty bad," I heard Slim say. "We've got to clean this cut; it's clear to his skull."

SWEET JUSTICE

151

I could hear the others askin' what they could do, but their voices sounded distant and faint. My head throbbed somethin' fierce. Everythin' was blurry, and I felt my eyes roll back in my head. I heard Slim tellin' me I was going to be okay and that I had a friend here.

"Hey, Bill, it's me, James." That was the last thing I heard before I went out again.

"He's goin' to be alright," James told them. "I've seen him take some pretty good beatings in his day. The man's tougher than iron."

"How do you know 'im?" the kid asked.

"I've ridden with him many a time in the last ten years and fought with him in the war. He's one of the best cowhands I've ever seen and damn good with a gun, I can tell you that."

"You don't sound Southern," Ben said.

"Southern? Hell no. I ain't Southern, partner," James said.

"Well, Bill is," Ben replied. "You sure you're not mistakin' him for another feller?"

"You can't mistake William Saunders for anyone, my friend," James shot back. "Once you get to know Bill, you don't forget him, that I can assure you. Bill here is true blue. If you're a friend of Bill's, he'd give you the shirt off his back if it was the last one he owned, and I'd venture he'd take a bullet for you if it came down to it."

"How did you fight with 'im in the war if ya'll were from different sides?" Ben asked with a little irritation in his voice.

"Bill here fought for the North, partner," James explained.

"Well, that would explain why he was fightin' his cousin," Stumpy exclaimed.

"Why would he do that? Fight for the north, I mean, when he was from the South," the kid asked.

"He wasn't the only one that did," answered James. "There were many that understood the importance of the union and more who saw slavery as somethin' that needed to go away. Slavery was on its way out long before the war started. Anyone who was payin' attention to the writing on the wall already knew that."

"Did his family know he fought for the North?" Jed asked.

"I don't think so. He told me he snuck away one night after his family went to sleep. The way he had it figured was they was goin' to come recruit him eventually, and he told me if he was goin' to have to fight anyway, it might as well be for the side he agreed with."

"Well, hell, that explains part of the reason he felt he couldn't go home, I guess," said Slim. "He told us he came close but just couldn't do it."

"That could've been part of it, I reckon," James said, "but somethin' happened to him at Gettysburg, and he just wasn't right after that."

"He killed his cousin," Ben blurted out.

Slim frantically waved his arm, told him to keep his voice down, and not to bring that subject up again.

"He killed his cousin?" James asked in a whisper. "Holy crap, no wonder he was off. I had no idea."

"No one did until he told us, and he was a little off after that too." "Well, I'll be damned," said James. "No wonder he lived life on the edge like he done."

"What do you mean?" Stumpy asked.

SWEET JUSTICE 153

"Well, I reckon you fellers wouldn't know anything about that, so I'll tell ya. Whenever there was a scrape, Bill was always at the front. It always amazed me how he never got shot because if lead was flyin', it was a flyin' around him. Two or three men could be shootin' at him, and before the smoke cleared, they was dead, and somehow Bill would come out with nary a scratch. If there was danger on a drive or problems with them Injuns, Bill was always the first to volunteer to go and get done whatever had to be done. He was in a posse with Wild Bill Hickok. Did he ever tell you that?"

"Sure didn't," the kid said as he saddled up next to him for more details. Everyone else gathered around to hear the tale, sure to be entertained by yet another story of Bill and his adventures.

"It was back in '70," began James. "Bill was bringin' in a herd to Abilene for John Chisholm. He'd been up in Montana for a spell, and on his way back, he caught Mr. Chisholm about two days into his drive. He told me John damn near shot him because he thought he was tryin' to wrangle his herd, until he recognized him. When he saw who he was, Chisholm was glad to have him there because they were three days late gettin' started. Some of the riders were late, and when they showed up, they was two men shorter than what was expected.

"I guess they assured him they was a day or two out yet but not to worry they was comin'. If any of you know Mr. Chisholm, you know that he ain't what you'd call a patient man, so he said, 'To hell with them. If they can't be on time, they can kiss my ass.' So needless to say, Bill came along at the right time. He has a knack for doin' that.

154 MARK INKLEY

"Anyway, when they got into Abilene, I was comin' in too with a herd from Texas, and we'd all been told that if we hurried back, there'd be another herd to bring in. Double pay right before winter sounded good to me, so when I ran into Bill at one of the saloons, I told him about it. Bill seemed eager to put more gold dollars in his pocket too. So we set off as soon as we could to be the first ones standin' in line when it came to hirin'. We hadn't seen each other since the war got over and had some catchin' up to do. Best damn ride I'd had in a long time. The war had a way of creating a brotherhood that can't be undone with time, and even though we had families, there was no way they could understand what we'd been through. So to spend time with someone who understood was a breath of fresh air."

"That don't sound like no ride with Hickok to me," Jed stated impatiently.

Everyone laughed when he said it.

"You'd do well to learn to hang on to your horses, Jed," Slim told him.

James continued with a smile. "When we got back to Gonzales, Texas, there was a herd waitin' alright, but the feller that was supposed to be the trail boss wasn't. Someone suggested they give a fella by the name of John Hardin a go at it and assured the owner that he came from a clan that knew cattle and that he'd get the job done alright. Problem was the owner of the cattle knew that this here John feller had been accused of killin' a Negro he'd wrestled and lost to in a fight for money. I reckon it didn't sit well with him to get his ass whooped by a colored fella, so he caught him on the road and told

SWEET JUSTICE   155

him he wanted a rematch. When the man refused, rumor has it he killed him.

"But due to the late season, the owner finally relented, and the drive was on. Bill formed a relationship with John, as was his nature, because he liked the way Bill could shoot, so through the better part of the drive, those two talked a lot, and John opened up to him about his past, braggin' about the things he'd done, tryin' to impress him, I reckon. Bill found out that not only had he killed the Negro but that he'd also killed the union soldiers who'd come to arrest him, and he seemed right proud of it. I reckon he thought Bill would be okay with it, considerin' he was from the South, but he didn't count on the fact that Bill didn't share his views on the colored people or that he'd fought for the North, so Bill didn't take to his actions liked he expected.

"Bill told me afterwards that he wasn't gonna stir the pot 'til the drive was over because there was a job to be done but that he intended to have him arrested when it was over. He continued to maintain the relationship so John didn't get wise to his intentions, and the rest of the drive went without a hitch until the end. When we got to the outskirts of Abilene, there was a backlog of herds because the railroad yards couldn't keep up with the cattle that were stackin' up, so it fell to the cowboys to try and keep our herds from intermingling with each other. A herd bein' driven by a crew of Mexicans didn't do such a good job of it, and when their herd started gettin' mixed up with ours, John saw red. "No one knew if it was the cattle gettin' mixed up or if it was the fact that he was a racist bastard and just didn't like the Mexicans, but whatever it was, he went over the edge and started

156 MARK INKLEY

screamin' at the foreman of their herd somethin' fierce. The Mexican took a pot shot at him and blew a hole right through his hat. Don't know if he was just a lousy shot or if he was just tryin' to shut him up, but John was tryin' to retaliate and would've killed him, I reckon, but his old gun misfired, so his shot hit his target in the leg instead. Bill stepped between them and told everyone to calm down before someone got killed and reminded them that the money we'd all earned was goin' to be tough to spend if they was dead. Like I said, it takes nerves of iron to step between two people shootin' guns, but he did, so a truce was called, or so we thought.

"All of a sudden John took my gun and shot that Mexican right through the heart. That's when all hell broke loose. Everyone dove for cover, and before it was over, six of them Vaqueros were dead. John shot five of them; Bill shot the other in self defense. Kill or be killed is what he told me. When the shootin' started, Bill was out in the open and saw one of them take aim at 'im. Little did that poor feller know he was drawin' on one of the fastest guns I've ever seen. He killed him so quickly that to this day he probably doesn't know he's dead. The rest of them scattered, and the fight was over as fast as it began. We took our herd in and got paid; Bill went to the peace officer in town."

"Wild Bill," Jed shot out.

"Yeah, Wild Bill," James said with a chuckle. "He went to tell him what he knew about this John Hardin but found him drinkin' with John at the saloon. They seemed right friendly, so Bill decided to bite his tongue until a better opportunity presented itself. A few days later, there was a shootin' contest in town. It was two dollars to enter, and the winner took all, so Bill put his

SWEET JUSTICE 157

two dollars down, and him and Hickok spent the rest of that afternoon sendin' people away two bills poorer 'til it came down to the two Bills." Everyone chuckled at the wit of James's statement.

Jed could hardly contain himself, and in his excitement asked, "Who won?"

James said "Hickok won but not by much. It was truly exciting to watch, I can assure you. So the two of them went to have a drink. Hickok told him that since he had given him a run for his money the drinks were on him. Before John invited himself to their party, Bill got the chance to spill the beans on Hardin, and Hickok told Bill he'd keep an eye on him and that he'd check out his story. John came up as the conversation was ending and asked who they was talking about. Hickok assured John that it wasn't him, trying to avoid guns bein' drawn in the crowded saloon but gave Bill a wink as he walked away. That night John decided that the man in the room next to him was snoring too loud and shot through the wall to shut him up, but he hit him in the heart and killed him. John was smart enough to know Hickok, friend or not, wouldn't let him get away with it in his town, so he jumped out the window to escape.

"He was correct in his assumption: Hickok got madder than hell and formed a posse to go after him and asked Bill if he'd ride along. Bill was more than happy to go after him and to ride with the famous Wild Bill Hickok. They got to be pretty good friends and were always happy to see each other after that. When he was killed in Dead Wood, Bill took it pretty hard and rode all the way up there just to put his second place ribbon on his grave."

James spent the next couple days checkin' on me and entertaining our cellmates with stories of my past, embellishing them whenever he could, as was his habit when he told his tales. In my subconscious state, I traveled forgotten trails and relived many of my experiences and lots of my childhood. The next conscious thing I became aware of was James tellin' of the time I avoided a fight with some Navajos who thought we were part of the group who'd been stealin' sheep from them.

"Navajos tend to be peaceful but can become ferocious when they think they've been wronged," James told them. "So when a group of us were comin' out of the gold fields in the Colorado Territory, we just happened to enter the outskirts of their reservation at the same time some other cowboys were makin' trouble. We didn't speak their language to understand what they were accusing us of, but fortunately for us, Bill had learned some signs from other Indian tribes he'd dealt with and was able to convince them we weren't the ones they were looking for but told them we'd help them get their sheep back."

"Why didn't you just shoot 'em and be done with it?" Ben asked. "One thing you'll learn about Bill, partner, is he don't kill no one that don't have it comin'. Besides, he's got a soft spot for them Injuns and will justify their actions at the drop of a hat. He says we should share the land with them instead of takin' it, avoid a whole lot of killin' is what he'd say if 'n he was tellin' the story. Anyway, we didn't have to search long to find which way they went and rode up on 'em as they were cooking one of the sheep for dinner. As we approached, one of the men went for his gun, but Bill shot it out of his hand and yelled, 'If you wanna see tomorrow, boys, you'll stay

SWEET JUSTICE   159

away from them there guns.' 'You workin' with Injuns,' one of them yelled, 'that's un-American.' Bill shot back that they are just as American as we are and warned him to keep his big mouth shut. Then turned and told the Navajos to go collect their sheep and to take one of their horses too for the inconvenience.

"'If you give 'em one of our horses, we'll hunt you down and kill you,' one of them shouted. 'You'll try and you'll fail, but I got a hankerin' for a good fight, so let's get it done right now,' Bill said coolly. The one with the big mouth yelled, 'Those are big words, considering we're unarmed.' Bill put his pistol back in his holster and told that feller to go ahead and pick his up. He did and stood there facin' him. He licked his lip a couple of times when he saw that Bill was serious. Finally, he shouted, 'They can have the damn horse. We're outta here.' The leader of the Navajo bunch walked over to Bill and handed him a feather out of his headdress and called him a word Bill translated as brother and invited us to come and eat the sheep them fellers was cooking."

None of them realized I was awake until I said, "You left out the part where he tried to give me his daughter to be my wife."

Everyone turned when they heard me and seemed right glad I was okay.

"How you feelin'?" Slim asked. "You took a pretty good whack to the head, my friend."

"I feel like I took a whack to the head."

"It's good to see you up, you old buzzard," James said with a smile. "I thought you might not see me before I got outta here."

"How long have I been out?"

"Four days," replied Slim. "We weren't sure you was goin' to make it."

"I told you he was tough as iron," James exclaimed.

"Did Virgil beat you, Bill?" asked the kid. "He told us you tripped with your shackles and hit your head."

"Sure did, and if you look under my shirt at the bruises, you'll see it wasn't no fall that put me here."

"Was it over the woman?" asked James. "The boys here kinda filled me in a little."

"Yes and no," I told him. "He wanted me to stay away from her, but there's got to be more to the story than that. The man's comin' unhinged, like he's tryin' to cover somethin' up, but I can't put my finger on it."

"Could be he's just plumb loco, and it really is just about the girl," James pointed out.

"Well, it's definitely about the girl," I assured him, "but do you remember that time when we hunted for that crazy man that hurt that girl outside of San Antonio?"

"Oh yeah," James replied with a chuckle, "that man sure wasn't right in the head."

"We didn't suspect him at first, remember? He was part of the group tryin' to find out who was responsible, but the closer we came to the truth, the more he tried to keep us from connecting the pieces and the more violent he became to prevent it until he just went off his rocker altogether."

"Yeah, I remember, Bill. But what's that got to do with this?"

"Don't know. Maybe nothin', but it has that kind of feel to it. There's more to this stew than what's floatin' on top, and I ain't found the spoon to find out what."

Artwork by Mark Inkley

CHAPTER NINE

Hell's Angels

ONE OF THE GUARDS CAME around and announced dinner. When he looked in and saw I was awake, he asked how I was. "Hungry," I said with a forced smile.

"You sit, Bill," said the kid. "I'll get your food for ya."

"That's alright," I told him. "I need to move anyway." I didn't realize how beat up I was until I stood up. That's when the pain of a whoopin' combined with lyin' down for four days hit me. I staggered over to the cell door, and everyone moved out of the way and allowed me to get my food first. I staggered back. James tried to help me by offering to hold my tin while I sat down.

"I'm alright," I snapped. "Just leave me be." "Okay, partner. Jeez, Bill, just tryin' to help."

My whole body ached, but my head was takin' the brunt of it. "I don't need help," I said irritated. I looked at my friend who by now was starin' at me with a shocked look on his face. "I'm sorry, James," I said in a softer tone. "I'm just mad at myself for allowin' this to happen. I didn't mean to take it out on you."

SWEET JUSTICE 163

"Well, hell, Bill, it's not like you could've prevented it. Out in the real world you'd never've allowed it too, but that's tough to do with shackles on. If you ask me, that guard's a yellow coward."

"You have no idea," I told him, "but you will if you stay here very long."

"I ain't stayin' here, Bill," he assured me. "I'm just waitin' for my day with the judge."

"I hate to tell you, James, but if you're in here, they've already decided you're guilty."

"No, I'm waitin' for witnesses to come that can prove I wasn't with those fellers when they was robbin' that bank. The only reason I'm not in the jailhouse is because it's full up."

"How'd ya come to be with them?"

"I'd set up camp by the creek when I heard one of them yell, 'Hello, that coffee smells damn good.' 'Come on in and get some,' I told them. You know me, Bill, I'd rather have danger where I can see it instead of sneakin' around in the dark. So I grabbed my Winchester and let 'em come on in. They seemed like alright fellers, and I was glad to have the company. I'd just started to cook the rabbit I'd killed when I heard horses in the distance. All of a sudden, they came outta the trees without announcing themselves, so I went into defensive mode and jumped behind the log. The others that were with me weren't so smart and started shootin' like crazy; there was lead flyin' everywhere. Dumb bastards lacked sense, I tell you. Two dropped like flies at the end of horses tail and another one took a bullet right above the knee. Two more met the butt end of that posse's rifles and probably wished they'd been shot after the beatin' they took.

"When the shootin' part was over, I wasn't even sure if they knew I was there, so I just stayed put. That's when I heard one of them call for me to come out from where I was hidin. 'I ain't hidin', I said to him. 'I don't even know what this is all about.' A fat one with a smart mouth said, 'Oh, you don't, huh? I suppose you was just out for a late-night stroll and just happened on these here fellers.' I asked him if he was born stupid or if that came with age and then pointed out that it was obvious that he was standin' in a one-man camp and that they'd happened onto me."

"That probably didn't work so well for you, I reckon," I said with a slight chuckle.

"You reckoned right. They rounded us all up and brought us into Tombstone. After a couple days there, they put us on a train and sent us here, even after I told them I could prove I was innocent."

"Same thing happened to me," I told him. "From that very jail. So why were you down Tombstone way?"

"I was comin' to take a job protecting some ranchers herd from Mexicans."

I started to laugh at that point, and he looked at me with a perplexed look on his face. When I saw it, I told him that he and I were two peas in a pod and then explained that not only were we both innocent, but we were both on our way to work for the same man. After a second or two, he found the humor in it, and we laughed together. Even though it made me hurt all over, I couldn't stop, and my mind drew comfort that I had an old friend to share it with. After the laughter died out, James asked what I'd done to get in here, so I quickly gave him a

SWEET JUSTICE 165

rundown of the situation up to the point of what that Earp fella told Emily.

James was silent for a moment as he drank in all I told him, and then he said, "Three years you been in this dump? Damn, Bill, I wondered why I hadn't come across you anywhere for a while." And then outta nowhere he said, "Old Charlie is a deputy in this town. Maybe he could put a word in for you."

"Charlie's a deputy here in Yuma?" I repeated.

"Yep," he said, "at least that's what I heard. Came here 'bout four, four and a half years ago I guess it's been now. You know Charlie, he never did like them cows anyway, and we all know he wasn't much of a cowboy, so he took a job more to his likin'."

"Charlie's been here this whole time? I sure wish I'd known that." "I'll bet you do. Hell, he'd vouch for ya, partner. He always kinda idolized you anyway, and he can prove you was even a law man for a time, maybe get you outta this hole and away from that guard who's out to get ya."

"That's sure a ray of light in dark clouds. Things might be lookin' up indeed."

James wanted to sit and reminisce after that, but my body was cravin' sleep, so I told him we'd talk in the morning. "Sure, Bill, get some rest."

"Hey, James. I'm sorry I snapped at ya."

"Hell, Bill, don't you worry none about it. I owe you too many to get my chaps tied up about that. You sleep good, partner."

I pulled my hat over my face, wonderin' how I could get in touch with old Charlie and listenin' to Slim cough. It was gettin' worse, and the humidity wasn't helping any.

I've gotta get him outta here was the last thing I remember thinking before I went to sleep.

The next morning I woke up to Stumpy tappin' my boot. "Hey, Bill, Spencer's at the door. Says he needs to talk to ya. Seems a little anxious."

I looked out the window and could tell it was too early for breakfast, so I shook the sleep outta my head, grimaced in pain as I stood up and staggered over to the door.

"Morning, Spence," I said. "How's your letters comin'?"

"Fine, Bill. I'm not supposed to be talkin' to ya, but Virgil decided to go get some breakfast, and I thought you should know that none of us believe his story about what happened to ya. Miss Watson doesn't either and said to tell you she's sorry and that she's been outta town with her father. She wants to come see you but doesn't want to make trouble for you unless you say it's okay."

"Hell yeah, it's okay. You tell her I need to talk to her and that it's important, if she doesn't mind."

"I'll tell 'er," Spencer said, "but it has to be where Virgil can't see.

He's a lot grumpier than usual lately, and I can't lose this job."

"Well, come around when you can, and we'll work on your readin'." "Miss Watson's been teachin' me," he said with a smile, "and I owe you one for gettin' me started. She came by my place to check on you and caught me sayin' my letters. I tried to hide them from her, but I guess I looked like a fox caught in the hen house, so I told her what you was tryin' to do for me and that I hoped we could finish when you was feelin' better. I wasn't tryin' to move in on your girl."

"Why do people keep sayin' that to me? She's not my girl."

"Well, she seemed right pleased that you'd help me, even in your predicament, and said she hoped you recover soon too." He paused a moment and then said, "She wants to see you, Bill."

"Well, that don't make her my girl. She's just tryin' to help me get outta here, that's all."

"Maybe," he replied, "but there was somethin' about the way she said it."

"You tell her to come, Spence, and thanks for stickin' your neck out for me."

"I'm much obliged, Bill, but I did it for Miss Watson." He looked at his watch in his pocket and commented, "Hell, I best get goin'. Good luck, Bill," he said as he hurried away.

I tried to go back to sleep, but the kid came over and reminded me that I still had the rest of 'em that I could teach. Then he smiled and said, "But you ain't as pretty as that Watson gal, so if she wants to teach us too, you might have to find another job."

"I wouldn't blame you, kid," I told him, "not even a little."

It wasn't long after that when Virgil came around to give us breakfast. It was the first time I'd seen 'im since the day he took me to one of his parties. As my turn came to get my portion, he looked at me with a sinister smile and said, "You best watch where you're walkin' when you got shackles on, Bill. You almost killed yourself."

"You best watch where you're walkin' all the time, if I ever get out of here, Virgil," I shot back with a stare that made him nervous. "Before, if I was to get out of here, I'd a probably just gone away, but now you and I have a score to settle, and I always finish what I start, my friend."

"You'll never get out of here, Billy. I'll make sure of that."

"You best hope you're right, Virgil. In fact, if you're not a prayin' man, this might be a good time to start."

"If'n I was you, I'd be the one prayin'," he said smugly. Then he got real close and reminded me of his offer and begged me to be reasonable and think about it.

"Nope. I think I'll hang around and find out what it is you're so desperate to cover up."

"I ain't tryin' to cover anything up," he said nervously.

"I think you are, Virgil," I stated accusingly, "and I aim to figure out what it is."

"You're crazy, Bill. I think that bump on your head made you loco." "Maybe. Time has a way of bringin' bones to the surface, though,

don't it, Virgil?"

He stared at me for a moment and shifted in his position a couple of times—all signs that I was closer to the truth than he wanted me to be.

"You're plumb crazy, I reckon," he said, finally walking away.

I sat down to eat when James came over and asked me if I thought my approach was the best way to fight this fight.

"You're not the first one to ask me that."

SWEET JUSTICE 169

"Well, damn, I can see why. The man just beat you pert near to death and still has the power to do it again."

"Sure, but I've put up with that animal for three years, and I ain't about to back down now."

"Does he hold the power he seems to think he does?"

"I don't think so. If he did, I'd be dead already, sure as shootin'."

"Well, a few more beatin's like the one you just took might not kill you, but it could keep you from ever thinkin' straight again. It's somethin' to think about, partner."

"James, this place is gonna kill me anyway," I assured him. "If I don't hang, I have seven more years in this hell hole, and to tell you the truth, I think I'd rather hang. So if he kills me, it don't make no difference to me. But if I let that pile of horseshit think he broke me, I'd be killin' myself."

"Then let's hope this gal can help ya, because that man is worse than an enemy, that's for certain."

We sat in silence for a second, so I turned to him and asked if he wanted to give me a hand. "I think I may have bitten off more than I can chew," I told him.

"Sure, Bill, what do ya need?" he offered.

I called everyone over and brushed the straw away to expose the dirt underneath and said, "Boys, James here is gonna teach you how to turn those letters you learned into words." I turned and smiled at him as he gave me that look he had in the past, when he knew I'd volunteered him for one of my crazy ventures. In all fairness I'd done it to him more than once.

We spent the rest of the morning helping giddy grown men sound out words like *cat* and *dog,* genuinely havin' a good time doin' it. When lunchtime came 'round, there were two guards, which was never a good sign. It meant they were there for someone, and there was always apprehension on our side of the bars. Virgil smacked his stick against the door as he stared me down and then yelled for James to step forward. "Judge wants to see you," he told him as the other guard put his shackles on. "Had I known you was an old friend of Bill's, I'd a put you in solitary while you were here."

"I thought they was kiddin' me about you, but I can see now you really are an asshole," James shot back.

Virgil raised his stick like he was gonna hit him.

"Careful, partner," James said coolly. "I'm gonna be free this afternoon, and that there stick will have to be washed after I get done with ya. That is, if you can get it out again."

Everyone laughed, and Virgil told us all to shut up. The man was such a coward that sometimes I almost felt sorry for him.

Most of the time, though, I'd burp or something else like it and realize I was mistaken. I got in line to get my grub and wondered if I would ever see James again and thought that if seein' him again meant things didn't go well with the judge, I hoped I wouldn't. Most men deserved better than the hell hole of Yuma, and those that didn't, deserved the gallows, which made this here prison a waste of space as far as I was concerned.

After lunch I spent the rest of the day teachin'. Everyone caught on real quick, everyone, that is, 'cept Jed. He struggled with it a bit, but everyone was good to help 'im, and I figured when we were done, he'd be able to muddle through alright. Late afternoon brought

SWEET JUSTICE   171

wind, so we were forced to call it quits for the day. The wind died down a little sometime after dinner, and I sat there hopin' James was in a saloon somewhere, enjoyin' his freedom. But Slim's words that there was no justice in Yuma kept runnin' across my mind. Slim came over and asked if I was feelin' alright, but the wind had irritated his lungs something awful, and he had a tough time talkin' without coughing.

"It's startin' to catch up with me, Bill."

"I know, Slim, and I'm sorry. We'll figure out a way to get you outta here, my friend."

"It's a nice dream, Bill," he commented with very little hope in his voice, "but I think this is the end of the line for me."

"What was it you told me," I reminded him, "somethin' 'bout not givin' up?"

"Well, if it is or if it ain't, I sure have enjoyed the company. You done good things for these here boys, Bill, and I'm right proud to have gotten the chance to know ya."

He laid down and coughed a few times while he tried to keep talkin', but the cough seemed to be winning the battle, so I said to him, "I am too, Slim. You're a good friend," and started tellin' him about a man in Wyoming he reminded me of. Somewhere through it all, he went to sleep. So I pulled my hat down over my eyes and joined him.

The next morning a little after breakfast, I could hear heated voices echoing down the corridor. It sounded like one of 'em could've been Emily, so I sat up in anticipation, hoping that I might get to see her. But as quick as the voices came, they ended, so I relaxed in a feeling of deflation and struck up a conversation with the kid.

"You been thinkin' about what you might do when you get outta here?"

"Sort of," he said. "Sometimes I think maybe I'll go home and have my pa teach me how to be a smithy, but every time I do, I hear another story about you and change my mind again."

"You can only believe half of what James tells you," I assured him. "He's the only person that can turn a six-inch fish into a twelve-inch one, just by tellin' a story."

"I want to see and do the things you have, Bill."

"I promised you that when you got out I'd teach you the ropes, kid, and I intend to keep that promise. But you need to understand that the law's comin' to the West, and with wire fence goin' up everywhere, my era might be takin' its last few breaths, so you best have a backup plan." "Well, I guess I don't need to know right now. I've got three years to figure it out."

"You're right," I told him. "You don't need to know right now, but havin' goals and somethin' to look forward to will sure make the time go by faster."

"I'll keep thinkin' 'bout it. Promise." "That's a good plan, kid."

I went to see if Slim was feelin' better after some rest, and he assured me he was and said thanks for caring. I asked him if he heard me tell 'im about that feller from Wyoming, and he said that he heard most of it and expressed to me how much he'd like to go there. "Maybe you will, Slim. Anything's possible. He shot me a look like I'd lost my mind and told me he'd go there with me anytime. About that time I heard the outside door open

SWEET JUSTICE   173

and Virgil's voice saying, "He's right this way, Mr. Mayor, sir. I'll go get 'im for you."

"We'll come with you, Virgil," Emily said.

"Sure, Miss Watson. Anything you say," Virgil replied nervously. "Well, imagine how much easier this would have been if you'd had that same desire this morning, Virgil," she said sarcastically. "It just wasn't a good time then is all," Virgil told her.

As they came into view, I was taken back at how beautiful she looked and had to stop myself from rushing to her. I drank in the sight and felt my chest get warm as I did.

"William, you have company," Virgil said as he got the shackles ready to put on me.

"Those won't be necessary," the mayor said.

"Of course not, sir," Virgil replied. "I just brought 'em just in case. It's protocol, after all, but we can overlook it this time." Virgil escorted us to the courtyard and then hovered over us after we sat down. He looked nervous, like his deeds past and present were about to be exposed. I guess he thought that if he was there, somehow he could control the conversation.

"Tell me your story, son," the mayor coaxed, "start to finish and a little about your background, and we'll see if we can't get to the bottom of this. When we're done maybe you can explain that gash on your head." He turned and told Virgil he didn't need to hang around and that he was sure the people of Arizona were payin' him to do more important things.

"The prisoners aren't supposed to be left unattended, sir," he stated. "I think I can handle the situation here, Virgil," the mayor assured him.

"This man is a killer, sir. I don't think that's a good idea." Virgil uttered desperately.

"You have been dismissed, and your concern will be noted." Virgil began to protest again when his attempts were met with the mayor's stern voice, "You have been given an order. Don't make me tell you again."

Virgil shot me a threatening look, and I could see nervous perspiration coming from under his hat. He lingered a little too long, however, and was told in no uncertain terms that he was beginning to become an irritation.

"I can call one of the guards who don't have a problem with listening to remove you if you'd prefer," the mayor stated coldly.

Virgil turned and walked away at that point but turned once or twice and made eye contact with me. His unspoken words rang clear, and I knew he was tellin' me to keep my mouth shut or I'd get more of his form of justice. I was fully aware, however, that this might well be my last chance of seein' another year and that I'd better figure out how to convince the mayor I was innocent, even if the repercussions brought more pain and discomfort.

I spent the next twenty minutes retelling my story and tried desperately to remember every detail and then reminded him of what Mr. Earp had said about witness testimony that was in my favor leaving Tombstone but somehow not being introduced at my trial.

He turned to Emily for confirmation, and when she nodded to the affirmative, he assured me that he'd get to the bottom of it then told me if I was caught lyin' to him it would not go well for me.

"If there is anything you're not telling me, now is the time to come clean."

"I'm not holding anything back, sir. That's God's honest truth." "You have a reputation that's preceded you to Yuma, young man.

But my daughter sees something different in you, and since I have faith in her premonitions, I'm going to try and help you, but only if you can convince me you're not just the troublemaker some say you are."

"Well, sir," I began. "I guess that would hinge on what they say; I can't defend myself without having that information."

"They say you've killed some men in your time," he said accusingly. "I have," I confessed, "but only when they were guilty of terrible deeds. Though contrary to what might've been said, I never hired out as a heavy that just killed because someone was payin' me to. The men I killed, sir, were given every opportunity to give themselves up or to just ride away, and they always took the first shot before they met my answer to their challenge."

"Are you sure there's not a mountain of justification in your statement, William?"

"There is not, sir," I assured him. "The Western frontiers are full of men that do awful things, men that break people's spirits and step on their freedom to succeed, simply because they have money and prestige. I told myself long ago that they weren't gonna get away with it as long as I was around to prevent it."

"We have laws and men to enforce them, son. You can't just go and take those laws into your own hands," he stated forcefully.

"I don't mean no disrespect," I said in my own defense, "but the land is vast, and it would be impossible for a few sheriffs, marshals—or even the military, for that matter—to ever enforce the laws. And even where they can, the cold hard fact is they're usually in the pocket of those they should be goin' after. No sir, if there is to be justice for all, like our Constitution says, sometimes it has to fall to those who are willin' to supply it."

He chuckled at my words and rolled them around in his head for a minute, then stated that I should be a lawyer or politician instead of a cowhand. I assured him that I wasn't diplomatic enough for either one of those ventures and that when I thought somethin' needed to be done, I was more apt to make it happen right then and there rather than waste time and energy tryin' to get people on my side.

"Maybe a future in law enforcements would be more up your alley." "Been there, done that," I said and quickly told them the story of my stint as sheriff up in Wyoming. Both he and Emily seemed surprised when I told them the story, so I asked them if that was so hard to believe. "Of course not, William," assured Emily. "I can see you in that role, and I bet you made a fine sheriff." The mayor implied that it was a good thing to know because not only would it help my case, but he was startin' to feel better about his daughter's interest in me. When he said it, I saw Emily blush a bit, and I in turn was glad that somethin' about me had impressed her father.

"Where did you grow up?" asked the mayor.

"I lived in Arkansas until I was thirteen. Then we moved to Texas." "What part of Texas?"

SWEET JUSTICE   177

"Sherman. My family was wheat farmers there." "Are they still there?"

"No sir. Last I knew they were in Amarillo, but I ain't seen them since the war."

"Did you fight in the war?"

"Yes sir. Right up to the end," I stated boldly.

"That was a terrible thing," he said. "It's too bad they couldn't have worked it out some other way without all those boys getting killed."

"I s'pose it needed to happen that way. It managed to hold together the union anyway."

"I'm surprised to hear you say that, William. Most Southern folks didn't want the union to stand," he said.

"I didn't fight for the South, sir. I fought for the North. I didn't agree with slavery, and I'd been taught the importance of holdin' the union together. I hope that doesn't change your mind about helpin' me." He looked at Emily, and they both smiled at each other. I wondered what kind of a hole I'd dug myself into until he told me in a quieter tone that he and Emily had left the South for the same reason and that he admired my courage to proclaim it so boldly. He stood up and assured me that he'd do everything in his power to help me and told me that he enjoyed the visit and hoped there might be others. I didn't want him to go because I thought that it meant Emily would be leaving too, and I really wanted a chance to visit with her. He quickly put my mind at ease when he said, "I'm sure you two have things to discuss, so until next time, Mr. William Saunders." He bowed just a bit and shook my hand. As he approached Virgil, he put his hand on Virgil's shoulder and told him somethin' we couldn't hear. But Virgil must not have liked it 'cause he shot me a look that could kill before he disappeared with the mayor. I turned back towards Emily and said, "It's nice to see you again,

Miss Watson."

"William, please. I thought we were better friends than that. I told you to call me Emily."

"I'm sorry. It's just that I haven't seen you for a while, and I didn't want to be disrespectful or presumptuous."

"Well, I certainly have put forth the effort to come and see you sir," she said coolly, "but it seems you can't keep yourself out of trouble, and from the looks of that gash on your head, real trouble indeed. Is it infected? Come over here and let me have a look at it."

I assured her that Slim had been takin' special care of it and that it didn't feel infected.

"I'll be the judge of that, William, if you don't mind," she replied. I was embarrassed by how I must've looked and, worse, how I smelled, so I told her I was fine and that I didn't want to get that close to her without a bath.

"Oh, William," she said compassionately, "don't you worry about that. I'm aware of the conditions and would never judge you for something that's out of your control. Now get over here and let me have a look."

I got up and walked over to her and bent my head so she could see clearly. When she took hold of me to control her vantage point, her hands felt so soft and warm. She pulled my head in close to hers. It was as close as I had ever been to her, and I felt my heart race as I fought the urge to kiss her. She smelled sweet, and her skin was so beautiful that I longed to always be where I was at this moment. When she was done examining my

SWEET JUSTICE 179

wound, she switched her hands so that she had one on each of my cheeks and pulled my head to where our eyes met. Her eyes were a deep blue, and they seemed to look right through me.

"We're going to get you out of here, William. You wait and see," she told me confidently.

That was the moment I realized without a doubt that I loved her. My heart ached as the knowledge that I didn't deserve her and probably never would sunk in. I pulled away from her because bein' that close was more than my heart could stand. I told her I wanted a favor from her if it wasn't too much to ask.

"Anything, William," she offered. "You name it, and if I can, I'll do it."

"I want you to see if you can get Slim out of here. He's dyin', and he didn't do anything—well, not anything anyone else wouldn't have done in his place. I'd like to see his last few years spent in freedom."

"If they found him guilty, there is probably very little I can do to help him, but I'll try."

"That's just it. He wasn't found guilty; he just had the terrible misfortune of killin' a judge's friend."

"I'll certainly look into it. Anything else?"

I hesitated, afraid that she'd done enough already, but she could tell there was more and prodded me to speak further.

"I wonder if you could look into another matter for me as well. There's a good friend of mine in here with me—Ted's his name—that as far as I can tell is bein' held without a trial for an act he committed when he was cornered and out of his mind and, as far as I'm concerned, was self defense in its own right. I'm not askin' for you to stick your neck out to get him released, but I do think he deserves a trial so at least he knows his fate, instead of rottin' away in here indefinitely."

She looked at me for a moment and then said, "You are one of the most selfless men I have ever met, William. Of course I shall look into it, and I'd be proud to help you in any way I can."

"Thank you, Emily. You truly are an angel."

"No, but I'm glad you think that way of me, William."

"There's one other thing," I said hesitantly. "My friend that just got outta here yesterday—do you know which one I mean? He just came in about a week ago."

"Yes," she said, blushing just a bit. "I know who you mean. He wanted me to let you know that if you found a way to get out, he would be working for the rancher outside of Tombstone and hoped you'd come and help him."

"I'm glad he got out, and I hope he didn't embarrass you. He's a good man. A little rough around the edges, but a good man nonetheless."

"What about him?"

"He claimed we had a friend that was a deputy here, but I haven't seen him or heard his name since I got here. I was just wondering if you could confirm it. If you could, he might be able to help you in gainin' my release. His name was Charlie . . . something—I can't really remember. Not much use for last names out on the range."

"Charles Goodnight," her voice broke when she said it. "That's it!" I said excitedly. "You know 'im then?"

The color drained from her face, and she looked as if she was about to cry. "Yes, I knew him, William. He's dead."

SWEET JUSTICE   181

"Dead! How'd it happen?"

Emily started to cry at that point and had a hard time gaining her composure. I took her hand and begged her forgiveness. "I didn't mean to stir up sadness, Emily."

After a moment she was able to talk again and told me it was alright. "It's just that I haven't heard that name spoken out loud for a long time now, and it threw me off. I'm all right now though. He was killed about four years ago when he went after an outlaw who had raped a girl here in town."

"You knew him well then, I take it?"

"You might say that, William. He was my fiancé. He used to tell stories of a friend he admired named Bill who had a way of figuring out things when no one else could and the courage and skill with a gun to correct it once he did. He told me he wished Bill was with him the day he left to go after the man that inevitably took his life, but I never put you two together until now."

"Did they catch the man who did it?" I asked.

"According to Virgil, Charles shot the man in the face but only grazed him. That's why I come to see the prisoners when they come in, to see if any of them are carrying the type of scar one would get from a bullet. When Charles returned fire at the man, Virgil claimed Charles was knocked off the cliff behind him."

"Wait a minute, why was he out with Virgil?"

"Virgil was just a guard then, and the sheriff was out of town. So he went to find someone with the authority to ride along. Virgil seemed eager to go, which surprised us. Virgil is rarely the first to give up his comfortable bed."

The cogs in my brain were spinnin' fast at this point as I absorbed this new information I was hearin' for the first time. The pieces started to fall into the missing holes, so I asked if Virgil and Charlie were friends before they went out together.

"They knew each other," she said, "but Virgil didn't like anyone who held my affection. Like I told you before, he's loved me since I moved here, so I wouldn't call them friends by any means."

"Was there ever a time Charlie could've shared his stories about me?"

"Charles spoke of his friend Bill often," she surmised, "so I suppose the answer would be yes."

"That explains a lot of things," I said. "What things, William?" Emily asked.

"Well, this gash on my head for one, if my assumptions are correct, and why Virgil has had contempt for me since day one."

"I'm afraid I don't understand."

"I'm not positive I do either, but I have a feeling that if someone were to question Virgil about the day Charles died, some new light might be shed on an old story."

"What kind of light?" she questioned anxiously.

"Don't you see, Emily?" I stated excitedly. "My problems with Virgil didn't start until you came to see me the first time. He was content to let me rot away where he could keep me under his thumb because he knew if I had access to the pieces, I had the potential to figure out what happened to my friend. You and I were a threat if he allowed us to get together. That's why he kept tellin' you I was causin' problems and that I was in solitary all the time; it was a way to keep us apart."

"You mean you weren't in solitary?" she asked.

SWEET JUSTICE 183

"I never left the cell, Emily, not once," I told her. "When you told him to leave us alone the first time you came, he immediately saw me as a threat on two fronts: I was pullin' your attention away from him, and he was under the assumption that I knew my friend had been here and what happened to him. If you and I were to keep talkin', the connection between you and Charlie would become evident."

"You think Virgil killed Charles?" Emily asked in disbelief.

"I do, Emily. In fact, if truth be known, I'd be bettin' my life on it."

Emily quickly made the connection between my accusation and last statement. "Did Virgil do that to your head, William? According to him, you fell when you were being brought back to your cell."

I shook my head and told her that if he knew we were talkin' 'bout it, he'd do it to me again and then carefully lifted my shirt to expose the bruises from his stick. Emily looked in disbelief at what he'd done to me and began to move closer to look at them; I quickly pulled my shirt down to deter her and said, "He did this to me while I was in full shackles, Emily. He's lost his mind, and the closer we come to uncoverin' his secret, the more irrational he'll become, I'm sure of it."

"I'm so sorry, Bill. What do you want me to do?"

"I've seen his kind before, and they become dangerous real fast, so I'm not sure I want you to do anything, to tell you the truth."

"Well, I'm certainly not goin' to allow him to do this to you again," she said absolutely, "so I'm not askin' for your permission; I'm askin' for your direction."

"Well, if it were me," I said, "I would have an attorney open the case of Charlie's death again and, if at all possible, make Virgil think that his testimony is vital to the case. He'll either become arrogant because of his newfound importance or he'll become nervous and agitated—it's hard to say. But he can't know it was you that requested it, or he'll see right through it. And that's when he'll become dangerous to us both." "I'll have new attorneys reopen the case," she said. "They do it all the time, trying to create work for themselves, so it shouldn't arouse his suspicion."

"Good. The other thing you have to do is leave Virgil with the idea that you and your father are givin' up on me and that you're now convinced I'm guilty."

"But that will bump you up on the list to be hanged," she said passionately. "I don't think I can do that. I don't want to do that, William."

I assured her that she had to and that I was willing to take that chance to find out the truth.

"I don't think I could live with myself if they hanged you. I know you're not guilty."

"I don't think they will," I assured her. "Besides, there's probably somethin' I'm guilty of if it came to that. But I know Charlie didn't deserve what he got, so it's a small price to pay for justice." I looked into her eyes before I continued. "And for you, Emily."

She started to cry at that moment and told me to stop talkin' like that. "All I've seen is goodness and compassion from you, William," she said boldly. "I find it hard to believe the world would be better off without you in it, and I don't want to be responsible if it had to be."

"It has to be this way, Emily, for both our sakes. So we'll just have to take the chance and see which one wins the race."

She rushed to hug me as Virgil came back through the doorway, so I stopped her by shouting, "Fine, Miss Watson, if you don't wanna help me anymore, you can just go to hell."

She got a hurt look on her face but caught on quickly and replied that it was impossible to help someone so callused and cold, and for good measure she continued with, "Virgil was right about you all along." Virgil's face lit up when he heard it, and he immediately raced to Emily's rescue. He called for another guard to come escort me back to the cell and quickly put his arm around Emily and began to comfort her. He turned to me as I was bein' put in shackles and assured me that there would be punishment for speakin' to Miss Watson that way as he led her out of my presence. I hoped it wouldn't be the last time I ever saw her, and the realization that it could be made my heart feel heavy. *You've lived a full life, Bill,* I told myself. I was convinced I was right about Virgil. The only problem was there were no witnesses to his crime, so the only way he'd be found guilty would be a breakdown under questioning, inconsistency in his testimony, or maybe, if we got real lucky, they'd catch the man who Virgil claimed was the man that killed Charlie. As I walked back to my cell, I hoped my plan would work because my desire to live and my plans for the future had changed direction over the last two months, and I looked forward to the experiences that I hoped were now laid at my feet.

CHAPTER TEN

The Loss of a Friend

"How'd it go?" the kid asked on my return. "Are you gettin' out or what?"

"Not today, kid," I told him. "In fact, that was probably the last time she'll come to see me."

"Why? What happened?" asked Slim.

"They think I'm guilty," I replied loud enough for any listening ears that might be lurkin' about. Everyone gathered around me when I said it, wantin' to know the details.

"Sure sorry to hear that," Ben said. "I thought for sure you was gettin' outta here."

"We're all gettin' outta here, one way or another," I said with a smile. "What changed her mind?" asked Jed. "I was thinkin' you two were kinda likin' each other."

"I was kinda likin' her," I said with a laugh, "but as for her likin' me, I don't think that would ever happen, not even if I was the last man in Yuma."

"Yeah, she's way too good for the likes of you, I reckon," Ted chimed in, reaching for a laugh. But when his attempt didn't receive the desired reaction, he quickly followed it with, "Sorry, Bill, I's just pullin' your leg."

Some chuckled at his comment, including me, but truth be known, I knew he was right, and it killed me to realize it. I had nothin' to offer her and no real prospects of ever havin' anything at this point in my life. *That's what happens when you don't establish roots or prospects, Bill.*

It's your own damn fault, I told myself. Still, I loved her and wanted good things to happen in her life, and if I could help put this chapter of Emily's life behind her, it was well worth the gamble, even if it didn't win her heart.

Everyone consoled me—the best a room full of rough-cut men could, anyway—and left me with my thoughts. I wanted to tell them not to feel bad for me and that there was more to the story than I was leadin' on, but I just couldn't take a chance on the plan comin' undone, so I had to let everyone think that what I told them was the truth. About that time Spencer came around with lunch, and I was glad because I was hungry enough to eat it for a change.

"Miss Watson left here cryin', Bill," Spencer said coldly. "I don't know what you said to her, but you had no right to make her cry like that."

I wanted desperately to assure him that I hadn't done anything to hurt her but, again, couldn't take the chance, so I allowed him to keep on thinkin' it. It hurt, though, because I liked Spencer and didn't want him to think less of me.

"Well, that's just too bad, Spencer," I said, continuin' to play the part. "Maybe she should grow tougher skin if she's gonna come 'round here, shouldn't she?"

"You're an ass, Bill," he said bravely. "And I thought I liked you." "Oh, get over it, Spencer. And you best think twice before you talk to me like that again."

"See, I told you, Spencer. The man's a worthless killer that deserves to hang," I heard Virgil's voice echo. He was lurking just out of sight, eavesdroppin' on our conversation, and I was relieved I hadn't tried to convince Spencer that Emily wasn't cryin' from anything I'd said to her. "You're a cowardice weasel, Virgil," I shouted as Spencer plopped my food on my tin.

"Maybe so, tough guy, but I'm free, and you're gonna hang soon, so I wouldn't change places with you, no sir," he said with a laugh.

No sooner had I sat down than Slim came and sat next to me. "You tryin' to get yourself beat up again, Bill? I don't know if you'll get as lucky next time, and after the way you just spoke to Spencer, I'm not sure I'd want to help you if you did."

"You don't understand, Slim, so let it lie."

"I understand perfectly well," he replied with irritation. "The man was defendin' Miss Watson's honor, and as good as she's been to us lately, I'd think you would understand that. I'm sorry she can't help you, but good hell, boy, she tried to, Bill!"

Slim's excitement got him to coughing, and it sounded worse than ever, so I went to get him some water and could feel the tension in the room that let me know I'd upset more than one person in it. I couldn't tell if he was mad at me or the cough that wouldn't stop until he was reluctant to take it from me.

"Come on, Slim," I coaxed. "Drink the water."

He finally took it but, because of his cough, wound up spillin' most of it before he even got it to his lips. So I went to get him some more. I helped him drink it this time, hopin' it would soothe his throat.

"We've got to get you outta here, Slim."

When he finished drinking the water, his cough subsided a bit, and he replied that he wasn't ever gettin' outta here and that he wished I'd just quit sayin' it. "I done what I done Bill, and that's just the way it is, so give it a rest already," he said. "Besides, if they ain't goin' to help you, why would they help me? I was caught dead to rights killin' that bastard."

I pulled Slim to the far corner and told him that givin' up was goin' to kill him faster and that he needed to fight even if he didn't think he could win.

"Miss Watson promised to plead your case to the courts, Slim," I told him, "and I believe she will. You just have to give it time."

"Well, she might not now since you got her all riled up, Bill."

"I didn't really upset her," I whispered. "We just want Virgil to think I did."

"Why?" he said out loud. I waved my hand in an attempt to keep him quiet because I didn't know who was listening.

"Why?" he asked quietly this time. "Ain't you got enough trouble with Virgil already?"

"I can't tell you right now, but Miss Watson could be in danger if she keeps comin' here, and we need Virgil to believe she no longer wants to help me, for her safety and hopefully mine too."

He started to prod me for more information, but I cut him off and said, "Silence is the key, Slim. No one can know this, even if I lose friends over it, understand?"

He nodded to let me know he did.

"Don't lose hope, partner, and don't lose faith in me," I said to him. "If I'm right, justice might well find its way to Yuma yet."

I finished my lunch and looked at the faces in the room. Strange, I thought to myself, how many times my circle of friends had changed through the years and how important each one had become to me in their own way. I started to look at each one individually and wondered who most they reminded me of from my past. The kid was easy—he reminded me a lot of William Bonny and, if truth be known, a little of myself as well. Ben, on the other hand, reminded me of a kid I'd gone to school with back in Arkansas; he was kinda quiet too and always seemed a little sad as well. I found myself wishin' I'd've taken the time to figure out why, but kids don't think that way. Kids tend to think that everyone has the same environment and lifestyle as the one they do and spend more time tearin' each other down and teasin' than they do frettin' 'bout why someone might be down or scared. Funny thing is, though, it's those experiences that shape who we become later in life. The thought made me wonder about men I'd come up against in my life and how easily they could've become somethin' different than what they had. It made me twinge to think that a lot of 'em would never get the chance to change because their opportunity was taken from them by the dangerous end of my gun.

Ted was a little harder to pinpoint because I could see a little of a lot of fellers I'd known like him. Ted was a cowboy's cowboy: tougher than a square nail and energy to spare. But after watchin' 'im for a moment, I saw him smile at something the kid said, and it became clear as a bell: he reminded me of Tanner, one of the boys I'd worked with for a short while up in South Dakota. *What do you s'pose happened to him?* I thought. I had damn near forgotten about him, but there was no doubt after it came to me that he and Ted were a lot alike.

Stumpy was easy; he reminded me of a Mexican I'd worked with in New Mexico that had a way of seekin' vengeance when he thought he'd been wronged and had a hard time lettin' it lie until he did. It was him that got us stirred up to go after the skunks that were takin' refuge under our bunkhouse, and it made me chuckle when I remembered that he was the first to get skunked. *That's kind of what had happened to Stumpy as well*, I thought. He went after those that had invaded his space, and even though his brother offered a good alternative, he couldn't let it lie. His skunkin' came from gettin' caught, and the stink he received from it was windin' up here.

Slim reminded me a little of my ma's brother. He had a way of comin' and goin' like the wind, and no one ever knew when he'd blow back in. But when he did, ol' Uncle Dan always had a bag full of stories and adventures to share with us, even though my pa would spend the time rollin' his eyes and makin' verbal sounds to let him know that he didn't believe the yarn was bein' spun. I realized it was Uncle Dan that made me wanna see what was over the next hill and around the next bend.

As I looked at Jed, my mind traveled back to an experience that took place at a trading post in the panhandle of Texas in '74. Some merchants out of Dodge City, Kansas, had decided to set up shop to supply the buffalo hunters in the area with the goods they'd need and some they wouldn't as they went about their task of, as I saw it, slaughterin' the great herds of bison that grazed the great plains of the larger surrounding area.

Early that spring, I was given the job of takin' a small herd of cattle down to them, I supposed, for meat to sell in the butcher shop, which made me laugh, considerin' the amount of buffalo meat that was left to rot each and every day. It irritated me a bit because the herds of buffalo were bein' wiped out for two main reasons: one, for their hides; and two, for the purpose of starvin' out the Indians and endin' their way of life. The first didn't bother me too much, but the other did a great deal.

The sad part about it was that they weren't usin' the meat for anything but buzzard and coyote feed, and it saddened me to think that such a magnificent animal was being hunted to near extinction, and people weren't even being fed by it. But a payin' job is a payin' job, so at the time, it didn't matter to me much, as long as there was gold coins at the end of my trail.

The feller that was offered to me as a companion was a black man that'd spent the first part of his life as a slave and the remainder, to date, as a cowhand. His name was Samuel, and even though he struggled in social situations due to his lack of education, we hit it off right from the get go. He worked hard and was good with cattle, but the thing I liked about him was his wit. The man was funny and had a unique way of lookin' at things most

SWEET JUSTICE   193

would just pass over with nary a thought. I remember the
first time he took his shirt off in my presence. The scars
from where he'd been whipped were large. I could tell
that at the time they were received that they were deep
and painful, and my first thought was how could a man
that'd suffered so much find humor in anything? It sure
made me admire 'im more than I did before.

When he saw me lookin' at them, he said, "What's
the matter? Ain't you ever seen a whipped nigger before?"

It took me by surprise when he said it, and I quickly
turned away, ashamed that men I called my kinfolk could
be capable of such savagery. "Don't you fret none about
it," he continued. "Come the end of that there war, I kilt
the man who done it to me."

It was one of the few times I cheered the death of
someone, and I thought to myself if there were people on
this earth that were able to do that and still sleep at night,
the world was better off with them no longer walkin' it.
He knew I was from the South by my accent, I gathered.
He quickly assured me that he didn't blame me and that
I wasn't to worry none when I slept.

"I ain't gonna kill you, boss," he said.

It became clear to me at that moment that he figured,
because I was Southern, I must've done somethin' similar
in my life.

"I hope not," I replied, "because I didn't fight for the
South, my friend; I fought for the North. And don't call
me 'boss'. I never owned any slaves and never would. Me
and you are equal partners in this venture."

A big, broad smile came to his face when I said it,
and he gave me a friendly smack on the back that damn
near knocked me to the ground. That's when I realized

that years of forced labor had made him a mountain of a man, and I drew comfort that I wasn't goin' to have to fight 'im.

If you didn't have access to your guns, Bill, I told myself, *this man would turn you to sausage for sure.*

The remainder of the drive was pleasant, and we had lots of time and opportunity to come to see each other as men that were equal regardless of our colors or background. And before it was over, I couldn't see color anymore. Just another friend to add to my list, and I was damn proud to put him there.

Our pleasant journey wasn't meant to last, however, because a Comanche medicine man named Isa-tai had got it in his head after a sun dance that they could defeat the buffalo hunters and save their way of life and promised those in attendance that he'd seen in a vision, that none of 'em would lose their lives if they were to pursue the fight. They formed an alliance with the Cheyenne, Kiowa, and Arapaho Indians led by chief Quanah Parker and set out to rid the plains of buffalo hunters.

We delivered the cattle without a hitch but didn't get clear before the Indians attacked the post. As near as I could tell, there were about seven hundred of them. When I turned to look at the numbers on our side and only counted about twenty-eight, I turned to Samuel and said, "I survived the war and many a skirmish, my friend, but it's gonna take a miracle to get us outta this mess."

"Come on, Billy," he said with a smile. "If we all shoot four Indians every minute, we'll be done by supper."

I chuckled at his comment and found myself invigorated by his words and soon found out that Bat Masterson and Billy Dixon were among the crowd. It brought comfort and courage back to me as I loaded my rifle and side arm to prepare for the fight that lay ahead.

The battle was intense and was full of near misses and injuries. On the third day of fightin', Samuel took a bullet to his arm that caused severe injury and forced me to drop the fight to slow the bleeding and make a tourniquet with my bandana. My attention was quickly pulled back into the fight, however, because of the amount of our already small band that were out of the fight due to wounds they had received, which meant that those of us remainin' had to fight even harder.

I found myself counting in my head so that I could tend to Samuel's tourniquet when it was time. The last thing I wanted was to let him bleed out or to be responsible for restricted blood flow that would cause him to lose his arm. The worry—added with the fact that I hadn't slept much for three days, and even when I did, it was in spurts—quickly ended by the noise of battle that just kept goin' on and on. It just made it seem more daunting than it already was, but when I turned to take care of him, I found he was back in the fight and tendin' to it himself. The man was tough—probably the only good thing that'd come from bein' a slave. Most men would be succumbin' to their injury and be outta the fight altogether, but not Samuel. Years of verbal and physical abuse and bein' forced to keep goin', even when he wanted so badly to stop, had made him stronger and turned him into a survivor.

The war had taught me not to waste ammunition, so I was tryin' to make each shot count. The man that was deliverin' ammo to us as we needed it pointed out that we'd lost a lot of men on one wall and expressed his concern that it could cause a breech if we didn't defend it better. I turned to Samuel and asked if he was goin' to be alright. He assured me he would and yelled good luck as I took off on a run to defend it. As I approached I could see that the enemy had realized it was vulnerable too and were fashioning a makeshift ladder to get over the wall. I stood up and put myself in a dangerous predicament so I could push it away from the wall when an arrow kissed the side of my neck. *You lucky bastard,* I said to myself as I was diving for cover. I found a hole in the wall and began to shoot as fast as I could cock my rifle and managed to send them running for cover once again. Bat Masterson noticed I was in need of help and came to my assistance, and I spent the remainder of the fight with him as more men dropped out each hour.

The skirmish continued for another night and most of the next day before about a hundred men came to join in the fight. When the Indians realized there were fresh bodies to continue the fight, they lost heart and began a hasty retreat, which was a relief to those of us who were 'bout as worn out as a man could be. As I turned to find and offer some assistance to my friend, who by now had lost a lot of blood, I thought to myself that the miracle I said we'd need to get out of this mess in the beginning had come at last.

Yep, I said in my mind, *Jed reminds me of Samuel for sure.* His early life was full of fear and beatings from his pa, and he learned to take it as it was dished out. Even though he wasn't the sharpest tool in the barn, it made him tough and loyal to a fault to those he chose to call a friend. I wondered where Samuel might be at that moment because he didn't return with me after that.

Turns out that some of the buffalo men had seen him fight and were impressed with how tough he was, so they asked him to join with them and stay on. That was the last time I ever saw Samuel, but I sure did like him and hoped he was happy wherever he was.

*****

I was shaken out of my deep thought by the sound of two guards comin' down the corridor. Everyone stiffened as they came because two meant they were probably comin' for someone. When they arrived at the door, I heard Virgil yell, "Stumpy, front and center. You're goin' to see the judge."

The color drained from his face as he got to his feet, and Virgil, as usual, didn't think he was doin' it fast enough.

"Move it, Stumpy," he said, "or I'm comin' in after you." "Try it, Virgil," I said tauntingly. "We'd all like to see that."

"I would think at this point you might want to keep your big mouth shut, Billy," Virgil said, tryin' to hide the fact that my comment had changed his mind. "Considering that any hope of escapin' this place without a rope burn on your neck walked outta here in tears this morning."

Slim, afraid that I might be coerced into blowin' the secret, quickly spoke up and said, "Don't make things worse for Stumpy, Bill. He can take care of himself, I reckon."

"You best not take your hatred for me out on any of these boys, Virgil," I threatened, "or I'll find a way to kill you, ya hear?"

"Now, Billy, why would I want to do that?" he said laughing. "I'm havin' too much fun takin' it out on you."

Jed and Ben called to Stumpy as he was leavin' and told him good luck. The rest of us quickly joined them as he disappeared behind the wall. Virgil shut the door with a slam and looked at me coldly. "Won't be long, Billy, and we'll be back for you. And if things go good this month, maybe we can turn this room back into the supply closet it was meant to be and put somethin' in it worth keepin' for a change."

I watched Ted swallow hard at Virgil's words, so I reminded him that Virgil was all talk and that he didn't have near the power he liked to think he did. "Besides, they can't hang you without a trial," I assured him, "and if Miss Watson does what she said she would, you might get one yet."

"What if they find me guilty?" he asked. "What then, Bill?" "They might, partner," I said as compassionately as I could, "but what's the alternative, rottin' away in here? At least with a trial, you know your fate, which beats the hell out of wonderin' every day, don't it?"

He didn't sound too convinced, so I quickly added that if he was found to be out of his mind in court, they'd just put him back in here anyway.

"I reckon you're right, Bill, but what about you?" he asked. "What you gonna do if Virgil finds a way to get you hanged now that Miss Watson ain't gonna help you?"

"Things have a way of turnin' out," I assured him. "And if they don't, I'll take the hangin'. It's better than sittin' in this hell hole for seven more years for somethin' I didn't do."

SWEET JUSTICE

"But there's lots of life yet to live, Bill," he reminded me. "You ain't gonna be that old when you get outta here. Maybe you could saddle up to Virgil and just get through it."

"No. It don't matter now what I do or say to 'im at this point. He's been out to get me ever since the day he laid eyes on me, and nothin's gonna change that now. Besides, I'll be forty years old when I get outta here, out of practice with my guns, and too old to start wrestlin' cows again, and that's all I've known since I was seventeen."

"Maybe you could be a sheriff or something again," suggested Ted. "No town wants a sheriff that's done ten years in the Yuma prison,

Ted," I reminded him. "Besides, I ain't given up hope of gettin' outta here, so don't you worry none about me."

"Hey, Bill, what d'ya think's gonna happen to Stumpy?" asked the kid.

All ears in the room perked up to hear my reply. I guess they thought since I'd been here for three years that somehow I must know everything. I could tell they wanted it to be good news, but I didn't have the heart to lie to them.

"Can't say for sure," I said, "but I'd be lyin' if I was to tell you that it'd more than likely be alright. The man killed some fellers, boys, and bein' Mexican ain't gonna help him none."

"But they was stealin' silver off his land," Jed pointed out.

"I reckon so, Jed, but Stumpy can't prove that it was his land without the deed from the Spanish government, and too many people are gettin' rich off it. They ain't gonna let it go without a fight at this point, and their fight is easy. All's they have to do is pad the pockets of the right judges and politicians, so I would venture that it sure don't look good for him."

"That's too damn bad," said Ben. "I really like ol' Stumpy." "Me too, Ben," I told him, "me too."

Dinner came and went, and we hadn't seen Stumpy yet. It bothered me some because I would liked to have seen him one more time before they hanged him. His absence got me thinkin' I wouldn't get that chance. I figured it must not have gone well in court and that he'd probably be hung in the morning. The sound of the gallows was somethin' you learned to tune out because it sure had a way of stealin' the fire from anyone on this side of the bars, especially those of us in this part of the prison, seein' as we were only a stone's throw from where it rested. As men came and went over the last three years, there always was one or two that didn't figure out what the sound was on their own, and when someone told them, they would cringe every time the thump filled their ears.

It's a sad thing to see how many young boys, full of vim and vinegar, start down the path that eventually winds up here, thinkin' they could never get caught because they were smarter than the system and those that controlled it. Or the ones that never stopped to think of the consequences of their actions until that awful thumping sound's echoin' in their heads, for hours sometimes. That's when regret steps in and drives a man who'd never cry in front of his peers to tears, knowin' each thump meant someone just like them was breathin' their last breath. It was more than they could take, and some would sob out loud, wishin' like hell they would've listened to their mamas when they were tryin' to steer them right and stayed away from the whiskey they thought was goin' to make them men because they drank it. And the gun they just had to have. Whiskey made men do things they might not otherwise do, but truth be known, the tool that landed most here was the gun.

Funny thing about a gun—it can be a blessing from heaven or a curse from hell, dependin' on how you use it. It can save your life, protect your property, and supply you with food, or it can lead you down dark paths that end in stealin', strong armin', and murder. Those who chose to follow the path that way tended to live short lives; they either met their end at the wrong side of another man's gun or wound up here, waitin' to be hung. But one thing's for sure: I never saw a man seconds from dyin' either way who didn't have regret written on his face, and I never got used to it, no matter how many times I saw it.

"He's not comin' back, is he?" asked Ben.

"It sure don't look good," Slim replied. After a short pause, he continued with, "Damn, I hate this place."

"He still could," Jed interjected. "Maybe things will turn out okay." "Maybe so, Jed," I said, tryin' to make him feel better.

The mood in the room was somber to say the least. Everyone had come to like Stumpy a lot. It wasn't that way at first, though. Slim had the honor of bein' here the longest. He was referred to as the old timer. Ted came after him, followed by me and then Stumpy. Jed and Ben came at about the same time and then, of course, the kid. Others came and went, but they were never here long. Some were moved to the higher security area as soon as a bed became available; others were never here more than a week before they were dragged to the noose. Those whose crimes were so heinous to deserve immediate hanging weren't missed when they were gone. They had a way of suckin' all the joy—what little there was, anyway—outta the room and creatin' contention while they were here. The ones waitin' for a bed weren't much better, but to tell ya the truth, I felt sorry for them. Doin' time in a cell not much bigger than the two cots that were in it didn't sound too invitin' to a person whose room ended where the sky touched the ground, and I was sure I'd rather take the noose.

When Ben and Jed came to join us, Stumpy was still angry and mean, combined with the fact he was no longer the new guy, which he wore like a crown for two scared kids who were convinced their world was gone forever. He took his anger out on them and used them as his whippin' post to make himself feel better. Ben was scared of 'im and avoided him like a plague, which wasn't easy in a room as small as we were in. Jed, on the other hand, grew up surrounded by men who were abusive, to say the least, so it was just another day to him.

Jed took it on the chin for a while, but when he'd had a gut-full, he told Stumpy, in Spanish, that he didn't scare him, even though he could probably whoop him and to give it a rest because he was tired of listenin' to him whine. I knew just enough Spanish to know he wasn't bein' what one would call nice, so I readied myself for a fight. To my surprise, however, Stumpy's whole countenance changed. He was elated that there was finally someone in here who could speak his language and quickly apologized for his actions and struck up a conversation with Jed just like they was old friends.

When the tension left the room, I said to him, "Hell, Stumpy, is that all we needed to do was speak Spanish to you to stop you from bein' so damn mean? Had we known that, we would've a long time ago. Ted here speaks Spanish, and I speak some too. What 'bout you, Slim?"

"I speak some," he said.

Stumpy smiled for the first time since he'd arrived. That's when he told us his story about how he came to be here, and we could all see why he was angry about it. Jed was able, in a few spoken words, to do what the rest of us couldn't for months. After that, Stumpy wasn't as full of anger, and bein' able to share his story with men who empathized seemed to help him deal with his situation. He kind of became a big brother to Jed and Ben after that. I likened the situation to a pack of wolves, and it made me smile. When new pups are born, their worst enemies are the wolves born the year before because they are still tryin' to find themselves in the pack. New pups are a hindrance and competition to them, but once they prove they have somethin' to offer, those same wolves become their teachers, and harmony comes back to the pack.

We sat sharin' stories 'bout Stumpy, and though they made us laugh, they made us sorry for our friend and sure brought a sadness into the room.

"Do you remember that time Stumpy tripped with his lunch and wound up puttin' his face into it?" asked Ben.

We all started to laugh because the memory was priceless. Stumpy had beans all over his face and didn't cotton to us laughin' about it. He wiped 'em off as he scowled at us, but when he looked up again, he had one still hangin' from a strand of hair, so we all started to laugh again. When he turned his head to growl at us, it came 'round and stuck to his cheek. Everyone had tears streakin' their faces from laughin' so hard. Fortunately, Spencer was the guard on duty, and when he came back to see what we were laughin' at, he offered Stumpy another tin full.

"What about the time he talked Ted into bein' his partner so he could show us how the señoritas danced in old Mexico?" Slim said excitedly. "I can still see 'im with that piece of straw in his mouth he said was a rose."

"Oh yeah," I said. "The way he was lookin' at Ted before he dipped 'im got me kinda worried for ol' Ted there."

Everyone started to laugh and poke at Ted a little when he said, "I was startin' to worry myself."

"I don't know what was funnier," Slim continued, "Stumpy dippin' Ted or the look on their faces when they realized the guards were standin' at the door watchin'. But I sure remember the thud Ted's head made when he dropped 'im, that's for sure."

We all started to laugh, and Ben asked Ted if that goose egg had ever gone away, and when Ted said mostly, we all were rollin' on the floor.

"You know, I never thought much about it 'til now," Ted reminded us when the laughter subsided. "But whenever one of us was sick, it was always Stumpy who nursed us." The mood changed to almost reverence as each one of us remembered Stumpy bringin' us water or savin' his bread to settle our stomachs. If one of us threw up, Stumpy was the one to gather the straw and throw it out the window to save the rest from smellin' it.

SWEET JUSTICE 205

"He turned out to be a great man," I said, "and I reckon we'll all miss him for sure. Hopefully, his selfless actions set him straight with his Maker because I can't think of anyone who wouldn't have fought for what was theirs just like he did. Even those that condemned him would've done the same, had the roles been reversed, I reckon."

"Here, here," Slim chimed in. "Difference is, Stumpy wouldn't have set them to hangin'. He'd've stood with 'em and helped 'em fight for it." He paused a moment before he continued, "Yuma justice is a sack of bullshit."

The room was quiet after that, and each one of us drifted to sleep with thoughts of Stumpy on our mind.

The next morning I hoped it would be Spencer who brought us breakfast because I knew he'd share any information he might have about Stumpy's fate. But to my dismay, it turned out to be Virgil, and he immediately set out to eggin' me on. I did my best to ignore him because I wasn't in the mood to deal with contention but to no avail.

"No lip today, huh, Bill? Maybe I done figured out how to shut you up. I'll just send someone you know to the noose as often as I can. Then I won't have to listen to you anymore."

"Why don't you just shut the hell up, Virgil!" I shouted. "Stumpy was our friend, and he didn't deserve no hangin' for what he did."

"Maybe he didn't hang for what he did; maybe he hung because he was your friend. Did you ever think about that, Billy?" he said coldly. "If I thought there was any truth to that, I'd kill you, Virgil," was my reply.

"Big words for a man on the locked side of the door," he taunted. "No, Virgil, those are big words for a man on the unlocked side of the door," I assured him, "because if that there door were to fly open right now, you'd piss yourself."

Everyone snickered when I said it, and Virgil's face turned red but quickly turned pale again when I asked him if he was absolutely sure I hadn't figured out how to get outta here.

"There's no way outta there," he said. The tone of his voice sounded like he was assuring himself more than me.

"But you can't know that for sure, can ya, Virgil?" I asked with a quiver of threat in my voice.

Virgil stammered uncomfortably about how they'd fill me full of lead if I was to try and that he wouldn't do anything to stop 'em if they did. My intention at this point was to pull the rug out from underneath his confidence, so I continued makin' him uneasy by asking if he remembered James.

"Of course I remember that worthless cowhand. And had I known he was your friend from the beginning, he'd still be in here just so's I could get under your saddle some more."

"Did you know he was friends with Charlie?" I asked with extra emphasis on Charlie's name.

Virgil went white when I asked him that, like he'd just seen a ghost. He was speechless and just stood starin' at me, lickin' his lips, so I continued.

"Did you know I was friends with Charlie too, Virgil? Who's to say that James ain't worked out a way to get me outta here?"

SWEET JUSTICE

"What's that got to do with Charlie?" he asked uncomfortably. "Nothin'," I said. "I just wanted you to know that we have connections you may not have known about and that I could still get outta here, even without Miss Watson's help."

"You won't ever get outta here. You're just dreamin'."

"You might be right," I replied, "but if I do, I swear I won't leave this town until you and I have squared up. That I can assure you."

"Charlie didn't have them kind of connections, Saunders. He was as dumb as the rest of you," he shouted. "He got himself killed goin' out after someone that was better than him with a gun. I didn't have anything to do with his death."

"I never said you did, Virgil."

Virgil's face twisted up like a kid who just got caught stealin' cookies, when he realized what I said was true.

"Seems to me you know more than you're lettin' on," I said accusingly, "and the part about someone bein' better with a gun than Charlie I find hard to swallow. I know how smart he was, and I'd venture a guess that if he was shot, it was done when he wasn't lookin'." I paused to let my words sink in and then said, "Maybe in the back . . . by a coward."

"What you tryin' to say, Bill?" Virgil asked defensively.

"I'm not tryin' to say anything, Virgil," I replied. "What is it you're tryin' *not* to say?"

Virgil started to sweat at that point because he knew he'd said too much already. "I'll see you hang, Bill. You can count on that, just like your friend Stumpy's goin' to in about two hours," he finished as he scurried away.

"I'm sure you'll try, Virg," I called out, "but not as much as you'll hope you can now, I reckon."

When he was good and gone, Slim asked me how come I couldn't just let sleepin' dogs lie.

"I was goin' to," I answered, "but he always has a way of bringin' out the worst in me."

"Well, partner, he's gonna wind up hangin' you 'fore your plan has a chance to get off the ground if you keep at 'im like that," he replied. "That plan ain't for me, Slim. It's for Emily, for Charlie, and for justice, and if it works, it'll be sweet justice indeed."

"Well, I reckon if it works for you too, that'd be a nice bonus," said Slim, "so try and tone it down a bit and ignore that son of a bitch. If not for you, do it for those that have the unfortunate habit of likin' you."

I turned to catch the smile on his face as he said it and was glad that I had people who cared around me. It made me want to set things straight with the others in the room, but I talked myself out of it and hoped that time would do it for me. The sounds of people gatherin' outside got the kid up and lookin' out the window. He was definitely a caged bird longin' to fly.

"What you see, kid?" I asked.

"Just people gatherin' for the hangin'. There sure are a lot of 'em." "It's been awhile since they had any hangin's, so there's probably goin' to be more than a few gatherin'."

"Do you think Stumpy is one of them?" Ben asked, even though he knew the answer.

"'Fraid so," I replied with a little sadness in my voice.

"I'm gonna miss him," said Jed. "He kinda grew on me some."

"He grew on us all, I reckon," I said as a hundred memories ran through my mind. "He was a good friend, that's for sure."

The hangin's went on for more than two hours. When it was over, we all said goodbye to Stumpy for the last time with heavy hearts. "So long, Stumpy," I whispered. "You're free, my friend."

Chapter Eleven

Voices on Paper

It'd been about a two weeks since the day Stumpy was hanged, and there was still a sadness in the room. When you live as close knit as we do in this cell, the loss of a face has a way of creatin' a void that's hard to miss. And with all the time we had on our hands, it was difficult not to think about 'im. I kept hopin' to see Spencer to get some information, but it was like he'd dropped off the edge of the map. As risky as it was for me to rub Virgil, it'd become a way of makin' the time pass and helped keep my mind off things, but unfortunately, we hadn't seen much of 'im either, so when Spencer appeared outta the blue and announced that I had a couple letters, I was ecstatic, to say the least.

As I walked to the cell door to get them, I wondered why I had two. I was expecting one pertaining to Jed and Ben but couldn't imagine who the other might be from.

"Imagine that," Spencer said. "You've been in here for three years and never got so much as one letter that I know of, and now you go and get two on the same day. Looks as if you've become popular all of a sudden."

"Not with you, I reckon. You still sore at me?" I asked.

"Nah," he said, "Miss Watson told me what was goin' on. Besides, Bill, I couldn't stay mad at you anyway."

I was afraid Virgil might be lurkin' about, so I told him not to say that too loud. Spencer laughed and said that I didn't need to worry none because Virgil was over at the courthouse tellin' his side of the story about what happened when he and Charlie went out after the crazy man. He handed me my letters and said, "He sure weren't happy about it either. He griped that he'd already told 'em what happened and couldn't see what difference it'd make now anyway."

"He doesn't know Emily stirred the pot, does he?" I asked.

"No, she done a good job coverin' her tracks," Spencer said. "They told Virg the reason they was askin' questions was to see if there was an award due to him for bravery. Somethin' 'bout service beyond the call of duty," he said with a chuckle.

"How's it goin'?" I asked.

"Don't rightly know. I've been gone a couple of weeks, but the other guards here sure ain't missed him much, I'll tell you that for sure."

"I thought you just quit comin' 'round because you were mad at me.

I'm glad to hear you was on vacation."

"I wasn't on vacation, Bill. I was over Tombstone way, workin' for Miss Watson."

"How'd you pull that off?"

"I told Virgil I had an uncle pass away," he said laughing. "It weren't a lie either; I actually did. But I wouldn't cross the street to attend his funeral. I had to go have Miss Watson read the letter to me, and when I told her I wasn't gonna go, she asked if I would be interested in a trip to Tombstone to collect information for your case instead. She paid my wages and passage, and I got to get away from Virgil for a while."

"Well?" I pressed him. "Well what?"

"Were you able to get any information?" I asked impatiently.

'Oh yeah. Duh," he said embarrassed. "The owner of the Bucket o' Blood told me out right that you didn't have nothin' to do with that gal's death, 'cept maybe not tryin' your best to stop it is all."

"That's not entirely true, but I'll let it slide if his testimony will get me outta here."

"Well, that's where the problem comes in, Bill," he said reluctantly. "He also said he wasn't comin' clear to Yuma to testify, if he had anything to say about it."

"He won't have much choice if they subpoena him," I told him. "The question is will they."

"Don't rightly know, but it sure made Miss Watson happy, I'll tell you that. Well, I best be gettin' lunch ready. Enjoy them there letters, Bill."

"Thanks, Spence, for everything. I'm much obliged to ya." "Don't fret it, Bill. It was my pleasure," he replied with a smile.

As he started to walk away, I yelled after him, "Spencer, one more thing before you go."

"Sure, what is it?"

"Well, I'm sure I know the answer," I started, "but I have to hear it anyway, just to put it to rest."

"What's that?"

SWEET JUSTICE   213

"Did they hang Stumpy, and if so, where did they bury 'im?" "No, Bill, they didn't hang 'im," Spencer said with a smile. "His brother showed up with proof that the mine was on his land and promised that if they'd let 'im go that he'd take him to Wickenburg and that they wouldn't ever see him again."

"Spencer, you truly are a walkin' barrel of good news today. You've had a pretty somber crowd in here for the last couple weeks, I reckon."

"Glad to help, Bill. Best be on my way."

I thanked him again as I looked down at the envelopes and saw that indeed the one on top was from the Triple C. I hoped it'd be more good news for my friends because we sure could use some around here. When I flipped it under to see the other one, my stomach dropped as a gasp escaped me. The top corner had my full name written in a penmanship I immediately recognized as my ma's. I wondered how she knew I was here, and at the same time, I was ashamed that she did. I hesitated to open it because for years I'd convinced myself that runnin' away in the night, fightin' for the North, and then not comin' home again had somehow turned them against me. And what if they had found out how Jimmy died? The thought filled me with dread, and for a moment, I almost didn't open it. Then my thoughts turned to the fact that they were gettin' on in years and that perhaps it was bad news of another sort altogether.

Maybe, I said to myself, *it would just be easier to pretend I never saw it and move on.* I wasn't sure I had the courage to read it either way. I felt foolish that I was so nervous about it. Me, the man who'd been on every cattle trail, fought Indians, and faced death in more than one gun fight, was now afraid of a little piece of paper that sat in my lap. I started to open the other letter, tryin' to convince myself that it was more important and that it had nothing to do with avoiding the other, but I knew I was lyin' to myself.

"Damn it, Saunders, just open it," I said out loud, "and get it over with." I slowly tore the envelope open and peaked in like somethin' was goin' to jump out at me. Once I saw the writin', I could hear my ma's voice clear as day. I felt warm in my heart, and in an instant I was a kid again, sittin' with her by the stove as she read to me.

> *My dearest William,*
>
> *You have no idea how much joy was in our home the day we found out you were still alive and well or how much we've missed you all these years. Your pa sends his love, as well as your sisters, who are both married now and, fortunately for us, still live here in town. Sarah is married to a great man named Jacob who owns the hardware store, and they have a small pig farm to keep their boys busy. Yes, William, you are an uncle, and your sister tells them about their Uncle William quite frequently. She has always loved you and cried tears of joy when she found out you were alive and immediately asked her husband if they could take the train to come see you.*
>
> *Olivia married a fine young man named Ezra who is currently serving as deputy sheriff but owns a small cattle ranch with his brother. When he was courting*

SWEET JUSTICE 215

Olivia, she told us that one of the reasons she liked him was his love for cattle and that it reminded her of you because that's all you seemed to talk about before the war. She has two little girls and is expecting another soon. They are hoping for a boy to help with the cattle, and she told her husband that if it were to be a boy, she wanted to name him after you. Your pa's missed you, William, and said that if he thought he could take the trip, he'd come and see you and expressed how happy he would be if you came here when you got out. He can't really work the farm anymore, but a few years ago, we paid it off. At the moment we're leasing it to the farm to our north. Pa said that he knew you didn't like farming much but wants you to know that it's yours when he passes.

William, please come when you can. We know you fought for the North and respect you for standing up for what you believe in and don't care either way; we just want to see and hold you again. Miss Emily Watson said that you are not guilty and that she and her father are trying everything they can to prove it. She told us the chances are getting better every day. We have missed you, son. If you can, please come home as soon as possible.

Love always, William,
Ma

When I finished readin' and wipin' my eyes sufficiently enough to keep my reputation, I turned to share the news with everyone.

"Looks like I'm an uncle," I said as proud as a rooster on the fence. "Poor kids," said Slim, jokingly.

"You got that right," I replied. "My little sister's talkin' 'bout namin' one after me."

"You got a letter from home, Bill?" Ted asked. "Dang, that's good news."

"How'd they find you here?" asked Ben.

"Miss Watson wrote 'em and told 'em what was goin' on, I reckon." "Well, looks like she helped you in some way," Jed stated. "That's gotta count for somethin', don't it?"

I winked at Slim when he said it and replied that she sure had and proceeded to share the letter with them all, pausin' to let everyone try to sound out the words so I could see if I'd been wastin' my time teachin' them to read for themselves. It made me happy to see that they were gettin' better. When we were finished, I didn't feel so bad 'bout leakin' around the eyes when I read it the first time because they all seemed to be havin' the same problem.

"It's lunchtime, fellers," Spencer yelled in. "That was a nice letter, Bill," he said. "I'm glad your ma and pa are doin' well."

"Me too, Spence. I'm much obliged to ya for bringin' it to me. Had it come when Virgil was workin', I might've never gotten it."

"Yeah, you would have," he said slyly. "It came to Miss Watson's address for just that reason."

"It's nice to have friends on both sides of the bars."

SWEET JUSTICE 217

"Sure is," he stated, "because Miss Watson sent pie for ya'll today."

Everyone let out a cheer but quickly quieted down when Spencer told them we were sworn to secrecy and that Virgil wasn't to find out about it.

When everyone had their food and left to go eat it, Spencer quietly told me that when Emily had come by, she said that Virgil's story didn't match his original statement and that he got nervous and agitated when the attorney called him on it. He told them that he couldn't be expected to remember everything four years after the fact and reminded them that he was the one that stuck his neck out goin' out there in the first place.

"What did they say?" I asked him.

"Mayor Watson told 'im that it was his job to give aid to the sheriff and his deputies and his responsibility to remember details better. And then he reminded him that a man had died and that those who loved him deserved to know the entire story."

"How did he take that?"

"Not well, according to Miss Watson. And he damn near fainted, she said, when the marshal suggested that perhaps the best way to remember might be a return to where it happened and have Virgil show 'em how it played out."

"What did Virgil have to say to that?" I asked.

"He told 'im he wasn't even sure he could remember exactly where it was. And then I guess the marshal let 'im have it and told 'im that he could ride back to any place he'd lost a friend in the line of duty and that it showed irresponsibility that he couldn't."

"Well, unless it happened just the way he claimed, that'd be tough to find a place on a whim that'd match his story."

"Do you think he really killed Charlie, Bill?" Spencer asked. "He sure has the temper to, I guess, but he's always been more talk than action. And why Charlie? What would've been the motive, I wonder." "I don't know how he was as a youngin'," I pointed out "but I'd venture a guess that he was a bit of a bully."

"That he was," Spencer agreed, "especially to those of us younger than 'im."

"How was he with people who got to close to Emily?"

Spencer thought about it for a minute before answering. "I can't say for sure how it was all the time because they're both older than me. But I can say there was more than enough chatter that went 'round, claimin' that unless you wanted a fight you best not get between them. Everyone knew how he felt about Miss Watson, that's for sure."

"Did Emily ever lead him to believe she shared his feelings?" I asked.

"Not that I know of. In fact, until Charlie came along, I can't remember her ever bein' tied to anyone."

"There's your motive," I said. "Even though Emily never returned his affection, she also didn't share it with anyone else, and then when she finally did, his world came unraveled."

"Damn, Bill, you're smart to put that all together," Spencer said. "When you live by the law of the gun," I told him, "you learn to put pieces together to form a picture. That way you always know you're fightin' for the right side and if the man you're huntin' deserves it or not.

Now, I'm not sayin' that I'm absolutely right, but I do believe that time will tell if I am."

"Well, your argument sounds good to me, but what's your stake in all of this?"

"Me and Charlie were friends before he came here," I told him, "and if he was murdered, I aim to find out who done it, be it Virgil or the man with the supposed bullet scar on his face. If it turns out to be the latter, the first thing I'm gonna do when I get out of here is go find the son of a bitch that killed my friend so Miss Watson can put it behind her and quit lookin' for him every time a prison wagon rolls in."

"You like her, don't ya?" Spencer teased. "Can't say I blame ya. She certainly is easy on the eyes."

"She sure is," I agreed with a chuckle. "I think she has feelings for you too."

"What makes you say that?" I asked intently.

"Just the way she beams when she talks about you. I'm not the brightest, but even I can see things. That, and she seemed real sad when you told her to quit comin' here to see you. I know you were both actin' that day, but her tears were real, I can assure you."

"I was worried about her. Virgil was startin' to see me as a threat. That's why he beat me up, I'm sure, and I didn't wanna take the chance of his violent behavior findin' its way to Emily. Besides, once I put my deductions together, I didn't want him to think Charlie's case was bein' reopened because of our conversations. So as much as it killed me inside, I did what I thought was best for her."

"Well, if your inkling turns out to be right, I reckon you've gotta be one of the best detectives I ever seen,

220   MARK INKLEY

Bill," said Spencer, "and I hope you're right because not working for Virgil anymore sounds too good to be true, and I can't think of any of the guards that wouldn't agree with me."

"I just want it to be over for Emily," I said. "She deserves the chance to move on with her life, and I think this is keepin' her from it."

"I'd agree with that. She sure is a nice enough gal and well liked here in Yuma, that's for sure. Well, hell, I best get on with my rounds, in case Virgil gives us a surprise visit. It was nice talkin' to ya again, Bill." Then he looked past me and reminded everyone that they best keep their mouths shut about the pie.

When he started to walk away, I yelled after him, "Let Emily know I miss our conversations."

"Sure thing, Bill," he said with a sly smile. "I'll make sure she gets the word."

I looked down at my tin, knowin' my food would be colder than usual because I'd plumb forgot about it while I spoke with Spencer, but I didn't care. The information he brought was music to my ears, and knowin' that Spence and I were again on friendly terms felt good. But I was hungry, so I sat to choke it down anyway.

"Who's the other letter from?" asked the kid.

I had almost forgotten about it until he reminded me, and then I was anxious to read it, so I slid the rest of my lunch to one side and quickly turned to the golden-crusted piece of heaven because, rest assured, as excited as I was to look at the letter, it sure didn't trump a piece of Emily's pie.

"Let's have a look," I said with my mouth full, as I motioned for Ben and Jed to come over.

SWEET JUSTICE 221

"Whatcha need, Bill?" Jed asked.

"Got a letter here that pertains to you two," I said.

"Is that the letter from your friend?" Ben asked excitedly.

"Sure 'nough is. Let's see what it has to say." I pulled it out and stared at it but didn't say anything for what was just a moment, but it must've seemed like a lifetime to Jed.

"What's it say, Bill?" Jed asked impatiently.

I smiled because it was just the reaction I'd anticipated. "Oh, you want me to read it out loud?" I said jokingly.

"Hell yeah!" they both replied at the same time. "How about I let you read it to me?"

They both looked at me and then each other before answering. "Okay," Jed said, "give it to me."

"Bill, it was gewd . . . good to hee . . . are from . . . yoe . . . you,"

Jed corrected himself. "We . . . wee . . . ree . . ." "Were," I said.

". . . were starting to te . . . hink . . ."

"Remember the *t* and *h* together make a different sound," I reminded him.

"Oh, yeah," he said. "Think you mig . . . hit be dead . . . might be dead," he deduced with a smile. "Sorry . . . to here that you . . . aree . . ."

"Are," I gently coaxed.

"We're gonna be here all day," Ben said in exasperation. "He's doin' fine, Ben. Just let 'im try."

"You try, smart guy," Jed said, red-faced and embarrassed.

He handed it to Ben, and I gently grabbed Jed by the scruff of the neck to let him know he did okay. Ben took the letter and picked up where Jed had left off.

"Sorry to hear you are in troe . . . ub . . . lee . . ."

"Trouble," I said as Jed chuckled.

"Trouble," he went on. "If there is anything we can do to help . . . plee . . . ase . . . please let us . . . ka now . . . ka now?" he asked puzzled.

"Know," I said.

"Why the hell is it spelt that way?" he asked a little more than frustrated.

"Because *no you can't* is a different word than *do you know*," I said. "That's just too damn confusing. You best finish it, or we won't be done 'til our release day," said Ben. "Ain't so easy, is it?" Jed interjected.

"Don't get discouraged, you two," I told 'em. "You'll get it, I reckon.

Just takes time."

"Will you just read it, Bill?" Ben asked. "I don't think I can wait much longer."

"Sure," I told him.

I was more than happy to read it for them, partly because of the time it was taking lettin' 'em have a go at it but mostly because correspondence from the outside had been a long time comin', and it had a way of transportin' me back out to the world I loved. As I began to read, I could hear the voice of the man who wrote it and longed to be there, workin' the cattle again. Funny, I thought as it carried me back, how the labor that used to seem mundane becomes somethin' you miss when you don't have the freedom to perform it. The sounds you used to take for granted suddenly become songs you'd kill to

Sweet Justice · 223

hear again, sounds like the creak of saddle leather as you bob back and forth, escortin' cattle into the pens, the bellowin' of the cows in the dark when takin' your turn on night watch, and the cry of a newborn calf as it calls out to its mama—these were sounds I hoped to have fill my ears one more time before I died, without a doubt.

"Hey, Bill," I heard suddenly, "are you goin' to read it or not?" "Oh, sorry. I was just thinkin'."

"We could see that," said Ben with a chuckle. "We said your name three times 'fore you heard us."

"Sorry, fellas," I said a second time as I started to read the letter again.

> *Bill, it was good to hear from you. We were starting to think you might be dead. Sorry to hear you are in trouble. If there is anything we can do to help, please let us know. You wrote about two friends that need a job in a month or two. I don't usually hire men that I don't know, but for you I am willing to make an exception. Please tell them that they are fortunate to know you because there is always a job here waiting for you and anyone riding with you whenever you come this way. So if they come with a recommendation from you, we'll find a place for them as well. Please let them know they must come however because I need men now, but I am willing to wait, if they are serious. I know you tend to be a wanderer, but if you was to get the chance to come with them, we'd love to see you.*

My wife and I pray that this letter finds you well, and we wish you good luck always.

Signed, Rubin Cook

"Well, boys," I said with a smile, "sounds like you got yourselves a job."

"Yee haw!" Jed shouted. "That sounds damn good to my ears, sure as shootin' it does!"

Ben, bein' more of a thinker, seemed to have mixed feelings, or at least that's the feelin' I got from the look on his face.

"Is that not the news you hoped for, Ben?" I asked a little confused. "Well sure, Bill," he replied. "I just don't know how we're gonna get there is all."

His question made me stop in my tracks because, truth be known, I hadn't thought much about that part either. My mind started racin' because Texas was a far distance without a horse and even farther if you were tryin' to get there on an empty stomach. Then all at once I remembered that I had two hundred and twenty-five dollars when I was arrested in Tombstone and knew that I would get it back when I was released. The problem, I realized, was how to get it before then so I could help them get that far.

"I got some money, Ben," I assured him. "You let me worry about that part."

"I don't want to take your money, Bill. What will you use when you get out?"

"I'll be okay. There's 'nough to go around, I reckon, so don't you fret none about it."

At that moment Slim started coughin'. It sounded worse than ever, so I attempted to go to his aid but was quickly drawn back into the conversation when Ben spoke again.

"I'm much obliged, Bill, and I'll pay you back. I promise."

"I know you will," I said with a smile, "because I know where you'll be."

Ben looked at me for a moment like I was bein' serious, and the blank stare on his face made me laugh.

"I'm just pullin' your leg," I assured him as I knocked him a little with my elbow.

"I know you were," he said with a sigh. "I was just thinkin' how much I'd hate to have you after me if 'n you wasn't."

"The only way I'd be comin' after you is if my friend tells me you were slackin' once you got there. But that ain't gonna happen, is it?"

"No sir," both of them said absolutely.

"Then I guess we don't have anything to worry 'bout, do we?" "Nope, sure don't," they said simultaneously.

"Good answer, boys. Now if ya'll will excuse me, I think Slim needs some water for his cough," I said as I headed for the water barrel.

"Hey, Bill, thanks again," Ben called out.

"My pleasure, Ben," I said, feelin' mighty good inside.

I made my way over to Slim, who by now had been coughin' way longer than usual. He seemed to be hidin' somethin' in the straw that was spread around him.

"How ya doin', partner?" I asked as I handed him some water. "Not bad. Just a little cough is all."

"It's not little. Sounds pretty bad, my friend." "It's nothin'," he said, tryin' to brush me off.

I looked at him intently, tryin' to get him to open up to me because my gut told me there was more to it than that, but I didn't want to overstep my bounds. When he started to cough again, I took his cup to fetch more water. That's when I noticed that the water at the bottom seemed to be a pinkish color. I dumped it out and used the dipper to rinse it before I filled it again, concerned that it was blood. When I returned I asked him if he was bleedin' from the cough, but he hesitated to answer me.

"Come on, Slim," I coaxed. "I'm here to help if I can."

"Don't fret none about it, Bill," he said. "I'll be fine. Besides, there ain't nothin' either one of us could do if 'n it was from the cough anyways."

"Was it?" I asked more firmly.

"Yeah, it was," he finally said, "but don't tell no one, ya hear." "If that's the way you want it, partner."

"This place is finally winnin' the fight, I guess," Slim said sadly, "but I really don't care much anymore, to tell you the truth. I'm damn tired of bein' here, and if this is my out, I hope it comes fast."

"I'm goin' to find a way to get you some fresh air, if I have to break you out myself."

"Well, you can't, Bill, but I'm much obliged," he said as he started to cough again.

I took him by the arm and led him to the window where at least he could breathe cleaner air and then went to get him more water.

"Dinner, boys!" I heard Spencer yell.

Sweet Justice 227

I rushed to the door in hopes that somehow he might be able to take Slim out into the open air and quickly explained the situation to him.

"I don't know, Bill," he said. "What if Virgil was to show up?" "I understand."

Truth was, I knew how much trouble he would be in if that was to happen, and I didn't want him to lose his job. He could see the concern on my face, however, so he told me that he would see if he could later when there was no chance Virgil was gonna show up.

"Much obliged, Spence. I know you will if you can." "I might not, so I ain't makin' any promises."

"I understand."

"I'll tell you what though. I'll make sure Miss Watson knows about it, seein she's been tryin' to have the courts release him for a couple weeks now. She doin' a right nice job of arguin' his case. She should be a lawyer, I reckon."

"Has she really?" I asked excitedly.

"Near as I can tell. I overheard her a couple of times when I've been over at the courthouse."

"Well, hell, that is good news," I said with smile. "Damn good news indeed."

I got my food and filled Slim's tin at the same time, then quickly went to share the news. When I was finished relayin' what Spencer had told me, he seemed to perk up a bit and even looked better than he had all afternoon.

"That would be somethin' to get outta here," Slim remarked. "I don't even know where I'd go if I did."

"You got some money if you was to get out?" I asked.

"Damn well better," he said, "considering I had a thousand dollars on me when I came here."

"A thousand dollars! Damn, Slim, I don't think I ever even seen a thousand dollars in my life. I had no idea I had a rich friend."

"Well, right now it's the warden's safe that's rich," he said with a chuckle.

"A thousand dollars," I said again in disbelief, "Where did you ever get your hands on that much money?"

"I used to be a stagecoach driver," he said proudly. "Then I hauled freight for a while. That is, until I decided to play pharo with a judge's friend."

"You never told me that." "You never asked."

"Reckon you're right there. So what, you just never spent money in between runs or what?"

"I did, but haulin' freight pays good, 'specially when you're willin' to take on the dangerous runs."

I spent the rest of the evening listenin' to Slim's stories in between fetchin' water to try to quell his cough. I found out he was married once and that he had a daughter that he figured lived in New York City with her ma.

"She loved me, I think," he said, "but didn't cotton to my bein' gone all the time." Slim went on to say that she came from money and that he figured his daughter was better off with her.

"One day I came home to find the house empty," he continued, "'cept for my stuff and a note. That was the last time I ever saw either one of them."

"I'm sorry."

"Me too," he replied regretfully. "But that was a long time ago. Near as I can tell, she'd be about your age by now, give or take."

"How old was she when she left?"

SWEET JUSTICE   229

Reckon about fourteen. It's like another lifetime when I think about it." "I know what you mean. Thinkin' back to when I was fourteen seems like another life to me as well."

Slim was in the middle of a story about a run-in with Apaches he had once when Spencer came and offered to escort him out for a while. That was music to Slim's ears.

"I'm gettin' out of here twice in less than two months," he proclaimed. "I think I've already died and somehow made it to heaven." I smiled at his comment as I watched him walk out with Spencer and was glad for him. *If he could get out of this dirty musty hell hole*, I thought, *he could live a long time.* I drifted to sleep with hopes that Emily could find success in her attempt to accomplish it.

Chapter Twelve

Changing of the Guard

THE NEXT MORNING I WOKE up later than usual. I'd been dreamin' about ancient writings my companions and I had come across while searchin' for some lost cattle up in the top of the Arizona Territory. It was around the Canyon de Chelly where the Navajos hid out when Kit Carson was tryin' to round 'em up and relocate them to a reservation. We'd seen lots of the petroglyphs here and there, but these were different. No one knew for sure who put them there; all we knew for certain was that they were old and that the people who were responsible for them were long gone. The interesting thing was that they seemed to leave all at once, and judgin' from the artifacts that were left at their dwellings, their departure was in a hurry. In some places it was as if they left in the middle of cooking meals, and their tools, pots, and clothing items were left as well. I pondered from time to time what event would cause a people to leave so quickly that they would abandon stuff that obviously took so much time to make. Some said they believed that climate change forced them to move on, but that explanation didn't hold water with me. It didn't address the hasty departure or explain why they didn't pack their things with them.

Others claimed they were wanderers and must've finally settled down somewhere else, but I didn't accept that explanation either. For one thing, the time and effort put into building the structures they lived in didn't lead me to believe they were wanderers at all, and judgin' from the corn cobs lyin' everywhere, provin' they were farmers, told me they couldn't have been. Comin' from farming stock, I knew all too well that planting to harvest meant they were tied to the land with very little time to do anything else, let alone wander.

Bein' a soldier I was leanin' more to some kind of war as the explanation—one they were losin', obviously, and that when they were discovered they fled for their lives. The evidence, to me anyway, backed up my theory. When I saw their writings the first time, I immediately labeled them as savage cave men who weren't smart enough to write, but the more I studied them, the more convinced I became that they were an industrious people with a deep understanding of agriculture and the seasons. That, added to the fact that they obviously traded with one another and their craftsmanship in pottery, basket making, and structural engineering, soon had me thinkin' that I had strongly misjudged them. The thing that finally convinced me that they somehow knew more than I'd given them credit for was the writings we stumbled across.

The bulk of their writings were in places where all could see them as they traveled, and as near as I could tell were put there to give direction or point to something like a stash or water. Some seemed to be warnings of danger and perhaps advertisement for a safe place to take refuge or a place to eat maybe. Others seemed to be more spiritual. Often I came across whole walls that were covered with different pictures like big horn sheep, deer. Snakes and signs I didn't understand at all, but more often than not, there was always a place of honor where three figures, who seemed to be revered, were painted as if they were lookin' down on the rest. My first thought when I saw 'em—probably because of my ma's Bible teachings as a boy—was they were the Father, Son, and Holy Ghost. I chuckled the first time I thought it, but the more I came across them, the more my insides told me I was right. That's why these particular writings affected me so much when we found them.

I almost walked past them without looking because I'd seen so many up to that point, but something made me stop and look. When I did I almost fell over backwards. There were the three figures as usual, but this time one of them seemed to be pointing, and the way the others below them were cowering led me to think they were receiving a warning or punishment of some sorts. Above their heads in what seemed like the sky were men on horses, an animal I hadn't seen drawn anywhere else before or since. The men had big hats on, something else I hadn't seen on any other drawings. There was a group made up of people and animals that seemed to be runnin' from them, leading me to think they were sweepin' 'em away or drivin' 'em out. On top of all that, the figures on horses were carryin' what appeared to be a flag with stripes on it. Indians were never known to carry a banner, so to me it just made it more intriguing. Knowing that these writings were ancient, put there centuries before the

SWEET JUSTICE   233

white men came here, got me wonderin', and I continued to stare like I was in a trance.

I stood in amazement as I drank them in and wondered if they really knew this was goin' to happen in the future or if it was just coincidence. I'd half decided I was reading more into it than was actually there, but my last glance took me back to the three figures as I rode away, and it'd stuck with me ever since.

I hadn't really had what one would call religion in my life since the night I snuck away to join the war, so it intrigued me that I would dream of that day and that the thought of the three figures being the Father, Son, and Holy Ghost was still something that I just couldn't shake. I shook the sleep out of my head, and as I looked around at my companions, my eyes fell on Slim, and I found myself praying in my mind.

Dear God, I thought, *if you really are up there, Slim could sure use your help now.* I laughed inside myself when I realized what I'd done, but immediate comfort came to me as if someone had heard me and was aware of the situation.

The kid was standing at the window, unaware that I was awake. "Virgil's goin' into the courthouse," he said to anyone who might be listening. "The mayor and Miss Watson are standin' next to a dandy on the steps."

"Must be a lawyer," I commented.

"Oh hey, Bill, I didn't know you were awake," said the kid.

"Just barely," I replied. "I've lived a long time without coffee, but I'd kill for a cup this mornin'."

"Did you have to mention coffee?" Ted said in exasperation. "Now I wanna cup too."

"Sorry, I was just thinkin' out loud. What're they doin' now, kid?" I asked.

"Looks like the lawyer and Virgil are in a heated quarrel, and the mayor is tryin' to quell the situation," he said. After a pause he continued, "Miss Watson is lookin' this way, tryin' to ignore 'em, I reckon."

At that I joined him at the window. Despite the chuckles from the others, I couldn't help myself or my desire to see her.

"Ain't you the one who told the kid to stay out of the window?" Slim asked with a smile.

"Some things are worth seein', but unfortunately, I only caught a glimpse as she went through the door."

"S'pose ya'll should've been faster," he said.

"You seem to be a little better today, Slim," I said, tryin' to change the subject.

"That I am, and I'm much obliged to ya for gettin' me out in the air last night. Sure did me good."

"That's good. Your color looks better, that's for sure."

"Good enough to look after that split in your head," he replied. "Looks a little infected, my friend."

"Probably is," I said. "I ain't taken very good care of it, I reckon."

Everyone had to come have a look after he said it, and I felt boxed in and embarrassed.

"I'm alright!" I exclaimed. "What are you guys, my ma or somethin'?" They all took a quick step back like I'd scared 'em. That's when I remembered my altercation with Spencer and realized that they all still thought Miss Watson really had figured I was guilty and that my cold words to Spencer and Slim were real.

SWEET JUSTICE 235

"I didn't mean to be so rough," I said apologetically. "You can look if you want."

"We don't want to rub you the wrong way," Ben found the courage to say.

"Sit down," I told 'em. "I got somethin' to tell ya."

I quickly explained the real story and how I thought that Virgil had more to do with my friend's death than he was sharing. I assured them that Spencer was in on it and that we were puttin' on a show to assure the safety of Emily and to keep me from receiving another beating at the end of Virgil's stick. Everyone caught on 'cept Jed; he had to have it explained to him, and we all got a good laugh at his expense.

"Well, after breakfast I'm gonna clean it," said Slim as he stared back at my head. "And it's gonna hurt, but it's your own fault, so I don't wannna hear any whinin', ya here?"

"Okay, saw bones," I said jokingly.

I made 'em swear that if the need should arise, that they needed to play along so Virgil wouldn't catch on. Considering the respect they all had for Emily, they were all too happy to comply. We all talked 'til Spencer came with breakfast, and the tension that'd filled the room seemed to be gone.

"Good hell, Spencer, you look like somethin' the cat drug in," I said as he plopped my beans on my tin.

"I feel like it too," he replied. "I'm pullin' a double shift, what with Virg bein' in court this mornin'. And to make matters worse, I'm a guard down today."

"How's it goin' in court?" I asked.

"Not sure. I only get tidbits here and there, but Miss Watson did tell me that Virgil's explanation as to the whereabouts and details of Charlie's death were vague and that the attorney grilling him was relentless. He wanted to know if he buried Charlie before he came back to town."

"What did he say?" I asked.

"He said hell no, that Charlie was at the bottom of a cliff, and that he wasn't goin' to hang around to be shot. I guess the judge and marshal told him he should've and that they were disappointed in him for not doin' so. When the marshal suggested that they go back and give him a proper burial, Virgil shot back that the buzzards and cats had made short work of him by now and that he didn't have time. He then assured them that he had told the truth and was growin' tired of repeating himself."

"What's your gut tell you?" I asked. "Do you think he's holdin' somethin' back?"

"I can't say," he replied, "but they sure ain't arrested him or nothin'." "Well, it was worth a shot. I still think he knows more than he's sayin'."

"I reckon if he does he'll take it to his grave. "You do realize," he pointed out, "that if he ever figures it was you that started all this, it could get ugly for you?"

"I'll take my chances," I said boldly. "Besides, I'm still hopin' he'll break."

"Well, he better do it quick then," Spencer said, "'cause I'd say they're close to puttin' this one to pasture. I don't want a man to pay for a crime he didn't commit, but it sure has been nice not havin' him hang around so much, that's for sure. And bein' the one in charge has been good for me, I think," he said with a proud grin.

"For all of us," I said with a smile. "Any word on how things are goin' for Slim?"

SWEET JUSTICE 237

"Not much that I've heard. But I know Miss Watson keeps bringin' it up whenever the opportunity presents itself."

"The wheels of justice turn slow, I reckon," I said, more to myself than to him.

"Well, at least they're turnin'," was his reply.

"Can't argue with you there," I said with a chuckle.

"Hell, I best get breakfast to the rest," Spencer said hastily. "They sure get powerful mean when they get hungry, and there's a train full of prisoners comin' in this morning that's goin' to keep me busy, what with Virg bein' in court. But I'll keep you informed of any developments as I get 'em, Bill."

"Thanks, Spence," I said gratefully. "I'd be much obliged if you would."

As I sat eatin' my breakfast, the conversation in the room was one of doom and gloom. Ted brought up the fact that he overheard Spencer mention that there were more prisoners comin' in today and reminded everyone that the prison was already full, according to James.

"What does that mean?" Jed asked.

"It means that they's gonna have to make room," Ben replied. "Do you think they'll put more in here with us?" inquied Jed. "That or hang some more," Ted answered.

"Don't go gettin' everyone worked up, Ted," I said sternly. "You don't know what's gonna happen."

"No sense frettin' 'bout things you can't control," interjected Slim. "Sorry, boys," Ted said. "I just get nervous not knowin' what they'll do to me, and if they were willin' to hang Stumpy, they sure won't have any problem hangin' me."

"Well, first of all, Ted, they can't hang ya without a trial," I reminded him. "Second of all, they didn't hang Stumpy."

"What?" Ben and Jed said almost simultaneously.

"Nope, sure didn't," I said. "Sorry, boys, I meant to tell ya, but it slipped my mind after I read them letters."

"Where'd he go?" asked Slim. "Did they move him to a cell?"

"No sir," I said with a smile. "His brother brought proof that the mine was on their property, and I guess he went with him up to Wickenburg."

"Damn, that's good news!" Ben exclaimed.

"So don't go gettin' yourself all lathered up, Ted," I said. "Things have a way of workin' out sometimes."

"Well hell, that sure does make me feel better."

"Good. I don't want to get your hopes up, but Miss Watson is pleadin' to the courts to give you a trial. I don't know what the outcome will be, but then at least you'll know."

"You asked her to do that for me?" Ted asked humbly. "You are a good friend, Bill."

"Well, I couldn't let you rot away in here. And she agreed with me." Everyone seemed to be in better spirits after that, and the conversation turned to brighter horizons. We spent the rest of the morning reminiscin' 'bout our lives on the other side of the wall. When the conversation slowed, Ben hit me up about sharing some stories of the Indians I'd fought and reminded me that I had promised him I would.

Ben, being from the South, hadn't had the experience of growin' up or livin' among them for very long, so his perspective was taken more from dime store books written

SWEET JUSTICE   239

by men from the East who really didn't have a clue and who embellished their stories to appeal to the reader and their pocket books. His interpretation was that they were savages that would kill you sooner than look at you. In his mind he saw their villages with scalps on every teepee and war paint on every Indian. He'd never experienced the family unity of a tribe or watched as everyone in it did their part to raise the children. He'd never seen the elders go without food to ensure the woman and children ate first or sat around a fire as generations of wisdom were passed down and taught. And he had no idea that their love for the land and their understanding of it made them less savage than the white man in a lot of ways. So I sat for a moment thinkin' of how I could change the way he thought of them and how to get him to understand that they only fought for what was theirs and to maintain their way of life. About that time one of the new guards announced lunch, so we dispersed to grab our tins.

"You'll still tell me, right?" Ben asked eagerly. "Sure thing, Ben," I assured him.

When my turn came to receive the daily slop, I asked the guard where Spencer was.

"He and the sheriff are waitin' on the train," he said. But he wanted me to tell a feller named Bill that there is a judge reviewing Slim's case and that he didn't see where it was anything but self defense. And then he asked me if I could pass on the message.

"Oh, I will," I said grinning. "I just happen to know Bill real well." I turned, excited to share the news with Slim and could hardly contain myself. As I walked, thirty feet seemed like thirty yards as I hurried to get to him. I put my arm around him and said, "Partner, your days in here might just be about over." "How so?" he asked apprehensively.

"A judge's reviewin' your case today."

"Well, as much as I'd like to share your jubilation," he said, "I've been here before."

"But not with Emily in your corner," I said matter-of-factly, "and this judge told her that it looked like self defense cut and dry."

Slims' face lit up as I finished tellin' 'im, and he looked better in that moment than he had in a long time. He stared off into space and smiled. "Wouldn't that be somethin'," he asked, "if the face of justice found its way to Yuma?"

"Well, it's got a good map this time, my friend."

We ate lunch together, and Slim couldn't wipe the smile off his face. I sat and wondered how many more times I would get to eat with my friend before he joined the long list of the many I'd left behind. Friends had come and gone a lot in my life, and I cherished their memories, but Slim would always have a place of honor in the list, and I would always be grateful I knew him.

Wasn't long after we finished eating that Ben started troublin' me to tell 'im my stories. I knew he wouldn't stop 'til I did, so I got myself comfortable and readied myself to share. I told him about my first encounter on my way to Montana and about the ones I fought with Samuel, my black friend, makin' sure he heard the word *friend*. Change comes from understanding and tolerance; whereas hate and division come from ignorance and bad examples. I hoped my words would cause him to see the black people and Indians in a new light. I told him about the ones that John Chisholm let take some of his cows to get through the winter and the Navajos I helped to get their sheep back. In the end I think everyone had a little different view of the Native Americans.

"If Andrew Jackson had taken the information about the Indians that some tried to share with him," I told them, "our relationship might've been a whole lot different than it is now."

"Why, what did he do?" Jed asked.

"He got it in his head that the white people deserved this land and that the Indians were savage locusts that needed to be wiped out," I replied. "When really, they, for the most part, were willing to share the land until the United States government started breakin' treaties and lyin' to 'em. Take it from me, they were not all murdering savages, or at least they weren't at first anyway."

"Jeez, that's definitely a different way of lookin' at 'em," Ben exclaimed. "Not at all what you hear from most people."

"That's because most people judge others from what they hear and not personal experience," I said. "There are some Indians who'll kill you, rest assured, but there are a lot of white people that will too."

"Bill, you've sure lived more in thirty-three years than most will live in a hundred," Slim exclaimed.

"That's what happens when you're runnin' from yourself, I s'pose," I said.

"But look at what you've seen and experienced, partner," pointed out Slim.

"I have very few regrets, Slim," I assured him, "but the ones I do have left deep scars. Killin' Indians for protecting what was precious to them make up a few of the deepest."

"But you'd be dead if you hadn't," Ben pointed out. "They kinda had it comin', didn't they?"

"You're right, Ben, to a point. But what if another nation invaded tomorrow?" I asked. "Would you lay down and let them take it, or would you fight even if you knew you probably wouldn't win?"

"I'd fight. Sure as shootin' I would."

"Well, that's all they are doin'," I explained. "And the sooner we learn to live with one another, the less of us there will be that have to die. So forget what you've heard from others, and find a way to find tolerance for those that are different because there are always enough enemies to go around without creatin' any more, I reckon."

CHAPTER THIRTEEN

Justice Comes to Town

THE SOUND OF THE PRISON wagon brought the kid to his feet and directly to the window as it made its usual stop in front of the courthouse. It was a scene that'd played out many times since I'd arrived here, but I joined the kid at the window anyway, just to see Emily again. There were nine prisoners this time, and I watched the guards herd them up in a line. It wasn't long before Emily appeared to go through the same ritual she'd performed many times over the last four years. I watched her look them up and down and found myself jealous of them for gettin' to be so close to her when I couldn't be.

She looked at the first four with the same disappointment she had so many times in the past, but when she arrived in front of the fifth, she shrank back, and from where I was standin', it looked like she was goin' to faint. *Who was he?* I wondered. *Could it be the one she'd searched for all this time?* I couldn't be certain, but the guards immediately took him into custody and escorted him into the courthouse. When I looked back

243

to find Emily, she was sittin' with her father, sobbin', and he was doin' his best to comfort her.

I searched the crowd that had gathered around her and caught a glimpse of Virgil slipping away down the street. He kept lookin' over his shoulder. Somethin' big was happenin', and I wished like hell I could be out there.

"What do you s'pose that was all about?" asked the kid.

"I'm not sure," I said, "but it looks like her search may have ended today, from the looks of it."

"That or the guy had a real ugly face," the kid said, laughing.

Everyone wanted to know what had happened so they could be in on the joke. I told them what we'd seen up to the part where I saw Virgil makin' his getaway down the street.

"I didn't see that part," the kid said with surprise.

"Well, let that be a lesson to ya then," I said. "If you wanna follow in my footsteps, kid, you best learn to pay attention to everythin' goin' on around you, or you might fall victim to an ambush."

"Why do you s'pose he was slinkin' away?" asked Slim.

"I don't know for certain he was," I replied, "but it sure looked like it to me. Maybe he saw a ghost."

"A ghost!" Jed exclaimed. "Do you believe there's such a thing?" Everyone started to laugh, and Jed's puzzled look kept 'em goin'. "I think he means that a part of Virgil's past may have just caught up with him," Slim explained.

"Oh," Jed said with the same look on his face.

Ted and Ben started to chuckle again, but I waved for them to stop. "I think, Jed, that Virgil's story about someone shootin' my friend Charlie may have just come undone," I explained. "I get it, I think," Jed said.

"Well, that could be good or bad for you, Bill," said Slim. "If your assumption is right, I mean."

"I know. If his story matches Virgil's, I'm in for a rough ride, I'm afraid."

"But if it don't though," Slim pointed out, "it might just be what pushes ol' Virg over the edge. That's good, ain't it?"

"Could be," I replied. "But that could mean Emily's in danger." "How so?" Slim inquired. "I don't understand."

"Because, my friend, up to now it's been an inquiry, not a trial," I explained. "But if it becomes a trial and he fingers Virgil as the killer, Virgil might come completely unhinged, and she'll have to testify."

"Why would she?" Ben asked.

"Because they'll look for motive, and Virgil's lifelong shine on her'll certainly be brought to light."

"I still don't get it," said Ben.

"I'm not sure I do either," Slim joined in.

"Well, I might be makin' mountains outta mole hills," I explained, "but if my gut's tellin' the truth, Virgil's already a little off-center. He's learned to take rejection from Emily through the years by convincing himself that it's just a matter of time 'til she comes around. He's spent his whole life makin' sure no one gets between them, and I'll bet if you went to his house, he has a shrine of sorts filled with things she's touched or articles, maybe from the paper, things like that."

"How could that put her in danger?" Slim asked again.

"Well, think about the girl you love and desire sittin' in a public gathering, airing all your actions in an attempt to destroy your character. Not only does it put him under scrutiny, but the affection he always hoped for will be dashed to pieces in front of the whole town. If he's as unstable as I think he is, it's hard to say what he might do when the love of his life cages him."

"I see what you're sayin'," said Ted. "It could be like trappin' 'coons: some cower in the corner and some become vicious as hell."

"Exactly, Ted," I agreed. "And the older the coon, the more vicious they are because they sense that if they don't fight then and there, they won't get the chance to."

"Well, if his story does match Virgil's," Ted asked, "won't things just go back to the way they are now?"

"No way," I replied, "because if it goes to trial, there's a good chance Virgil's gonna figure it was Emily and I that started the whole thing in the first place. Then he'll turn on me for sure, and possibly Emily too, only with a vengeance."

"Damn, Bill, I figured you was smart," the kid said, "but if you turn out to be right about this one, I'd have to say you're the smartest feller I ever met."

"Well, I guess all we can do is let it play out at this point," I said, "and let time tell if I am or not."

It wasn't long after that they brought dinner around, and again I asked where Spencer was only to be told that somethin' big was goin' on over at the courthouse and that Spencer was still processing the new prisoners because no one was sure where Virgil was.

"He must be damn tired," I said.

"Yeah, I wouldn't want to be in his shoes," the guard said. "He was lookin' forward to Virgil replacin' 'im, that's for sure."

SWEET JUSTICE   247

Knowing I'd play hell gettin' any more information from him, I took my beans and sat down to eat next to Slim.

"Virgil's missin'," I told him.

"Missing?" exclaimed Slim. "What d'ya mean?"

"I'm not sure, but the guard told me he didn't come to replace Spencer tonight."

"Sounds like you might have hit the nail on the head, Bill," Slim replied.

"Yeah, well, for Emily's sake, I hope not," I said fearfully.

"Well, I reckon there's nothin' you can do 'bout it, partner, so put it out of your head."

"She could be in danger, Slim, and you know how I feel about her," I replied with a hint of panic in my voice.

"She's a smart gal, Bill," Slim assured me. "I'm sure she's aware of the danger. There's no sense gettin' worked up 'bout somethin' you can't control."

"Reckon you're right."

I spent the rest of the evening trying not to worry about it but found little success. I tossed and turned for a long time 'til sleep finally found me.

The next morning I awoke early and immediately started worrying again about Emily and the danger I was sure she was in. *What have you done, William?* I said to myself. *"Why didn't you just do your time and keep your big mouth shut? At least then she wouldn't be in trouble."* I paced back and forth like a caged animal, feelin' totally helpless to prevent the consequences of somethin' I'd created.

My movement must've woken Slim because he usually slept longer in the morning. As soon as I realized I did, I had a whole new thing to beat myself up over.

"You're gonna wear a trench in that there floor, partner," Slim commented.

"Sorry, Slim. Hope I didn't wake ya."

"You did, but that's alright," he said chuckling.

"Why do I always have to stir the pot?" I asked myself out loud. "Are you still keyed up about Virgil's disappearance?" he teased. "I didn't know you cared so much about him."

I tried to laugh at his comment because I knew he was just tryin' to get me to relax, but I was beyond relaxing. My need to make things right and the part of me that wanted to put all the pieces together until the picture was clear were engaged at full throttle. On the other side of the wall, I could take my guns and wit and right a wrong or offer a solution, but in here I couldn't do anything but wonder and worry.

"She's okay, Bill," Slim tried to assure me.

"How could you possibly know that?" I asked with a hint of irritation.

"Have you heard any commotion out there?" "Can't say I have."

"Don't you think if the mayor's daughter were in trouble you'd a heard somethin'?"

"Probably," I answered, feeling a little better.

"Sure you would've, my friend," Slim said calmly. "Your not typically one to lose your head when the chips are down. Don't let a girl stop you from bein' rational. You might need that trait before this is all over. Besides, Virgil probably just went on a drunk or somethin'."

"You're probably right, Slim. I'm just not thinkin' clearly."

"I understand. If I was twenty years younger, with a girl like that hangin' 'round, I might be actin' the same as you right now."

My face turned a little red with his comment, and my heart ached to be where I could protect her from any danger that might come her way. The emotion made me feel foolish because I wasn't even sure if the feelin' was mutual, and I knew in my heart Miss Watson could probably take care of herself just fine.

"I just wish I knew what the hell was goin' on," I said. "Spencer'll let you know soon enough," he assured me. "Spencer's probably in the deepest sleep of his life right now."

"Maybe," said Slim, "but he can't sleep forever, my friend, so why don't you come and tell me some more about Wyoming and try to get your mind off things you can't control before it drives you crazy."

I spent the rest of the early morning describing sights and smells of Wyoming, Montana, Utah, and any place else I could think of, tryin' to keep my mind off Emily. I was grateful to Slim for seein' what I needed at the moment and being willin' to give up his sleep to give it to me.

Eventually, the sun made it through the window, and somewhere in the middle of my stories, Slim drifted back to sleep, a sleep he deserved, and whether he heard what I said or not, it didn't matter because he had accomplished what he'd set out to do either way. One by one, faces I'd grown fond of started to join me as hunger and heat stirred them awake. There was a strange feelin' in the air, one that had a smell of change.

I couldn't quite put my finger on it, but somethin' in my gut told me things were goin' to be different from now on, but I had no idea how soon that would be.

The last to stir was Slim. When he awoke again, he had a deep line in his face, put there from the sleeve on his shirt after he used his arm as a pillow. Ted noticed it first, and it made 'im chuckle. When the rest of us turned to look and see what he found so humorous, we quickly joined him. Then, for reasons that can only be explained by deep friendship and a bond that could only be formed in a situation such as ours, we began to laugh—not at Slim anymore so much, but just because in a hell hole in Yuma, Arizona, we'd found moments of joy. And for a brief second, I was happy to be there.

It wasn't long after that I heard footsteps start down the hall, bringin' breakfast. I hoped it was someone that could give us some news, but I only had to listen a second more before I realized they were the steps of Virgil. Funny, I thought, how through the course of my time here I'd come to recognize them and how they always brought out the worst in me. But today they sounded heavier; they didn't echo with the same cocky confidence that usually accompanied them. As his face came into view, he looked tired and nervous. I thought perhaps I was imagining it 'til he made eye contact with me and quickly looked away without any comment at all. He called us for breakfast and plopped food on our trays without sayin' a word. And as quickly as he came, he left again.

"What the hell do you make of that?" Ted commented. "That was a first, if ever I saw one."

"Somethin's got his goat, that's for sure," Ben said.

SWEET JUSTICE   251

"A hangover like none other, probably," Slim pointed out. "I'll say," agreed Ted. "I wish he'd drink more often."

We all started laughin' 'til we heard him returnin'. I half expected him to shout in some vile comment like he usually did when he sensed we were laughin' at 'im, but instead he simply looked in and told Ted he was appearin' 'fore the judge after breakfast so to get himself ready. Ted looked quickly to me with dread in his eye and confusion written all over his face.

"What d'ya reckon that means?" he asked.

"Sounds like you're finally gonna get your day in court," I said, trying to sound reassuring.

"What if they decide to hang me?" he asked in a shaky voice.

"Well, it won't be today, Ted," I told him "More likely as not, they'll just set a court date, after they ask you some questions."

"You sure?" he asked apprehensively.

"I'm not sure about anything, but I do know how it's supposed to work, and from the sounds of things, the new judge does too."

"It's gonna be alright," Slim assured him, "so you best get yourself presentable."

Ted shoveled his breakfast down his throat and started to brush himself off.

"How do I look?" he asked.

"You best do somethin' with that mop," suggested Slim. "You look like you been wrestling a wind storm."

Ted got his hair wet and started runnin' his fingers through it about the same time Virgil and another guard came to get 'im. Still, Virgil seemed preoccupied. I had a hankering to ask him about it but bit my tongue to stop myself. *No sense wakin' a sleeping bear*, I told myself, so instead I watched him and Ted disappear.

"You really think it's gonna be alright for Ted?" asked Ben.

"It will be today," I said. "What I told him was true. However, Ted did kill some men, so I can't say for sure how it'll all turn out."

"What if it don't turn out," Jed asked, "and they do hang him?" "Well, hell, I reckon I don't want to think about that, Jed, but hangin' can't be much worse than rotting away in here, I s'pose." "Here's better than dead," he shot back.

"For you and I maybe," I said, "because we have a release day to look forward to, but Ted has no idea, my friend, if his is tomorrow, next year, or a hundred years. There are some fates worse than death, I think, and that'd be one of 'em."

"I have a feelin' he's goin' to be just fine, Jed," said Slim, tryin' to make him feel better.

The kid was standin' at the window watchin'. When Ted came into view, the kid gave us all a play-by-play description of what was happenin', all the way to where he disappeared through the doors as he entered the courthouse. He started to turn away when a flash of movement drew him back.

"It's the mayor and Miss Watson," he stated, "and they're enterin' the courthouse too. And there goes Spencer right behind 'em."

"Are you sure it was Emily?" I asked with relief.

"I think I'd know Miss Watson," the kid said sarcastically. "See, I told you, Bill," Slim said. "She's just fine."

SWEET JUSTICE   253

"Let's hope it stays that way," I commented.

"You got it bad for her, don't ya, Bill?" the kid asked teasingly.

I paused a moment before answering because even though I knew he was right, I'd never admitted it out loud to anyone.

"You might say that," I replied.

"Might!" Slim said with a chortle. "I'd say so. You should've seen 'im this morning," he continued. "I never seen anyone with it so bad."

Everyone started to chuckle at his comment. "Alright," I said. "I love her. Is everyone happy now?"

"'Bout time you came clean," Ben commented, "but we all knew you did anyway."

The kid broke in and saved me from any more teasin' by announcin' that there sure were a lot of folks enterin' the courthouse.

"If the man Emily saw yesterday is the man I think he is," I pointed out, "I'll bet most of the town will be there."

"From the way they're stackin' up outside, it looks like half the town is there already," noted the kid. "I reckon the courts are gonna be busy for a few days, what with overcrowding and all."

"Does that mean more hangin's?" Jed asked.

"For some, I reckon," I replied, "but for others it might mean an early release, so it could be good for some, I s'pose."

"Wish I was one of 'em," Ben said with a sigh. "How long did they give you anyway?" I asked.

"Three years. Been here 'bout a year and a half, give or take." "That'd be about right, I reckon. Seems like you came about February," I said.

"It was. Funny, I remember thinkin' that at least I'd be warm for winter and I'd eat for a change."

"Warm maybe," Slim cut in. "The eat part I'm not so sure 'bout.

Are we callin' it food now?"

We all laughed at his comment and shared our colorful words for what we thought of the food here.

"I've had to eat worse," Ben said seriously. "But I'd kill for a piece of jerked beef for a change, that's for sure."

"I don't remember what month I came," said Jed, out of the blue.

"You came in October," Slim reminded him. "I remember because it'd just started to cool down."

"How long does that make it for me then?" Jed asked. "A year and ten months," answered Slim.

"How long did they give you?" the kid asked. "Two years," he replied.

"Two years!" I said excitedly. "Hell, you're almost done, Jed."

Jed's head perked up, and he sheepishly asked, "How almost done exactly?"

The kid started to laugh. "Don't you know how many months are in a year?"

"Not really," Jed grinned with embarrassment. "I don't even know what all the months are called."

"Unbelievable," the kid said in surprise. "You really didn't go to school, did ya?"

"I already told you I didn't," Jed replied defensively.

SWEET JUSTICE

255

"You have two months," I said quickly, tryin' to prevent a fight. "Or eight weeks, if that helps."

"Really?" he said joyfully. "That's it?"

"That's it?" I assured him. "Or maybe sooner from the looks of things."

"Yee haw!" he yelled. "Reckon that's good news, ain't it." "Reckon it is," I told him as I gave his hair a jiggle.

"Well, there's a smile that ain't goin' away," Slim said. "Good for you, Jed. You're almost done."

Artwork by Mark Inkley

CHAPTER FOURTEEN

Bittersweet Goodbyes

IT WAS WAY AFTER LUNCH before Ted was escorted back, and the perplexed look on his face enticed all of us to ask how things went in court.

"They want to send me to see some kind a doctor," he said. "And get this, if he says it's okay, they might let me go, that is, if my boss'll give me my job back."

"Will he?" I asked.

"I don't know, but Spencer said he'd send a letter for me."

"Well, that's good. If Spence said he would, you can count on it."

"I s'pose."

"What's the problem, Ted?" I asked. "Aren't you excited you're gettin' outta this hell hole?"

"Reckon I'd have to be plumb crazy if I weren't," he stated. "It's just . . ."

Ted let his sentence end there, like he'd run out of breath. After waitin' for a moment for him to continue, I finally asked, "Just what, partner?"

257

Ted looked up at me to reply, but his mind was somewhere else. "Just what?" I asked again.

"It's just that I killed some men," he said finally. "And after spendin' time with you, the reality of my actions and the knowledge that I took everythin' from them is hard to swallow, and I wonder if maybe I really do deserve to hang for it."

"Do you remember anything about that day?" I asked.

"Kinda," he replied. "There were lots of times when they poked at me or questioned my orders that I fantasized about doin' what I did, but I never acted on it until that day when I broke. When I pulled my gun, part of me knew I was doin' it, but in my mind, I was just doin' what I'd thought of many times, and somehow it didn't seem real. The longer I shot, the more like a dream it became, and for a while I convinced myself that's exactly what it was. So by the time they got me to town to see a doctor, it didn't seem real, so in my mind it wasn't."

"Somethin' clicked in your brain, Ted," I assured him. "You can't be totally responsible for what you did. It's not like you hunted 'em down with the intent to kill 'em."

"But they're still dead, Bill!"

"I understand, Ted," I said, searching for words to soothe him. "But you're sorry for it now. Maybe you can take this second chance to make amends or somethin'."

"What? How could I possibly make amends?"

"I don't know, Ted, but you sure can't if you're dead. So look at it as a chance to try anyway, and watch for an opportunity."

"It just don't seem fair, that's all."

SWEET JUSTICE 259

"Well, those were tough men in a tough country, Ted. They have to bear some of the weight of your actions," I assured him. "You were their boss, and they should've respected you in that position. I'll tell you this much, if a group of men started gangin' up on me, I might shoot and ask questions later even with a clear mind."

"Well, hell," he said, "it still hinges on gettin' my old job back anyway, and I doubt that's goin' to happen."

"It might, partner," I reminded him. "You did work for him thirteen years. That says somethin' for ya and how much he liked you."

"He was a good boss and friend."

"Well, even if he don't, Ted, don't go beatin' yourself up 'bout it anymore. You might get a second crack at it, so use this gift to do somethin' good, ya hear?"

"Okay, Bill."

"When'll you go see the doctor?" asked Slim.

"Not sure," Ted answered. "I was so overwhelmed that they weren't gonna hang me I quit listenin', I think."

We all chuckled, and Ben told 'im he probably would've done the same. But the room broke into laughter when Jed, poking' fun at himself, said, "Hell, I probably wouldn't have understood what they was sayin' to begin with."

We spent the rest of the afternoon talkin' about what might lay in store for Ted if everything worked out for him. I described in great detail the trail Jed would be on as he made his way to the triple C. The more I talked, the more excited he became, and by the time dinner came 'round, he was like a kid in the general store standing at the candy counter. Slim, bein' the good man he was, helped feed the flame, and I think he genuinely enjoyed doin' it.

"You might be next," I reminded him.

"Might," Slim said, "but I ain't gonna count my chickens 'til they're hatched.

"Who wants dinner?" Spencer yelled in.

"How come you're workin' tonight, Spence?" I asked.

"I'm not," he said. "I just wanted to come and bring you some news, so the guard asked if I'd bring your supper to ya, seein' as I was comin' down here anyway."

"Well, I'm glad you did," I said, "because I'm dyin', wonderin' who the man was Emily saw yesterday."

"I figured you'd be wonderin' that. I was sure the kid was standin' at the window watchin'," he said teasingly.

We both looked at the kid who by now had changed to a shade of red.

"Sure was," I said, poking at 'im.

"It's gettin' to be I might not recognize the building without his face in that there window," Spencer said with a laugh.

"I ain't there *that* much," the kid said defensively.

"Oh, I know you're not," Spencer said, rolling his eyes. "You do have to sleep."

We shared a laugh for a moment—well, everyone but Ted, that is. When it comes to mealtime, Ted takes it pretty serious and probably wouldn't hear a word you were sayin' until he was done.

"So who was he?" I finally asked.

"His name is Terrance," he started, "and he's the one your friend Charlie and Virgil went after for rapin' that girl four years ago."

SWEET JUSTICE 261

"Figured as much. How'd Virgil take to seein' him?" I asked intently. "He was white as a ghost," Spencer replied quietly, just in case Virgil was lurkin' about. "And, Bill, he didn't have no scar on his face."

"Doesn't surprise me," I commented. "I'm sure the real truth ain't been told—well, not all of it anyway."

"That's what Miss Watson said to her pa after they escorted him into the courthouse," Spencer stated.

"Did they question 'im about that day?" I asked.

"No, they were convicting him for the rape. They might question him in a day or two about it, but the courts are extremely busy right now. I guess the rest he came in with went on a killin' spree up north, and I'm sure they'll hang as soon as the judge can try 'em."

"Is that what he was brought in for?" I continued to press.

"No," Spencer answered, "he was caught red-handed, rapin' another girl, is what I heard."

"Great guy," I said sarcastically. "Sounds like he'll get the rope for one of his crimes anyway."

"Ya, this new judge ain't one that can be bought," he assured me. "Plays it pretty close to the book, that's for sure."

I changed the subject by askin' if he had any word on Slim's fate and thankin' 'im for helpin' Ted with his letter.

"No problem," he said. "Glad to help 'im. As far as Slim goes, I ain't heard nothin' new, but the judge agreed with Miss Watson that it was self defense as far as he could see, so I guess time will tell on that one. How's his cough anyway?"

"Better, since you let him out in the air, and again, I'm much obliged to ya for that."

"I do what I can, Bill, but you're welcome."

"So I guess Ted's probably sayin' his goodbyes, huh?" Spencer continued.

"Should he be?" I asked.

"Judge told him his transfer would be in the morning, Bill," he said, sounding surprised. "Didn't he tell you that?"

"Ol' Ted didn't hear anything after the word release," I said with a grin.

Spencer found that funny and got a good chuckle out of it before he spoke again.

"Yeah, he's gonna see a new kind of doctor we got in town," he stated. "One that pokes your thoughts, not your belly."

"What kind of doctor is that?" I asked with a little bit of doubt in my voice.

"I don't remember what they call 'im," Spencer said. "I just know he's from back East, and he's kind of a wet noodle."

His description of the man tickled me, and I about spit my beans in his face when he said it. "Met a few of 'em in my day," I said, "but I hope he can help Ted. If he can, I won't judge him too hard."

After a moment of silence, I thanked Spencer for comin' to keep me apprised like he promised he would.

"Sure, Bill," he said, "but there's one more thing, and it's important." "What is it, Spence?"

"Miss Watson wanted me to tell you she hasn't quit tryin' to prove you're innocent, but," he hesitated, "she's havin' a hell of a time findin' the positive testimony that came in with you from Tombstone."

"I think Virgil took it," I accused.

Sweet Justice 263

"Well, she wanted me to make sure you didn't lose heart and that you knew she's goin' to keep tryin' 'til she succeeds."

"I believe it. Make sure she knows I'm much obliged to her, and tell her thanks for contacting my family. It sure meant a lot to me."

"I'll be sure to do that," he promised as he walked away.

I turned to find Ted and found him still looking bewildered. I was happy that he was gettin' outta here, but I was sad at the same time. Ted had become a good friend to me while I was here, and I was real tired of watchin' good men come and go throughout my life. I decided then and there that it was high time to settle down somewhere and establish some roots.

"Ted!" I yelled in a friendly manner. "You're gettin' outta here in the morning, partner."

"In the morning?" he asked surprised, "You sure, Bill?"

"Spencer just told me that's what the judge said today," I said grinning. "You best get the wax outta them there ears, my friend."

"Reckon I ought to at that," he agreed.

Everyone gathered around him, pattin' him on the back and offerin' their congratulations, and like true friends they were genuinely happy for him.

"I'm gonna miss you, Ted," said Ben. "It's been nice havin' you around."

"I'm gonna miss all you too," he replied, "but maybe we'll see each other again."

Everyone smiled, but we all knew full well it'd probably never happen, and the knowledge caused a deafening silence for a moment.

"Maybe," Ben said finally.

"It might be sooner than later," Ted said, "because they was pretty particular that my release hinged on me gettin' my old job back, and if I don't, I s'pose they'll put me back in here."

"You will, Ted," I assured him. "You just gotta be positive is all." "Hope so," he replied.

"You will, Ted," we all said in unison.

We spent the rest of the night sharin' all the stories we could remember about Ted and had ourselves a damn good time doin' it. In fact, we laughed so hard a couple times that the guards yelled for us to keep it down. Slowly, one by one, we all drifted to sleep without fully grasping how different this hell hole would be once he was gone.

The next morning we all took turns tellin' him goodbye and wishin' him good luck, until Spencer came with breakfast and escorted him away. I stared at the door after they were out of sight and felt an empty pit as the realization that I might never see 'im again sunk in.

"Good luck, Ted," I whispered.

I turned to look at the rest and found 'em all looking at the same door. I knew the blank stares on their faces meant they were all thinkin' somethin' similar as our friend left for the last time. As I watched them one by one come back to the moment, I thought how much bigger the cell was startin' to feel now that Stumpy and Ted were gone and remembered that Jed wasn't too far behind 'em.

"Hell, when you leave," I said to him, "the rest of us might get some well deserved peace and quiet 'round here."

SWEET JUSTICE 265

Jed looked over at me just to make sure I was kiddin', and the smile on my face put him at ease.

"Probably not for long," the kid said. "I'm sure they'll bring more in to replace them."

"Reckon so," I replied, "but it won't be any of that bunch that just came in, I'd imagine. I have a feeling most of that lot will get their necks stretched for too long."

"Why, what'd they do?" asked the kid.

"Killed some folks for no apparent reason," I answered. "Some men just need to be hung because they're bad to the core, and they certainly fall into that category."

It wasn't long after dinner, however, that my prediction was proven wrong. We'd just sat back to relax and digest another well-cooked tin of slop when we heard commotion comin' from the front office.

"Make sure them shackles are painfully tight," Virgil barked.

One of 'em was cluckin' like a chicken after he said it, and I heard the thud of Virgil's stick as it made contact with his body. It had the desired effect, though, because the cluckin' came to an immediate stop. "You're a son of a bitch!" someone yelled. "You didn't have to hit him that hard."

Then I heard Spencer tell another one to hold still. Finally, the familiar sound of the door squeaking from someone comin' our way made its announcement, followed by the noise of the most unruly bunch I'd been around in a long time.

"Move back, dogs," Virgil called in. "You have visitors."

All of us moved to the back wall as they were escorted in and had their wrist shackles removed.

"Sorry, fellas," Spencer said when he saw us, "we're out of room." "Shut up, Spencer," Virgil demanded. "They don't deserve any explanation. They're no better than the rest of these pieces of shit." "Takes a piece of shit to know one, Virgil," I said without thinking.

With four guards in the room, he had the courage to smack me with his stick and the desire as well. Not to mention a need to show his authority so he didn't lose the respect from our new friends. He only hit me once, fortunately, but it hurt nonetheless and hindsight told me that I'd probably asked for that one. The guards finished what they were doin' and left us oldtimers to face the glare of the new guys as they familiarized themselves with their new surroundings. There was tension in the room as this new group attempted to assert themselves as fellas to be reckoned with. Well, all but one, that is; he was nursin' a lump on his head that I could see from where I was sittin'. So I attempted to break it by ignorin' them and findin' a place to lie down. The rest of my companions followed suit, and it looked like all was going to be okay 'til the man with the tattoo on his face told Ben to move out of his spot.

"I was here first," Ben said with a quiver in his voice.

"You think I give a damn?" the man shot back in a heavy Russian accent.

Ben, tryin' to avoid contention, got up and moved with a wave of his hand to indicate that the place was now his, but as soon as he sat down, the same man told 'im that he was in one of his friend's places now.

"Well, to save me from havin' to move again, can you point out a spot that's not one of your friend's so I can sleep?" Ben asked politely.

"Over there where we piss," he said laughin'.

"Go to hell," Ben said with all the courage he could muster.

"Did you just tell me to go to hell?" the man shouted. "Those might be the last words you ever say, boy."

As he headed towards Ben, I stood up to stop his approach and took 'im by surprise.

"Leave him alone," I said firmly. "He didn't do nothin' to you." "What are you, his pa or his guard dog?" he said as his companions laughed. "Because I can beat the hell out of you too."

"Give it your best shot, partner," I said, starin' him in the eye.

He hesitated for a moment, not sure how to react to the fact that I wasn't afraid or intimidated by him, before he threw a punch. I dodged it and quickly fired back with a stiff straight punch to the gut that knocked the wind out of him. He threw himself at me and managed to take me down to the ground as he fell, and the weight of his shoulder landed square in my chest. As pain from my injuries inflicted by Virgil earlier shot through me, causin' me to wince a bit but at the same time managin' to make me mad, I shoved him off me with my foot. But that only helped him back to a standin' position, and as he gained his balance, he came at me again and grabbed me by the neck hair. As I was standin' up, he shoved me hard into the kid and Slim. They both instinctively braced themselves and quickly helped me secure a good foothold right before he was on me again. This time I met his motion with a solid punch to his chin that made his eyes roll back in his head, like he'd been kicked by a mule, followed immediately with a hook across his temple and eye. He tried to shake it off as he approached again, but his wild punch fell short as I met his challenge with the palm of my hand and felt his nose pancake against his face, resulting in immediate blood to indicate I'd broken it. He stood there starin' at me in a state of shock, so I asked him if he was done, giving him a chance to end it then and there. But like a wild animal, he came again, so I finished it myself with an uppercut to his chin. When he went down that time, he didn't get up again.

His friends moved to the far corner and sat down, content to play nice if I would too. I was hurtin' somethin' fierce and in no mood to take on another, so I sat down to show them the fight was over. Ben came over and told me he was sorry.

"Don't worry about it, Ben," I said. "He was itchin' for a fight and, like the coward he is, decided to pick on the one he thought was the easiest target. He deserved what he got, if 'n you ask me."

"Yeah, but you sure didn't deserve to get beat on my account," continued Ben apologetically.

"You're my friend, Ben, and I sure wasn't goin' to let him push you any further, that's for sure."

"I'm much obliged, Bill," Ben replied. "You're a good friend. That man would a killed me."

"You're welcome. But in the future, don't sell yourself short before you try. You never know what's inside you until you dig it out, and you might be surprised at what you get when you do. Men like that are bullies, and sometimes what a bully needs is a good ass whoopin' to change his mind."

"Looks like you changed his real good, Bill," the kid stated with a smile. "I almost felt sorry for him when you punched his chin because I knowed what that feels like firsthand. Don't tangle with Bill Saunders, would be my advice."

"Well, he'll sure feel it come mornin'," I said as I looked at his friends who, after hearin' my name, seemed obliged to look the other way rather than meet my stare, tellin' me it was safe to lie down and pull my hat up over my eyes in an attempt to find that horse of mine for a ride to the cool mountain meadow I went to each night.

CHAPTER FIFTEEN

Visit from an Angel

"MORNING, SPENCE," I SAID WHEN Spencer came to the door with breakfast. "Any news from the outside?"

"I've got all kinds of news today, Bill," he replied, "and all of it should sure please you."

"Well then, get on with it," I coaxed in a friendly tone, "'fore you forget what it is."

"Alright," he said chuckling. "First of all, I have it from a pretty good source that they're thinkin' about lettin' Ben out early, seein' he has a job to go to and all, and due to the fact that we're bustin' at the seems right now."

"How early?" I asked.

"Same time as Jed there," he said, "so they can travel together. He'll have to check in with the law when he gets there and keep his nose clean, however."

"He will," I assured him. "He's a good kid."

"I know he is," Spencer concurred, "but don't say nothin' to 'im 'til it's for sure, ya hear?"

"That's probably a good idea," I agreed. "That's good news for sure, Spence, thanks."

SWEET JUSTICE 271

"Wait, it gets better," he said excitedly. "And this one I know for sure. Your friend Slim there will more than likely be outta here by the end of the week. The new judge said his case was self defense cut and dry and that the territory would be lucky if he didn't sue them for unlawful incarceration."

"Slim's not that kinda man," I told him. "He'll just be happy to be out, and I'm damn happy he will be."

"Me too," agreed Spencer. "And now the best news of all. Emily will be here in about an hour to see you, and she seemed genuinely excited about it."

My heart leapt at his words and then sunk again just as fast. "Damn," I said, "I look like a bum, Spencer. I don't want her to see me like this." "Got you covered, my friend," he said with a smile as he handed me a comb, soap, and a straight razor through the hole in the door. "You sure are a good friend, Spencer," I said thankfully.

"Oh, don't I know it," he replied with a proud laugh. "You don't have to tell me."

"Wait a minute! How did you get this past Virgil?"

"Virgil won't know," he assured me. "That's why Emily chose to come today. Seems there were some prisoners that needed pickin' up about twenty miles from here, and the mayor insisted that Virgil be one of the men to go get 'em."

"Oh, I'll bet that set 'im off," I said with a chuckle. "You don't know the half of it," Spencer said laughing.

Reflecting on the amusement he got as he said it and the euphoria I felt from the good news, I shared the laugh with him, and we continued 'til we had tears comin' out of our eyes. As the laughter died down, Spencer reminded me that I best get freshened up and excused himself to go feed the rest of the inmates. He waved his hand and said he'd see me later. I quickly got my hair wet and ran a comb through it and then asked Slim if he could give me a shave.

"You gonna trust me with a razor?" Slim asked in disbelief. "You do have nerves of steel."

"I don't really have much choice. I don't want to see Emily lookin' anything but the best I can."

"I can give you a shave," the new guy stated. "My pa was a barber in Santa Fe."

"You sure you want to do that, Bill?" Ben blurted out. "Why wouldn't I? He says he can do it, and I need it done."

"You beat up his boss," Ben stammered nervously. "How do you know you can trust him?"

"Can I trust you?" I asked as he was looking at Ben with irritation.

"Hell yeah," he said. "Then I can tell everyone I gave Bill Saunders a shave."

"There you go, Ben," I said with a smile. "He says I can trust 'im." "Brag to who?" Ben continued like he didn't hear me. "You're gonna hang for killin' them folks anyway."

"Killin' what folks?" the new guy asked in surprise. "I never killed no one, and as far as that man thinkin' he's my boss, he can think it all he wants, but I answer to no one."

"Didn't you kill them people just for fun?" Ben asked. "That's what Spencer told Bill."

"Don't go turnin' these fellers against Spencer," I said sharply. "Well, that's what he said, ain't it?" continued Ben.

Sweet Justice

"Hell, son, is that what ya'll think?" he shot out. "Those fellers took our cells. That's why we're in here with you. The worst thing I ever did was let that man there," he said pointing to one I beat up, "talk me into robbin' a train."

"Then you didn't kill anyone?" Ben asked apologetically. "I just figured it was you when you came in the same time they arrived."

"Well, you figured wrong," he said. "You should ask questions before jumpin' to conclusions, I reckon."

"Well, in all fairness to the boy there," interjected Slim, "your partner didn't leave room for askin' much."

"Yeah, I know," he replied, "and I think I speak for everyone here when I say I sure am sorry 'bout that."

"Water under the bridge," I said anxiously. "Now, about my face." "I'm real sorry," Ben said as the new guy soaped up my face. "I just thought—"

"Don't sweat it," he said, "but you best know what you're talkin' 'bout in the future before ya go accusin' a man of murder, or he might be guilty of it after that."

"You're right," Ben said. "I'm sorry again anyway."

As I sat listenin' to the scrapin' blade of the razor as it went to work cuttin' my beard that had pastured on my neck and face way too long, I could hear Slim coughin' in the far corner—the place he'd started retreatin' to whenever a coughin' jag came on, just in case it was accompanied with blood again. That's when I remembered the news Spencer told me before he mentioned Emily coming.

"Hey, kid," I hollered, "get Slim some water, will ya?"

Slim took it and drank it down. It seemed to quell the irritation some, so I called him over to share the good news.

"You okay, my friend?" I asked him.

"Reckon so," he replied. "I think the dust and the extra bodies just got the best of me is all."

"You're gettin' outta here next week, partner," I told him.

My words seemed to hit him like a ton of bricks, and he staggered back when I said them. "Really?" he asked in disbelief. "Am I really?" "Just got the news from Spencer. Said the new judge called it self defense and that you shouldn't be in here, so as soon as the paper work's done, they'll release you."

Tears welled up in his eyes, and he tried to choke 'em back by squinting. He sat in disbelief for a moment before speaking again. "Bill, I sure don't know how to thank you. This never would a happened if it wasn't for you."

"I'd like to take the credit, Slim, but it's Emily Watson who made it happen. I've been in here with you, 'member?"

A broad smile came to his face. "Maybe in the end," he said, "but friends like you come along once in a lifetime, if a man's lucky, that is. I'll forever be grateful to have knowed ya, Bill."

"Same here. You deserve this, and I'm just glad I could help. Now quit distractin' the barber here 'fore he cuts off my nose, will ya?"

Everyone gathered around to congratulate him, and he took center stage. I was grateful for it because my stomach was doin' back flips as I waited for Emily to arrive. *Does she feel the same for me as I do her,* I asked myself, *or am I just wishful thinking?* Seconds became minutes and minutes became hours as I listened for the

SWEET JUSTICE 275

familiar squeak of the door that led to the corridor. When it finally announced itself, everyone stopped to wish me luck as I listened to the sweet sound of Emily's footsteps comin' towards me.

"Bill, you have a visitor," Spencer called in and then smiled when he found me standing at the door.

"Hello, William," Emily said. "It's been awhile, and may I say you look nice."

"You look lovely as usual, Emily," I replied, tryin' to keep my composure.

"Come on you two," said Spencer. "I'll take you to the courtyard."

"I have so much to tell you, William," Emily said, "and my dad took care of Virgil for us."

"Oh he did?" I said, tryin' to sound surprised. "That should make things more pleasant, shouldn't it?"

"Anytime he's not around is pleasant," she stated. "He hovers over me all the time—always has—and whenever he's gone, I feel free."

"That's no way to live," I replied. "Why haven't you ever told him that?"

"I tried, but Virgil just hears what he wants to hear." "Sounds like a prison of sorts to me," I replied.

"That's an interesting way of looking at it. I never thought about it that way before. But enough about him," she continued as she threw her dress forward to sit down, "I want to talk about you."

"I'll talk about whatever you want to, Emily," I told her and without thinking continued with, "I sure have missed you."

Emily's face began to blush a little when I said it, and I quickly apologized for embarrassing her.

"What I mean to say is I like our visits," I said, tryin' to cover my forwardness.

"I know what you meant, William," she said pleasantly. "I've missed you too."

We looked into each other's eyes for a moment, and I desperately longed to kiss her at that moment.

"Did Spencer tell you about Slim?" she asked, breaking the trance I was in.

"Sure did. I sure am obliged to you for makin' that happen, and so is he, I assure you."

"It looks like your efforts to find Jed and Ben a job is going to work out for both of them as well."

"Yeah, well, they both need another shot at it. I was just in the right place at the right time, I guess."

"Don't be so humble, William. Your efforts have helped a lot of people. Both Ted and Stumpy made sure to let the judge know that it was you who steered them straight and helped them know where they went wrong and how to avoid going there in the future. Spencer told the judge about your helping Ben and Jed find work and even confessed that it was you that got him started in learning how to read. He also told the judge that if all the prisoners were like you, there would be no need for walls or bars. That was quite a compliment, if you ask me. And Slim would have rotted away in here until he died if it wasn't for you. His case was buried away and would have stayed there forever if you hadn't brought it to my attention."

"Well, they're all good men. I'm just glad I could help 'em." "William, you don't see it, do you?" she asked in surprise. "See what?" I asked, a little confused.

"What a good man you are. You not only took the time to befriend these men but sincerely tried to help them, all while being locked up for something you didn't do. A lesser man would have let his anger make him mean and uncaring, but not you, William. It's almost like you were supposed to be here at this time."

"I've always tried to make the best of where I am when I'm there," I explained. "It's not a big thing."

"Oh, but it is, William, it is," Emily shot back. "You called me an angel once, do you remember?"

"How did you know that?" I asked surprised.

"Spencer informed me, and he said you took a lot of ribbing for doing it," she said with a smile.

"Yeah, well, I meant it, and I'd say it again."

"*You're* the angel, William. These men needed you, and they had no one else to help them. You put yourself to one side and set out to help those around you. I find that to be one of the most admirable traits I've ever seen in anyone I've met in my entire life."

"Well, I'm glad there's somethin' about me you like," I said, a little embarrassed.

"There's more than that. That's why what I have to tell you is so hard for me to say."

"Then just say it. There's no need to hold on to an unbreakable horse."

After a pause, Emily explained, "The judge said that unless the statements of your innocence can be found, your case can't be brought up for trial again, and with the overcrowding of the prison…."

Emily broke down at this point and started to cry uncontrollably, and no matter how hard she tried, the tears kept comin'.

"With the overcrowding of the prison, I'm to be hanged," I said, finishing the sentence for her.

At that moment she rushed into my arms and held me tight. "It's not fair," she sobbed. "It's just not fair that someone who has helped so many should have to die for something he didn't do."

I held her tight and told her it was alright and thanked her for tryin' so hard to help me, even when it put her in a dangerous position.

She stopped cryin' at that moment and looked into my eyes. "There you go again," she pointed out. "How can you be so strong and selfless even when things look so bleak?"

"I'm not strong. I just don't want you to blame yourself is all. You did all you could to help me, and if I have to die here, I'm glad I got the chance to meet you before I did. When you leave here today, you hold your head up and know that I'm eternally grateful for your efforts."

"I would cross mountains to help you, William," she cried. "I haven't stopped searching for the evidence, and I promise I won't stop until I find it."

"I'm much obliged, but if you can't, I don't want you blamin' yourself, ya hear?"

"I admire you more than anyone I ever have before. I've thought about you every day since the day we met. It's hard to explain, but it's as if I knew you or I was supposed to know you. I don't know what I'm saying— But I knew you were innocent and that I was meant to help you or maybe you were meant to help me, I don't know. I just wish I hadn't waited so long because now it's too late."

SWEET JUSTICE 279

I put my fingertip to her mouth and looked into her eyes. Our lips found their way to each other, and in an instant the dread of the news I had just received washed away, and I was overcome with joy to think that an angel such as Emily Watson could ever see anything in a man like me. And for a moment nothing in the world mattered anymore.

All of a sudden, Virgil's voice shot out.

"What the hell is this? I didn't give anyone permission to be here today."

"I said she could come," Spencer said defiantly.

"Yeah, well, you just cost yourself a job, Spencer," he shouted. "Get your shit and get the hell out of here before I kill you myself."

"He did it at my request, Virgil," Emily said boldly, "and my father knows about it, so I wouldn't be too quick to fire him."

"I'm the boss here, Emily, not your pa. I decide what goes on here. And as for you, Billy," he continued, "I have half a mind to tell the courts you were in the process of rapin' the mayor's daughter."

"That's a lie, Virgil," shot out Emily. "He was doin' no such thing." "It don't matter anyway," he said coldly. "You'll be hanged before too long anyway, so I'll just look at it as a goodbye kiss. But I think you and I will have ourselves one of them there chats tonight anyway, Billy." "If you hurt him again," Emily stated bravely, "I'll make sure *you* lose your job, and I'll bring charges against you myself."

Virgil looked hurt when she said it and a little surprised as well. I panicked as the scene played out, angry with myself for allowin' our plan for Emily's safety to come unraveled.

"Haven't I always been nice to you, Emily?" he asked. "Didn't I always watch over you and protect you when we was youngins?"

"More like mauled me, Virgil. Anytime I got close to anyone you perceived to be a threat, you pushed them along until they were afraid to talk to me at all."

"I did that to protect you from gettin' hurt."

"Ironic," she replied, "that by trying to keep me from being hurt, you were hurting me all along."

"That wasn't my intention," he said defensively. "It's just that I always loved you is all."

"Well, I don't love you, Virgil," said Emily, courageously. "I never have, and I never will."

Virgil looked at me with hate when she said it and grabbed me by the neck, giving it a squeeze. Her words hit 'im hard, and he was on the verge of insanity. The crazy look in his eye and the foam forming around his mouth made me worry more than ever for Emily's safety.

"Do you love 'im?" he asked as small drops of spit hit me in the face. "Is this what you love, a murderer and criminal? Hell, I can be a murderer right now if that's what you like in a man."

"You already are," I said in a raspy voice while he continued to choke me. "You killed Charlie, and you know it."

My words made 'im push me to the ground, and he looked like a caged animal.

"I never killed no one," he shouted. "The man that done that is locked up right here and is fixin' to hang real soon."

SWEET JUSTICE   281

"Not until he's been questioned about Charlie's murder, he isn't," cut in Emily. "I'll make sure of that."

"They have enough on him to swing him now," Virgil said smugly. "He's waitin' on death row as we speak, so you're gonna have to take my word that he killed your man and get over it already."

"I wouldn't be too sure about that, Virgil," I said with challenge. "Things have a way of comin' to the surface sooner or later."

"Well, you won't be around to see it, Billy," he said with a sinister smile, "'cause you'll be joinin' him 'fore too long, and you can ask 'im yourself. As for you, Miss Watson, I'd let sleepin' dogs lie, if you know what's good for you."

"Is that a threat?" asked Emily.

"Not at all," he replied. "But there ain't no use prolonging the execution of Charlie's murderer by muddyin' up the water. Now I think it's time for you to leave, Emily," he said as he grabbed me by my arm and twisted it hard behind my back. "Billy here has to go inside now."

Emily hesitated to follow Virgil's request, so he called for another guard to escort her out.

"This isn't over, Virgil," she said as she was being led towards the exit, "and I would advise you not to lay a hand on him if you know what's good for you. And *that*, Virgil, is a threat."

I watched as she disappeared through the doorway. Even though Virgil was pushin' my arm near to breakin', I knew things were gonna go from bad to worse when we didn't make the corner towards my cell. Virgil continued to shove me until we found ourselves at the far corner of the building, in what looked like a cellar of sorts. Upon our arrival Virgil shoved me hard to the ground.

"I told you to leave 'er alone," he whispered angrily. "All's you had to do was obey, and I would've helped you get outta here. But you just had to stir the pot, so now you get to spend the last few days of your miserable life in here, and I'm gonna make sure you don't enjoy them." He lifted his stick in a threatening manner and took a step forward before realizing he'd failed to restrain me. Virgil sized up the situation and nervously licked his lip, not sure now of his next move.

"Tell you what, Virgil," I said calmly. "You promise to leave Emily alone and forgive her for tryin' to help me, and I'll quietly stay in here. Hell, you can come beat me every day if that will make you feel better. But don't take your anger for me out on her; she was just tryin' to do what she thought was best. In a week or so, I'll be gone, and so will the man that killed Charlie. Things will go back to normal, and you might still have a chance with her."

"I don't stand a chance with her," he said. "Not now anyway." "You might," I lied, "but not if you don't treat her nice. You go find her and tell her that I confessed to killin' that girl and that she doesn't need to come back here anymore because I don't want to see her."

"But she was kissin you'," he pointed out. "Maybe she wants to see you."

"She was just givin' me a kiss as a last request," I said, trying to calm him down, "'cause she knew I was gonna be hanged, that's all. Now put some shackles on me and know that you were right all along and that you finally won."

Virgil thought for a moment about what I'd said, and a smile replaced the scowl on his face as he turned towards the door.

"I'd be lyin' if I said I was gonna miss you, Billy."

"Same goes for you, Virg," I replied, "but it sounds like I'm leavin' whether we're gonna miss each other or not, so go do what I told you, and I promise not to give you any more trouble."

When he left I prayed that my actions would keep Emily safe. I told myself that if I was going to die soon, at least I got one kiss from the only girl I had allowed myself to fall in love with since I was a kid. Sayin' it out loud softened the blow of what was comin' and gave me the courage to face it. I found a spot where I could lie down sorta comfortably, pulled my hat down over my eyes, and soon I was ridin' along a mountain stream once again.

The next week and a half or so went by in a blur, broken up by an occasional meal bein' shoved into a cracked door and footsteps comin' and goin'. I was grateful now for all the time I had spent alone through the years, because the lack of conversation and the silence of solitary had a way of breakin' most men. But I used it to my advantage. I gathered all of my life's decisions into two piles and faced them head on: the regrets went to one pile to be dealt with later; the rest—friends, family, experiences and Emily—went to another. I boxed them into a beautiful treasure chest and was grateful for each one of 'em and the chance to call 'em mine. Then I wrapped it up with all the laughter and joy each had brought me and labeled it as my life. I then set out to clean the room it would rest in by comin' to grips with the regrets that littered the floor.

I thought of each man who'd met his end from the barrel of my gun. I thought of Jimmy and the day he died. I thought of lesser men who I wasn't as kind to as I could've been.

And my biggest regrets: sneakin' away from home without sayin' goodbye, and not goin' back when I should've. The thought of all the years I could've spent helpin' my pa, watchin' my sisters grow up, and listenin' to my ma read from the Bible pained me, and I desperately hoped that they would all forgive me. I hoped that those who I had wronged in any way somehow had moved on without lettin' my actions steer them one way or another. I thought of each encounter that ended in violence and bloodshed and searched my mind to see if there was any other way to have dealt with it or if my eagerness to right a wrong made me act in haste. Last of all, I prayed that if my life was to end soon, somehow Jimmy'd still loved me and would meet me there, if there really was a hereafter.

Peace came to me as I dealt with family first, and I knew in an instant that they somehow understood and loved me just the same. I sure was grateful at that moment that Emily, in her wisdom, had sent them word and that I'd received some in return. Reflectin' on my actions with others, the thought came clear as a bell that I'd always attempted to be decent with anyone I met and was always quick to make amends and say I was sorry if I was wrong. As far as those who found themselves on the wrong end of my gun, I always tried to give a man a way out before pullin' iron, and I knew in my heart that their deaths were brought on by their own actions. And last of all, I found myself prayin' to God, who I'd long abandoned, and felt his lovin' hand of comfort on my shoulder as he touched my heart with words of assurance that Jimmy was waitin' for me and loved me still.

Tears came to my eyes, but they weren't tears of regret but, rather, comfort. In my mind I peacefully took myself back to the high mountains of New Mexico for one last ride on my favorite horse and one more inhale of the fresh alpine air.

Chapter Sixteen

The Call of Love and Duty

I awoke to footsteps comin' down the hall, and I knew that they were comin' for me. I was slowly dyin' from starvation and dehydration, so they were almost comforting to hear.

"This is it. My time has come," I said to myself. *"Face it like a man, William."*

"Where the hell could he be if he wasn't in there, Spencer?" I heard the mayor ask in a state of panic. "What did that maniac do with him?" "I don't know," he said dreadfully. "I just hope he hasn't killed 'im like he always wanted to."

"Why would he want to kill him?" asked the mayor.

"Bill figured out that Virgil was the one that killed Charlie a long time ago," explained Spencer. "And he sure didn't cotton to Emily and Bill bein' together, I can tell you that."

"I should have listened to her years ago," the mayor stated regretfully. "She tried to tell me he was off-center, but I didn't do a damn thing about it."

286

"You can't blame yourself, Mr. Mayor. We all kind of knew it all along."

"Yeah, well, now gettin' her back lies with the experience and grit of a man we can't even find and, worse than that, a man that should've never been here in the first place."

I tried like hell to call out to them, but my thirst had swollen my tongue and robbed me of my voice, so all that came out was a faint whisper. When I sensed that Spencer was by the door, I found the strength to bang my boot against the floor, creatin' a thud I hoped he would hear.

"He's in here, sir," said Spencer, excitedly. "Behind this door." "Well, get it open!" the mayor shouted.

"I don't have a key. Only Virgil had a key to this door."

"Well, find it!" the mayor continued to shout. "Damn it, man, he has my daughter."

I heard Spencer run towards the front office and the mayor callin' for me to hang on.

"They're not here!" Spencer yelled down the corridor. "I don't know what he did with 'em."

"The bastard probably has them on him," the mayor said in exasperation.

"What do you want me to do, sir?"

"How should I know? Just think of something."

"We're going to get you out of there, Mr. Saunders," Emily's pa said more calmly. "You just hang in there."

The next thing I heard was horse hooves comin' towards me. The echo bouncin' down the adobe hallway was deafening, When they came to a stop, I heard chains bein' strung through the bars in the window's opening, the distinct slap of someone's hand makin' contact with horse flesh, and then, in an instant, the loud crash of the door bein' ripped from its hinges and adobe shards splashing in every direction.

"Damn!" Spencer said when he saw me. "You look like hell, Bill." "I feel like hell," I mumbled incoherently.

"Don't try to speak, partner. I'll fetch you some water."

Spencer was back in an instant and reminded me not to drink too fast. Then he helped me up by takin' my arm and leadin' me towards the front office. By this time there were five or more people around me, and I heard the mayor shout to give me room. Spencer helped me into a chair and brought me more water.

"I'm sorry, Bill," he said as he handed me some bread. "I had no idea Virgil had done this to you. He wouldn't let me back in after firin' me, even after the mayor gave me my job back."

"Where's Emily?" I asked as my energy began to return. "What's going on."

"We're not sure. We think Virgil's got her."

"He does have her," the mayor tried to say calmly but with little success. "We have to get her back."

"We'll get her, sir," I tried to assure him, "but we can't just go runnin' off without puttin' some pieces together first. When did you first know she was gone?"

"We don't have time for this," said the mayor, exasperated. "She's out there, and every minute we waste, she gets farther away."

"I understand how you feel, and believe me I want her back myself," I told him, "but I need to know what led up to it."

SWEET JUSTICE   289

"The man went berserk, that's what led up to it," he replied. "That's not gettin' us anywhere, sir," I said firmly. "You need to calm down and be rational. Now, how long has she been gone?" "About eight hours," replied Spencer as he tried to feed me bread and jerky.

"Has anyone gone after her?" I asked between bites.

"Four men left this morning when Virgil was nowhere to be found. But we didn't know Emily was with him then. They crossed the river but lost his tracks when he took to the rocks. That's when they came back and informed us that there was two riders. That's when we realized Emily was gone too."

"Why was he running, Spencer?" I asked.

"Willy—that's the man that Virgil said shot your friend—fingered Virgil as the real killer in court. And as near as we can tell, Virgil must've overheard him somehow."

"Where was Emily at that time?" I continued to press.

"She was in the courtroom. And when Willy looked her in the eye and swore that he didn't do it, she left to go find Virgil to confront him about it, or at least that's what we figure."

"Why wasn't the sheriff sent after him at that time?" I asked with irritation in my voice.

"He was. About ten minutes later. That's when they realized Virgil was gone. Looks like he was ready to leave at the drop of a hat in case it went that way, so the sheriff rounded up some men and lit out after him. The only reason they came back after losin' his trail is because they weren't supplied to be gone more than a day at the most, and when they came back, he confessed that he didn't have the trackin' skills, so he was just a needle in a haystack."

"Do we know for sure what way they went?"

"That much we know for sure, Bill. The tracks leaving Virgil's corral were easy to see and easy to follow in the sand. It was those damn rocks that helped 'im get away."

"There is always track," I said confidently. "You just have to know what to look for is all."

"There's something else you should know," said Spencer. "When they busted into Virgil's house, they found just what you predicted they would. It's eerie. He had pictures of her and newspaper clippings from all her charity and fundraiser events. They also found a doll he had made that had her real hair he had collected over the years. But the most disturbing thing, I think, was the dress that disappeared from the swimmin' hole years ago. It was lyin' on his bed and looked like it'd been there for a long time. They also found the papers that stated you had nothin' to do with that girl's death in Tombstone. You were right about everything, Bill."

"Then we're dealin' with a man that's outta his head," I concluded. "His kind is capable of anything, and that sure makes him dangerous."

"Can you find her, William?" the mayor asked hopefully.

"I'll find her, sir. That I can guarantee you, but I'll need two good horses and supplies for at least four days."

"Two horses?" he questioned. "Why two?"

"'Cause if I'm goin' after a mad man, I'm takin' the kid with me, that's why."

"Now wait a minute. Not even I can pull a man out of prison," the mayor said. "But the sheriff and his deputies will go with you."

SWEET JUSTICE 291

"No, they won't," I said firmly. "The last thing I need is a parade. What I need is another man that's damn good with a gun and one that's not soft. This is a tough job for tough men, and I know the kid's got what it takes to see it through, so you best figure out how to get him for me and you best do it fast, mayor, because like you said, we're wastin' time."

"Fine, I'll see what I can do," he replied.

"No disrespect, sir," I said back to him, "but when I leave here I'll want another gun with me, or you might be signing both Emily's and my death certificate."

"He'll be out in an hour, William," he said without hesitation this time. "You go get whatever you need and tell them to put it on my tab. I'm really sticking my neck out, William, so you better bring him back when you bring my daughter."

"We'll be back, sir," I told him. "You have my word on that."

I turned and headed to the livery stables to find two good horses that could ride long and hard. Spencer accompanied me and asked what he could do to help.

"Do you have more to eat?" I asked him. "I feel like I'm starvin' to death."

"You look like it too." He handed me some dry biscuits. "You best start with these, stretch out your stomach a little. I'll go round up some jerked beef for energy and meet you at the smithy's."

"Thanks, Spencer," I said gratefully. "Once again, always lookin' out for me."

"Do you really think you can find her?" he asked before walking away.

"I can find her," I assured him, "but will I find her alive is what's got me worried."

"You think he'd kill her, Bill?" he asked with concern in his voice. "Not on purpose, I reckon," I replied, "but he's riding fast and hard, and she ain't used to that. If they're in them rock cliffs on horses not used to bein' there, I can tell you they're both in danger. Add that to the fact that Virgil's outta his head and runnin' scared, and what you got is a dangerous situation, to say the least."

"You'll find her, Bill," Spencer said, more to convince himself than me. "I know you will."

Spencer disappeared into the crowd, and as I came around the corner, I found Slim standin' outside the freight building. He looked shocked when he saw me and ran to hug me when he was sure it was me. "It's good to see you, partner," he said. "I was afraid you were dead." "I'm too ornery to die, Slim," I said. "It's good to see you on the outside. What you still doin' in this hell hole?"

"Got myself a job haulin' freight. When you didn't come back, we all figured you got yourself hung. What happened?"

"I'll tell you when I get back, Slim," I said, brushing him off. "Virgil's kidnapped Emily, and I'm on my way to bring her back."

"Well, then, I'm goin' with you, partner," he said without hesitation. "I owe that gal my life."

"You pay her back by livin' it then, my friend," was my reply. "I'm ridin' hard and fast, and you're not in any condition to keep up."

"Reckon you're right," he said sadly. "I wouldn't want to slow you down, not with something this important.

SWEET JUSTICE 293

You take care of yourself, partner, and bring her back, ya hear?"

"I will, old friend. You can count on it," I said as I hurried away.

It was about an hour later that I picked up two freshly shoed horses and met the mayor and the kid in front of his store.

"I didn't mean to volunteer you for something without askin' you first, kid," I said when I saw him, "but I need you on this one."

"Bill, I told ya I'd have your back anytime," he said with his cocky smile, "and I'd a been offended if you didn't volunteer me. Besides, Miss Emily Watson needs our help, and I just wouldn't feel right if I didn't give it to her."

"You ready then?" I asked.

"Let's ride," he replied as he two-stepped and jumped on his horse's back from behind. "You got me a gun?"

"Sure do," I said with a grin. "But seein' you're a prisoner, I think I'll give it to you on the other side of the river."

"Bring her back to me, William," the mayor said, "and I'll give you whatever you want."

"We'll be back, sir, and she'll be with us," the kid shouted.

"Get up!" I yelled, and in a flash we were chasin' the setting sun.

*****

There was no moon that night, so darkness came on fast. The kid and I pushed as long as we could before stopping. My desire was to get to sleep quickly so we'd be saddled and ready to go as soon as the crack of dawn said good morning. Even though I was hungry, I was too tired and concerned to talk myself into cookin' anything, so I ate jerked beef instead while I boiled some coffee.

"Damn, there's a smell I've missed," the kid said excitedly. "My thoughts exactly."

When it finally came to a boil, I quickly filled two brand new tin cups to the top and handed one to the kid before settling back to savor one of the things I'd missed the most since the day I was arrested.

"Did they let Ben go with Jed?" I asked between sips.

"Sure did. Not joyfully, though. We all thought you might be dead when you didn't come back that day."

"Another week and I would've been," I said somberly. "What happened?"

"Virgil showed up just as I was kissin' Emily. And it was the straw that broke the mule's back. He lost it, my friend, and mentally I saw him snap, so I had to do something to protect Emily."

"Did he beat you again?"

"No. That's kinda how I knew he'd cracked; he just didn't have the heart when he saw the kiss. That was compounded when Emily informed him that she never had and never would love him."

"Yeah, I can see where that would hit 'im like a ton of bricks."

"It did," I assured him. "I watched a scared and confused animal turn vicious, and I instantly witnessed Emily turn herself from loved and protected to hated and vulnerable, so I did the only thing I could think of. He already knew I was up to be hanged, so I let 'im think she

SWEET JUSTICE 295

was fulfilling a dyin' man's request, and I promised him that if he didn't harm Emily, I would remain silent until my execution day."

"Where were you?"

"In a cellar farther down our corridor. Sometimes I could hear ya'll, but it was muffled. Every once in a while, Virgil would bring me some food and water, but about four or five days ago, he quit comin' altogether."

"Yeah, that was about the time he went to testify against your friend's killer. The guard told me his story was full of holes. We didn't see him after that either."

"When did they let Slim out?" I asked.

"Two days after you disappeared. He cried when you didn't come back. Bill, we all thought you were dead."

"What did Jed and Ben do for money?" I asked, tryin' to change the subject.

"Don't know," he said. "I plumb forgot they was goin' to get it from you."

"Hope they're okay," I said with a little concern. "The two or three dollars they got when they were released won't get them too far."

"Me too," the kid said, yawning. "I like them two a lot."

"Well, hell, we best get some sleep, I reckon. It ain't gonna be easy pickin' up a trail tomorrow."

I laid down and tried to put all the pieces I had gathered together and thought of Virgil's actions, reactions, and personality in an attempt to decipher his next move. I knew he hadn't spent much time away from a town in his life, and I hoped that meant he didn't have a clue what to do if he got too far from water. If he didn't, tracking him would be easier, unless he did something stupid, that is.

I also drew comfort that no matter how hard he pushed, Emily would only be able to go so hard, and I hoped that his infatuation for her would bring compassion. If it did, we could easily catch them. My last thought was on Ben and Jed again. Without money they didn't stand a chance of reaching Texas.

"When this is done, Bill," I told myself, *"you best go out after them."* I closed my eyes and was out in an instant. Only this time I was too tired to go to the mountains, so I settled for the bunkhouse in New Mexico instead.

"Please help me, William," I heard echo off the rock. I ran through the sand, but it seemed to claw at my feet like demons pulling me under. *"Please help me,"* I heard again. I attempted to free my legs, but they held fast. I clawed at the sand with my hands like I was swimming as her screams became more frequent. Clawing for a hold, I found a cactus, and in spite of the needles cuttin' into my hand, I gripped it firmly and pulled with all my might, strugglin' to free my legs. *"He's going to kill me, William!"* she screamed in terror. I grabbed the cactus with both hands and watched as the pricks went through my palms, tearing the flesh as they exited. Finally, my legs began to break free. When I felt the release, I ran towards the rocks and the protection they offered as the sandy cold fingers from hell kept tryin' to grasp them again. *"You have to get up the wall,"* I heard echoing in my head. That's when I realized I had lost my boots. I started to climb, searching for places to put my feet, but each time I found one, it would melt away, leavin' me hangin' by my fingers. Looking down I could see that my feet were cut and bleeding, leavin' blood streaks on the cliff face. A blood curdling scream from

SWEET JUSTICE

above hastened my climb until I found myself looking at Virgil, but somehow it wasn't him; it was more like death himself holding Emily in its grip. *"You want her?"* he said eerily. *"Go get her."* Laughing, he released his hold on her, and she began to fall into blackness. I dove over the edge to grab her, but as I looked back up, she was still standing next to him, and as I fell, he let out a demonic blood curdling laugh. Just before I hit the ground below, I jerked back to a conscious state so intense that I flipped my blanket completely off me, and I found myself saturated in sweat. The laugh was still there in the back of my mind, gripping me with terror. "It was just a dream, Bill," I said out loud, but oddly my feet and hands hurt just the same.

I looked to the east and could see the sliver of grayish blue on the horizon, and I knew it would light enough to see soon, so I knocked my boots together to rid 'em of any critters that might've crawled in during the night, put them on, and started to build a fire.

I don't remember takin' my boots off, I realized all of a sudden. *You're losing it Bill,* I thought, as the flame began to dance on the wall behind me.

The smell of bacon and coffee brought the kid back to the conscious world, and the first thing out of his mouth was "Sure beats the beans in Yuma. don't it?"

"Hell, yeah," I said with a smile brought on by the realization that I really was free. The frenzy of the situation and the panic brought on from knowin' the girl I loved was missin' drowned out the moment I had looked forward to for three long years. My mind and body had immediately jumped to action, and it took the kid pointin' it out to open my eyes to the reality of it all.

For a few seconds, I stared off into space, wrappin' my head around it.

"Hey, Bill, you okay?" the kid asked.

"I was sure I'd die there, kid," was my reply. "Came mighty close too."

"Damn glad you didn't, Bill," the kid said sincerely. "I sure don't wanna lose another friend."

"You best get some coffee in ya, kid," I said, pointing to the fire. "There's a long, hard day in front of us, and I'd venture we're gonna find out what kind of men we are today."

We finished our breakfast and started to saddle our horses when I looked down and noticed dog tracks in the sand, I lifted my head to follow their path and realized that they were all around us.

"Hey, kid, did you see or hear any dogs last night?" I asked. "Dogs? There ain't no dogs out here, Bill, not that I seen anyways." "Take a look at the sand," I replied, pointing with my head. "Well, I'll be damned, Bill. Where the hell do you suppose they came from?"

"I don't know," I answered as I walked the perimeter of our camp. "But near as I can tell, it never left."

"What?" the kid said with a chuckle. "You're losin' it, Bill, 'cause there ain't no dog here now."

"See for yourself, kid," I said seriously. "There aren't any tracks leading in or out of here."

The kid took a quick circle around the first time, full of cocky youth, sure he was gonna prove me wrong. He circled a second time, tryin' to figure it out.

"That don't make no sense, Bill," the kid said apprehensively. "How can an animal come and go without leaving tracks?"

"There's only one explanation that comes to mind, but I never put much stock in it. It's time to go. You ready?"

"Yep, let's ride."

We rode in silence for about a half an hour as the sun made it the rest of the way over the horizon. I could tell the kid's head was buzzin' with reasons for the tracks, but each one must've fallen short because each time his body signs indicated he was about to speak, he fell back into thought again. Finally, he asked, "What's your explanation, Bill?"

"If I told you," I said, grinning, "it'd scare the hell outta ya." "I don't scare that easy, Bill," he said confidently.

"Me neither," I assured him, "but when that old Navajo Indian told me about it, the hair on my head stood straight, I can tell you that."

After a minute or so of silence, he asked if I was going to tell him. "Not now, kid. We've got bigger things to deal with."

"What's our next move then?"

"The sheriff told me they lost Virgil's tracks where the trail makes a T," I told him, "so we ride 'til we find it then try to figure out where they went after that."

"Do you think you can?" he asked "I mean, how do we find tracks on rocks?"

"There's always tracks, kid," I answered. "We just have to look 'til they're done hiding."

"Yeah, but," he started to say and then stopped.

"Yeah, but we didn't find the dog tracks," I finished for him.

"I know you're a good tracker, Bill," he said apologetically. "I didn't mean to doubt you none."

"Don't fret none about it. I've tracked animals and men across all kinds of terrain. We'll find her, and you can take that to the bank."

It wasn't long afterwards that we came across the T the sheriff mentioned. I immediately eliminated the trail south because of the lack of cover and water.

"Only a man that knew the terrain would take that road," I said to the kid. "Anyone else would be turning themselves into buzzard feed."

"You said he was crazy," the kid pointed out. "Maybe he did." "Out of his mind and stupid are two different things, partner," I said confidently. "Virgil's lived in the desert his whole life. I'm sure he knows that trail is suicide, so we can eliminate that one."

"Do you think he's headed for San Diego?"

"Don't know, but I doubt it. Too many people would recognize Emily there. But I can tell you this much: he didn't go forward, on this road anyway, and he sure as hell didn't go back. So we search the rocks and canyons."

I sent the kid west on the main trail with the instructions to search for horse tracks entering back onto it in an attempt to eliminate the possibility that they took to the rocks to brush away the track for a while and then to come back to the main trail when it was safe. I searched for any sign as I went but was focusing mainly on side canyons that looked like they might access the terrain above. It took about three hours before I saw a scratch on the rock entering into one of these canyons that looked promising enough to search farther up its jagged mouth, so I gave the kid a whistle. Fortunately, he'd picked up my trail when his search turned up nothing, and he was only a hundred yards behind me when I called him in.

SWEET JUSTICE

"Find something, Bill?" he asked anxiously.

"Not sure," I told him, "but this rock will end as we enter this canyon. If that scratch there is anything, we should find tracks when we get back to the sand."

"Well, lead on, partner," the kid said. "This day ain't gonna last forever."

I chuckled as I coaxed my horse forward, glad to have a friend along. I could see prints in the sand before I got to them. The sand was soft and angled slightly, and it was easy to see that one of them was loaded to capacity.

"You think that's them?" the kid asked when he saw them.

"It's them alright. Looks like three horses, and one of them is packing something heavy. Virgil must have secret life," I continued, "'cause there ain't no way he just happened on this canyon."

"What the hell's he doin' out here?" the kid said, more to himself than anything.

The canyon began to narrow the farther we went, until there was barely enough room on both sides to slip through.

"I hope it widens out up yonder," I said to the kid, "'cause backing these animals outta here could prove interesting."

"Maybe we'll find Virgil wedged in," the kid said laughing.

I pictured it in my head and started to laugh with him. "If we do, I'm gonna shove on his horse's ass and leave 'im there."

It tickled the kid. I'm sure it was the walls on both sides that kept 'im on his horse. It was only another hundred feet or so that the canyon made a sharp ninety-degree angle. The flash floods had washed out the sandstone, creatin' a cathedral into the cliff face, leavin' a pool of water in the bottom with ferns growin' on the wall.

"Holy cow!" the kid said when he beheld it. "I aint never seen anything like this in my life."

"You should see the canyons up north, my friend," I replied. "Words can't do them justice."

We let our horses drink their fill. When they were finished, I looked at the sand dune opposite the undercut. I could see where two horses had climbed the side to get to the top of it. So I nudged my horse to follow them. As soon as I came to the top, I immediately saw the fire pit and indentations where two people had slept.

"This is where they stayed last night," I pointed out.

"That means they're not too far in front of us," the kid stated excitedly.

"Problem is, Virgil obviously knows this canyon well, so if we want to close the gap, we best be on our toes."

I climbed off my horse to get a better look at things, not wanting to miss any clue that might be to our benefit. The kid doubled back across the top and disappeared behind the vegetation that had made its definite claim to what little ground there was for anything to grow on.

"Hey, Bill! You gotta see these!" the kid exclaimed.

I walked around the mesquite bush to see what he was talkin' about, and I had to step back to take them all in.

"What do they mean?" he asked.

"Not sure" I said "I don't reckon anyone does."

"The people who wrote them do," he stated out of ignorance. "Those people are long gone. These are a thousand years old or maybe older."

SWEET JUSTICE

"Who do you think they were?"

"The Navajo refer to them as the ancient ones, but I ain't never seen their writings this far south before."

As I studied them, my eyes were drawn to the three figures I had seen so many times before. Again, my first thought was the Father, Son and Holy Ghost. I don't know why, but that's what my gut told me they were. From there I saw the same references that I was sure were giving instruction to any that saw them. Things like hunting grounds, food caches, and water, but as I glanced farther, I could see people in chaos, holding bows, arrows, and spears. When I got to the other end, I involuntarily shuttered. There was a figure that was half man, half wolf, who seemed to be enjoying the mayhem. I stared at it more intensely. Was it a wolf or a coyote? Or maybe . . .

The word escaped my mouth after it hit me like a charging bull. "DOG!"

"What?" the kid asked.

Not wanting to jinx our mission by putting any apprehension into him, I said pointing to wall, "This one kind of looks like a frog."

"Looks like a lizard to me," he said with a chuckle. "You're probably right. We best get going."

We mounted our horses and traversed the sand dune back to the bottom of the canyon. It was about an hour before we broke out of it and found ourselves on broken, semi-flat ground that was a field of sandstone slabs. At first it was easy to follow the tracks in front of us, but it didn't take long before we were losin' precious time. Every time the tracks switched from sand to stone, it became a hunt to see any sign of where they led to because they never seemed to connect to a precise point.

"He's doing this on purpose," I concluded. "He's tryin' to throw off anyone who might be following."

"What we gonna do?" asked the kid.

"I want you to backtrack."

"Backtrack?" he exclaimed with irritation. "We're already losin' precious time."

"I know, kid, but wandering aimlessly isn't helping that. I want you to follow our trail back an eighth of a mile or so. I'm gonna to hold this position. When you get to a point where you start to lose sight of me, stop and look at me."

"Alright, Bill," he said loyally, "but I can't see how that's gonna help none."

As the kid began to cover our tracks backwards, I was amazed at how much we had crisscrossed. *You're smarter than I gave you credit for, Virg,* I thought.

When the kid reached the point that he felt he had to stop, he turned and faced me. I dismounted my horse and put a stone on her reigns and walked back about three hundred feet to where I'd seen the kid cross earlier, looked at him, turned swiftly and looked at my horse, and then called for the kid to come in.

"What did that tell you?" he asked a little exasperated.

"That they're heading that direction," I said, pointing to another canyon in the distance.

"How did you decipher that?"

"He meandered to confuse his pursuers, but he has a destination that he's headed to nonetheless, and we just figured it out."

"I'm still not following you."

SWEET JUSTICE   305

"Think about it, kid. If you're headin' somewhere that doesn't have a trail, what do you do?"

"Pick a focal point and try to head towards it as straight as possible," he answered.

It took a second or two for him to catch on. When I saw he got it I asked, "So which way do you think he's headed?"

"I think he's headed that direction too," he said, grinning.

"And I'll just bet that if we keep our eyes open as we beeline towards it, we'll come across their tracks again and again, and if we don't, we can always come back here and try again."

"Never should have doubted you, Bill," said the kid. "I knew you was smart."

"Old and experienced, kid," I stated, "old and experienced."

CHAPTER SEVENTEEN

The Demon Dog

THE SUN WAS KISSING THE western horizon by the time we neared the mouth of the canyon. On our arrival we saw that what we thought was one canyon turned out to be the gateway to three. I knew that they'd taken one of them. We'd crossed their tracks several times as we made our way there. We again found ourselves on solid sandstone, and following their tracks proved to be difficult, especially in the fading light.

"You see anything, kid?" I hollered as we swept back and forth, looking for any telltale signs.

"Nothing definite."

"Keep looking!" I shouted. "We're about out of day light."

"Got it!" he yelled "Looks like they're headed for the middle one." We brought our horses to as full a run as we dared on the slick rock until we were back on sand. Only problem was there weren't any tracks goin' into the canyon.

"Damn it!" I shouted "Where the hell did they go?"

"Sorry, they sure looked like they was headed this way to me." "It's not your fault. We're gonna have to make camp here, though,

I'm afraid. It's too dangerous to ride in the dark."

"We'll find it in the morning, Bill," the kid said, tryin' to comfort me.

"You're damn right we will," I said boldly. "The thought of what Emily's enduring with that man is more than I can take. The sad thing is all the ground we made up this afternoon we'll lose in the morning again while we figure out where that son of a bitch went."

We freed our horses of their saddles, and the kid started a fire. "I'm gonna cook you something to eat, Bill," the kid offered. "You ain't eatin' much today, and from what the mayor told me, not much for a while 'fore that."

His words reminded me that my body was still reeling from the lack of nourishment, but my concern for Emily's whereabouts had kept my mind from thinkin' 'bout it.

"Much obliged, kid. Maybe I can think clearer if my belly's full."

When we finished eating, I washed it down with a good cup of coffee and said, "Where'd ya learn to cook, kid? That was mighty tasty." "My ma was a cook for one of the hotels in town when I was a kid.

My pa liked to stay at the blacksmith's shop late into the night, so she taught me how to fend for myself."

"Well, it was damn good. Maybe you should be a cook." "No thanks. I'm not much for towns."

"You could always be a chuck wagon cook," I suggested. "They make better money than the cowboys do."

"Never thought about it," he stated. "It's somethin' to think 'bout, I reckon."

"Well, I'm bushed," I told him, "so I'm gonna think about lookin' at the back of my eyelids."

"Me too," he agreed. "You plumb tuckered me out today."

I laid there, waiting for sleep to overtake me and stewed about what Emily was going through and how she was dealin' with it. I wasn't concerned so much that she was petrified into submission because I knew she was strong and that she was a survivor. My concern was more for her mental welfare. Was she lyin' there, wonderin' if anyone was comin' for her, and if they were, would they be able to find her before Virgil did something to harm her? Or was she planning an escape? That one brought me more apprehension than the thought of her with Virgil. This was a harsh country, and there were Apaches here, hidin' from the cavalry, and they'd been known to do abhorrent things to women. The last thing I remember thinking before I fell asleep was, *Emily don't do something foolish. Just stay where you are until I can find you.*

I'd only been asleep about an hour or so when something woke me up. It wasn't a noise but more a feeling I had that somethin' wasn't

right. The breeze comin' from the canyon carried a hint of somethin' foul every once in a while. I sat there and listened, trying to hone my senses or catch movement in the darkness, but nothin' ever came, and soon I was asleep again.

Somewhere in the middle of the night, I was awakened again by sound of the kid cocking his rifle and breathing like something had scared the hell out of him.

"What is it kid?" I whispered urgently.

"Don't know," he said back in a shaky voice. "Somethin' touched me."

"Did you see it?"

"If I'd seen it, I'd a shot it!" he shouted back frantically. "It's like it was there, and then it wasn't."

"Were you dreaming?"

"Hell, no, I wasn't dreaming Bill," he said angrily. "Somethin's out there."

"Okay, kid. Calm down and keep your eyes open."

The moon was just startin' to cast its light over the top of the cliff, illuminating the desert in front of us just enough to make out shadows. "There it is!" the kid exclaimed. "What the hell is that? Look how fast it's movin'!" "Don't know, kid."

"Should I shoot it?" he asked in anticipation.

"No!" I said urgently. "It's too far away. Besides you'll give away our position to Virgil, and we need the element of surprise. It's the only chance Emily has."

We watched as it disappeared into the shadow of the cliff. As it reached its edge, it turned to look at us. Its eyes were blood red and shone into the night. The hair on my body stood at attention, and in a second, it was gone.

"What the hell was that?" the kid pleaded "What the hell was that, Bill?"

"I'm not sure," I told him again, "but we can't let it rob us of our sleep."

"I ain't goin' to sleep with that thing out there," he said in a shrill voice. "That ain't goin' to happen, no way, no how."

"We'll sleep in stints," I told him. "You go first, and I'll keep watch.

Don't worry, kid, I got your back, and I don't miss with a rifle."

At first he leaned up against his saddle and stared into the night, but eventually his eyes grew heavy, and he went to sleep again.

The words that the old Navajo medicine man had shared with me years before rang in my ears. "Be wary in the canyons at night, my white brother," he warned in broken English. "Evil things, evil things."

I turned to my interpreter and asked what he was trying to say. "We don't talk of it," he said. "If we do they come for us."

I pressed him anyway. "What might come for you?" "Skin walkers," he replied in a whisper. "Very bad, Bill." "Skin walkers? What the hell is that?"

"No talk," he kept saying. "Very bad."

Suddenly, the medicine man stood and motioned for us to follow him. When we arrived at the rug door of his Hogan, he told my companion in Navajo to wait. Seconds later he came out and began to remove my shirt, and then handed me a paste. With his hands he indicated that he wanted me to eat it. Afterwards he drew marks on me and again beckoned me to follow him. We wound up at what looked like a small tee pee made out of sticks, and he opened the hatch door for me to enter.

"What is it?" I asked the interpreter.

"It's sweat hut," he replied. "Never seen white man inside. Very honorable."

We sat for what seemed like forever while the heat began to permeate the small space. Finally, the medicine man started to chant or sing.

"What's he doing?" I asked.

SWEET JUSTICE   311

"Chase bad spirits away. Make so none can hear."

When the song ended, he again handed me some more of the paste he had made as he chanted. This time I knew what he wanted, so I used two fingers and put it in my mouth. It was bitter, but I did my best not to show it. This seemed to please him, based on the almost toothless grin he gave me after I swallowed it.

"Bad medicine," he began. "Very bad, angry brothers, kill family." "Is he telling me about the skin walkers?" I asked my companion. "Yes," he replied in a hushed tone.

"What does he mean 'kill family'?" I pressed. "Does he mean my family?"

"No," he assured me, "he mean skin walker have to kill a person in own family."

I stared at him with a look of shock.

"What the hell for?" I asked in disbelief. "What do they hope to gain?"

"Change."

"Change from what?" I inquired, a little confused.

"Dogs, wolves, many things. They witches, Bill. Want to hurt, want to make trouble, bring evil."

"Watch in canyons," the medicine man warned again, using his fingers to point at his eyes. "Very bad, very bad."

"Why is he tellin' me this?" I asked the interpreter. "Not know. Skin walker only make trouble for Navajo."

He then asked the medicine man why he was tellin' me this. The old man began to waif the smoke towards his nose with his eyes shut and softly chant again. Suddenly, his eyes shot open, and he grabbed my wrist and with terror in his eyes began to speak quickly in his native

312 MARK INKLEY

tongue. I couldn't tell what he was sayin', but I did grasp that he was warnin' me.

"What did he say?" I pleaded.

"He say that he see a vision when skin walker will want to keep you from stopping something bad. He ask ancestors to put protection around you so dog cannot kill you."

The medicine man spoke again and drew a circle in the air as he did so.

"He say draw circle around camp to keep out," my Navajo friend said. "The spirits will protect you."

Then the old Navajo patriarch went back to a trance and began to chant again.

"We go now. He must stay for two days to cleanse spirit."

I hesitated for a moment, feeling bad that my question would force him to stay in this confined space when I heard my companion forcefully say, "We go now, must hurry, Bill."

The experience stuck with me for a while, but as the years went by, I had tucked it away and allowed the dust in my mind to all but cover it up. When the moments of quiet reflection would uncover it again, I would brush it off as the rants of an old Navajo and tuck it back away. But lookin' into the darkness now and thinkin' about the situation, I hastily stood, drew a circle around our camp, and once again felt the urgency of the warnin', making the hair on my arms stand on end. *What was it?* I thought. *Is this what the medicine man had seen in his vision? What does this thing want to stop me from accomplishing? Certainly not the death of Emily. After all, why would he care about that?* I reasoned she didn't know the Navajo, so her actions one way or another would have no bearing on them. My thoughts then turned to Virgil. What could he be doin' that the skin walker wanted to see continue? And how did he know this country so well when anyone who knew him claimed he hated to be away from town and his comfortable bed?

My mind kept tryin' to put the pieces together as I kept watch in the canyons like the warning from years before had told me to do. Before I knew it, the bluish grey of an approaching morning announced itself. "Well, at least the kid got some sleep," I muttered as I went about buildin' up the fire again.

The smell of coffee made the kid stir, but when consciousness hit 'im, he jumped, grabbin' for his rifle. It took a few seconds for him to focus and realize that all was well, and then he got an embarrassed look on his face and calmly sat back down again.

"It's okay, kid. I was scared too."

"I wasn't scared," he replied defensively. "Just keepin' on my toes is all."

"Okay, kid," I said with a chuckle. "At least one of us wasn't."

He stared at the ground for a moment, shakin' the sleep from his head before speaking again.

"I thought you were gonna wake me up to take a turn at watch," he commented.

"I was," I told him, "but my mind was tryin' to make sense of things, and before I knew it, it was time for breakfast."

"What was it, Bill? Did ya figure it out?"

"Indians," I said, hopin' that would satisfy his curiosity. "That weren't no damn Indian," he shot back.

Knowing that I wasn't lyin', I said, "Believe me kid, it was."

While we ate breakfast, I told him the story of meetin' the medicine man and what I was told, and that what we saw might've been this skin walker.

"You believe that?" the kid asked. "I mean, do ya think it's real?" "Don't know, kid, but I do know that the Indians have lived here a lot longer than us, and they believe it."

"But if they only trouble their own people," the kid pointed out, "what they after us for?"

"Don't know, partner," was my reply "Don't know. It's almost light enough to be on our way though, so we best get saddled."

As the approaching light of the morning began to illuminate our surroundings, the kid saw my circle around our camp and pointed it out.

"Nothin' to fret over, kid," I assured him. "I put it there." "So you do believe it."

"I won't say one way or the other, kid," I replied sheepishly, "but after what we saw, I figured it sure couldn't hurt."

"Well, I reckon I'd a done the same. Don't know if it was your circle, but there ain't no dog tracks around this mornin'."

"Forget the dog tracks. We're lookin' for horse prints."

"I'd a bet the farm they was headed this way," the kid let me know again.

"He's makin' it hard to follow him," I pointed out, "and it was gettin' near dark, so don't beat yourself up over it."

SWEET JUSTICE   315

After makin' a quick scan for any evidence we might've missed, we started to turn to pick up the trail at the last place we'd seen it. That's when I took one last look into the mouth of the canyon and noticed what looked like material blowing in the wind.

"Hold on, kid!" I yelled. "I need to check somethin' out."

I made the hundred-yard gallop to its opening and could tell that fabric was cotton and that it hadn't been there long.

"What d'ya find, Bill?" the kid asked as he rode up.

"Good and bad. This here material looks as if it came off a woman's riding trousers, so I'd venture to guess ya'll was right; they did go down this canyon. They must've dragged somethin' to cover their tracks."

"I knew I was right," the kid said in his cocky tone. "So what's the bad?"

"There are dog tracks that start about fifty feet up yonder." "Shit. That is bad."

"Thought you weren't scared," I said teasingly.

"I ain't scared, Bill," he said in a shaky voice. "Are you?" "Nope. Just keepin' on my toes is all."

The kid looked a little embarrassed when I said it as his own words echoed in his ears.

"We goin' in or what?" he asked, trying to sound undaunted. "After you, my friend," I said. "You're the one that tracked 'em to this point. It's only fair you lead the way."

He looked at me and licked his lips then kicked his horse and rode bravely into the canyon. We only went a hundred yards when the horse tracks we were lookin' for showed up in front of us once again.

"If it hadn't been for the piece of cloth," I pointed out, "it might've been this evenin' 'fore we found 'em. Emily must've done it on purpose when she saw Virgil wipin' their trail away."

"She's pretty smart."

"Good thing, too. Lettin' 'em get another day in front of us could be a life or death situation."

We rode until about noon or a little after to a spot where the canyon widened out and three smaller canyons joined. At this point two more horses joined up with them before heading up the biggest of the three conjoining canyons.

"It looks like they're headin' back up to where we just came from," the kid speculated.

"Back up, yes," I agreed, "but this canyon appears to come out on the other side of the mountain from where we camped, and we best keep our wits about us, kid, 'cause the horses that joined 'em are Apache."

"You sure, Bill?" the kid asked apprehensively.

"I'm sure. They ain't got shoes on, and no white man would ride a horse in this country without them."

"I hate to ask this, but do ya think they might've killed 'em?" "Nope," I shot back, hoping I was right. "If they was goin' to kill them, they'd've done it here. I don't know if they're prisoners or not, but no one got off their horse, and the weight on the shoed horses ain't changed none."

"Well, that's good, ain't it?"

"It sure is, kid. But now our fight just got tougher, and it's with Apaches to boot. If they get a hold of us, they'll torture us as slowly as possible 'fore we die. Ya know that, right?"

SWEET JUSTICE 317

"Why you gotta say that, Bill?" he asked "As if the damn dog tracks ain't got me scared enough."

"I just want you to be fully aware of your fate if this turns out bad is all," I told him firmly. "You've been good to ride this far, and I'm much obliged to ya. So if you wanna turn back now, I wouldn't think any less of ya."

"Turn back? Hell no! I ain't turnin' back, Bill. I told ya I had your back, and I meant it, so let's go get your girl and get the hell out of here." We followed the five horses until they left the bottom of the canyon and started up a heavily traveled game trail that as near as we could tell led up to the mountaintop, which meant water and a cooler elevation. "Reckon I'll be damn glad to get out of this dry canyon," commented the kid. "The horses need water."

"Sure do, but we're goin' to stop here for the night anyway." "What?" the kid said in disbelief. "We got an hour of sun left. That's more than enough time to at least get up to them trees there."

"You're right, kid," I said, "but we don't know where in them trees they stopped or how many Indians may have joined 'em. I ain't in no hurry to run full on into a shootout right before the sun goes down. We'll get rested up and leave fresh in the mornin'. That way we'll have our wits about us, and if we have to fight, we have all day to do it instead of some Apache sneakin' up on us during the night. That's just my thought, kid, but you're leadin' us, so if you wanna head for them trees, let's go."

"I think we'll stay here tonight," he replied.

"That's a good idea, kid," I said facetiously. "Sure am glad I brought you along."

After we lightened our horses' loads, the kid started to collect firewood and stack it by his makeshift pit.

"No fire tonight, kid," I said.

"How we gonna cook? I'm starving."

"Eat some jerked beef and biscuits. If we light a fire, the glow is gonna illuminate this canyon and give away our position. It's too dangerous. I'd just as soon let 'em wonder where we are. Maybe keep them from gettin' sleep, worryin' 'bout us sneakin' up on them."

"Maybe they don't know we're here."

"If those dog tracks are from what I think they are," I pointed out, "they know we're here alright, so let's keep 'em guessin'. What d'ya think?"

"I think you're damn smart, Bill."

"Well, I hope that don't change," I said apprehensively, "when I suggest you give the remainder of your water to your horse."

"It won't," he replied, "but what we gonna do if we don't find water in the mornin'?"

"We'll deal with that when it comes, kid," I answered. "But if our horses can't get us outta here, it won't matter much whether we do or not."

"I reckon you're right" he agreed, as he poured the remainder of his canteens into his hat.

I rose to do the same, and as our horses drank, the kid looked at me like he wanted to say somethin' but hesitated to do so.

"Somethin' on your mind, kid?" I asked.

"Well, I don't want you to think I'm scared or nothin', but you think you'll be drawin' that there circle around us tonight?"

"There's nothin' wrong with bein' scared, kid," I assured him. "It's how you react to it that matters. But yeah, I'll be drawin' that circle tonight for sure."

"Good," he said, still tryin' to sound brave. "Just a precaution, right?"

"Right, kid," I agreed with a chuckle.

We stared up at the stars for a while in silence, each of us comin' to grips with our situation at hand and makin' plans in our minds as to what we might do and how we might react come tomorrow if and when the showdown took place. The kid finally broke the silence.

"Ya think we'll find 'em tomorrow, Bill?" "Reckon it's possible. You nervous?"

"Little bit. I ain't never fought no Indians before, and it don't help that my first will be with Apaches."

"Just watch your back, kid," I warned. "They're sneaky and know how to blend in with their surroundings. Hopefully, they haven't met up with any others."

"What if they have?"

"If we get into a mess of 'em, kid," I stated firmly, "you high tail it outta there, you understand? Don't worry 'bout me; you just run like hell. Ya hear?"

"I would never leave you, Bill," he assured me.

"If we're outnumbered by Apache, kid," I said, looking him in the eye, "tryin' to be loyal will get you killed. So promise me you'll run, or you ain't goin' with me tomorrow."

He swallowed hard, and even in the darkness, I could see his Adams apple travel down his throat.

"I promise, Bill," he said "Good. That's real good."

After that we both went back to our own thoughts, both of us a little nervous about our nightly visitor but unwilling to speak about it.

"It sure is dark," the kid suddenly said.

"Moon should be up soon," I said, tryin' to offer comfort. "You okay for first watch?"

"Reckon so," he replied nervously. "You must be tired." "Dog tired," I said without thinking.

His head whipped around when I said it, and he gave me cross look. "Sorry, kid, it just slipped out," I said apologetically. "Do you want me to take first watch instead?"

"No, I'll be alright," he replied bravely. "You need to sleep, and I might need you more tomorrow against them Apache."

"Everything is goin' to be alright, kid," I stated while drawing a circle. "Wake me up when the moon is over your head."

I pulled my hat down over my eyes, hopin' that the night would be peaceful for a change 'cause what the kid said was true: I was tired, and I knew in the back of my mind that come sun-up I'd need every faculty I had, if more Apache had joined them. I hoped that if Emily was in the presence of Indians she wasn't a prisoner because at least that way she might be safe from any harm they would normally dish out whenever they came across white women.

The fact that they hadn't been killed on the spot led me to believe that they weren't captives, and it got my mind racing as to what Virgil's relationship with them might be. I pondered about the third horse that was loaded up, and then it came to me. Virgil was dealin' somethin' to them, and Apache only wanted two things from the white man's world: guns and whiskey. *Idiot,* I thought. More than one man had let greed rob him of his judgment about providing these two things to Apaches.

Both in their own right could be dangerous but when combined and fed to Indians, the repercussions were almost always explosive and violent. *Doesn't he know,* I thought, *that once they get what they want the first to fall victim to them is usually the provider? You've put yourself on dangerous ground, Virgil. And if it was just you, I'd say you deserve it, but now your stupidity has Emily on that same ground with you. If your guess is correct,* I told myself, *you better find her tomorrow, Bill, or it might be too late.*

I took one last look at the kid before closin' my eyes. He was sittin' pale-faced, starin' deep into the darkness. *You're in good hands* was my last conscious thought before the dream world took me to the mountains again.

The next thing I remember was the kid shakin' me awake. When I rolled over to look at him, he didn't notice that his efforts had worked 'cause he was starin' wide-eyed up the canyon.

"What is it, kid?" I whispered, sensing the danger. "Our friend's back."

"Did you see 'im?"

"No, but can't you smell it?" he shot back.

The smell hit me at almost the same time he said it, and I recognized it from the previous night. It was the odor that preceded our mystery guest's arrival.

"Keep your eyes open, kid," I warned, "and don't panic. We're bein' watched. I can feel it."

I stayed low to the ground and took my position between two small boulders just inside the circle I'd drawn in the sand. The kid's position allowed him to see up and down the canyon, but the rocks he was sittin' on robbed him of seein' anything in front of 'em. I had moved to that spot so as to cover all vantage points. That's when I noticed the dog tracks in the sand just outside the circle. Whatever it was, it was smart, because it had managed to come within fifty feet of us unnoticed. I tuned my ears to listen for any movement in the darkness. In a flash his eyes appeared out of the darkness, and it growled at me while lookin' at the drawn circle in the sand. Then just as quickly, it was gone. I thought I heard a faint scratch from the towering wall at our backs.

"Get undercover, kid," I said in a loud whisper. "I think it's on the wall behind you."

No sooner had I said it a large rock came down and crashed right where he'd been sittin' just seconds before.

"Holy shit, Bill. You saved my life," the kid said in a state of shock. "I only prolonged it if you don't keep your wits about you," I stated in a tone indicating we weren't out of trouble yet.

Another rock came down, hitting close to where the kid had moved to. "How come he's only after me?" he asked excitedly.

"He's not," I assured him, "but I think you're the only one he can see. Keep his attention. I'm gonna crawl outta here and come up behind him if I can."

I removed my spurs and then shimmied on my belly, keepin' myself hidden behind the stones that littered the ground until I crossed the circle I had drawn hours earlier. At that point there were large rocks I could stand behind without being seen, and I looked for any kind of shelf in the cliff that would allow me to gain access to the ledge that the rocks were being hurled from. I found a path that I thought would get me there, but because of the steepness of the wall, I knew I would have to take

SWEET JUSTICE 323

four steps without stopping, and doin' it without makin' noise was gonna be tricky.

"Damn it! Think, Bill," I said to myself. Then it came to me. *Take your boots off; it'll give you better traction and make less noise.* I quickly slid them off and stood to begin my assent. That's when I felt my feet sink into the sand. I couldn't keep the memory of my nightmare from creepin' up on me. I hastily took a step to the wall, just in case I sank farther and stepped on a tumbleweed that'd been blown into two rocks that lay at the base of the wall. The stickers on it found their way between my big toe and nail, causin' a shearing pain to shoot through my foot and up my leg. I stumbled a little while I freed my foot from its grasping hook and lost my balance as I fell towards the rock. Instinctively, I put my hand out to stop my fall, but it was the hand that had my rifle in it, and I didn't want the butt to crack against the rock. So at the last moment, I turned my hand, rotating the rifle towards me and wound up stopping myself with the back of my hand, rolling the skin back as it brought my body to a stop. So now my foot was bleedin' and my hand as well, and I still hadn't scaled the wall.

Whatever it was up above me was still tryin' to hit the kid with rocks, so I waited until I heard one hit the ground and shatter before I moved, hopin' it'd mask any noise I might make. My timing was impeccable, and I easily made the four big steps up the cliff face. From there I'd have to get around a cactus that'd found a spot between the stones to prove to them that it could and would live there whether they liked it or not. But as I skirted around its upper side, there was only about a foot or so between it and the cliff behind. The ground was steep, and my shoulder found the cactus's finger like needles, grabbing hold of my shirt and holding fast. I knew that if I kept moving forward that it'd tear my shirt and give away my cover I had thus far suffered to obtain. I gently put the rifle down and went to work in an attempt to free myself without losin' my balance again on the steep hill.

After what seemed like an eternity, I finally found success and again picked up my rifle and made my way through two huge boulders that acted as a threshold into the shelf that was above the kid, As I approached the position where I thought our midnight guest was, I could smell the stench so strongly that it burned in my nose. I paused a moment and thought of Emily and the danger she was in. As much as I wanted to shoot this creature that had robbed me of sleep and time, I couldn't take the chance of blowin' our cover with a gunshot. I flipped my rifle around to use as a club instead before makin' my attack. Hand and both feet bleedin' now, I took a deep breath, came out of the boulders, and took the thing— what turned out to be an Indian in a wolf's skin—by surprise. His black eyes stared at me in terror, and then his face seemed to morph in an instant. He growled and showed yellow, sharp teeth, and just before the butt of my rifle hit him full on the head, his eyes turned blood red and shined in the darkness.

The impact of my gun hit him hard, and even in the darkness I could see the blood spray as he fell over the edge of the cliff, landing about twenty feet from the kid.

"Is he dead?" I called down.

"If he's not, he's goin' to be, judgin' from the blood he's losin'," the kid replied.

"Hold on," I said. "I'm comin' down."

We looked at 'im, neither one of us wantin' to touch 'im, partly because of the fear he'd put in us, but mostly because of the stench that permeated him.

"Let's get 'im the hell out of our camp and get some shuteye," I finally said.

We drug him out of the circle I'd drawn and quickly threw some sand over him to mask the stench and then laid down to get some shuteye.

"What d'ya think he wanted with us, Bill?" asked the kid.

"Don't rightly know," I answered, "but I have an idea. The part that's got me bothered some is how and why a Navajo skin walker is clear down here in Apache country."

"Maybe they's workin' together," the kid commented.

"I don't think so," I replied. "Navajo are peaceful unless you provoke them. Apache, on the other hand, are warriors. The two are bitter enemies."

"So what's your idea?"

"I think Virgil's sellin' guns and whiskey to the Apache. And I think they have somethin' big planned for 'em, some kind of raid or somethin'."

"So do you think the skin walker is in on it?"

"Maybe not directly, but I do know that the medicine man told me they like to see evil and chaos. Guns and whiskey in the right Apache hands would certainly deliver both. The problem is if I'm right, Emily's in grave danger, and her only hope now is us, kid, so we best get some sleep. Sun'll be up before we know it."

We pulled our blankets up over us, and as tired as we both were, it wasn't long before we were asleep.

Artwork by Mark Inkley

CHAPTER EIGHTEEN

Indian Troubles

A COYOTE CRY WOKE ME up, and I saw it as a good thing 'cause the light of a new day was peakin' over the horizon. I loved the early morning sky this time of year because Venus and Jupiter were brilliant in the eastern sky, and both were visible in the crack of the canyon. I started a little fire to get some coffee goin', knowin' I might be takin' a risk but fully aware that we were both goin' to need it today. I made a curtain of sorts to keep its flame from lighting the far canyon wall. The kid rose up when he smelled it and quickly joined me in anticipation of gettin' some.

When it was ready, I handed him a cup and asked if he remembered my instructions.

"I do, Bill," he assured me, "but I still ain't happy 'bout it." "You're young, kid," I reminded him, "with a lot of life in front of you. Don't throw that away on a fight you can't win."

He sat in silence for a moment, drinkin' his coffee before speakin' again. "You're a good friend, Bill, and I'm sure glad I got the chance to know ya."

327

"You say that like I'm already dead."

"I just know how you are," he pointed out, "and if there is a mess of Indians, I'm sure you're not leavin' Emily behind, even if it means your life."

"I'm sure not," I agreed, "but this is my fight, and if it comes to that, you just know I chose it. Your fight will come another time, and you'll know when that is, when the chance of gettin' killed will pale in comparison to what you're fightin' for."

"The last few months have been good for me, I reckon," said the kid. "After gettin' to know ya, I've got a clearer perspective of where I wanna go and the kind a man I want to be, and I'm much obliged to ya for that."

"Well, that's good, kid. I'm glad I could help, but I ain't dead yet, and I don't plan on bein' that way, so what d'ya say we go win this here fight and I'll go with ya?"

"I sure like the sound of that, Bill," he said with a smile. "Yes sir, I like that a lot."

The coolness of the night was quickly being chased away by the approaching day, and I could tell it was going to be a hot one. The Mojave was the only place I'd ever experienced frying pan heat and bitter cold all in the same twenty-four hours. As the chill in my extremities began to flee, I knew today'd be no exception.

"We best break camp, kid, and take advantage of the remaining darkness to put some distance behind us."

"You think that's safe? If they can't see us, that means we can't see them."

"Well then, we'll just have to keep our eyes open, I reckon. Besides, I'm sure they're in the trees up yonder. After makin' coffee we're in need of findin' water 'fore it gets too hot, so we're just gonna have to chance it."

SWEET JUSTICE 329

We saddled our horses and packed our gear in silence as our minds carried the burden of anticipation and apprehension of our predicament and duty. When we were ready to leave, the kid headed towards the rocks below us.

"Where ya goin'. kid?" I called out.

"Gotta pee," he said, "and I wanna take one last look at our friend you killed before we go."

I shuttered when he said it as the events of the night before came to the surface and the conscious reflection reminded my brain that my feet and hands still hurt. The years of rough and tumble combined with the war had trained me to push things like pain and fatigue to the back of my mind so I could face the challenges at hand. That is, at least, 'til somethin' brought 'em to the surface, which is what the kid's comment had done.

"He's not here, Bill," the kid exclaimed.

"What?" I answered in disbelief. "There's no way he survived that fall. You sure you're lookin' in the right place?"

"Hell yeah, I'm sure," he shot back. "He ain't here."

Damn it, I thought. *If it survived, then they might know where we are, and they' ll be anticipating our coming.*

"Come on, kid. Let's ride," I coaxed. "I reckon our job just got tougher."

The approaching light allowed us to see in front of us, but it also cast shadows that had a way of trickin' the mind when anticipating trouble around any corner. It made the kid jumpy and a little trigger happy.

"Breathe, kid," I said. "Just take it easy and keep your eyes open. I'll let you know when to shoot."

"I thought I saw somethin' is all," he replied.

330   Mark Inkley

"They ain't in this canyon kid," I assured him. "Least not here anyways."

"How do you know, Bill?" he asked a little irritated.

I could sense that he was nervous so I answered him calmly. "'Cause, kid, there's no place for an ambush on sheer cliff walls. Besides, they're in need of water just as bad as us. I can almost guarantee you they're up in the trees where this here canyon starts."

"If you say so," he replied with a shaky voice.

"I say so, kid. You've gotta relax, or you're not gonna make it out of here alive," I warned. "Keep your wits about you and think before you act, or this is as far as you go, ya hear?"

"Okay, Bill," he replied after taking a deep breath. "I'll try." "Don't try, kid. Do," I said absolutely. "You know why your friends died tryin' to rob that ore wagon?"

"Jeez, Bill, what ya gotta bring that up for?" he asked.

"They died because they didn't think before they acted, and the only reason you're still alive is 'cause the man ridin' shotgun did."

"Yeah," he answered after a short pause, "I get it."

"Good. Now, let's go save Emily's life while keepin' our own. What d'ya say?"

"I say that sounds good, Bill. Let's do it," he said in a calmer voice. We continued in silence until the sun chased us up the canyon, bringin' the heat, and it wasn't long before the lack of water took its toll on us and our horses. Fortunately, I picked them wisely, anticipating long distances between water holes, and they didn't disappoint, but I could tell the kid wasn't as used to it as they were.

"You gonna make it, kid?"

SWEET JUSTICE 331

"Think so. I got a powerful thirst, but it ain't killed me yet." "Suck on a pebble," I told him.

"Do *what*?" he asked in a tone like I was tryin' to speed up his dehydration.

"It's another trick I learned from the Navajo. It'll help create spit and keep you from breathin' through your mouth."

He looked at me like he still didn't believe me but bent over and grabbed one off a ledge as we passed and popped it in his mouth.

"I hope this works," the kid said, rollin' it on his tongue.

"It'll work," I guaranteed him, showing off the one in my mouth.

It was about another hour before we left the cactus behind and started seein' juniper trees take their place.

"Okay, kid," I said breaking the silence. "This is where we keep sharp, understand?"

He nodded that he did, as he sucked on his pebble.

"See that canyon with the greener trees up ahead?" I gestured. "That's where we'll find water, I reckon, but it may also be where we find trouble."

He followed my finger as he spit the pebble out of his mouth. "Let's do this, Bill," he said confidently. "I'm damn ready to be outta this desert, even if it means goin' back to prison."

"Me too, kid," I agreed with a smile, "me too."

As we came around the last bend leadin' into the canyon, the horses' heads perked up, and it spooked the kid some, I could tell by the way he tensed up.

"I think the horses hear somethin', Bill," he said anxiously.

"Give 'em some reign," I replied calmly. "Could be they just smell water."

"Well, hell, let's go get some then," he said. "I'm dyin' here." "Remember what I said 'bout thinkin' 'fore you act?" I reminded him.

"They might be up there too," he said proudly.

"Now you're gettin' it. What d'ya say we tie our horses and sneak up and have a look see?"

The kid seemed happy that I'd ask his opinion, and he replied, "I say lead the way, Bill."

"Tie your horse good, kid," I said firmly. "They want water real bad, and if they can get away, they'll bolt for it and give us away."

"Good thinkin'," he agreed as he tied another loop around the tree. We moved slowly as we went, and before long we could hear a small spring trickling. The sound made my mouth dryer than it'd been as my body craved the coolness it offered. About that time I heard a horse whinny in the distance and motioned for the kid to get down. "Did you hear that?" I asked.

"Sure did. How far d'ya think they are from us?"

"Where they are and where they tied their horses might be two different places, but I'd say a couple hundred yards or so."

"Didn't think about that. Sure am glad you're here, Bill."

"I'm glad you are too, kid," I replied. "Now keep your eyes and ears open, Them Injuns can be five feet in front of you and you might not see 'em if you're not payin' attention."

We came to a spot in the ravine where we thought there'd be water, but in August it was runnin' far below the boulders that littered the ground. The sound of it rushing under our feet was a teasing menace as we continued tryin' to get closer to our target. I signaled to the kid to cross over to the other side and keep pace with me. I had two reasons: one was to broaden our scope of the terrain in front of us; the other was to keep us from bein' attacked at the same time—if and when it happened—because we were too close together.

I motioned for him to pull his knife and keep it handy just in case. I was glad I did because all at once I heard the blood-curdling holler of an Indian as he leapt at the kid from his hiding place with his hatchet the Apache were so fond of. Fortunately, the kid saw it comin', and as his attacker pounced, he was able to avoid takin' it to the head directly, but it did find its way into his arm tearing at the flesh as it went, causin' the kid to yelp in pain but also sendin' him into survival mode. The Apache warrior rolled to one knee and leapt at him again, but this time the kid side-stepped and drove his knife deep into the side of the Apache's stomach, tearin' at his guts from the momentum and stoppin' him cold. The Indian started to scream, and the kid shut him up with the butt of his rifle, bringing the sound of rushing water back to the ravine. He looked at his arm bleeding quite heavily and then at me in a state of shock.

I had just started towards him when I felt a searing pain in my leg. When I looked down to see what it was, I saw an arrow stickin' out just above my knee. Before I could react, I was on the ground with an Indian straddling me, knife in hand and a wild look in his eye. He hesitated goin' for the kill, drinkin' in his victory. His excitement and youthful cockiness allowed me to grab a rock and hit him in the face, knocking him off balance and giving me the advantage to roll him off of me. He came to his feet, clearly upset and prepared to attack again. I searched for my knife that'd been knocked out of my hand, but it was too far away to get to, so as he lunged at me. I did the only thing I could: I punched him in the face, knocking most of his front teeth out of his head as his knife found its home in the meat of my shoulder. My punch, true to form, had knocked him flat on his back, and the astonished look on his face was only wiped away when I took his knife and drove it deep into his chest.

By this time the kid had found his way over to me, looked at the dead Indian and asked if we could go get some water now. His comment made me laugh in spite of the pain, and soon he was laughin' with me. "Sure, kid," I said between gasps of pain and laughter, "but can I get this damn arrow outta my leg first?"

I reached down and broke the projectile off at the back of my leg and instructed the kid to pull it out from the front.

"You sure, Bill?" he asked apprehensively. "What if it hit an artery?" "If it did, kid, I'm gonna die anyway. But if we don't get it out now,

it's gonna swell, and then it'll kill me for sure. Just grab it and pull. And, kid," I pleaded, "don't hesitate. Just yank as hard and fast as you can, even if I scream."

The kid grabbed it with both hands and tugged with all his might.

The pain was excruciating, but once it was out I found relief.

"Much obliged, kid. Now let's get ourselves patched up. We need to finish the job we came to do."

SWEET JUSTICE

335

From the amount of blood that had saturated the kid's shirt, I expected to find a worse wound than I did. Turned out to be more flesh than muscle, and it had almost stopped bleeding by the time I got to it. However, enough hide had been removed that infection was a real threat, and I knew my wounds were worse so I anxiously said, "Now we have to get to some water, kid."

"Sounds like it's under our feet," he pointed out. "Let me move some rocks."

In spite of my pain, I grinned when he said it and then gently informed him that it was probably two or three feet down and that it would take longer to move the stones than it would to follow the stream bed 'til we found it on the surface.

"That makes more sense," he agreed.

After about fifty yards we, found a spot where it cascaded down a waterfall of sorts. It was still behind rocks, but the falling water splashed out as it hit the boulders underneath, allowing me to soak our bandanas enough to scrub out the dirt.

"I wish like hell I could get a handful of that," the kid said wantingly. I took his bandana and soaked it to the point of dripping and told him to squeeze it into his mouth. He did so quicker than a bullet and then looked at me sheepishly for not thinkin' of it on his own. The second and third time he eagerly did it on his own, however, happy to have learned a new trick.

"Not too much, kid," I warned. "Wait 'til we find it above ground 'fore you drink anymore."

When I was finished, I took my bandana and began to scrub his arm, knowing it could be days before we'd see a doctor. I wasn't gentle about it either. I wanted to get it as clean as I could before wrapping it. He grimaced from the pain but took it like a man until I was finished. "Now take yours and make a bandage, kid, and make sure you cover the whole wound."

I then peeled my shirt back to see what damage I had to my shoulder. The knife had entered the muscle just as it begins to roll into the arm and tore out the side as my attacker fell. As near as I could tell, it'd barely missed the shoulder bone, but I knew I needed to stop the bleeding. After I scrubbed it as good as I could, I told the kid to keep pressure on it while I took yucca plant fibers and rolled them together, making a primitive thread, then fashioning a cactus needle to accept the thread.

"You have to sew it up, kid," I said. "I can't do it with one arm." "I ain't never done this before, Bill," the kid stated with apprehension.

"It's alright," I assured him. "I'll talk you through it. Soon as you pull the bandage away, pinch the center of the tear and quickly poke the needle through."

"I'm not sure I can," he said with shaky hands.

"Yes, you can, kid," I said firmly. "Just take a breath and steady those hands and be true when you commit. We don't have time to make another needle, understand?"

The kid swallowed hard and removed the bandage, pinched the flesh together, and shoved the needle through. The pain went clear to my toes, and when he saw my reaction, he hesitated for a moment.

"Don't stop. Come around and do it again and then pull on the thread to close the gap. But not to hard or you'll break the strands."

SWEET JUSTICE

After the second time through, the kid got a feel for it, and before long it was closed enough to stop most of the bleeding.

"Not bad, kid. Maybe you should be a saw bones."

He knew I meant doctor when I said it but questioned why us old-timers called them that. It reminded me of our age gap, and I realized that the war was over before he was even born.

"Because, kid, doctors in the Civil War spent more time sawin' limbs off to stop gangrene than they did anything else, that's why."

"That must've been hard," he said solemnly, "bein' in that war, I mean."

"We're in one now, kid," I said, trying to change the subject, "so I reckon we best stay focused."

The wound on my leg was pretty clean, all points considered. The hole in the back was only as big as the arrowhead that entered there; the one in the front was a little bigger but not by much. As luck would have it, the arrow was released close enough to me that it didn't really have time to go into a spin. It was obvious that it'd missed my artery, so I tore a piece of my shirt off to create a tourniquet I hoped would slow the bleedin' 'til we were in more favorable circumstances where I could cauterize it. When we were done, I told the kid we needed to move on and asked him if he was up for it.

"Let's go," he said eagerly, in spite of his injuries. "We got a job to do."

"You got sand, kid. You'll do just fine."

"Much obliged, Bill," he said proudly. "What's our next move?"

"You sit tight and keep your eyes open. I'm gonna bring the horses in for water."

"I'll go, Bill. I ain't nearly as beat up as you—or old," he offered with a smile.

"My granddad always said you're only as old as you feel," I said in response, "and right now I feel damn old so I'll let ya, but keep sharp, kid, understand?"

"Got it. I'll be right back. With any luck we'll be on our way home tonight."

I watched him walk away, thinkin' to myself that I was lucky to have him along. If that attack had happened when I was by myself, they would've killed me for sure. I turned back to scan the horizon, searching for any danger that lay ahead, determined to avoid walkin' into an ambush again. I fine-tuned my vision to look for anything that looked slightly out of place, tryin' hard not to stare at any one thing for too long. Your mind can play tricks on you when it switches to tunnel vision and not only make you see things that aren't there, but also make you miss things that are. I moved rocks to expose water for the horses to drink, tryin' to avoid lettin' it happen to me.

It was about fifteen minutes or so 'fore I caught the movement of another Indian just above the trail we'd have to travel if we were to continue forward. The only way to avoid it would be to backtrack a quarter of a mile and come in way above them, and that idea came with a whole new batch of negatives. One was the loss of time it would cost and two was there was no way to tell if our new route would feed us back into the canyon or put us into cliffs and rockslides.

Not knowin' the terrain, I didn't wanna take that chance, so I quickly went to work deciphering a plan that'd put us on the offensive instead of the other way around. Their choice of terrain for an ambush was almost perfect; the trail would lead us into a bottleneck with no place to run and allow them clear shots down on us as we passed through. The one flaw to it was the fact that there was a horseshoe bend that preceded it that would put us out of their vision for at least seven or eight minutes. I hoped for the latter because if the idea I had was going to work to our advantage, we'd need all the time we could find. It wasn't long 'fore I could hear the kid bringin' the horses up the draw. It amazed me how noisy horses could be compared to a man on foot. This worked well into my plan because ears tend to lock onto the loudest noise and focus there while all other noise is blocked. The horses drank eagerly as soon as the kid gave them leave to do so.

"See anything?" he asked as he slid in alongside me in the rocks. "Yep. There's more Injuns up on that ridge there."

"How many?" he asked nervously. "Could you see?"

"No," I said flatly, "but there's at least two. They never run alone." "Looks like that's our only path up," he pointed out. "What we gonna do?"

"You sure you want to do this, kid?" I asked, giving him a chance to opt out. "This sure could get hairy."

"I'm with ya, Bill," he stated firmly, "all the way to the end if needs be."

"Okay, kid, but no hero stuff, remember. If the odds are against you and you can get away, you make damn sure you do, ya hear?"

"I know," he shot back in exasperation, "I know. Jeez, how many times you gonna tell me that?"

"As many as it takes 'til it sinks in, kid. Men your age think they're invincible, but you're not. I sure don't want your life to end on my watch."

"Got it. So what's the plan?"

"I'll tell you on our way up there."

"What if there's more between here and there?" the kid asked in a heightened voice.

"They know we're comin', and they have a good ambush spot," I replied. "So I think we're pretty safe 'til we get there."

"How can you be so sure?" he asked, hoping for a good answer. "'Cause they don't know I saw 'em, so they think they have the advantage. The best thing we can do is let 'em keep thinkin' that. By ridin' like we think we won, that'll keep 'em dumbed down with confidence and give our attack the element of surprise."

"Your wisdom sure never disappoints, Bill. I trust your judgment, so let's go dance the dance."

We mounted our now freshly watered horses and rode the trail lookin' like we were out for a Sunday stroll and tried our best to look like the sitting ducks they though we were. All the while I was bringin' the kid up to speed on my plan, workin' out any deviations that might occur 'til we came to the bend that put us out of their vision.

"Guns loaded, kid?" I asked hurriedly.

"Yep," he replied, "Rifle and two pistols."

"Wait for the horses to get around the bend 'fore you move," I reminded him, "and then don't hesitate to get up that hill. If you can keep me in your line of sight once I get up my side, we'll try and move in at the same time."

SWEET JUSTICE   341

"Got it."

"Then let's do this," I stated confidently.

We slid off our horses and gave them a sharp smack on the ass to get them runnin' and took off on foot up the steep hills on both sides, hopin' that our horses' runnin' would mask the sound of slidin' rocks under our feet. My leg hurt somethin' awful, and I struggled to get up the steep terrain as quickly as I felt I needed to, but the thought of Emily kept me goin', even though the exertion started it to bleedin' again. The plan worked perfectly. I figured because now we were in the cover of junipers and, as near as I could tell, undetected to boot. I motioned to the kid to move forward slowly, and with my two fingers pointing to my eyes, tellin' him to keep a close watch for danger, I hoped that our attack earlier would remind him of how well they could blend in and hide and keep him on his toes. I hoped he could really shoot as well as he claimed he could. I had seen lots of men that could shoot targets, cans, and even moving objects without missing but fall apart when bullets were bein' shot at them. It was a whole different animal when death and danger were thrown into the mix.

I didn't have to wait long to find out, however, because as soon as our horses had come into view, minus their riders, our attackers realized quickly that they'd been fooled and were up in the state of chaos I'd hoped they would be. Before they could put two and two together on where we might be, we were on top of 'em. The first one to notice was about fifty yards away when he saw the kid, and in a state of panic he took a wild shot at him. The kid didn't hesitate to return fire, and his bullet found its mark, hitting him in the heart. After that, bullets were flyin' everywhere, and the fight was on. The kid kept his cool and was able to keep 'em at bay, allowing me to sneak undetected behind them across the ravine, which by now had turned more into a flat meadow of sorts filled with sagebrush and early fall flowers. The contrast between the rugged beauty and the ugly fight crossed my mind as I watched the three remaining take turns firin' at the kid.

Unnoticed, I was able to take my Henry and patiently put the one that seemed to be bravest in my sights. The distance between us was about four hundred feet, so I was glad for the time to take a deep breath and slowly squeeze the trigger without havin' to dodge bullets. I watched as he fell, knowin' that my bullet had found 'im long before the sound of my gun had. The other two scrambled to find cover once my location was realized, and in so doing one of them accidentally put himself, for a split second, into the kid's line of fire, and he didn't miss his chance. I heard his gun at the same time I watched his intended targets feet leave the ground as the bullet hit him square in the chest.

The last one, realizing he had no way out but death, quickly threw his gun down and put his arms in the air. I kept my gun pointed at him as I rose up and headed his way. The kid, judging that we must've won from my action did the same, and we closed in on what was now our prisoner. When I got to him, the first thing I noticed was that he wasn't Apache like the others but rather a young Navajo boy who as near as I could tell was about seventeen years old.

"What are you doin' with these Apaches?" I asked him.

SWEET JUSTICE   343

He didn't answer but just stood there wide-eyed and frozen. With what little Navajo I'd learned, I let him know that we was friends with his people and attempted to ask my question again.

He surprised me when he answered in broken English. "Fighting for my people," he said defiantly.

"Your people have no need to fight," I reminded him. "They have their land and are a peaceful people."

"White man take Indian land," he said bravely. "We fight to get back."

"How?" I pressed. "What's goin' on here."

"White man and girl sell us guns," he said. "With guns we are same.

The more we kill, more guns we get."

"All your going to do is get yourself killed like your friends here," I pointed out, "and start somethin' that'll hurt your people not help them. If you start killin' white people, the military and everyone that barely tolerates you will hunt you down and kill every Indian they see in the process. That's not helpin' your people, my friend."

I watched as the words I spoke rolled around in his head and saw what seemed like such a good and brave thing become a foolish idea in his mind.

"Where is this white man and girl?" I asked.

Again he held his tongue like all young men will do if they think they're turnin' on their friends.

"Tell me," I coaxed calmly, "and I'll let you ride outta here unharmed if you promise to go home and rid yourself of these foolish ideas and if you promise not to bring any more harm to your people. Otherwise, you can join your friends here, and I'll find 'em myself."

"There are more Apache," he said. "They will kill me if I tell you." "Not if you leave now," I assured him. "The cavalry will catch up with them soon, and you best not be with 'em when that happens. Tell me where the girl is, and I'll let you go," I said again.

"They on way to Apache camp," he finally said. "'Bout day's ride from here." "How far ahead of us are they?" I asked impatiently.

"They leave when you kill friends this morning," he confessed. "We came to stop you 'fore joinin' them."

"Much obliged, friend," I said thankfully. "Now go home and stay outta trouble. That's how you can help your people."

He stared at me for a few moments, hesitating like he didn't believe me.

"Go, my friend," I coaxed. "We won't kill you; you have my word on that."

He started to leave and then stopped and turned around. "Take lower trail," he said. "Only Indian know about pass. Very fast."

CHAPTER NINETEEN

Running Out of Time

"WHAT D'YA SUPPOSE HE MEANT by that?" asked the kid.

"Not sure. But we've gotta catch up to Emily before they get to that Apache camp, or all our cards'll be on the table."

I started to search for our horses as quickly as my leg would allow. The climb and battle had taken its toll on it, and I could feel my heart beat as the blood found its way to the hole. It didn't take long to spot them where the spring created a pool, and I quickly started headin' that way.

"Damn, Bill," the kid exclaimed, "you're bleedin' real bad."

I looked down at the front of my leg, and the bleedin' didn't seem too bad, all points considered. "It's not that bad. Let's keep goin'."

"The back of your pant leg is saturated, Bill. We gotta do something now."

I twisted to see what he was so excited about and quickly realized he was right. If I kept losin' blood like that, I wasn't gonna make it very far.

345

"What can we do?" asked the kid, full of worry.

"Tie the tourniquet tighter is all we can do. We don't have time for anythin' else at the moment."

I dropped my trousers to retie the tourniquet and could tell that if I didn't get to a doctor soon this wound'd probably kill me. But my desire to save Emily pushed the fear to the back of my mind as I pulled the cloth as hard and tight as I could. I was about to pull my pants back up when our Navajo friend came out of the trees with some kind of plant and was tearin' strips from it and chewing them up into a wad.

"This help," he said as he undid the tourniquet and began to push the wad into the hole in my leg. "Stop bleeding. Numb pain."

After he had shoved more of the same into the back of my leg, he handed me more of the plant and told me to use it if the bleedin' started again and warned us to not forget the circle at night.

"Skin walker very angry."

Then as quickly as he came, he was gone again.

I could feel the pain subside almost instantly, so I tied the bandage around it again and stood to pull my trousers up.

"I'll go for the horses," said the kid. "You best rest here a spell." "I'm alright. We'll go together."

"No offense, Bill," he replied, "but I can move a hell of a lot faster without you."

The wisdom in his words rang true, and all I could do was motion for him to go.

"I'll hurry," he promised. "We'll be back on the trail 'fore you know it."

"Thanks, kid. I owe ya one."

SWEET JUSTICE   347

I laid down under the shade of a tree and closed my eyes. It wasn't the cool mountains in New Mexico, but it was as close as I'd been in a long time, so I took advantage of it to catch up on a few zzz's while I waited for the kid to return.

My instincts woke me from some much-needed rest when my subconscious sensed someone standin' over me. I drew my pistol like lightning without thinking.

"It's me, Bill!" the kid screamed with fear. "We gotta go." "Sorry, kid. I must've fallen asleep."

"It's alright," he said. "You'd think I'd a learned my lesson the first day we met, so I suppose I'm partially to blame."

"No, kid, you're not," I assured him. "The life I chose made me this way, I reckon."

"We've come a long way since the day we met, haven't we, Bill?" commented the kid.

"Sure have, kid, sure have."

We rode as fast as we dared push our horses for an hour or so when we came to a place where the trail split.

"I wonder if this was what our Indian friend was talking 'bout," the kid questioned.

"Don't know, but this is a low trail. What d'ya want to do?" "You askin' me?"

"I am, kid. What does your gut tell you?"

"My gut says that we can trust the Navajo," he answered firmly. "I think we should take the lower trail."

"Mine too," I agreed. "But with Emily's life on the line and the fact that we're runnin' outta time, I just wanted a second opinion."

We again brought our horses to a full gallop and headed for what at first appeared to be a box canyon.

By now we were in deep sand, and there was no trail to follow that would indicate anyone traveled it. I started to wonder if our friend had led us on a wild goose chase to allow Virgil plenty of time to reach the Apache camp safely. When we arrived at the back of the canyon, it looked like it came to a dead end, and I began to curse myself for not turning back when we lost the trail. I was about to tell the kid to turn around when I noticed that the natural formation was an optical illusion; what looked like solid rock at a glance was really the rock behind it. I continued forward, half expecting my horse to run into the wall but instead found myself at a place where two canyons met and, as luck would have it, another place where the water pooled after flash floods.

"That's the damndest thing I ever seen," said the kid. "It looked like the canyon just ended."

"And to think I was about to turn around," I said. "Glad you didn't. The horses are in need of water."

"Well, we can thank our Navajo friend for a lot today," I said gratefully. "I'm sure glad he wasn't the one I shot first."

After we filled our canteens again, we started up the sister canyon to the one we came down. It wasn't long before I could see why this route would save us time. The upper trail required a climb of a thousand feet or better to get around the drainage we found ourselves in; whereas, this way took us around the base of the mountain on relatively flat ground. With any luck we'd run into Virgil and Emily as they descended from the top.

It was about a forty-five-minute ride from there until we came across the main trail again. With a little tracking

SWEET JUSTICE   349

observation, I realized they were still ahead of us but not by much.

"They're right in front of us, kid. Keep your eyes open." "How far do you think?"

"Well, let's put it this way. If we hadn't stopped to water the horses, we damn well might've met 'em right here."

"That's unfortunate."

"Not really," I told him. "Our horses are fresh and ready to go; whereas theirs will be plumb tuckered out from the climb and decent they just went through. Virgil ain't gonna push 'em to hard now. He's gotta think we're either dead or way behind 'im and that he's home free." We rode hard, knowin' that time was precious. If what we was told about the Apache camp bein' a day's ride away was accurate, I figured they would have to camp one more night before finishin' the trip. I hoped this was the case because I had no desire to confront Virgil in my condition, anywhere near earshot of a mess of Indians. Hell, as far as that goes, I didn't want to in good condition either.

The flats we were ridin' appeared to lead back into hill country, and it concerned me a little when I noticed it. "Damn, that's not good," I muttered.

"What's not good, Bill?" asked the kid.

"Our trail leads us into those rocky hills, kid."

"I don't understand. What's the harm in that? We've been in canyon and hill country since we left."

I smiled at his inexperience before replying. "If Virgil gets high enough to see back on these here flats, the dust from our horses will tell 'im someone's comin'."

"I get it. But don't he think them Injuns are bringin' up the rear? Maybe we ought to lose our hats so from a distance we look like 'em." "Damn, kid, that's the smartest thing I heard come outta your mouth since I knowed ya," I told him. "Put his mind at ease. Good thinkin'."

"I had a good teacher," he said proudly. "Figured it was about time one of my ideas saved our asses for a change."

"Might just have that effect," I replied as I slipped my hat off my head.

The kid did the same, and we continued to ride headlong into the sun, hangin' low in the afternoon sky.

"Keep an eye out for danger, kid," I warned as we entered the first of the foothills.

"If it's all the same to you," he replied, "I think I'll keep both out.

How's your leg anyway?"

"Not bad," I said. "I don't know what that stuff was he put in it, but it seems to be doin' its job alright."

"Does it hurt?"

"Hell yeah, it hurts, but at least I ain' bleedin' to death."

The kid started to make small talk as we rode, and I had to remind him that becomin' complacent could get us killed. He immediately caught on and buttoned his lip and went back to scanning the surrounding country.

*****

It was now about two hours before sundown, and dread and panic started to grab hold of me. I knew if we didn't find 'em before sunset, the odds would go way down of comin' across them 'fore they were well into the unsafe zone for any kind of rescue.

"Calm down, Bill," I told myself. *"They're here somewhere close."*

About that time the kid rode up next to me and asked what the plan was if we didn't find 'em by nightfall.

"We have to, kid," I said passionately. "We can't afford to let them get any closer to that Indian camp, or it may be too late. Once Virgil delivers the guns and they start drinkin', I've got a feelin' that they just might kill 'im. And God knows what they'll do to Emily 'fore they kill her too."

We rode on somberly as the sun continued to hang lower in the sky until it just became too dark to see anymore.

"Dammit! I failed you, Emily," I thought as I took the saddle off my horse. *"I'm so sorry you're still with that son of a bitch. I'm sorry I didn't kill ' im when I had the chance and save you from this mess to begin with."* The kid started to prepare a fire, and I told 'im to keep it small. His response was that he was hungry and he sure as hell wasn't gonna eat cold beans or go without coffee.

I could tell it was fatigue and a sense of failure talkin', so I tried not to snap back at 'im. "We're deep in Apache country, kid," I reminded him. "I'm just lookin' out for your butt. If you start a big fire, the light might cast in all directions and give our position away to someone we don't want a visit from."

As soon as the words left my mouth, I thought, *That's how we can find them! Virgil doesn't have that worry. That means he has no reason to keep his fire small at all.*

"Get yourself somethin' to eat, kid, and save some coffee for me.

I'm goin' scoutin' for a while."

"Ya can't go out there by yourself, Bill," answered the kid, with worry in his voice. "I'll come with you."

"It's okay, kid," I replied. "Much obliged for the offer, but I'm doin' it alone this time. You get yourself fed and get some rest. If what my gut is tellin' me pans out, we'll be leavin' early in the mornin'."

I gathered my guns and began to leave camp when the kid said, "Hey, Bill? Remember what that Navajo said 'bout drawin' circles?"

"Did your arms fall off, or don't you know how to draw a circle?"

He wasn't sure if I was kidding or not and quickly defended his ability to make one.

"I just thought since it was you the medicine man said it to it would protect that maybe it ought to be you that draws it is all."

"Sure thing, kid. You might be on to somethin'."

After I finished my crude artwork, I slipped into the darkness, pausin' just long enough for my eyes to adjust before headin' farther in the direction that I hoped would bring me closer to Emily. I was only gone about forty-five minutes when I could see a faint glow on the wall in the distance.

"Be real quiet, Bill," I told myself. *"It could be them, or it might be Indians. Either way you don't want 'em knowin' you're here."*

I continued forward, movin' ever so carefully through the darkness, doin' my best to avoid anythin' that might cause noise or alarm any creatures that could give away

SWEET JUSTICE 353

my position. I came close enough to here Emily's voice, or at least the echo of it, and strained hard to hear what she was sayin'.

"They're going to kill us, Virgil," she said. "Just as soon as you give them their guns, they'll kill us for sure."

"No, they won't," Virgil replied smugly. "These here Injuns are my friends."

"Apache don't have white friends, Virgil," she shot back with a pleading voice. "They're just usin' you to get what they want."

"You're wrong, Emily," he said in a louder voice. "You don't know everythin', you know."

"I know they'll kill us both, Virgil," she stated boldly, "and if that's a risk you're willing to take then fine, but let me go because I'm not."

"You're never leavin' me, Emily," he said sinisterly. "I've loved you too long to let you go now."

"You killed Charlie because of that, didn't you?" she asked accusingly. After a slight pause that usually precedes a confession, he finally blurted out his reply defiantly. "You're damn straight I did," he said,

"and your precious William too."

"William was right all along," she said as she started to cry. "He didn't really have anything to do with that girl's death, did he?"

Virgil started to laugh when she asked it. "Nope, he sure didn't. But I hid the evidence that could prove that the day he came to Yuma." "Why, Virgil?" she asked, angry and surprised. "What right or reason did you have to meddle in a man's life like that?"

"Because I knew he was friends with Charlie," he replied defensively, "and I figured he knew what happened to him. Bill has a reputation for puttin' pieces together, and I couldn't take the chance on him gettin' wise to what I'd done."

Emily was crying uncontrollably now. Through her sobs she asked how Virgil knew so much about me.

"Because Charlie was always braggin' about bein' friends with Bill Saunders. He was always talkin' 'bout him. Between that and the fact that he held your affection, I couldn't stand the bastard."

"Why didn't you let William go, or at least try to, after you found out he didn't even know Charlie had been to Yuma? That would have prevented our coming together in the first place."

"For someone so smart, you sure are thick sometimes, Emily," he said rudely. "You think I didn't see the way you looked at 'im the day I brought 'im in? I could always read your face like a book, and I knew there was fire between you two. I knew you'd try and help 'im. The only thing that surprised me was how long it took for you to do so."

"It was because my heart was broken over the loss of Charlie," she said, crying harder than ever. "I felt like I was betraying him."

"Well, you don't have to worry about either one of 'em now," said Virgil, coldly, "because they're both dead, and if you ever try to leave me, you will be too."

"I'd rather be dead than be with a vicious, crazy murderer," she replied courageously.

"That can be arranged, Miss Watson," he threatened, "so don't try any funny stuff, ya hear?"

"We'll both be dead by this time tomorrow, Virgil," Emily shot back. "So I guess it won't matter if I did."

"Tomorrow we'll be rich with gold, Emily. And then you'll finally love me. Just you wait and see."

"I'll never love you, Virgil!" she screamed "Why can't you get that through your big head?"

"After tomorrow I'll make you love me," Virgil replied confidently. "Your going to die tomorrow," Emily said in a softer, sad voice. "And you'll take me with you because of your arrogance. But I don't much care anymore. At least I won't be with you."

After that, there was silence, and I wanted to run to her and manifest the fact that I wasn't dead. It hadn't crossed my mind that she thought I was or that Virgil was under the impression that I was too. I attempted in the dark to make my way up to where they were, hopin' I could sneak in undetected and overpower Virgil without any gunfire. I wasn't sure how far away the Apache were, and I knew that in the quiet of the night, gunfire would carry along way. As I came into a clearing, my nose was instantly filled with the pungent odor of the Navajo witch that'd tried so hard to stop us each night.

I frantically searched all around me in an attempt to find him. My limited vision exposed nothin', yet my senses told me he was there. Quickly, I used the butt of my rifle to draw as big of circle around me that I could. No sooner had I finished and looked up again, he was standin' right in front of me, yellow-jagged teeth and blood red eyes. I pointed my rifle and informed him that I knew he could bleed and therefore die and that I had no hesitation to prove it. But I was lyin' to him and myself because the last thing I wanted to do was fire my gun.

He began to circle me just outside the perimeter I had scratched in the sand. At first, I followed him, not wantin' to lose sight, in case he attacked. But a man would get dizzy in a hurry if he continued spinnin' like that, and if I was to stagger or fall within his reach, I'd be at his mercy. So I held my ground in the center and stared back at 'im each time he passed, doin' my best to make 'im believe I wasn't afraid. After a couple of hours, his steady pace began to take its toll on me, and I found myself gettin' sleepy. As my eyes grew heavy, he lunged at me in an attempt to make me jump from my position.

"This can't go on all night," I thought. *"I have to do something 'sides stand here. Emily needs me."* So I mustered my courage, and as he passed in front of me again, I stepped forward and swung hard with my rifle. He lifted his arm to protect his head and left his ribs wide open for the full impact. He let out a yelp that sounded more like an injured wolf than a man as he retreated to safety. I took advantage of the opportunity and quickly drew a bigger circle that would at least allow me to lie down. When he saw what I was doin' he ran in an attempt break the barrier 'fore I finished, but he was too late. He growled at me instead then lay down just outside of it like a guard dog keepin' someone at bay.

I sat for a while just starin' at him, angry that he was accomplishing his mission. Emily was just above me, hours away from bein' led like a lamb to slaughter. My nemesis was fully aware of that. He didn't need to kill me; he just needed to prevent me from stoppin' Virgil from delivering the guns in order to win.

"Should I just shoot him?" I thought. *"No. If I do, the place could be swarmin' with Indians by sunup, and Virgil' d know someone was here."* I was torn as to what I should do. *"If this thing keeps me up all night, my chances of savin'*

her will be dulled, and a lack of sleep' ll have a negative impact on my judgment and actions."

I watched as Virgil's fire died down. As the last flicker danced off the wall, I turned back to the dog man, his blood red eyes still starin' at me.

"He obviously can't get you, Bill," I said to myself, *"so don't let ' im keep you awake."*

I laid on my back and pulled my hat over my eyes. No sooner had I done so he was back at the perimeter, tryin' to keep me from sleeping by intimidating me with any threat he could come up with. I lifted my hat just enough to give him an uninterested look and then pulled it back again and closed my eyes. He kicked sand, growled, and ran around in circles, tryin' to keep me from sleepin', but I tuned him out and did anyway.

The last thing I thought before I went out was, *"You can only defeat me if I let you. And that's not goin' to happen, you stinkin' ugly bastard."*

CHAPTER TWENTY

Showdown at Daybreak

MY EYES SHOT OPEN AS the breeze of the approaching morning started to chase the cold out of the canyon. My head snapped in the direction of the skin walker's restin' place, but he wasn't there. I sat up with a jerk and started starin' into the grayish blue shadows, searchin' for him, but I couldn't see 'im. I started to wonder if I'd dreamt the whole thing until I glanced at the circle around me and could see where an attempt had been made to dig underneath it. At first I was hesitant to leave the safety barrier, but my duty to save Emily was more powerful than any fear I had at this point, and my window of opportunity was closing quickly. I cleaned my guns and made sure they were loaded, took a drink from my canteen, then stepped out of the circle in the sand. I half expected to see the skin walker run at me. When he didn't I took another step and paused again, then another and another, until I was confident he was gone.

"Probably went to nurse his broken ribs," I thought with a smile.

358

SWEET JUSTICE   359

I was afraid from the silence that Virgil had already left, until I heard a horse whinny from where I'd heard voices the night before. As quietly as I could, I made my way up through the scattered rocks, but as I stepped off of one, it became dislodged and crashed down the hill. I froze in position, and then heard Virgil's voice call out.

"Up here, friend!" he called out. "I wondered when you'd get here."

Knowin' I couldn't respond, I jumped behind a rock, hopin' he'd figure he was mistaken.

"Come on in!" he yelled again. "It's almost time to go."

I figured his voice must've woken Emily, when he said, "Well, good mornin', my love, you ready to be rich?"

There was no response, and I could feel the ice of her stare back at him from where I was.

I continued makin' my way up to where they were, careful not to step on any more rocks.

"Be that way then." When you see that gold, you'll be singin' a different tune. Are ya'll comin' in or what?" he yelled down again.

"Come have some coffee, Emily," I heard him say. "I'm real sorry we had words last night."

"Say something, Emily," I muttered. "Your voice will mask my footsteps."

"Words?" she shot back in a tone that said she couldn't believe how insane he was. "You confessed to killing the only two men I have ever loved in my life!"

"Good," I thought. *"Keep talking."*

"Yeah, but now we can be together, Emily," he said soothingly. "Don't you see? This is the way it's supposed to be. This is the way it was always meant to be."

"It was never supposed to be this way," Emily stated coldly. "You need help, Virgil. You're out of your head."

"You'll see," he replied like he didn't hear a word she said. "Very soon you'll see."

"Very soon you'll be dead, Virgil," Emily assured him, "and I can't say I'll be sorry."

Her words masked the last few steps I needed to get up the hill. "Well then, you best give me a kiss 'fore I die then," Virgil said as he grabbed her.

"Let go of me, you animal!" I heard her say with a scream.

As I stepped out from behind the rock and into view, Virgil was locked into a stare with Emily but caught my entrance with his peripheral vision and without lookin' to see who it really was said, "Just in time to see me kiss my future bride, boys, then we best get goin'."

"Let her go, Virgil!" I demanded. "Or I swear I'll blow your head off."

"William!" cried Emily. "You're alive!"

"You!" Virgil said in a state of shock. "How'd you get here? You're supposed to be dead."

"Well, sorry to disappoint," I stated flatly, "but I can guarantee you're gonna be if you don't let her go."

"You ain't gonna win that easy," he replied as he put Emily in front of him and stepped closer to the cliff. "In a few hours, I'm gonna be rich. And if you try to stop me, I'll kill her. Understand, Billy? Just like always, I have the power."

"You let her go, Virgil," I said lying, "and I'll let you go get your gold. If you don't, I will blow your head off, rest assured."

SWEET JUSTICE

"Do what you have to, William!" yelled Emily. "Even if it means my life. Do you know how many people will die if the Apache get those guns? This has to end here!"

"They'll kill you, Virgil!" I said, tryin' to buy time. "You know that, right?"

"That's what she said," he replied, jerkin' her around with his arm across her chest, "but I think you're both wrong. Why would they kill me when I'm their only source for more guns and whiskey?"

"Where you gonna get 'em next time, Virg?" I asked sarcastically. "You won't be able to show your face in any town for a thousand square miles now, and the Apache know it. You're worthless to them after today, and the gold you've been promised has been in the hands of more than one idiot if it even exists at all."

"You're wrong," he said. "They're my friends."

"Virgil, you don't have any friends because you're an ass."

"No one's gonna keep me from that gold, ya hear?" Virgil yelled, holding Emily dangerously close to the cliff 's edge. "Not you, not her, no one. And if you try, I swear I'll shove her over the edge."

"And what, Virgil? Add more to the blood that's already on your hands? You killed my friend and attempted to kill me for a girl you can't have. Now you're willing to kill her and who knows how many others for a bag of gold. Damn the consequences as long as you're happy, right?"

"I don't have friends because no one respects me," said Virgil, licking his lip like he always did when he was uncertain or nervous. "Emily never gave me the time of day because she was rich and I wasn't, and the folks in

Yuma only hold people with money in high prestige and give 'em the respect they deserve."

"And you think that gettin' rich by sellin' guns to the Apache is gonna give you that respect? Unbelievable. The people of Yuma would hang you, sure as shootin', even if your pockets were full of gold. So why don't you let Emily go and end this crazy notion before anyone else gets hurt. Come back to Yuma and take your chances in court."

"What chance would I have in Yuma?"

"Well, if you bring the guns and the mayor's daughter back," I pointed out, "they might have some leniency on you. At least, you've gotta chance that way. If you go through with this crazy deal with the Apache, I can guarantee you'll be dead 'fore the sun goes down."

Virgil mulled my words over in his head for a minute or two before answering. "No, Billy, I think I'll take my chances with the Apache, get my gold and the girl too. What d'ya think of that, honey?" he asked Emily, while sniffing her hair.

"I think I'd rather die," Emily said in disgust.

"That can be arranged," he replied as he licked her face, "unless you know how to fly."

"Let her go!" I yelled as he dangled her over the edge.

"Oh, I plan on it," he said demonically, "unless you put your gun down now."

I could tell Virgil was out of his head and desperate, and I sensed that his back was against a wall. He'd already proven that killing people gave him no pause or remorse, so I had no doubt that he'd let her go.

"Okay, Virgil," I agreed. "I'm puttin' the gun down. Just pull her back away from the cliff."

SWEET JUSTICE 363

"And your gun belt too, Billy."

"No, William, you can't. He'll kill you!" Emily pleaded as I threw my belt and rifle down.

"That's good, Billy," stated Virgil with an evil grin. "Now move away from the cliff," I pleaded.

Virgil took about four steps back, and then he got a crazy look in his eye that prompted me to be ready for anything.

"You want her? Come and get her!"

With that, he shoved her back toward the cliff edge, and I immediately dove to catch her before she fell. I managed to grab her arm at the last second and held tight as she swung back and forth. The bank started to crumble underneath me as I pulled with all my might to bring her up before we both went over. I struggled until I could reach down and grab lower on her body, all while Virgil was laughin' in the background. Finally, I was able to roll back with both hands on her now and bring her back up on the ledge.

We both lay there, pantin' and hearts racin', relieved that the ordeal was over. The struggle had popped the already delicate stitches on my shoulder, and it had started bleedin' again. Emily crawled over to me when she noticed it and immediately began to try and stop the bleeding. "Well now, ain't that sweet. Hero saves girl, only to be shot when he's done," Virgil said, placing his rifle barrel against my head. "What a shame."

"No! Don't kill him, Virgil!" Emily begged. "I'll go with you. Just don't kill him, please."

"You'll go with me anyway, Mizz Watson," Virgil said absolutely, "but I've wanted him dead far too long to pass this up. Say goodbye, Emily."

I heard the sound of a gun cocking and winced in anticipation of the sound of fire when I heard a familiar voice.

"Drop the gun, Virgil, or I swear I'll kill you where you stand."

I felt the pressure of the rifle leave the back of my head and turned to see the kid motioning for Virgil to move away.

"'Bout time you got here, kid," I said in relief. "What d'ya do, sleep in?"

"Well, I didn't have Mr. Morning there to wake me up," he replied with a chuckle. "What happened to ya?"

"It's a long story, kid," I told him. "Ask me later."

"Bartholomew!" Emily exclaimed. "How did you manage to get out of prison?"

"Someone had to be the hero," he said, giving me a wink, "What with Bill here gettin' shot by Injuns and almost again by Virgil there, I didn't dare let him come alone."

"Bartholomew?" I repeated standing up.

"If you want me to let Virgil have another crack at it, Bill," he said with a scowl, "just call me that again."

"Okay, kid. I s'pose I owe you that, but it's apparent now why you never shared your name."

"It's a good name," said Emily in his defense as she put her arm around me. "He just saved your life, so you let him alone, William."

"Alright, kid," I said, "what d'ya say we get outta here?"

Virgil started laughin' and not his regular I-have-power-over-you laugh but deep from his gut.

"What the hell you laughin' at, Virgil?" asked the kid. "Seems to me, considerin' what's in store for you when we get back, you'd be keepin' your mouth shut."

"Oh, your little celebration party tickles me, kid, is all," Virgil replied. "Ya see, ya'll think you won some kind of battle here, but truth is, if I don't take them guns in by noon, there's gonna be a mess of Apache gonna come lookin' for me. And when they do, you'll be dead, and I'll be rich. So I don't know what you're smilin' 'bout, kid, but considerin' what's in store for you, I'd be runnin' if it were me." He started laughin' again and then looked at Emily. "Seems to me you chose the wrong man now, doesn't it?"

"I would rather die here today with real men, Virgil," Emily said coldly, "then spend another minute with you."

"And you will, Miss Watson," he replied. "You most certainly will." "Kid," I said with a sense of urgency, "you have to get Emily out of here now."

"No, William," Emily protested, "we'll all go together."

"You don't understand," I told her. "What Virgil says is true, and I can't fight them and protect you at the same time."

"You're already injured," the kid pointed out. "You take her, and I'll stay and bring Virgil and the guns back."

"Much obliged, kid," I said appreciatively, "but what you make up in sand and courage, you lack in experience. I'm trustin' you to get Emily to safety. That's your part of the fight. Can I count on you to do it?"

"Absolutely, Bill," he agreed. "I'll do whatever you want me to." "That's what I want you to do," I said anxiously, "and I need you to do it now."

"I don't want to leave you again, William," Emily said sadly, hangin' on to my arm. "I thought I lost you once and don't think I can go through that again."

"You have to. We're runnin' out of time. I can't let these guns fall into the hands of the Apache, and I need to know you're safe, so let the kid take you back, and I promise I'll be there as soon as I can."

"What was it you said to me?" Virgil chimed in with a laugh. "Oh yeah, you'll be dead, all of you!"

I went after him just to shut him up, and like always he shrunk like the coward he was.

"Pretty brave," he shot out, "considerin' Barty there has a gun pointed at me."

"Put the gun down, kid," I said. "What?" the kid asked in disbelief.

"No, William," Emily pleaded, "not now anyway".

"Get goin', kid," I said relenting. "Put some space between us as fast as you can."

Emily hesitated to mount her horse and sat staring at me. "Get goin' Emily, please. The kid'll take care of you."

"But who's going to take care of you?" she asked, "You're injured, and that horse carrying the guns is about spent."

"I can take care of myself," I assured her while pickin' up my guns. "Been doin' it most my life. 'Sides, I'm goin' to rid him of the whiskey 'fore we leave. That'll lighten the load and, with any luck, slow the Apache down some."

"You make sure you come back to Yuma, William," pleaded Emily. "Promise me."

"I will, Emily. I promise. Now get goin'."

After a short pause, she climbed off her horse and ran to me. "I love you, William Saunders," she blurted out.

Then she kissed me and, without givin' me a chance to respond, climbed on her horse and began to ride away.

Her comment took me by surprise, and I didn't know how to react to it. I tried to respond, but when I opened my mouth, all that came out was, "You watch over her, and don't stop 'til it's too dark to ride, kid."

He raised his hand in a gesture that let me know he understood before coaxing his horse into a full run.

Virgil looked nervous as they rode away. "I suppose you're gonna kill me?" he asked apprehensively.

"Nah. Watchin' you go to prison will be more rewardin'. Besides," I continued, "the Apache will probably kill us both."

"We could take the guns in together, Bill," Virgil suggested out of desperation. "I'll split the gold with ya fifty-fifty. That's more money than you've ever seen in your life."

"Good plan," I responded. "There's just two problems with it: one is I don't like you enough to partner up with you; and two is I have a soul, somethin' you seem to be lacking."

"So what then?" he asked sarcastically. "We're just gonna try and outrun 'em?"

"Yep, that's the plan," I shot back.

"That's just suicide, Bill," he replied, "We don't stand a chance." "Suicide shouldn't bother you none," I reminded him, "considerin'

you were fixin' to ride into an Apache camp and hand over whiskey and guns. The way I see it, you were well on your way to killin' yourself anyways." I sat down and looked at Virgil while my words rattled around in his brain.

"Don't you reckon we ought to be goin'?" he asked urgently.

"We ain't goin' nowhere 'til you get the whiskey off that there horse." "Ain't you gonna help me?" he asked in a tone of exasperation. "Not a chance. I'm gonna watch you do it while I keep this here Henry pointed at ya. So if you're worried about time all of a sudden, I'd suggest you best get movin'."

Virgil hastily unloaded the hooch and, according to my command, stacked it so it would be easily seen by the Apache as they rode this way. I hoped that the allure would be too much for them to pass up and that our first night would be relatively safe as they slept it off. When he finished I tied his hands to his saddle horn and told him to lead the way. The sun was still hangin' in the eastern sky, and it brought me comfort knowin' that we had an hour or two before the Apache would become suspicious.

CHAPTER TWENTY-ONE

From Hunter to Hunted

"THAT HORSE WON'T MAKE THE climb that's comin'," warned Virgil. "Doesn't have to," I replied coldly. "Just keep ridin'."

It was a couple of hours before we started to leave the hills behind us and found the flat open space again. With any luck we'd be across it before there'd be any potential to stand out like sore thumbs to the Apache as they arrived to the spot we were at now.

The sun was hot for early September, and it made the journey seem even longer than it really was. I watched the mirage it created in the distance that looked like water, and I hoped the horses would make it to the real water the kid and I had found on our way in.

"The horses ain't gonna make that pass with no water," Virgil commented again.

"Don't you worry yourself none about it," I said. "I'm just sayin' is all," he replied.

"Well, don't say," I shot back. "It forces me to have to speak back, and you're the last son of a bitch I want to talk to."

369

"No need to be that a way," said Virgil. "We got a long ways to go yet."

"Did you bump your head?" I asked full of hate and anger. "Or are you just stupid? You tried to kill me, you killed my friend out of jealousy, and you would've killed Emily if I wasn't so quick. Believe me, I'd rather have my tongue cut out than talk to you, so shut up and don't give me any reason to shoot ya, ya hear."

We made it to the split in the trail pretty quick, considerin' we weren't tracking anymore like when we came in. I breathed a sigh of relief knowin' we weren't gonna be out in the open anymore. How we made it before bein' spotted was any man's guess, but there was no dust on the horizon to indicate we were bein' hastily pursued, so I told Virgil to take the lower trail.

"What?" he said in disbelief. "That looks like a maze of canyons. I think the trail over the top is the one we should take."

"It'll be a cold day in hell 'fore I give two bits for what you think, Virgil," I replied. "Just do what I say and keep your damn mouth shut." I looked overhead to see the position of the sun and knew that the odds were highly favorable that the Apache were just now figuring that somethin' had gone terribly wrong with the plan. Their horses were more suited to the climate and therefore could go farther without water at a higher rate of speed. Our only chance was if they got to the whiskey and gave into the temptation to have a little before they rode any farther. Otherwise, they'd catch us in the narrow canyon and easily overtake us. My desire was to be back into the trees on the other side of the mountain before we'd have to make a stand of any kind, and I knew that would require spendin' the night in the canyon. All my hopes rested on the knowledge that Apaches were prone to drink when it was presented and that their leader would give in too. Unfortunately, only time would tell if I was that lucky, so I continued to gamble as I pushed man and beast farther into the rocks.

By the time we arrived at the waterin' hole, the sun had moved far enough into the western sky to cast long shadows. I knew that the canyons would be too dark to traverse once it went to sleep, so I informed Virgil that this is where we would stop for the night.

"We got an hour before the sun'll be down," he said. "I think we should keep going."

"Once again your ignorance and stupidity precede you, Virgil," I stated. "Do you think I just got lucky findin' this here water hole?"

He looked at me blankly like he wasn't sure how to answer.

"Well, I didn't," I continued, "which means I know what's in front of us. And believe me, this is where we want to stay. Odds are they'll be on top of us 'fore we hit the next water hole, so I don't really care 'bout you. I want the horses to have their fill."

I helped him off his horse and proceeded to tie his hands and feet together.

"How am I supposed to sleep this way?"

"I don't care how you sleep or if you do at all," I told him. "Seems to me when you placed me on that floor and forgot to feed me awhile back it wasn't a concern to you how I would sleep, so consider this me returnin' the favor."

I pulled the saddles off the horses and relieved our pack horse of his load before startin' a fire to cook somethin' to eat. That's when it hit me that other than a little jerked beef this was where I had my last real meal. I realized how undernourished my body had become, so I pulled out all the stops and began to fry bacon and cook beans, all the while eating biscuits. Virgil stared, mouth watering, as the smell began to dance around him.

"I suppose you ain't plannin' on sharin' any of them vittles," he said dejectedly.

"You can have some beans," I replied. "Much obliged, Bill," he commented.

"That is, after I spit in 'em," I commented coolly.

He got a look on his face that was a cross between disgust and fear, mingled with his own words used many times echoing in his mind.

"See, it don't feel so good, does it, Virgil?" I asked as I handed him a tin of beans and bacon.

He took it from me and looked for a second, like I might have been serious.

"Don't worry, I didn't spit in them," I assured him. "Only a snake belly like you does things like that."

"To tell you the truth, I wouldn't care much if ya did," he confessed. "We ran out of real food the night before ya'll caught up with us."

"You mean to tell me I sent Emily away hungry this morning?" I asked angrily.

"'Fraid so."

"I ought a shoot you right here, Virgil. It's a good thing the kid knows how to cook, is all I have to say."

My thoughts turned immediately to Emily and her whereabouts. "With any luck they're in the trees next to fresh water," I muttered to myself under my breath. Then I found myself prayin' that they'd be safe. I made a vow

SWEET JUSTICE 373

that if I was to get out of this and back to Emily that I would find God and make him a part of my life because I sure had thought of 'im and asked for his help enough lately to give somethin' back. I pictured myself walkin' into a church with her by my side, and it made me feel proud just thinkin' 'bout it, even though I hadn't been in a church since I was fifteen years old.

"You say somethin', Bill?" Virgil asked with his mouth full. "Not to you, I didn't," I told him. "Not to you."

The last of the light was chased from the canyon shortly thereafter, and I rose up to draw a circle around our camp.

"You superstitious?" Virgil asked with a chuckle.

I was going to reply, but I was too tired, so I ignored him and laid down.

"You best get some sleep," I told him. "We're leavin' mighty early in the mornin'."

I pulled my hat down over my eyes and thought of what Emily had said to me 'fore she rode away. And for the first time in a long time, I didn't go to the mountains of New Mexico; I went, of all places, to the courtyard of the Yuma prison. And there I found Miss Emily Watson waiting.

The next thing I realized, I was awake. Something was out there; I could feel it. My stirring woke Virgil up, and he could see me starin' into the darkness.

"What is it?" he asked excitedly.

I motioned for him to button his lip and continued searching. It wasn't long before I spotted the red eyes in the distance just watchin' us. *He's keepin' us in his sights,* I thought. *So he can report our location, I'll bet. Must be tired of me hurtin' him. That's why he's keepin' his distance.*

"What the hell is that?" Virgil asked shrilly. "You don't want to know. Just stay in the circle." "Is it some kind of animal?" he pressed.

"It's a Navajo skin walker," I shot back in a whisper. "Now keep your voice down."

"They ain't real," he replied. "That's just a myth."

"Well, there's your myth starin' at you with red eyes. Why don't you go tell 'im he don't exist, and I'll go back to sleep."

"I'll pass," he replied with a shaky voice. "Just shoot it."

"Damn, you are dumb, Virgil. I'm not sure how you made it this far. If I was to shoot, every Apache on the map would know where we were."

"I see your point," he answered sheepishly. "Then what we gonna do?"

"We're gonna stay in this circle, that's what. And you're gonna keep your mouth shut."

It wasn't long before his eyes disappeared. I wondered if findin' us was its only objective until I saw him come from behind a rock just outside our circle. Virgil gasped and began to mumble something incoherently as it stood with its yellow sharp teeth and red eyes staring us down.

"What is it you want?" I asked calmly.

Using his finger he pointed to the guns on the ground, and then slowly like it was drawing a line in the air, his finger pointed at me.

"Well, come and get me then," I taunted.

He looked at me and then at the circle at his feet.

"Is that what's bothering you?" I inquired as sweat beads began to run down my face. Knowing that his report back could very well cost us our lives, I said, "I can make that go away."

He looked again down at the ground, and in a moment I knew that if he was to leave, our fate was sealed, so I came to the conclusion that I could either die tonight or in the morning and that I had nothing at this point to lose. I pulled my bowie knife out of its sheath and brushed the line away with my foot.

I heard Virgil scream, "What the hell are you doing?"

At the same time, I heard the growl of my nemesis lunging at me. I swung my knife in an attempt to finish the job early, but he was too quick. He came again, swipin' his dirty fingers and sharp long nails, like an animal would swing its paws. I spun to avoid him and caught one of his fingers in the process. The injury caused him to howl out eerily, but it only made him more angry as he spun and pounced on me like a cougar. As luck would have it, I'd learned through the years to keep my knife in front of me where it would do some good. As we fell to the ground, my knife found its way deep into his belly. He gurgled a putrid breath in my face as it escaped him, but the wound seemed to have very little effect on him otherwise. I pulled hard upwards as I twisted the knife from side to side, and I could feel a tremendous amount of blood saturate my shirt. He sat up on top of me, pulling the knife out as he went and raised his hand like he was gonna hit me, so I quickly drove the knife into his heart.

That stopped him cold but didn't kill him. It did, however, allow me to throw him to one side, and I continued cuttin' 'til I could reach in and grab his heart with my bare hands. When he felt my hand close around it, I could see fear for the first time in his eyes, and I knew I'd found his weakness. I yanked as hard as I could and tore the heart from his chest and held it, still beating in front of his face as I watched the life drain from him.

"Take that, you bastard!" I yelled as his body fell in a heap.

I looked at the heart in my hand and then to Virgil, who was starin' wide-eyed in disbelief at what he'd just witnessed. After a moment of silence, he asked how I knew I could kill it.

"I didn't," I replied breathless and panting, "but one of us had to die tonight. I just got lucky."

I drug his body out of the circle and laid down again. My body ached, and the cold of the night crept up on me in waves, each one bigger than the one before, until I shuddered with the involuntary motion the body uses to defend its self from hypothermia. I reached to pull the blanket up around me and noticed that the wound on my shoulder had started bleeding again. Knowing that a tourniquet would be useless, all I could do was apply pressure and hope the bleedin' would stop.

The wound on my leg ached like a bad tooth, but the medicine my Navajo friend had given me had stopped it from bleedin', so I chewed some up and put it on my shoulder as well. The instant pain it caused shot through me and seemed to find an exit at my toes.

"Maybe that's why he didn't put any there, Bill," I thought, grinding my teeth.

The pain began to subside after that, and I fell back to sleep, holding the pressure on it as best as I could.

When my eyes opened again, I could see Venus in the eastern hemisphere. I knew the sun would be pursuing it soon, so I got up and started a small fire for coffee. I was confident that the number of Apache that might be chasing us was significant enough to prevent them from makin' camp in the canyon, so I decided that they had stopped up on the flats to bed down. It was risky, but my body needed coffee this morning, so I took the chance. The smell brought Virgil back to the land of the living, but he sat in silence just watchin' me.

I handed him a cup and stared up into the morning sky.

"Been a long time since I've seen that," I commented. "A man sometimes doesn't know his treasures 'til there gone."

"Never look at 'em myself," replied Virgil.

"Well, you ought to," I suggested. "Seein' as to what might happen today, this could very well be your last chance."

Virgil shuffled out where he could see better and sipped his coffee as he took them all in. I reached over and cut the rope connecting his hands to his feet and felt his confused stare for a moment as he looked at me. Without sayin' a word, he again turned his head to the heavens. "There's so many," he said. "Kinda makes a man feel small and insignificant, don't it?"

"We are small and insignificant. That's why we have to make each day count."

"Don't suppose when we get back I'll have too many more days to do that," Virgil said sadly.

"You might, Virgil. Folks are a lot more forgivin' to those they know. Could be they might just let prison teach you a lesson and not hang you for Charlie's death."

"Maybe," he stated with little hope in his voice.

"He was a good man, Virgil. Whatever they do to you, you can rest assured you deserve it."

"Reckon you're right there, Bill," agreed Virgil. "I just couldn't stand the thought of anyone stealin' Emily from me is all, but I guess I've pretty much put that horse to pasture now."

"Your obsessive behavior put that to pasture before you even got out of school, Virgil," I pointed out. "Murdering Charlie was overkill in a desperate attempt to keep somethin' that was long gone, and in your gut you knew it, right?"

"Reckon I did at that. If it's any consolation, if we die today, I just want you to know I'm sorry for killin' Charlie."

"Funny, how facin' death brings a man back to himself. Sad part is for most, its too late by the time they get there, and most are only sorry because they got caught."

'Yeah," he replied. "I reckon I deserve to die if it does come, but I sure don't want to."

"Whatever's gonna happen to us is gonna happen. As long as Emily gets back safe, it don't matter much."

"That's a kind of love I never understood," commented Virgil.

"That's the only kind of love there is," I informed him. "If you think you love someone for what you'll get out of it, you've missed the stage. Love's all about what you can give to those you care about."

"Maybe I never really loved anyone," reflected Virgil, "'cause I don't think that a way."

"You can't love others 'til you love yourself, Virgil," I replied. "Maybe if they let you live, you can give that some thought while you're in prison. Come on, it's time to get movin'."

SWEET JUSTICE 379

"A little dark, ain't it?" Virgil asked.

"Maybe you'd rather let them Indians gain some ground on us instead," I answered.

"Reckon not. Though I don't see what difference it makes if I die here or back in Yuma."

"It makes a big difference. They ain't gonna torture you first in Yuma, and I don't plan on dyin' without a fight. Speakin' of which, come here and I'll untie you."

"Really?" he asked surprised.

"Really. We ain't gonna outrun them unless we can ride like hell, and you can't if your hands are tied," I said while cutting the rope.

I let Virgil rub his wrists for a second or two before telling him to load the pack horse and get his own saddled. I contemplated giving our midnight guest a shallow burial but then decided that his body might unnerve the Apache some, and we needed all the help we could get. I went and gave him a quick once-over just so I could rest assured he was good and dead this time before saddlin' my own horse.

We rode by moon and starlight for a while before the sun started to turn the sky its typical bluish grey. When it finally did, Virgil was able to see the mountain pass we'd avoided.

"Wish I'd known about this," he commented. "Sure did cut a lot of work and time out of it."

"If you had, you'd be dead right now," I pointed out, "and worse yet, Emily would be in the hands of the Apache."

"I reckon you might be right, Bill," said Virgil, "or I might be rich and on my way to San Francisco by now."

"I am right, Virgil. There never was any gold, and you'd be dead or wishin' by now you was anyway. The thought of what they'd be doin' to Emily should make us both glad she's with the kid instead."

The sun was blazin' hot by now, like it was tryin' to give it all it had 'fore winter would be along to combat it. Our canteens were runnin' dry, and our horses were startin' to foam at the mouth. I could tell they needed a rest, but I didn't dare stop out in the open. About noon or thereabouts, we came to the place where our trail joined the high road and turned to make the slight climb up to the trees that promised water and some protection if we had to fight. It couldn't come anytime too soon for the pack horse, who by now seemed to be on her last leg. "Another hour, girl," I said as I patted her cheek, "and I'll let you rest."

She looked at me like she understood the peril we were in, and she seemed to find the strength to push herself a little harder for my benefit. I spent the next hour continually looking over my shoulder in anticipation of a swarm of Indians approaching any minute and was never so grateful to see trees and cover when we cleared the last hill before the spring. I scouted for a place to make a hasty retreat in case our enemies arrived while we rested the horses. I knew how long the ride was from here to water again, and I understood that the animals needed a chance to prepare themselves for the challenge that lay ahead.

Virgil dismounted and headed immediately for water. "Where you goin'?" I shouted after him.

"For water," he stated defensivel.y "I haven't had any for a couple hours now."

SWEET JUSTICE   381

"You'll get your saddle off your horse and unload that poor mare before you get water," I commanded.

"I will," he said. "I just need a drink first."

"If you're thirsty," I asked, "how d'ya think that poor horse that's been carryin' your sorry ass is feelin'? Get your saddle off and unload the other one 'fore you drink, or I'll make you carry the load from here on out."

"Okay, okay," he replied in disbelief. "Keep your shirt on."

I took the saddle off my horse and found some dry grasses to rub him down with, checked his feet and made sure he knew how much I appreciated his service. It was somethin' I had done with all my horses, even though more than once I had taken some ribbin' for doing so. It didn't matter to me because my horses had always performed well under all circumstances—be they good or bad. On top of that, my horses always came when they saw me and stayed close by in case I needed them, somethin' those that teased me couldn't brag about.

I knew they needed rest, and truth was so did I. After I rubbed the mare down, I got a drink and filled my canteens. I found a spot where I could keep a close watch for approaching danger and sat down in the shade. Virgil pulled up under a tree and went to sleep.

Typical, I thought. Virgil never worried 'bout anything that wasn't bitin' his heels or the consequences of not bein' prepared. When situations would sneak up on 'im, his reaction was usually knee jerk and chaotic and resulted in hasty, usually wrong, decisions. His life-long relationship with Emily and decidin' to sell guns to the Apache were two good examples of that. If the Apache were to clear the hill right then, Virgil would probably pay with his life for not stayin' on his toes, but it didn't bother me too bad, considerin' the man got us into this situation in the first place and in so doin' put Emily's life in danger as well. Joined with the fact that he'd killed my friend, it almost made me wish they would for a moment, just to watch it happen.

We stayed for about an hour, givin' the horses time to drink their fill 'fore I kicked his foot to wake 'im up.

"Time to go, Virgil," I said with contempt. "Get the mare loaded." "Go to hell," he replied half asleep.

"Do it now," I barked, "or I'm leavin' you here."

Virgil was fully awake by then, and the dire situation at hand had again found its way to the front of his puny mind.

"Sorry, Bill," he stated out of fear. "I'll get right on it." "I know you will," I shot back.

The mare shrunk a bit when Virgil approached, and I felt bad that we were gonna make her continue to carry the burden, but I had no choice. There was no way I could allow the Apache to gain access to the guns, so I walked over and patted her down and spoke softly to her, explaining the situation in hopes that somehow she understood. I felt that perhaps she did when she nuzzled me while Virgil was loadin' her up again.

It wasn't long before we left the safety of the trees and entered back into the sea of standing cactus that decorated the view as far as one could see. They had their own unique rugged beauty and were a testament that life could survive anywhere and under any circumstance if the desire was there. It gave me courage, even though I knew we were now visible to any searching eye for miles around. If we were lucky, we could survive too.

SWEET JUSTICE   383

For the next few hours, we rode with as much haste as I dared push, and I spent more time lookin' behind me then I did in front.

Where are they? I thought. *They can't be that far behind us.*

It wasn't that I was in a hurry to fight 'em; it's just that I knew they was comin' without a doubt, and the anticipation of their arrival was more than I could stand. The battle was inevitable, and years of bein' in the thick of confrontation had made me become the hunter instead of the other way around because I didn't like waitin' for the other side to make the first move. It had a way of makin' you jumpy and gave you time to second guess your plans, which usually caused hesitation when the fight was finally on top of you, and a man that hesitates when there are guns involved rarely gets another crack at it. We continued to ride, unnerved by the knowledge that any minute they could be on top of us. But as the sun started to fall lower in the western sky, there was still no sign of them.

"Maybe they ain't comin'," Virgil stated hopefully.

"Oh, they're comin' alright," I assured him. "They ain't gonna let these guns get away from them now, I reckon."

"They'd have caught us by now if 'n they was," Virgil said smugly. "Unless they're doin' this on purpose," I pointed out. "Could be they're administering a form of mental torture, hopin' it'll wear us down before the attack."

"Well, they ain't gettin' to me," Virgil said boldly.

"Ain't they?" I asked sarcastically. "Seems to me you all been lookin' behind you as much as, if not more than, I have."

"Just want to be ready is all," Virgil replied.

"Whatever you say, Virg," I responded with a chuckle, "whatever you say."

The sun slipped behind the distant mountain, indicating that we had about an hour before it would be dark, but I knew it wouldn't be long after we reached that moment that the moon would come out of hidin' to take its place.

"Gonna have to make camp soon," Virgil said. "We'll be sitting ducks, what with no real cover and all, so we best find a good spot before we can't see anymore."

"We're not makin' camp," I informed him. "Not here anyway."

"What?" he shot out.

"You heard me. I said we're not makin' camp tonight."

"Why the hell not?" Virgil inquired angrily. "I'm tired as hell, and I don't think they're comin' anyways."

"So am I," I replied, "but we're a hard day's ride to water, and the horses will do better in the coolness of the night than they will in the blazin' sun tomorrow. "'Sides, our pursuers are comin', rest assured, and they won't be expectin' us to keep goin'. With any luck we can get across the rocky flats before they catch us."

"Probably break a leg on them rocks in the dark," Virgil said with contempt.

"Could," I agreed, "but it's a chance we'll have to take because we sure can't outrun 'em in those rocks, and I think that's where they want to take us down anyway."

"What makes you think that?"

"'Cause anywhere else we can make some kind of a stand. Even though we haven't got a chance, we'd take a

SWEET JUSTICE 385

few with us on our way out. On those flats they could pick us off with little risk."

"I'm startin' to see why ol' Charlie held you in such high esteem.

You're pretty damn smart, I'll give ya that."

We pushed forward without conversation. The sound of Charlie's name and knowin' I had his killer stirred up a ton of emotions inside me. We arrived at the spot where the Apache had joined Virgil and Emily days earlier, just as the last light disappeared and left us in almost total darkness.

"We'll wait here," I said. "Give the horses a break 'til the moon comes out."

"I s'pose you want me to unpack the guns again?" Virgil asked apprehensively.

"Yep," was my reply.

It wasn't so much for the horse's sake, if truth be known; it was just a good way to punish him for what he'd done. The dessert chill settled in and reminded me that fall was definitely on us now. I closed my eyes and tried to imagine the high mountains of New Mexico and Montana as they would look at this moment. The aspen trees would be brushed with yellows and reds, and the morning mists would add a mystical beauty to the scene. The majestic elk would be squaring off to find out who was the toughest and therefore which ones would have a part in the creation of the next generation.

I snapped to when Virgil stepped up to ask if there was anything to eat and reluctantly joined him as the images in my mind faded away. I hoped that I'd get the chance to see it in real life again as I rummaged to find some jerked beef for us to chew on. The moon introduced itself by casting its light into the canyon.

"Time to go," I announced.

"What!" Virgil said in disbelief. "I just got the horse unpacked." "Well, you best get her packed again," I replied.

"You did that on purpose," he mumbled. "Sure did. Reckon you had it comin'."

Virgil went to work without sayin' anything, and even the mare seemed to enjoy watchin' him do it. She had what looked like a smile on her face as she swung her head back to see what was going on, and I swear she looked back at me as if we were sharin' a moment that tickled us both.

With any luck I hoped we'd be back to the writings the kid and I had found and the water that shared the canyon before the comin' day provided any light. It was a couple hours before we came out of the mouth of the canyon where Emily had left us the clue that inevitably saved her life. The moonlight cast its shadows across the rocks and gave the terrain an almost other-world look. My concern was finding the canyon that would lead us to the water we now needed desperately. Even though I'd kept the rule of lookin' behind for landmarks to direct me on my returning journey, things had a way of lookin' totally different in the dark, and we didn't have time for any mistakes.

My deep thought was broken when Virgil stated he was sure his criss-crossing actions here would've thrown off any posse.

"Yeah, you almost fooled me for a while too." "How did you figure it out?" asked Virgil. "I'm smarter than you," I said.

"No really," he asked again. "How did you track me on solid rock?" "I made an educated guess," I answered, "and it proved to be right.

But truth is it was Emily that sealed the deal by leavin' a bread crumb at the mouth of the canyon."

"Damn," Virgil said in exasperation, "and I thought I was bein' real careful."

"She saved your life, Virgil," I reminded him, "so I reckon that was a good mistake."

"Well, we don't really know that, do we? Or if them Injuns are comin' at all, as far as that goes."

"Virgil, I'm tryin' real hard to tolerate you right now, so try not to say stupid things. Those Apache would've killed you for sure. And they're comin' alright, you can count on it."

I was grateful for the bright moon as we made our way along, not only for the sure footin' it gave to the horses but also because it allowed me to make out landmarks I had burned into my brain. When we came to the mouth of the canyon, I breathed a sigh of relief because I was sure that we were in the right place. I turned to look at Virgil who was asleep in the saddle, content to let his horse follow mine as we headed into the dark crack that lay before us. The deeper we descended, the more the canyon walls acted as a curtain hell bent on stoppin' any light from penetrating and blocking us from escapin'. In the cold blackness, they felt like they was closin' in on us, and the horses were skittish and reluctant to continue forward.

I leaned over and spoke softly into my horse's ear. "We have to do this," I whispered, "and I'm countin' on you to bring me to Emily."

I don't know if it was my desperation or the smell of water that kept him goin', but he did, and it wasn't long 'fore I could make out the silhouette of the overhanging rock and feel the slight temperature change from the pool of water.

"We're here," I said out loud, waking up Virgil. "Where's here?" Virgil asked groggily.

"Where you camped the first night with Emily." "That was fast. I must've dozed off."

"More like slept. I thought you were gonna fall out of the saddle a few times, and I had plans of leavin' you there if you did."

"Sorry, Bill," Virgil said half apologetically. "Do you want me to unload the guns?"

"No time," I told him. "It'll be morning soon. We're just stoppin' for water and somethin' to eat is all."

"What you got?"

"Cold beans," I said. "Might as well get you used to prison food now, I reckon."

Artwork by Mark Inkley

CHAPTER TWENTY-TWO

The Last Stand

WE LET THE HORSES DRINK their fill and made sure we had all the water we could carry and then sat a spell, waitin' for the crack of dawn to shed its light before we pushed on. As soon as we could see again, I started us out only to find that the mare was never gonna to fit through the skinny slot canyon with all the guns packed on her.

"How did you get her through the first time, Virgil?"

"I had to unload her," he stated with a tone of voice that indicated he thought it was a stupid question.

"Why the hell didn't you point that out when you asked if you needed to unload the horses?" I grumbled.

"I was tired."

"You're an idiot, Virgil!" I shouted. "We could've done this in the dark."

"Sorry, Bill," he shot back defensively. "I guess I wasn't thinking." "Dammit, Virgil. You never think. The Apache could be here any minute," I yelled as I began to unload the packs off the mare.

Virgil, realizing his stupidity quickly started helping. I led the three horses down the canyon to where it widened

390

SWEET JUSTICE 391

out again and went back for an armload of guns. It took three trips to get them all, and since Virgil was getting so good at packing 'em, I left him to get 'em loaded up again. The distance was about a hundred and fifty feet, and it cost us precious time before we were on our way again.

The sun was up and workin' on gettin' hot by the time we came out of the canyon. As I caught a glimpse of the stage trail, I knew we were close to Yuma.

"Another four hours or so," I said to Virgil, "and we'll be home free." "Well, one of us will be," he replied. "D'ya think we can make it before the Apache find us?" "Maybe," I said, "if we're lucky."

Our hopes were cut short, however, because no sooner had we hit the main road, our pursuers began to pour out of the canyon like roaches comin' from a crack in the wall after they were disturbed.

"Run!" I shouted.

Virgil was already gone like the coward he was, leavin' me to try and coax the mare along. We rounded the bend, and my eyes spotted some high ground where the cliff wall would offer some protection.

"Up there!" I yelled to Virgil. "Get up there and take cover!"

The horses, sensing danger, bounded up the hill, and even the mare made good time. I dismounted and took cover behind a rock just as the Apache came around the corner in hot pursuit. It only took them a second to figure out where we went, and then the fight for our lives took center stage, and unfortunately, I was the star.

True to form, some of the younger Indians let eagerness outweigh wisdom and immediately started up the hill. They were easy to pick off, and as they fell, they stopped the others from makin' the same mistake.

There were so many of them shootin' by now that it made it hard for us to return in kind without puttin' ourselves in the line of fire. I found a crack between two rocks that allowed me to take out three more that had a good vantage point on us. I turned to see how Virgil was doing and found him with his back up against the rock facing the opposite way he should've been to offer any assistance. He was frozen with fear and was mumbling somethin' to himself.

"If you have any intention of gettin' outta here alive, Virgil," I shouted, "you best get into the fight!"

"I can't move, Bill! I tried, but I just can't."

"Dammit, Virgil!" I pleaded "Get a hold of yourself and cover that hillside."

He continued to stare at me until I shouted, "Now!"

My command brought him to attention at the last moment, and he was able to stop two of them right before they cleared the last hurdle. I spotted three of them attempting to get to our horses that had scattered from where we left them to a safer place behind a rock about a hundred yards over and down from my position. As luck would have it, they'd gotten into a position that had the cliff wall on one side and a boulder that was too big to climb over on another, with enough cover in front to force the Apache to put themselves in our sights if they wanted them.

I took careful aim and took the one in front out 'fore he could get to them, causing the other two to take cover. It was shortlived, however, because my rifle needed to be reloaded, and there was another working his way towards me by bouncing from rock to rock. I knew I wouldn't have time to reload before he would be on top of me, so I pulled my six from its holster and took him out as he leapt to the next rock. As fast as I could, I loaded my rifle. It's a good thing I'd gotten good at loadin' it quickly because when I turned again, there were three runnin' towards my position. The cocking action of my Henry made it easy to remove all three before they could find cover. I glanced back towards the horses just in time to see one of them leading the mare away, so I put him in my sights and pulled the trigger. The bullet hit him square, and I watched as his feet left the ground.

I turned to look at Virgil, expecting the worst, but found him firin' like there was no tomorrow. I didn't know if he was hittin' anything, but his action was causin' a pause in the ranks, so I yelled, "Good job, Virg! Keep going!"

The non-stop firing began to subside as the Apache realized that they were just wasting bullets. Virgil turned to me and excitedly exclaimed that he had gotten six so far and then again took his position with courage.

He finally found his sand, I thought. *Too bad it came on the day he had no chance of winning.* It would take a miracle to get out of this alive. That fact was clear, but I sure wasn't about to tell Virgil that. As futile as it was, I wasn't goin' down without a fight.

"To the last bullet, Bill, and die with your boots on!" I said out loud as I turned to check the horses again. The last of the three was just grabbing the reigns when I found him at the two points on my gun and fired. His body was hurled forward in a scene of violence and carnage. Then the canyon went deathly quiet as the Apache huddled to come up with a plan that wouldn't cost so many lives.

The remainder of the morning and a large part of the afternoon was spent pickin' them off one by one as they tried different ways to gain access to the horses and to us, but each one failed and each one cost the life of another young warrior.

"Good thing you spotted this here site," Virgil yelled between shots. "We could hold them off here for days."

I smiled at him in an attempt to keep him positive, but in my mind I knew we had to be gettin' low on ammunition, and there were still a lot of apache out there. Like ants in an anthill, no matter how many you brushed away, there were two to take their place.

"Don't get overconfident," I told him, "and make each shot count." "We got loads of ammo," he said when my advice clicked in his head.

"If you think you can run a hundred yards across that hill, we do. The horses bolted from the get-go, and I've been doin' my damnedest to protect them ever since."

I watched the color drain from his face when he crawled over to confirm that what I had told him was true.

"You're doin' good, Virgil," I confirmed. "Hell, I even have a little respect for you now, so don't lose heart. It's not over, and who knows, we could win this thing yet."

"I guess dyin' here today beats prison and the noose," he said as he made his way back to his position.

"Your actions here today ain't gonna save you from prison, Virgil, but they might save you from the noose. So don't give up, ya hear? We're gonna take as many out as we can, and we're gonna do all that's in our power to

Sweet Justice

395

keep those guns out of the Apache's hands. And if we die, it will have been for a good cause."

I turned away to fire at three more that were attempting to get to the horses before finishing with, "When you get down to your last bullet, you keep it and use it on yourself."

"I ain't gonna commit suicide, Bill," Virgil stated flatly. "They'll have to kill me if they want me dead."

"They will Virgil," I affirmed, "but not before you've wished a hundred times that you'd have taken my advice."

Virgil licked his lip and stared at me for a moment, and I was afraid that I might've sucked the wind out of him.

"Well, until I get to that bullet," he exclaimed, "I'm gonna take as many out as I can."

"That's the spirit, Virgil. To the last bullet then?"

"To the last bullet," he responded. "To the last bullet," he repeated as he again took his position.

We continued to pick them off one by one as each attempt ended the same as the one before it. The sun was startin' to grow heavy and sink lower in the western sky, and our ammunition was gettin' lighter. "Looks like the light's gonna run out before our bullets," Virgil said hopefully. "We might live to see another sunrise."

"Virgil, when that sun sets, they'll swarm us," I pointed out, "and we won't stand a chance in hell."

"What's the plan then?"

"We ain't got nothin' to lose now, so I think I'm goin' for more ammo."

"You think you can make it?" Virgil asked, his voice full of doubt. "I'm gonna try," I replied. "If I can get there, I'll wait until dark and then bring the horses back over here, so be ready. If all else fails, maybe we can make a run for it."

I handed Virgil all the ammunition I had left before leaving.

Just keep movin', Bill, I told myself. *Bob and weave, bob and weave.*

Those words played out in my head the whole time I was runnin' as I watched bullets bounce off rocks all around me. My leg caused a limp as the dull ache pulsed through it, but it might've worked to my advantage because it prevented a consistent speed. A moving target is almost like a stationary one if the hunter can match the speed of his prey, but inconsistency makes that more difficult.

A hundred yards seemed like a thousand as my heart pounded like a drum in my head. I staggered a little on a loose rock and almost went down. That would've been the end for me, so I threw my wounded arm out to catch myself on a full run and tore it wide open again. I could feel the blood as my shirt soaked it up. The pain was excruciating, but my will to live and the thought of Emily kept me going 'til at last I found the safety of the rock the horses were behind.

Two Apaches had started out after me and were quickly closing in. There was no time to load my gun before they arrived, so I met them instead with my rifle butt and knife. The first to arrive met my stock across his temple, and it sent him to the ground with a large gash from there to his eye. The second got it on the back swing, but all it really did was give me a second to discard it and grab my knife. As he threw his rifle up to shoot, I threw my knife at the same time, causin' him to flail backwards as it became acquainted with his large intestine. As he fell, I relieved him of his gun. By now the first one was up and attempting to come at me, but the bone between his temple and eye socket was shattered, so I put him out of his misery with a bullet from his buddy's gun before turnin' it on the temporary owner of my knife.

I made short work of loadin' my gun in anticipation of more coming and dove behind a rock for protection. I could hear Virgil shooting as fast as he could. Our enemy decided we were somehow more vulnerable split up then together and rushed our positions. I began to easily pick them off. First those running at me and then, with my new vantage point, some others below me that were now easy targets. Virgil held his own, and they quickly saw the folly of their thinking and retreated back to safety.

We were in a standoff. We held the higher ground and couldn't be reached. They blocked our path of escape and knew that once it was dark they would have the advantage. So we just sat starin' at each other. I used the time to try and figure a way out of our predicament, but I knew in my gut that once the sun went down, we were dead men. The odds of stayin' high on the hill and gettin' to Virgil's location was slim, to say the least. Goin' down would put me right in the middle of 'em. If three or more could sneak up in the dark, they would at last have their victory.

I sat starin' up at Virgil, knowin' he'd come to the same conclusion. He held up the bullet between his finger and thumb lettin' me know it was his last. I thought about my life and my family and then about Emily and how nice it would've been to get to know her better. Then I got on my knees and prayed that somehow my life had merited a place in heaven. I then stood up and loaded my guns, mounted my horse, and smacked the mare hard on the ass, sending her runnin' headlong into the Apache. When she got to them and drew their attention, they did just what I hoped they would. They went after the guns she was carrying. At that point I shot as many as I could. Then I rode down the hill, rifle in both hands, with the intention of goin' out in a blaze of glory. But just as they stood to take me out, the sound of the cavalry bugle could be heard followed immediately by thundering hooves.

What a sight to see—the boys in blue as they rounded the corner. The Apache scattered but to no avail. The mare ran right in the middle of the army as they approached, without losin' one of the guns she was carrying. *She was the hero all along,* I thought, as the cavalry began to make mince meat of those who were chasin' her. The ones who stayed under cover began to bolt and run, so I did my part to stop as many as I could. Virgil took his last bullet and loaded it in his gun and made good use of it as well until, finally, those that remained left the cover of the rocks and came into the road with their hands held high.

In all the commotion, it took awhile for me to spot the kid. When I did he had already seen me and in his cocky attitude rode up to me with a smile on his face. "Looks like I saved you again, I reckon," he said.

"Yep, kid, it sure does," I replied.

"I was afraid I'd be too late," he stated as he looked at all the dead Indians on the hill, "but it looks like ya'll was holdin' your own."

"If you'd a been five minutes later comin', kid," I declared, "you would've been too late."

SWEET JUSTICE 399

"Glad I came when I did then" he replied, "'cause facing Emily, after I promised to bring you back, would've been the hardest thing I ever done, I reckon."

"Thanks, kid, for gettin' her home."

"Well, to tell you the truth, Bill, I only got her to the river," he confessed. "That's where we met the cavalry. I offered to show 'em where you were, but I really thought you'd be up in the boulder flats. I was surprised to find ya here, if you want to know the truth."

"Yeah, I tricked 'em," I said with a smile. "Rode all night. They caught us this morning comin' out of the canyon."

The kid looked down and noticed my bloody sleeve. "Your arm looks bad. We best get you to the doc—I mean saw bones."

"Hope not in this case," I shot back. "I'm kinda fond of this arm." "Looks like the cavalry has things under control here. Let' get you back to Yuma."

"Hold on, kid," I said, looking for Virgil. "There's somethin' I gotta do first."

I found him in the custody of a couple soldiers, and I was sorry that this wasn't as sweet for him.

"We made it, Bill," he said. "Damn if we didn't make it."

"We wouldn't've if it hadn't been for you," I pointed out. "If it's any consolation, I forgive you Virgil."

"For which awful thing?"

"For it all," I said sincerely. "Including Charlie's death."

"I don't deserve it, Bill," he replied, "but I'm much obliged." "Good luck, Virgil," I said as I rode away.

"I'll need it, I s'pose."

"What the hell was that all about?" the kid asked in disbelief. "Nothin', kid. It's just that I don't want to carry that hate around no more. Virgil and I are only alive because we worked together, and I felt I owed him that."

"Well, I'll be damned. I never thought I'd see the day. Well, one thing's for sure. If we wind up bein' cellmates, maybe he'll be nicer anyway."

"You could just ride off, kid," I reminded him. "Mexico is only a stone throw away."

"I could," he agreed. "But a real good friend of mine told me that I needed to pay for things I've done. He also told me to take the time to make things right while I was doin' it. So if it's all the same to you, I think I'll take his first round of advice."

"You're gettin' smarter every day, kid," I said proudly. "Yes sir, smarter every day."

On our way back into Yuma, I told the kid what'd happened the night I didn't come back to camp and about my last encounter with the skin walker as well.

"I'd like to say I wish I was there," the kid interjected, "but that would be a bare-faced lie."

"Yeah, it sure was hairy," I agreed. "I think Virgil might've pissed himself, but I didn't say anything to him."

The thought of what I said tickled the kid, and we shared a good laugh over it.

"I don't want to come across as soft or nothin', Bill, but I'm gonna miss having you around."

"I'll miss you too, kid. I'll make sure to let you know where I'm at from time to time. Maybe when you get out, you can come find me."

"I could warm up to that idea just fine," he said with a smile.

The sun was down before we got to the river, and I was too tired to go any farther.

"Kid, I'm spent," I told him. "I think I'm goin' to camp one more night next to the river 'fore goin' into town."

"Sounds good to me," he answered. "Want some company?" "Only if the company's cookin'," I said.

"He is," was his reply, "and damn happy to do it."

We spent the night starin' up into the night sky and talkin' about the experiences we'd had after we left each other.

"Emily thinks she might've scared you off when she told you she loved you," the kid said out of the blue. "I told her I thought you felt the same way."

"It did take me off guard," I agreed. "Reckon now that she's home, she might feel different."

"Don't think so. She's been pretty worried about you."

"Well, I reckon, we'll see what tomorrow brings." I laid down and got comfortable before continuing. "As for now, I have plans for a nice ride in the mountains, and I can't get there 'til I'm sleepin', so I'll see you when I get back in the morning."

"I'll be here. Good night, Bill."

*****

The next morning we slipped into town pretty much unnoticed, and I headed for the doctor while the kid went to get me somethin' to eat.

"Did you get him?" the doctor asked, referring to Virgil. "Yeah, I got 'im," I answered. "The military's bringin' 'im in."

"And the guns?" he pressed. "Did you stop the Apache from getting the guns?"

"Yeah, doc," I assured him. "I got the guns too."

"You'll be a damn hero around these parts now," he exclaimed excitedly while he scrubbed out my arm.

He kept on with the small talk, probably tryin' to keep my mind off the pain he was inflicting. I took it pretty good 'til he poured alcohol in it to kill any infection he hadn't dug out already.

"You withstood that better than most" he said admirably as he started to sew it up." Looks like you tried to do this on your own at some point."

"Yucca fiber and a cactus needle works pretty good, unless you have to keep usin' the limb its sewed into," I replied.

"You've got grit, boy, I'll give you that." When he was finished sewin' it up, he turned his attention to my leg. "You're gonna have to drop your trousers, son," he informed me as he drew the curtains.

"Actually, I think my leg's fine," I said. "Other than an aching pain, it seems to be okay."

"Do I tell you how to save mayors' daughters and fight Indians?" he asked.

"Reckon not, doc," I answered. "What's the—"

"Then don't try and tell me how to doctor," he said, cutting me off. "We all have our jobs to do."

"Alright, doc," I said as I slipped my pants down. "I hear what you're sayin'."

He pulled some of the pulp out of my leg and examined it intently. "What is it?" he asked.

"Reckon I don't know," I replied. "A Navajo kid gave it to me. Seems to work good though."

"Seems to work excellent," he added. "Your leg appears to have no infection, and the wound is mostly healed. I'd sure like to know what it is."

"Then you'll have to ask them. Not all Indians are bad, and the only part of them that's savage is the part we created."

He thought about my words for a second or two before he responded. "Well, they have a grasp on some medicines," he agreed. "I don't think I have anything that would've worked that well."

I had just finished pulling my trousers up when the door flew open. It was Emily, followed closely by the kid, and the mayor was bringin' up the rear as fast as he could.

"William!" Emily gushed as she threw her arms around me. "I was afraid I'd never see you again."

"I promised you I'd be along," I said smiling. "Didn't you believe me?"

She was at a loss for words as she stared into my eyes, so she hugged me harder instead.

Her father stepped up and put his hand out to shake mine, but at the last second threw his arms around us both instead.

"I can never thank you enough for bringing my daughter back to me," he said full of gratitude.

"Well sir, I'd like to take the credit," I stated, looking at the kid, "but it was Bart, here, that really brought her back."

"Don't open that can of worms again," the kid exclaimed. "If I had a gold piece for every time he's thanked me today, I'd be rich enough to buy my way out of prison."

"I am in debt to both of you," the mayor assured us.

More and more people started to show up, wanting to shake our hands. The doctor's office quickly became too small for the party, so it slowly worked its way to the courthouse where the judge came out to offer his thanks and congratulations to us.

"I reckon this town is in debt to you both," he said, more to the crowd than to us. "Your service won't soon be forgotten."

"Typical political wind bag," I thought as I shook his hand. "What are your plans now, Mr. Saunders?" I heard someone ask from the crowd.

I felt Emily's eyes fall on me when the question was asked, and pretty soon others wanted to know my answer as well.

"I have two young friends somewhere between here and Texas," I proclaimed, "who are probably out of money and a little worried and lost by now. I reckon I'll head out after them 'fore I make any longterm plans. I haven't seen my family in nigh on twenty years, so I reckon I'll go home for a spell."

"What about you, Bart?" they inquired "What are you gonna do now?"

The kid got a surprised look on his face when they asked it and then, without replying, stared off into the distant horizon. After a pause that caused a hush to fall over the crowd, he spoke sadly, "I have to finish my sentence first. I'm not sure what I'll do after that, but I can guarantee you it won't lead me back to prison."

A murmur traveled through the crowd like a wave bouncing off a wall. His statement reminded the mayor that the town's newest hero was a convict with a sentence to serve, and he found himself torn now with a pit in his stomach.

"Well, I can't profess to speak for the law, son," he boldly stated, "but the town of Yuma is not in the practice of putting heroes in prison."

At that moment all in attendance cheered to show their support. "What does the law have to say about it, your honor?" the mayor continued, putting the judge on the spot.

The judge pondered for a minute before speaking. "Well, I would say if a certain someone could convince me that he'd learned his lesson and promise never to cast a shadow on my courthouse steps again—and I mean never—I might be persuaded to turn him over to a mentor that could teach him a noble way to contribute to society."

"I could do that," the kid said excitedly. "I swear I could."

"Well, that's good," the judge replied, "because it just so happens I had your folder on my desk when you left, and somehow it got misplaced. I'm in no mood to bring your case to trial again, so raise your right hand and repeat after me."

The kid did as he was commanded.

"Bartholomew Smith," the judge said with authority, "do you swear to keep the laws of the land from this day forth and do your best to make sure others do also? And do you promise to stay within twenty miles of Mr. Saunders until your sentence of three years has reached its end?"

Everyone held their breath in anticipation of the kids reply.

"This is where you're suppose to answer, kid," I said, nudging him. "I do," he said in disbelief. "I promise I will, sir."

"Then with the power granted me from the United States government, the state of Arizona, and the people of Yuma, I release you from the custody of the Yuma state prison and into the custody of one William Saunders until the space of three years has passed, at which time you'll be free to come and go as you please."

When the judge finished speaking, the crowd sent up a cheer, and the celebration officially began.

Lacking the mood and energy for crowds, I hung back, found a place to sit in the shade, and watched as they hauled the kid off for a drink. Physically and mentally, I was wiped out and a little overwhelmed to boot, so I pulled my hat down over my eyes to rest.

"Hey, partner," I heard a familiar voice say.

I tilted my hat a little and peeked out from under the brim. "Howdy, Slim," I said, happy to see him. "Pull up a chair and sit a spell."

"I knew you'd succeed," he stated as he pulled up an old rocker sitting on the boardwalk. "I never doubted you for a minute."

"Yeah? I'm glad I didn't disappoint you. I thought I was a dead man a few times out there. How you likin' your new job?"

"Only been on one run," he answered, "but it's okay, I reckon. Got some good news though."

"I could use some good news. What is it?" "Emily helped me find my brother," he replied.

"That is good news," I said. "You gonna go see him?"

Sweet Justice 407

"Don't know. Reckon I'll write him for a spell and see what the future holds. Which reminds me, are you gonna go see your folks like you promised?"

"Sure would like to," I assured him, "but Ben and Jed cut out of here with little or no money, so I reckon I'll go out after them first."

"They left with plenty of money," I heard Emily say out of the shadows. "I gave it to them along with two good horses."

"I didn't know you were there, Miss Watson," I said, surprised. "Thank you for looking out for them."

"They promised to pay it back, William," she replied with a hurt tone of voice. "I just figured if you were willing to help them, then I would be too."

The last words kind of caught in her throat like she was holdin' back tears.

"Did I say something wrong?" I asked regretfully.

"You called me Miss Watson, William. I thought we were closer than that by now."

"I just didn't want to sound disrespectful."

"I told you I loved you, William. If you don't feel the same way, I understand, but certainly you could call me by name."

I rushed to her and held her tight as the tears formed at the corner of her eyes.

"I love you too," I gushed. "I just wasn't sure you really felt that way or if it was just said in the heat of the tense moment is all."

"I wouldn't say it if I didn't mean it, Mr. Saunders," she replied in retaliation. "You have stayed on my mind since the first day I saw you, and even though I fought it, I couldn't make you go away. Then each time we talked,

I felt so at ease with you and looked forward to visiting again. After a while I longed for it and missed it when Virgil kept me from doing so. Sometimes it wasn't easy to get clearance to see you, I'll have you know."

"I feel the same way," I assured her. "It's just that in my wildest dreams I never thought that you could see anything in me, so I guess I just wouldn't let myself believe it."

"I see myself with you for the rest of my life," she replied.

"I have nothing to offer you," I told her. "What would your father say?"

"My father knows how I feel, William," she said, "and I have plenty for us both."

As we spoke Slim kept quiet in the background until he found a pause to cut in. "Appears to me that some good may have come out of our time in Yuma after all, Bill. Reckon if you don't kiss her, I'm a goin' to."

We turned to look at him, smiled, then turned back to each other. "I love you, Emily," I said, "and I promise to stay by your side for the rest of my life."

I anticipated a similar verbal reply, but instead her answer came as she kissed me deeply. Slim chuckled, as some of the towns folk cheered. All my past and future were swallowed up in that moment, and all that mattered was now. I pulled her closer, in spite of the crowd and lived it to the fullest.

Chapter Twenty-Three

Going Home

"I reckon with this new development I best go have a talk with your father," I said as the people continued cheering.

"He's a tough nut," Emily replied with a smile. "You might want to take your guns with you."

"Bill," Slim cut in, "don't you be forgettin' your promise now, ya hear?"

"What promise would that be?" Emily asked.

"'Bout not lettin' paths keep 'im from goin' and seein' his family.

You promised, Bill."

"I did at that, partner," I agreed, "and I intend to keep it, but this complicates things a bit."

"That's just how it started for me," said Slim regretfully. "Don't wait 'til it's too late, my friend. You'll live to regret it."

"Sure thing, Slim," I assured him. "I said I would, and I will, just as soon as I'm healed up a bit."

"Not without me," the kid shouted from the crowd. "I'm afraid you're stuck with me now."

"I'm gonna have my sister's husband put you to work on the cattle ranch, kid. See if we can't work some of the cockiness out of you."

"I was thinkin' more along the lines of sheriff or marshal," he replied. "I kinda like that trackin' and searchin' thing."

"Well, let's get your sentence behind you first," I suggested. "Kinda hard to be in law enforcement when you're payin' a debt for breakin' a law."

"Cattle sounds good too," he said as the cavalry bugle sounded in the distance.

Everyone cleared the road as they rode through. The sergeant tipped his hat to me as he passed, followed by two of the Apache leaders and Virgil. He had his head hung in shame as they entered the gate of the Yuma hell hole. I started to follow out of curiosity when Emily called me back.

"Don't, William," she said. "I don't think I can see him right now after all the pain and death he's caused."

"I just want to see how the guards that used to call 'im "sir" treat 'im."

"They'll treat him as good as he deserves. Spencer is the boss now." "Good for him," I said enthusiastically. "He deserves it. Spencer made my time there tolerable, to say the least."

I watched from a distance as Spencer came out to collect his newest prisoner and smiled inside to think that justice had come full circle. And for the first time, I looked around at the town called Yuma and saw it the same way Emily did: a place where good people had found a way to build a community and fill a need all the while forming friendships and creating commerce

Sweet Justice 411

and a future for those that would come after. The cacti were just startin' to bloom, and the river ran blue and powerful, the rugged beauty was truly inspiring.

The town I thought I hated had given me good friends and purpose, a chance to help others, the time to come to grips with my past, and, best of all, the girl I hoped for all my life. What started out bad turned into something great, and Yuma seemed beautiful to me at that moment.

"Where you at, cowboy?" asked Emily.

Her question snapped me back again. "I was just thinking how lucky I am," I replied.

"I love you, William Saunders," she said, "placing her head on my chest."

The next two weeks went by in a flash as I healed from my wounds. I had plenty of visitors to keep me company. Emily, of course, kept by my side as much as she could, and Spencer came to see me as often as his new job would allow. He told me during one of his visits that the only reason he got the job was because I had started him down the path to reading.

"Emily should get the credit there," I told him.

"Sure," he agreed, "but if it wasn't for you, I never would've asked, and I'd still be stupid."

"You were never stupid, Spence," I assured him, "but I'm glad I could help."

I enjoyed our visits, but my favorite ones were from Slim. Slim had become a true friend and in a lot of ways acted as a father, dispensin' wisdom and givin' advice. If he hadn't been there when Virgil beat me so bad, I might be six feet under instead. It sure was good to see some color back in his face and not have to hear him cough so much anymore. We received a letter from Ben and Jed, tellin' us they got there and that they were pickin' up on things fast. They told me their boss wanted to know why I wasn't with them. They also thanked me for all I had done, and they kept their promise and sent Emily her money back. "They'll be fine now," I told myself as I finished reading the letter chock full of misspelled words.

Towards the end Emily and I took walks, and she introduced me to all her friends who truly seemed happy that she had found someone to fill the void that she carried so long. We even went to church together to keep a promise I had made when I had no one else to turn to, and I felt a peace I hadn't felt since I was a boy.

When the doctor came to see me, I asked him if I could travel. "Don't see why not," he answered. "Your wounds look fine, and you seem healthy enough. Sure would like to know what the Navajo used though," he said longingly. "I'd like to have some of that around."

"I'll see if I can find out, doc, and make sure you get some." "I guess this means you're leaving, then," Emily said sadly.

"Reckon so," I stated. "I haven't seen my family in twenty years, and I finally have the courage to face them. But you could always come with me."

"I can't leave my father, William," she replied. "I'm all he has, and he's not getting any younger."

"I understand," I replied, trying to hide my disappointment. "I wouldn't want you to."

"You'll come back though, won't you, William?" she asked hopefully. "I'll come back. I just don't know when that'll be."

SWEET JUSTICE 413

"I'll be waiting," she said as she started to cry. "However long it takes, I'll wait."

"Two or three months at the longest," I assured her. "Then no Apache, skin walker, or even Virgil will keep me away, ya hear?" I said, holding her face in my hands. "I promise."

"So many things can happen in three months," she said between tears.

"I promise I'll be back, Emily. I haven't broken a promise yet, have I?"

"No," she said, forcing a smile, "and you better not this time."

We ate dinner with her father that night, and he asked me what my plans were when I got back.

"I don't know, sir. There's only three things I know how to do—good 'nough to brag about anyways—cowboy, shoot, and farm. Unfortunately, pushin' cattle doesn't fit well into my plans anymore. I don't think this beautiful girl is gonna want me to go off hirin' myself out as a heavy, so that pretty much leaves farming. As near as I can tell, there isn't a whole lot of that going on here."

"Emily tells me your father has given the farm to you in Texas." "Yes sir," I replied, "but he could live a long time yet, and I don't think Emily has plans of leavin' you or Yuma, so I'll just have to find somethin' here, I reckon."

"Nonsense," he shot back as he looked at Emily. "Sweetheart, you can't let me keep you from living your life. This is your time. Besides, the elections are in a couple of months, and I've decided not to run again. There has been more than one generous offer for our mercantile and livery stables, and if William has no objection, I could join you in Amarillo when they sell."

"Absolutely no objection on my end to you joinin' us, sir," I said happily. "In fact, I'd be pleased if you did."

"Then it's settled," he stated, taking Emily's hand. "You deserve this sweetheart, so I would suggest you get the things packed you'll need until I can bring the rest with me."

"Are you okay with this?" I asked her.

"William, I would follow you anywhere," she stated as she hugged her father. "Thank you, Papa."

"You haven't called me that since you were a little girl," he pointed out with a smile. "I like it."

Emily went straight to work gettin' her things together, and I went to check on the kid to make sure he was ready to go and tell him of the change in plans.

"Sounds like I might just be in the way," he said with worry in his voice.

"Nah, kid," I assured him. "The farm's big, and there's plenty to do.

You'll earn your keep, I reckon."

The next morning we boarded the train headin' for Oklahoma.

Slim and Spencer came to see us off.

"You take good care of her, ya hear?" said Spencer. "Slim and I will be there for the wedding, so don't go gettin' hitched early."

"We won't, my friend," I promised.

"I'm much obliged for all you done for me," Slim said to us both, "and I hope all the best for you."

"You just make sure you're there for the weddin'," I said as I bear hugged him. "You're gonna be my best man."

"I'd be mighty proud to," he replied with a tear in his eye. "All aboard!" the conductor yelled as the train blew steam.

Everyone wanted a hug from Emily, and she paused as she kissed her father.

"You're a good daughter," he shouted over the clanking of the cars as they pulled tight, "and I'm proud of you."

"You come as soon as you can," she said. "We'll have a place for you."

"I will," he promised. "Now go."

Emily caught my hand, and I pulled her to me just as the train picked up speed the momentum threw her into me.

"This is where I want to be forever," she said, looking into my eyes. "Then I'll just have to accommodate," I replied.

As we rounded the last corner that gave us a view back on Yuma, I drank it in. Three years I spent there wondering if each day would be my last, but instead it was where my life began. Justice had come to Yuma at last, and it was sweet.

The End

Epilogue

Going home brought a peace to me I'd searched for in many places for many years. Funny that the place I'd avoided was the place I needed to go all along. In reflection, I could see that my journey was where I found myself, helped many along the way, and forged lasting friendships. It prepared me to see eye to eye with my father, who became my best friend in the end, and I was glad to share the remainder of his days at his side on the farm. We worked together 'til the day he passed away. It allowed me to find the love of my life, a girl who saw more in me than I could and helped me to see it too.

Emily and I spent the rest of our lives together, raisin' wheat and children—two boys and a girl. Our boys had a love for farmin' and eventually had the biggest farm in Amarillo and boasted the first tractor in the area. Our daughter, however, was more content with the horses and cattle and hung on all my stories whenever she could get me to tell 'em.

I kept my word to the God I came to know as I wandered, and Emily and I were in church every Sunday.

Emily's father did come and live with us and survived long enough to hear his grandkids call him Papa.

Slim lived another nine years in freedom and peace, doin' what he was good at. He died haulin' freight from

Yuma to San Diego but not before comin' to visit each time one of our children were born.

Ben and Jed worked for four years learnin' the cattle industry before startin' a prominent horse and cattle auction house called North & South Sales. They and their wives ate many of suppers at our house and stayed lifelong friends.

The kid finished his sentence and then wandered off for a few years, gettin' into the last of the cattle drives as the wire fences and railroad slowly killed 'em off. He explored the west and went all the places he wanted to see 'fore comin' back to settle down. He then became the town sheriff, then marshal, and finished his days out as a Texas Ranger, bringin' many in they said couldn't be caught. There was always a room for the kid at our house, and we were honored to have him there.

Before I got too old, we all went to New Mexico to hunt elk together. The antlers still hang on the barn to this day.

CPSIA information can be obtained
at www.ICGtesting.com
Printed in the USA
BVHW052242070723
666786BV00015BA/473